Searching for Nora

Searching for

Nora

AFTER THE DOLL'S HOUSE

Wendy Swallow

Peavine Mountain Press ✳ RENO, NEVADA

PEAVINE MOUNTAIN PRESS, Reno, Nevada USA
Copyright © 2019 by Wendy Swallow
Manufactured in the United States of America
Design by Kathleen Szawiola

Library of Congress Control Number: 2019911151

Paperback edition: ISBN 978-1-7331075-0-1
E-book edition: ISBN 978-1-7331075-1-8

This book is dedicated to the women
of the nineteenth century, who started everything.

And for Karlsgut.

Searching for Nora is the story of three quests.

At the heart of the novel is Nora Helmer's search for herself. It begins the moment she leaves her husband at the end of Henrik Ibsen's iconic play *A Doll's House* and carries her to places she could scarcely have imagined.

The second quest is that of the young university student Solvi Lange, who is searching for her missing grandmother—and for an escape from conventionality in post–World War I Norway.

The third quest is my search for both these remarkable women. Who are they, what will they do with their lives, and why do they matter?

Nora Helmer has always mattered to me, ever since I first saw *A Doll's House* onstage in college. My friends wondered how Nora could be a simpering wife-child in the first act, then throw off the chains of matrimony in the third, but not I. I recognized her manipulations and lies for what they were—the desperate measures of a powerless woman trying to manage as best she could.

My fascination with Nora deepened years later when I left my own husband and the home where we were raising two young sons. Heading out into the world as a single mother, I could only think how many advantages I had over Nora—a paying job, the legal right to care for my kids, an understanding community. Nora had none of that.

When I saw the play again I found I could no longer cheer when Nora slammed the door and walked out. Instead, my heart ached for her—so angry, so excited, so naive. I began to suspect that those who cheered were misreading Ibsen's play. Nora's decision feels today like an act of liberation, but for Ibsen's contemporaries, her final act was far more complicated. It was essential to Nora's soul, yes, but it was also impulsive, desperate, even self-dramatizing. For much of Ibsen's play, Nora believes her only escape from the shame and criminal liability of her forged loan is to commit suicide. This is no small hint. Ibsen knew the world of his day was far from ready for Nora, that she would face poverty, despair, and possibly the trap of prostitution on her solo path to self-knowledge. He knew that what she was doing would likely lead to ruin, even suicide.

Yet, at the same time, Ibsen gave Nora a survivor's drive and an adaptable nature. When she stops to think, she can be cunning and practical. When she gets past her own vanity, she can be thoughtful and caring. I believed she could figure out how to make her way in the world, despite daunting obstacles, and I wanted to give her that chance.

There have been other sequels to *A Doll's House*. Most are plays that ring with the authors' political persuasions, reducing Nora to a feminist icon rather than exploring her likely fate in nineteenth-century Norway. None gave me the story I wanted to read, which was how a young mother, with convictions and a heart, would take on her own flawed character in the effort to understand and rebuild herself.

I decided it was time to get Nora off the stage and give her space to roam, so I chose to write a novel. I knew she would struggle with the consequences of her choices, particularly the loss of her children. One of Ibsen's core themes is the tension between idealism and realism; I wanted to see how Nora would face the devils of her day and gather the courage to give up her masquerades and manipulations so that she could stand honestly before the world.

To understand her time, I researched Norwegian social and economic history and read about the scandalized reaction to Ibsen's play when it premiered in 1879. I traveled to Norway to interview Ibsen experts and emigration historians. I read about the Norwegian diaspora to America and grew haunted by the dark side of prairie life. Exploring the empty corners of Minnesota, I fell in love with the wide, quiet land, but also came to respect its rigors and challenges.

Solvi, a lonely girl with a rebellious spirit and fierce yen for the truth, sprang to life so I could view Nora through the prism of time and turn-of-the-century social change. I had to believe the fire in Nora's belly got handed down to a female descendant, and I wanted to know that girl.

For the past ten years, Nora and Solvi have lived in my imagination. When I started, I had no idea this novel would take me so far or teach me so much. In the end, I came away with a profound appreciation for the women of the nineteenth century, those early pioneers who started to fight—both personally and publicly—for equality and women's rights.

And for Henrik Ibsen, who understood what those brave women were up against.

A Note about Kristiania

The Kristiania of this story is the city known today as Oslo, the national capital and largest city in Norway. From 1879 to 1920, the years spanned by this book, the city was named Kristiania (a modification of the earlier "Christiania"). The city's original medieval name of Oslo was restored in 1925.

Searching for Nora

CHAPTER ONE

NORA

Spring 1919 ■ *Spokane, Washington*

When Anders and I boarded the train in Minnesota back in 1889, we headed west in search of obscurity.

We rode for days, through the interminable flat of Dakota, into dry Montana, and then beyond, to where the mountains rose on the horizon and trees appeared again. When the train stopped at Spokane, with its rolling grassland and forested hills, we got off. Familiar but not familiar. When we first saw the orchard, stunted by drought and neglect, I thought we should continue on to Seattle. But Anders pleaded with me: *I can save this place.* He meant that it could save him, and so we settled, one last time.

There are other Norwegians here but many more Germans and Swedes, so we manage to keep our distance. The orchard has thrived under Anders's care, and we keep a large garden, as well as chickens, pigs, sheep, and a few docile cows. Anders and Jens tend the trees, press the apples, and build furniture to sell. Jens married a German girl named Katrin he met at a dance, and they built their own small house at the bottom of the orchard. They have four children, who drift in to delight us every day.

Am I happy? Content, I would say, as I have learned not to wish for anything more. Over time I found my own small place in the community, a bit of purpose, and that has kept me from thinking too much about my past.

Until yesterday.

WHEN I SAW THE ADVERTISEMENT, I could only stare at it, dumbfounded.

Apparently I was dead, but now I might be alive.

I was tidying up before dinner, tossing the *Skandinaven* and other periodicals into a basket, when I glimpsed something familiar. The newspaper, published out of Chicago, mixed Norwegian news with political talk and gossip from the parlors of Kristiania to the docks of Seattle. Every Norwegian in America read it.

I picked it up again. Had Anders seen it?

No. He would have said something. Because there in the ad, of all things, was a picture of me. It was a picture I knew, though I hadn't seen it in years. In the photo I am young and astonishingly lovely. I'm clad in my dove-gray silk, the gown luminous in the studio's lights, with a froth of lace at my throat. My honey-blond hair is piled loosely on my head, my eyes level and my chin lifted as I smile for the photographer. On my lap sits Emma, imperious in her own billow of lace. Next to me is Torvald, handsomer than I remembered, in his crisp black frock coat. And there are the boys in their sailor suits, Ivar standing true and tall next to his father, Bobby leaning sweetly against my knee.

It was from before, before everything happened.

Before I started wearing black.

If anyone has information about the woman in this photograph, please send a letter to box 143 at the central post office, Kristiania, Norway. Nora Helmer was declared dead in 1885, but her family has reason to believe she is alive, perhaps in America. Reward.

I ran my fingers across the advertisement, as if to make sure it was real. I had lost my own copy of the photograph years ago, when I fell through the ice one warm March afternoon. I had put it inside my blouse that day, over my heart. It didn't survive the water.

I started to tremble. I couldn't believe I had the picture back.

With shaking hands I ripped the ad out of the newspaper, making a mess of it. Finally, just as Anders banged in the front door, it was done— the advertisement safely folded and hidden in the pocket of my apron, the mutilated newspaper stuffed into the stove.

NORA
December 26, 1879 ▪ Kristiania, Norway

I left late one frigid night. Torvald, too stunned to stop me, stood gaping in the parlor as I clattered down the apartment stairs and slammed the big front door. I wanted to shake the gossips from their beds, to send them to the window to glimpse the unthinkable: Nora Helmer, walking away in her traveling coat, with a satchel!

I did it to leave Torvald in a stew of scandalous talk because it was what he feared most, more than he feared losing me.

Outside, the cold knocked the air from my lungs. I grabbed the railing to steady myself and hesitated for a long moment, suspended between two worlds. Inside the lamps still flickered, and all that had been my world shimmered in the firelight—the chairs pulled up beside the stove, my embroidery hoop waiting on the footstool, my darling children asleep in the nursery. It would be so easy to slip back in and say I was sorry. To beg his forgiveness. To sink back into the suffocating eiderdown of my life.

But I was not sorry. Sorry would come later, pulling me down like grass in a mountain lake, but not now. Instead, a surge of exhilaration swept up from my feet. I was free, as if all the constraints and rules of my marriage had fallen away with the slamming of the door. I was just Nora—no longer Torvald's squirrel, no longer his wife!

I took a deep breath, then plunged into the icy street.

My boots skidded on the frozen ruts, so I hurried as best I could, skirting the gaslights and sucking in the electric air. Afraid that Torvald would come after me, I ducked down an alley, stumbling past ash cans in the knee-deep snow. I took other alleys and soon lost my way, but it didn't matter. I only needed to disappear.

I walked and walked, slipping past stately houses and darkened apartment buildings. I barely felt the weight of my bag, as I had taken so little, just a few clothes, my lotions, my pearls. But there were other burdens. Everything that had happened flickered through my mind. Torvald's words, in particular, cut like fragments of glass.

How had it come to this fevered flight? I knew, and I didn't know.

It happened at the sad end of Christmas. The overwrought children were finally asleep, and Torvald and I, limp with brandy, had lingered in the drawing room. And then he found the letter, delivered earlier. The letter from my blackmailer.

"What's this?" he said as he opened it and began to read. Then he gasped. "Is this true?" His eyes bugged out at me in disbelief, as if he'd never seen me before. "Did you do this thing he says, forge your father's signature, for a loan?" He looked at the letter again, then back at me, his face going scarlet. "And the man who loaned you the money is blackmailing you?"

"Yes. I did it to save your life."

"How could you!" he thundered. "And against my wishes!" He paced, breathing hard. "Do you have any idea what you have blundered into?"

"I loved you more than all the world, Torvald."

But he couldn't hear that. "None of your slippery tricks, Nora!"

He shouted, he called up my father's "flimsy values," and then said he should have known I would be no better. *Hypocrite and liar*, he called me, his accusing finger shaking with anger. Then, when he thought he was ruined, *criminal, disgusting, shameful*. And the final wound—that he could never trust me with the children again.

And so our marriage cracked open, and the life I'd known spilled away.

THE COLD FINALLY CAUGHT UP WITH ME. I stopped, lost in a jumble of weathered cottages, and slumped against a wall to breathe. And as I did, my circumstances settled gently on my shoulders, like snow. I had left home to wander the city alone at night, and I had left my children behind. I thought of them sleeping in their rumpled beds—Ivar with his long legs sticking out from the sheets, Bobby curled like a forest creature, Emma snuffling in her crib. She had a cold; would Nurse summon the doctor tomorrow? She could sicken and die, and I might never know.

I couldn't bear the thought of that, so I stamped my feet to make sure they weren't frozen and looked about. In the distance I could see the warehouses along the harbor.

After everything that had happened, I had come down to the fjord after all.

I walked toward the water. The big port was unusually quiet, emptied by the holiday. Darkened ships lined the bulkhead, and stacks of lumber loomed in the shadows. Snatches of fiddle music echoed across the bay from the drinking houses of Vika, the slum on the other side. Life went on, apparently, but so far away it didn't seem to include me anymore.

Instead, there was the sea, the beckoning sea. As I stepped out onto the dock, the thick cold of the fjord reached for me, like ghostly arms. Maybe this was how it should be. Throughout this awful Christmas, as my blackmailer circled in, there seemed to be just one way out: down, into this dark water.

At the farthest end I inched my toes out over the last plank. This would be Torvald's punishment, then, for all of it—marrying me, belittling me, accusing me. But it would also be a gift, as I would take my shame with me into the depths.

I gazed south down the fjord. The deeper water was quiet and forgiving, heaving gently under the crystalline sky. I could solve it all with one small step, no more than stepping off the stoop outside our apartment. I wouldn't have to crawl home to my aunt or beg for work. The children would grieve, yes, but in time they would recover and go on with their lives.

And Torvald? His honor would be restored, but at night guilt would climb into bed to lie with him.

I swayed, dizzy with possibility.

Then I looked down. Trash and flotsam pulsed against the dock; the water was the color of coal. My blackmailer was right—it would be an ugly death, sordid and final.

Not heroic, as it might seem onstage.

I stepped back and shook myself, as if waking from a tangled dream. What was I doing? I was young, strong. I could have a whole life ahead of me. Why must the heroine die to redeem the man?

Then, as clear as if an angel spoke: *because men write the plays, Nora, just as they write our lives.*

And with that, the refusal that drove me out the door coursed through me again. I stumbled away from the edge.

I needed warmth and a bed. I picked up my bag and headed to Kristine's.

A CONSTABLE found me crossing the promenade near the parliament building and insisted on guiding me through the dark streets to the apartment of my only friend. When we got there, it took several pulls on the bell before Kristine appeared, disheveled from bed and speechless to find me at her door with a police escort.

"Make sure she stays in at night," the constable said. "She was wandering down by the harbor."

Kristine pulled me up the stairs to her small flat. My knees gave out; she helped me to a chair.

"Nora, my goodness, you poor thing . . ."

I was shivering now, my teeth rattling in my mouth.

Kristine threw a blanket around my shoulders, stirred the fire, and filled the kettle. When she turned back to me her face was wary. "What have you done, Nora?"

"I've left home, Kristine," I stammered. "I've left Torvald."

Her mouth dropped open. "You've left Torvald? You can't do that!"

"I have, Kristine. I told him everything, as you said I should, but it came to ashes." I clenched my teeth to stop their chattering. "My miracle didn't happen, Kristine. Torvald will never forgive me, so I'm going back to Hamar. My aunt will take me in, and I'll get a job. I'll work, as you have."

"I never suggested you leave your husband!"

"He called me terrible things, Kristine, unforgivable things."

She stared at me for a long moment, then turned to prepare the teapot. "This is unthinkable. You have no idea how difficult it will be, what it's like to be poor. You're such a child—." Her voice caught, and she spun back around. "Your children, Nora! How could you leave your children?"

The thought of my children felt like a stone on my chest. "Perhaps they're better off with their nurse right now, Kristine. I'm no kind of mother. I need to figure out how to live in the world before I can be their mother again."

"Nonsense, Nora! They'd only be better off with their nurse if you were dead!"

There it was again, the appropriate solution. I just looked at her, speechless.

She softened, taking my bone-cold hands and rubbing them. "Nora, Torvald will not let them send you to jail for your forgery, and in time he'll forgive you. Go back. He loves you; he'll take pity on you. Don't be so selfish."

My cheek twitched. I was giving up everything. My future would probably be a cramped apartment like hers, with handed-down furniture and stained wallpaper. "How is this selfish, Kristine?"

"Because you're acting only on feelings," she cried, losing her patience. "You're being impulsive, as you always are!"

"Is it impulsive to do the only thing I can do? I cannot live with someone who considers me a criminal and a child. I can no longer be his wife."

Kristine poured my tea, and then tightened her robe across her spinster shoulders. I could feel her distancing herself.

"Go back to bed, Kristine," I said. "And thank you for taking me in. I had no one else."

"Do you need anything?"

"Yes. Could you please go to Torvald's tomorrow and collect my things? Have them sent to my father's house in Hamar."

"Of course."

I handed her a card with the address and a handful of coins. "I told Torvald I would take only what's mine. If he argues, let him have his way."

She lingered, unsettled. "In the morning things might look different. Perhaps you should pray on it, Nora."

"Perhaps I should," I said.

She sighed, then left me to God.

I DID NOT PRAY. I waited for sleep, but instead sadness seeped in like the tide. Sometimes a rift opened in one's life, a crack that snaked through everything, dividing before from after. But until the crack widened into a chasm, you could still see the other side, the life that was safe, the life that you knew. I had stumbled into territory that felt as barren as the moon, yet when I closed my eyes, all I could see was home—my piano stacked high with music, the boys playing with their tin soldiers on the rug, Cook calling us to dinner. Precious, known, and now lost. Fading already into nothing but memory.

THE NEXT MORNING I rose early, anxious to be gone in case Torvald came looking for me. The gaslights still burned as I crossed the city, dodging trams and people. I thought of my children having their breakfast and wondered what their father might have told them, or told the servants, or the servants their friends. The elegant parlors would ring with malicious talk of me by noontime.

At the station I managed to board a train to Hamar without detection, and the city of Kristiania soon vanished behind us as we clattered north, a welcome relief. Across the small compartment an older woman traveling with her husband watched me with a disapproving air, puzzled that a lady in a fine coat would travel alone, as if I wore my story on my sleeve. I smiled, but it did little good.

I turned to the window. The Norwegian countryside flickered past in the slanting winter light, the ghostly snowfields patched in between heavy walls of forest. The whole world felt black and white, the blank page of my future rimmed with the dark unknown. When I took this train south with my new husband, all those years ago, I had chatted with everyone in the car. Now I kept to myself. Stripped of my life, I couldn't think what to say.

Because how would I explain this? What would I say to my aunt, the only family left to me? She would demand to know why, but I wouldn't know where to start. Because it was impossible to say when unhappiness began. It crept in, like that damnable tide, and before I knew it, I was in up to my knees.

MAYBE IT STARTED the night Torvald began coughing uncontrollably at dinner. He'd been rasping for months—getting over a cold, he said—but nothing like he coughed that evening. I jumped up and held his heaving shoulders. When he pulled his handkerchief away from his mouth, my world tilted.

Our nurse stuck her head in the door. "The baby is finally asleep."

"Thank you, Anne-Marie."

Torvald shuddered. "I should lie down, Nora."

"That was blood, Torvald. I'm sending for Dr. Rank."

"No, Nora, it's nothing. Just a cold, I've told you. No need to waste money on the doctor." His face glowed with a pale light. He had always been a hearty man, filled with appetites, for wine and sport and me, but not recently.

"Go to bed, and I'll bring the hot-water bottle," I said.

We'd only been married two years, but I already knew it did little good to get his permission for anything. I helped him out of the room, then went into the kitchen to find the maid.

"Helene, please go for Dr. Rank. I'll do the washing up."

She nodded and grabbed her coat.

LATER DR. RANK AND I whispered in the hall.

"I'm so sorry, Nora," he said, cupping my hands in his. "It's probably tuberculosis. You must take him somewhere warm, somewhere in the South. As soon as you can, before he gets sicker."

I nodded, but it was just politeness. We couldn't afford to travel anywhere. We could barely afford Dr. Rank.

"Italy would be best, as it's cheap. Go to Rome. There are other Norwegians there; you wouldn't be alone."

I opened my purse, another ruse. "What do we owe you, Dr. Rank?"

"Nora, for goodness' sake, put that away. For my dearest friends? Nothing. Now, here's a syrup for the cough. Make him rest. Use your wiles."

I smiled faintly. "I'll do my best. Thank you."

TWO DAYS LATER, Torvald could barely raise his head from the pillow, but he bellowed nonetheless. "Never, Nora. I will never borrow money! I don't care if I shrivel up and die! I will not borrow!" He stopped to cough. "Only the weak borrow."

"But if you don't go south, you could die! Then what of me and the baby? What will we do without you?"

"I am not going to die, Nora; please calm down. I'll stay in bed and recover here. Surely Anne-Marie knows a few home remedies."

My mind skittered about, like a rat looking for an opening. "I'll ask her," I said, but then thought of something better. "I've got to run to the market, to, ah, fetch the newspapers."

"Don't be long, Nora. I hate it when you go out."

I kissed his hot forehead. Pink roses spotted his cheeks. How I loved him.

I THREW A SHAWL OVER MY HEAD, but instead of heading for the market, I walked to the pawnshop lane near the bay. It ran through a ramshackle neighborhood, where poor children sat on filthy curbs and questionable women in gaudy hats lingered at the corners. I asked around and soon found myself begging at the desk of a thin, bespectacled man in a worn vest. A Mr. Krogstad.

"You can't get a loan yourself, ma'am, as you're a woman. But if you have a male relative who would sign for you, I could consider it."

"My father," I said. "He'll sign for me."

"Good," Mr. Krogstad said, then coughed. "The interest, of course, because of the risk, would be, well, ahem . . ."

"I'm sure the terms will be fair," I said, giving him my most charming smile. "I'll speak to my father. Could you draw up the loan papers?"

"Tomorrow morning, I'll have them for you."

Giddy with relief, I went and bought all of Torvald's favorite periodicals. I would tell Torvald my father had given us the money, and then I would find a way to pay off the loan. I would take in sewing or copy documents for businesses, as I had done for my father.

When I was younger I would never have thought of such a thing, taking a debt onto my own shoulders, but the birth of little Ivar had made me stronger. If I had to take matters into my own hands, it was only to protect my husband and child. It wasn't as hard as one might have imagined.

I tucked the newspapers into my bag. With any luck, we would be off to Italy in a few weeks.

The next afternoon I told Torvald my father was ill, then took the train to Hamar with the loan papers in my bag. If my father didn't like the terms, he might just give me the money, I thought. It would work out fine.

But when I arrived at my childhood home, I found my aunt dressed in mourning. My father had died the day before, felled by his heart. It happened at the moment I was talking with Mr. Krogstad, as if my father's soul had refused to cooperate.

"Why didn't you write and tell me how badly he was doing?" I said, shocked by this complication, stung that she hadn't alerted me.

She quivered a bit, and her mouth went tight. "You knew he was failing, Nora. I didn't think I had to ask."

I flushed. "I'm sorry, Aunt, but Torvald is also ill, and there's the baby."

She just looked at me, unmoved. "And you his only child."

She went upstairs to rest, leaving me to sit with my father's body in the dining room. I looked at his marble-like face, considered the alternatives, then signed his name to the note and stuffed the mess in my bag. Who would ever know he had already died? Any woman would do the same to save her husband's life, I reasoned.

But even then, I knew. I knew I could never tell Torvald.

NOW I GLANCED at the imperious woman on the train, and the elixir of rebellion began to bubble again in my veins. From this moment on, I would do my best to stand on my own two feet. I would get a flat and live alone, eating sweets whenever I wanted. I would make friends and work in an office. I would be helpful and clever; men of industry would come to rely on me. If I earned enough, I might even take the children to the mountains for summer holidays—surely Torvald would see the value in that. There was no reason the children couldn't spend time with their adoring mother.

Yet beneath these bright dreams, reality crouched like a toad. My aunt would probably shrink from my company when she heard what I had done. And how to disguise my recklessness, the fact that I had left my marriage with little forethought? The truth was, I had neither plan nor money.

The train pulled into Hamar. Beyond the lights of the platform, I could see Lake Mjøsa, frozen, stretching to the mountains beyond. We climbed down; the wind whipped across the ice.

Landing back in the town I meant to leave forever felt like a reproof from God.

I headed uphill warily.

CHAPTER TWO

S O L V I

November 1918 ■ *Bergen, Norway*

Solvi slipped away before dawn, stealing out the servants' entrance while her mother slept. It was so easy it scared her, like stepping off a cliff. Simple but cataclysmic. She ran down the alley, her bag banging against her knees.

At the main street she caught a tram filled with housemaids bound for the sculleries of the gentry. She dropped into a seat and tried to catch her breath. The maids watched her with drowsy eyes, this fine young girl with her fur-trimmed cape and heavy case.

She turned to the window. The tram rattled past rows of elegant town houses still shuttered in the morning dusk, then headed to the harbor where the city was coming to life. Skiffs and small boats crowded the wharf, unloading goods as fishmongers filled their market stands. All so familiar to this Bergen girl, so beloved. Sadness wrapped around Solvi's heart like a weed.

At the station the early train to Kristiania rumbled with impatience. There was no time for her to reconsider, even if she wanted to; she jumped aboard just as it pulled away. By the time she was settled, the city lay behind her. She turned and, for a moment, caught a glimpse of the rooftops and steeples, with the islands and harbor and the gray Norwegian Sea beyond; then it was gone.

Tears welled in her eyes. Her mother would be rising, would find the note. *Please don't come after me. You're not strong enough, and it will do no good. I'm sorry to leave like this, Mama, but I'm drowning.*

Solvi tried to compose herself. She would not become her mother, weeping whenever life got hard. She was leaving so that she would not become her.

She took out a book, but it did little good.

THE TRAIN SWUNG EAST, beginning the long climb up the massif between Bergen and Kristiania. Solvi set her book aside and watched the wind-gnarled trees pass by. Snow soon appeared, a tattered lace flung across the landscape.

When her father was alive, Solvi often hiked these mountains with him, helping collect the alpine plants he studied in his laboratory. Because she was young, he would warn her about the *huldra*—the beautiful fairy women of the mountains who snatched children. But Solvi would just laugh and run over the next rise. She didn't believe in fairies; she believed in the good green earth.

Even as a child, she was unusually observant and soon developed an eye for rare mountain flowers. When she grew older she fancied herself his assistant, taking notes and photographing specimens with his field camera.

Sometimes her father would cup her face with his gardener's hands. "You have a rare mind, Solveig. Don't waste it embroidering pillows." How she missed tramping these hills with him, talking about the wide and luminous world.

Today, however, the clouds hung low and flurries blew past, scattering, lifting, then dropping again. When her father died just as the Great War started, Solvi felt like this—as if a winter wind howled through her. If only she could open the train window and let the snow swirl around her again, let it strip her clean and return her to grief. Because grief would be easier than what she felt now.

She could just imagine her mother's dramatics—dropping the note to the floor and stumbling back to bed, humiliated and wounded that Solvi would do such a thing. The maids would hover, applying compresses and salts but saying little. Solvi felt like a bird that had wriggled out of the snare, astonished to be free.

She gazed out at the blowing snow. But what if this escape cost too much? What if her mother never forgave her? *I'm sorry, Papa. Please understand.*

A PORTER BROUGHT TEA. Solvi wrapped her cold hands around the cup. How did she get here, on this train, leaving all that was familiar? She knew, and she didn't know.

Solvi's father had always wanted her to attend university, but when he died, that dream seemed to die with him. Her mother also changed. After his death, she grew anxious and took charge of Solvi in a way she hadn't before.

"Time to work on your trousseau, Solveig," her mother would say. "No more gallivanting about." When she discovered Solvi studying instead of sewing, she called it unseemly. When Solvi asked for an exam tutor, her mother bought her a fine silk dress instead.

But it didn't work. Her mother's hounding only stiffened Solvi's resolve to fulfill her father's ambitions. Besides, he'd left Solvi with a mission. A few days before his death, he gave her his field camera. "Go record this war, darling; whatever comes, take pictures," he said. "Someone should do it."

After his funeral, Solvi started carrying the camera everywhere. It was the size of a small book, with accordion sides that expanded when the front was snapped open. All Solvi had to do was slip a glass plate in the back, adjust the lens, and then press the shutter. It wasn't long before the camera became her refuge.

But finding evidence of a war happening far away wasn't easy. There was plenty to fear—that the Germans might invade, that Bolsheviks were infiltrating the shipyards—but little to photograph.

She tried capturing the subtle signs—empty market shelves, sailors smoking nervously on the wharf, cannons perched on the breakwater. Then, two years in, the war escalated, and German submarines began sinking Norwegian merchant ships. Solvi prowled the waterfront, hoping to spot a crippled steamer or perhaps even an enemy periscope. But the ships sank out at sea, and the drowned sailors left no mark, just holes in their mothers' hearts. Grief was private, difficult to catch.

Then Solvi thought of a way. In seafaring Bergen, the U-boat war had grown into a sorrow past imagining—half the fleet and two thousand Norwegian men buried in the cold ocean. One day Solvi found a knot of anxious mothers gathered at the newspaper stands, squinting at the lists of the dead, their faces grim. The photograph was even more powerful than she had hoped. This was what her father had meant.

But when Solvi showed it to her mother, she gasped. "How could you invade their privacy this way, Solveig?"

"This is history, Mama! It's my job to capture this strange time we're living through."

"I don't know what your father was thinking, giving you that camera." Solvi's mother straightened the frill at her throat and scowled. She didn't like her daughter roving about the city and worried incessantly. *Don't wander by the harbor,* she would say, or *Don't sit with boys in coffeehouses; people will think you're cheap.* And whenever Solvi put on her cape, *Don't go out in the cold and wet! You'll catch pneumonia!*

"It's always cold and wet in Bergen," Solvi would fume, stomping back up to her room.

And so Solvi started telling little fibs, just to relieve her mother's mind. That she was only going to Lisanne's house, that she always avoided the harbor, that she never sat with boys.

And in that way, a gap opened between them.

BY MIDDAY, the Kristiania train had reached the bleak Hardangervidda plateau, which it had to cross to reach the Oslofjord to the east. Solvi ate a roll with salmon paste and watched the tundra slide by.

In truth, Solvi and her mother had always been at odds. They were so different, Solvi asked her father once if she was adopted. He just laughed. *You are your mother's daughter, darling. She just had a different sort of father.*

He meant Solvi's grandfather, a retired banker who still dressed and went to the office every day to make sure they weren't giving away all the money, as he put it. He had a bearish way about him, affectionate but domineering. Solvi and her parents had always lived with him, as if there were no alternative.

Grandfather adored Solvi when she was young, spoiling her with treats and calling her *little squirrel.* But when she matured, he became protective and critical. Was it just his age? Solvi tried not to resent his ready disapproval, his concern over her *rebellious spirit* and *tramping about,* but her temper often flared as much as his.

By the time Solvi graduated from her ladies' academy, he had become fixated on finding her a husband.

No one spoke of university anymore.

ONE AFTERNOON, on a cool September evening, her grandfather handed her a letter as they gathered in the parlor before dinner. Solvi opened it, puzzled.

> *Dear Solveig: Our parents agree you and I would make uncommonly successful helpmates for the vicissitudes of life. Therefore, would you accept my hand in marriage? Someday the war will end; it's time to think about our future. I'll call on you tomorrow.*

It was from Stefan Vinter, a rich young man from one of the best families. Solvi scarcely knew him.

Her mother stepped into the parlor. "The Vinters, darling. How exciting!"

Solvi turned to her grandfather. "I'll have sherry tonight, as I'm apparently a grown-up now."

Her grandfather raised his eyebrows but poured her a glass. She drank it down and handed it back for more.

"Really, Solveig," her mother said. "There's no need to make a scene."

"I'm sorry. But I don't understand why you have to arrange a marriage for me."

"Solvi, it's a great honor," said her mother, rubbing her hands. "The Vinters have done well with their shipyard during the war, thanks to the Germans sinking all those ships, and Stefan's so handsome and intelligent. He talks about all the things you like: art, literature, politics."

Solvi remembered talking with him once; he spoke only of his hiking and rifle club. "But I want to go to university, like Papa wanted."

"Well, I'm sure your father would not advise that now, not with this wretched war," her mother said. "There are few good men left in Norway, between those leaving for America and those who've drowned. Your friends will be snatching husbands as soon as an armistice is signed, mark my words."

"You don't know what Papa would advise," Solvi said. She hated it when her mother spoke for him.

Her grandfather cleared his throat. "I can't imagine why you think you would enjoy university, Solveig. It's dreary work—all that Greek and Latin. I took little pleasure in my education."

"But I loved school, and Papa said I have a rare mind," she said. "Besides, I want to work, to contribute in some way."

Her grandfather grumbled. "Your contribution—and it is no small thing—is to raise children and care for your husband and aging parents. Why aren't you young ladies content with that? Frankly, it seems ungrateful."

Her mother took her hand. "Darling, you don't seem to understand. The Vinters are very well off. You would have nannies, even a lady's maid. You could still take baskets to the poor."

"I don't want a lady's maid," Solvi said. "I'm not sure we should have maids at all!"

"Whatever do you mean?" Her mother's eyes widened in surprise.

"I mean that it's wrong to hide in this . . . this luxurious cocoon!" Solvi said, sweeping her hand around the elegant parlor—the green damask walls, the brocade drapes, the glowing rosewood furniture. "Haven't we learned that from this awful war?"

Her mother's mouth grew tight. "Once you're living in a dank little room doing your own washing, you will sorely miss your cocoon, Solveig."

Solvi looked at her. It was maddening how elegant she was, with her silks and high-collared lace. As if her perfection absolved her from wrong thinking.

"I just don't understand why you won't let me find my own husband."

"Because you don't seem interested in husbands," her mother cried. "You're too busy taking those awful pictures!"

"You're the one who told me not to talk to boys, Mama!"

"There's no need to shout, Solveig," Grandfather said, patting her shoulder. "I understand that love is confusing. When you're young, you don't know whom to love, so you either love everyone or you love no one. We're offering guidance."

Solvi tried to swallow her anger, so they would stop looking at her as if she were mad. She finished her second glass of sherry, then turned to her mother. "Mama, how did you know you wanted to marry Papa?"

Her mother relaxed; this was the kind of discussion she preferred. "Well, Solveig, to be honest, I didn't know. But your grandfather did, and I knew to trust him."

"But I want a modern marriage—a marriage I pick for myself, to someone who'll treat me as his equal," Solvi said. "Don't you want me to be happy?"

"Of course we do," said her mother, "but marriage is not just about what you want. It's about security and position. We live in unstable times, Solvi; we're trying to provide for you." She gave Solvi a sly glance. "Besides, you could have a modern marriage with Stefan. We'll get you one of those adorable short wedding dresses, all flounces around the knees and sheer up top. And once you're married, all you need do is use your feminine wiles, and you can have it any way you want."

Solvi blushed, suddenly ashamed for her.

"All we ask is that you try to like Stefan," her grandfather said.

"And be polite when he comes tomorrow," her mother said.

"I'm always *polite*, Mama."

Her mother pulled the bell for dinner. "If you say so, darling."

THE NEXT MORNING Stefan Vinter came for coffee. Solvi's mother left them alone, so he could declare his love in private. Instead, he chatted about his father's shipyard. Solvi watched him, trying to make out what she meant to him. Then she saw it; it was as if she'd already said yes.

Arrogance. It was what she disliked most about her kind.

When her mother asked later how it went, Solvi just smiled. She needed to buy herself time.

THE TRAIN TO KRISTIANIA finally started its descent toward the Oslofjord. Solvi stood to stretch, then pulled her photo album from her satchel. She had to stop thinking of home. Perhaps this would help.

Before she left, she had put all her photographs in chronological order, so that she could see how her technique was developing. She flipped the album open to the beginning. Her early pictures were blurry shots of plants and flowers, including one of her father crouching beside a mountain stream examining a fern. Then several photographs of her parents and grandfather, beside a blazing Christmas tree, lunching in the garden. Then a shot in through a door ajar—her father in his sickbed. It was her first good photograph, she could see that now, but when she took it she felt only despair.

Then she turned to her pictures of the housemaids. Solvi had started with Mathilde, her family's maid. When Mathilde asked Solvi for a portrait to give her young man, Solvi told Mathilde to put on her Sunday best, then she seated her in the parlor. And there was Mathilde, the woman she could be if she wasn't a maid.

Soon, Solvi was photographing other young maids in parlors. But the more time she spent with them, the more she wanted pictures of them at work, cracking gourds with cleavers and starching shirts in brimming kettles. Before long the maids let her shoot whatever she liked.

Solvi paged through the pictures that captured the world of these young servants. Some were filled with movement and light, like the picture of several laughing girls pulling sheets off a clothesline in a windstorm, the linens flying like jibs. Others were dark and sad—a maid leaning wearily against a door with a heavy basket on her hip, a scullery girl with her head and shoulders in an oven, a bucket of dingy water at her knee.

One particular image always made Solvi feel like crying—a picture shot from below of a young maid lugging coal scuttles up a narrow stair, holes in her stockings. It felt like a statement of some kind, notice of a wrong that should be corrected. The maids she met worked ungodly hours, often to exhaustion; it didn't seem right.

But when she showed the pictures to Lisanne, her friend just shook her head and teased her for turning Bolshevik. After that, Solvi kept the album under her bed.

SHE GLANCED OUT THE WINDOW. The train had left the tundra behind and was winding through a forest alongside a river that ran for the sea. Her heart skipped a few beats. It wouldn't be long now.

She turned to the last set of photographs in her album. One of the best was a haunting image of an old schooner tied up at the wharf shrouded in mist—beautiful but also strange, as there were two figures being carried ashore on stretchers in the foreground. She came to realize only later that she had captured the first evidence of the terrible illness that swept Bergen in early October.

It was the great influenza that was marching across Europe, and it had arrived in Norway by sea. Soon, ships were unloading their dead before anything else came ashore.

The illness struck quickly and left its victims leaking blood and gasping for air. Within days of the flu's arrival in Bergen, the city shut down. Schools and churches closed; stores emptied of goods. Solvi's mother tried to quarantine her, but Solvi slipped out one afternoon and took pictures of the houses draped in crepe, hunched figures lined up outside the hospital, and finally, sickeningly, a wagon stacked with bundled corpses. She couldn't stop herself.

When Grandfather coughed up blood a week later, Solvi's mother locked her in her room.

Solvi, frantic to help, banged on the door. "Let me nurse him!" she yelled, but her mother ignored her. Solvi knew her mother was protecting her, but she couldn't help feeling that her mother had decided to die with him.

As if he needed her more in death than Solvi needed her alive.

Grandfather's influenza soon settled into pneumonia, and several days later his heart seized. They thought he was abed, but he was up rummaging through his study when he collapsed. Solvi's mother was out searching for bread, so the maids—unsure what to do with his body—unlocked Solvi's door. She helped them lift him onto the polished dining room table. When her mother returned to find Solvi sitting beside him, she fainted and had to be carried to her room. By dinner, she was coughing blood as well.

This time no one thought of locking Solvi away. The doctor came and told her what to do—fluids, cold compresses, and plenty of blankets. Solvi took notes, trying not to panic.

As he left, he said one last thing. "Handle her as little as possible, and wash your hands carefully if you must mop up. Many leak blood from their eyes and noses or vomit blood. But don't be alarmed; it doesn't necessarily mean she's dying."

Solvi could only nod.

OVER THE COURSE of the day and evening, Solvi's mother grew hot to the touch and slept fitfully, throwing off the covers one moment and crying for them minutes later. That night, Solvi tried to doze in an armchair in her mother's room, but it was impossible. Worries, one after another, rose before her. If her mother died, where would she live? Who would care what happened to her? How would she go on with no one to love her?

All she could think was that she would have to marry Stefan Vinter because she'd have no one else.

THE NEXT MORNING, as Solvi sat watch by her mother, Mathilde handed her a photograph—an old studio portrait of a couple with three children. It was singed at one end.

Solvi had never seen it before. "Where did you find this, Mathilde?"

"Under the stove in your grandfather's study, when we went in to tidy up."

"Did he try to burn it?"

"He was burning letters and other papers. We found fragments in the ashes when we cleaned the stove."

Solvi peered at the photograph again. The clothes were so old-fashioned. Then she sucked in her breath—the man was her grandfather, young, handsome, and proud. But Solvi didn't recognize the others. The woman, elegant in gray silk, sat smiling softly, her chin high. There were two boys in sailor suits, one standing very straight next to her grandfather, a younger one leaning against the woman's knee. And a baby, swathed in lace, perched on the woman's lap.

Solvi turned the photo over. There was no family name, just the stamp of a photography studio in Kristiania: *Stenberg's Photography Atelier, 365 Mollergata, Kristiania. October 9, 1879.*

She slipped it in her pocket.

BY NOON Solvi's mother tossed with pain, her breath growing labored. "I'm poison," she babbled. "Leave me. Let me go with Grandfather."

"No, Mama," Solvi said, stricken. "Stay with me! I'm the one who needs you."

But her mother just shut her eyes.

Later, the doctor brought medicine. "She must cough to live; mustard compresses will help," he said. Then one last admonition: "Don't upset her."

The day passed in a blur. When her mother slept, Solvi puzzled over the mysterious photograph. Was this a family Grandfather had before her mother was born, or was the baby her mother? Solvi checked the date. Her mother would have been two—that must be her. But who was the woman? Solvi's mother always said her mother died giving birth to her, but this woman looked like . . . Solvi squinted at the image. The woman looked so much like Solvi's mother, it must be her grandmother.

Then Solvi looked more closely at the boys. They would be her uncles, and perhaps . . . perhaps . . . Could these people be alive?

Solvi glanced at her mother, back at the photograph, and then something shifted. She had always wondered why she had no other relatives, no aunts or uncles, no cousins. Now—just as she feared she was losing everyone—there could be other family. Uncles, at least, and they might be married; perhaps she had cousins!

Solvi peered again at the woman in the photo, her grandmother. And what if she were alive? Alive and wondering if her daughter had a child?

Mathilde brought a custard for Solvi's mother, who opened her eyes only long enough to push the food away. Solvi took the bowl into the hall and wolfed it down, then returned to the sickbed and gazed down at her mother. What other secrets was she hiding?

When the rainy skies finally went dark, Solvi retreated to a sleeping pallet on the floor. She couldn't stop wondering about the people in the photograph. Then it came to her—maybe she could find them. They weren't here in Bergen, or she would know them. The next most likely place to look was Kristiania. That was where the photograph had been taken, so they must have lived there at that time.

Perhaps her uncles were working and going about their lives in Kristiania right at this moment!

Then, another thought: the university was in Kristiania.

She turned those ideas about in her head until she fell into an exhausted sleep.

HOURS LATER, Solvi woke with a start. Her mother stood over her, swaying, clutching a bloodstained cloth.

"Mama! What are you doing?" Solvi jumped up and grabbed her arm.

Her mother just looked at her, eyes blazing.

"Mama, get back in bed," Solvi said, pulling her across the room. "Lie down."

Her mother plucked at Solvi's sleeve. "I'm afraid for you, Solvi," she said in a rasping voice. "I'm afraid you'll be alone."

Solvi's chest tightened. "I have many friends, Mama. Lisanne's family will take me in."

Her mother shook her head. "No, now listen. You must marry Stefan. Promise me."

Solvi just looked at her.

"Promise!"

"I cannot marry Stefan," Solvi whispered. "I just can't."

"Solvi, you don't understand; you'll have no one." Her mother started to weep, bloody tears that dripped onto the sheets.

No one? Solvi pulled out the scorched photograph and held it up to her mother's face. "Mama, is this your family?"

Her mother looked at it for a moment, then turned away.

"Is that Grandfather?" Solvi said, pointing.

"Yes," she whispered.

"Is that you?" Solvi stabbed at the baby in lace.

Her mother nodded.

"And is that your mother?" Solvi's voice rose.

Her mother just looked at Solvi, her eyes brimming.

"Are those your brothers? Mama, are they alive?"

"I don't know."

"Where are they?"

Her mother closed her eyes. "I don't know! I don't know!"

"How could you not know!" Solvi shouted.

Her mother shrank into her pillows and turned to the wall.

Don't upset her, the doctor had said.

Solvi stepped back and after a few moments relented. She went to the window. Outside, a sliver of moon hung above the rooftops, appearing and disappearing as the wind drove the clouds across the sky. Family . . . she had other family—Solvi was sure of it.

THAT EVENING Solvi's mother suddenly started struggling to breathe. Solvi propped her up, fighting an urge to climb into the bed and throw her arms around her.

"Mama? Can you hear me?"

Her mother's lungs rattled, but she opened her eyes.

"Mama, please don't die!"

Her mother gazed at her for a long moment, then sighed and turned away.

Solvi started to weep. "I'm sorry I can't promise, Mama! I'm sorry! Please don't die!"

COOK FOUND SOLVI kneeling beside her mother, sobbing. She took her downstairs and settled her by the kitchen fire with a bowl of soup. They talked of small things—the rain, the larder.

Later, Solvi took her place again beside the bed, but her mother asked no more of her. Solvi held her hand and waited for death.

SOMEHOW, miraculously, Solvi's mother did not die. She lay suspended for several days in a coma that looked like death, then opened her eyes and asked for a boiled egg.

Two days later she caught Solvi's hand as Solvi passed by the bed. "Sit down, Solveig."

Solvi sat, dread rising in her chest.

"I remembered something last night. I remembered that you wouldn't promise."

Solvi flushed with shame. She'd hoped the illness had erased that moment between them.

"It was my deathbed request, Solveig."

Solvi twisted her hands. "I cannot marry him."

"Nonsense. Of course you can, if he'll still have you." She patted Solvi's knee. "Go get my pearls from the jewel box."

"Your pearls?"

"Just get them, Solvi. I want you to see them."

Solvi went to the dresser and pulled out the string of lustrous drops. Something felt wrong.

Her mother took them and dangled them in the light. "Grandfather gave me these when I married your father. I always meant to give them to you when you got engaged, darling. Aren't they lovely?"

Solvi flushed again, but this time the shame was for her mother. Did she think Solvi could be bought? "I don't love him, Mama. I will not marry someone I don't love."

"Oh, Solvi, don't be a child. Love is the last thing. It comes, but later, after you've shared a table and a bed. Early love is a bad sign; that's what Grandfather always said."

Solvi stood up. Something was gathering inside her, and if she didn't speak of it, it would wither and die. "I'm going to Kristiania to take the matriculation exams, Mama, to see if I can be admitted to the university."

Her mother's eyes widened. "Solvi, no. I need you; I have no one else!"

"You have the servants, Mama; they care for you. And it's not forever. I'll study and then come back to Bergen, maybe to teach, maybe to marry."

"You can't possibly pass the exams, and you have hardly any money, only that little bit your father left you," her mother said, picking at the blanket in agitation. "Besides, we know no one in Kristiania, so there's nowhere for you to live. It's quite impossible."

"But my academy teachers said I should try, and there's a study house for women. I can live there," Solvi said.

"Some old matron watching over a house full of young ladies? That's not acceptable."

Solvi just looked at her in stubborn silence. Her mother pulled out a handkerchief and dabbed at her eyes. "I don't understand why you must leave Bergen. It will break my heart."

"I don't mean to break your heart, Mama, but no one in Bergen understands me," Solvi said, thinking of her album hidden under the bed so as not to offend anyone. "I'm different; I'm odd; I want things other girls in Bergen don't even think about. I'm not just different from you; I'm different from everybody."

"Solvi, I'm sure you could find more friends if you put down that camera and tried. Besides—what would I do without you?"

"Live your life, Mama. This precious life you're lucky to have."

"But you're my life, darling. You're my everything."

Solvi picked up the breakfast tray. She didn't mean to be hard-hearted, but she was fighting for air.

"Then I'm sorry for you, Mama."

A FEW NIGHTS LATER Solvi and her mother ate dinner in the awkward silence that had settled between them.

When she was done, Solvi's mother put down her fork. "I've made a decision. You may not go to Kristiania. Just put the idea out of your head."

"I wasn't asking permission, Mama."

"But it's my job to protect you, especially now that our menfolk are gone. If you want a job, you can find something suitable here in Bergen. Besides, you have little money, and I'm not going to finance it."

"University's only part of it," Solvi said, pushing her potatoes around her plate. "I want to go to Kristiania for another reason, Mama."

"What, for God's sake?"

"I want to find your family, our family."

Her mother sucked in a breath. "What are you talking about?"

"The boys in the photograph. Maybe we do have menfolk! If they're alive, they're probably in Kristiania. I might have cousins, maybe even a grandmother!"

Her mother's mouth dropped open. "No, Solvi. Don't even think that."

"But the photograph of your family was taken in Kristiania. You must have lived there then."

"We've lived in Bergen as long as I can remember," her mother said, turning away and ringing the bell.

"Don't you want to find your brothers?"

Her mother looked at her. "Solvi, if you must know the awful truth, my mother died shortly after that photograph was taken, and my brothers went off to school the next year and, well, died there. Of typhus or something. That's when Grandfather and I moved here."

A shadow passed over Solvi's heart. They died? "But why did you never speak of them?"

"I barely knew them and did not miss them when they were gone."

Solvi narrowed her eyes. How could she not miss her own brothers? "And why did you tell me your mother died in childbirth if that wasn't true?"

Her mother busied herself folding her napkin. "Oh, I don't know. I thought that if you knew my mother died when I was young, you would worry about losing me. The truth is, I was raised by my nurse, Anne-Marie. It was as if my mother died in childbirth."

Solvi sat back in her chair. "So we don't have other family?"

"No, Solvi, we do not. They're gone, gone forever. And, by the grace of God, I beg you to leave them in their graves."

"What was your mother's name?"

Her mother blinked. "Why, Solveig Fallesen, of course. Surely you remember you were named for her."

"I was? I never knew that. What were your brothers' names?"

Her mother rose. "I hardly remember. I was a little girl when they died, and your grandfather never spoke of them." She gave Solvi a long stern look and then turned away. "I'm tired. I'm going to bed."

BACK IN HER ROOM, Solvi sat studying the photograph of her mother's family. How could her mother not know the names of those sweet little boys? If they had died, the family would have been bereft, the names carried as tender talismans forever.

No, her mother was lying—that was the only explanation. And if she was lying, there must be a reason.

Solvi gazed at the image of her grandmother. There was something about her, something bold and open that Solvi felt as kindred. Her mother didn't have it—her strength was brittle, dependent on her comforts and station. Whatever her grandmother had, it didn't pass to Solvi's mother.

But maybe it passed to her.

A FEW DAYS LATER the church bells started ringing and didn't stop. The Germans had surrendered; the war was finally over. Solvi ran out with her camera and took pictures of the crowds that filled the harbor, celebrating.

The next morning Stefan Vinter came by for Solvi's answer. When she opened the front door, the image of her grandfather as a young man—self-satisfied and proud—flashed in her mind. No wonder he selected Stefan for her.

This time Stefan did profess his love, but it didn't help. When Mathilde brought in the tray of coffee and sweets, Stefan was gone.

A few minutes later Solvi's mother peeked around the door. When she saw her daughter alone, she swept in.

"You didn't!"

"I did. Stefan Vinter is free to marry someone else."

Her mother put her face in her hands, as if to weep. "I'm afraid for you, afraid you'll never marry!"

Solvi just looked at her, unmoved. "If I marry, I want someone who'll run away with me on a grand adventure, not someone who will just go to work for his father the next day."

"Oh, Solvi, that's just childish talk," her mother sobbed.

"Mama, I'm tired of this," Solvi said, taking a cake and shoving it, in a most unladylike fashion, into her mouth. Then she went upstairs to pack.

CHAPTER THREE

NORA

Spring 1919 ▪ *Spokane, Washington*

After Anders headed out to do his chores the next morning, I took a lantern down into the root cellar so I could examine the advertisement again, in private. I hated keeping it a secret, but to tell him would only breed worry. I needed time to decide what to do, or even if I should do anything.

Because what if I had never seen it? Suppose the bundle of newspapers bounced off the wagon and was never delivered? I would be none the wiser, and neither would Anders. And we could have continued as we were, safe in our little vale of solitude.

But it was delivered, and now I faced a difficult question: Should I tell Anders?

I kept secrets from Anders for many years. I thought they were little more than shadows, but they came to loom over my everyday happiness and held me apart in everything I had with him. It didn't end well, trying to bury the truth.

I would keep this secret one week, I told myself, to give me time to figure out what to do. And then I would tell him everything.

IN THE ROOT CELLAR I turned over a bucket and sat down. The dank coolness of the exposed earth reminded me of the old sod house, how it smelled of death. And sadness rode in with that memory. Since the moment I spotted the advertisement the night before, everything seemed to push me back into the past I had tried so hard to forget.

I pulled the scrap of newspaper from my pocket. Despite the ghosts it revived, I felt drawn to the picture. How astonishing to see it again, after so many years. I had forgotten what the children looked like back then, how beautiful they were, how much they were already themselves: Ivar, proper and well behaved; Bobby, dreamy and excitable; Emma, a tiny princess destined to be a queen.

So which was looking for me? It must be one of my children, as no one else would care. But did my children even know I was alive? And, if they did, why seek me now?

I last saw them nearly thirty years ago. By now, they would be more than grown; they would be middle-aged. Emma would be forty-one, the boys a bit older. Every Christmas, and on each of their birthdays, I had tried to picture them marching steadily into their adulthood, but their images in my head remained childish, as those were my memories of them. Their grown-up selves could only be conjured through a haze.

Then, a thought—perhaps there were grandchildren. It was easier to imagine them, little Ivars and Bobbies and Emmas.

I savored that idea for a long moment. Grandchildren might be more forgiving. But I shook the notion from my head. It was too much to hope for.

Instead, I examined the text below the picture again: *Nora Helmer was declared dead in 1885, but her family has reason to believe she is alive, perhaps in America.*

Reason to believe? Ivar knew more than that. Ivar, my perfect boy.

I picked a few turnips out of the loose soil and dropped them in my basket. Ivar was the one who proved true, the one who had believed I was alive, even when Torvald insisted I was dead. Ivar was the one who had wanted me back.

NORA
December 27, 1879 ▪ Hamar, Norway

On the cold night I returned to Hamar and my childhood home, I stood outside for a long moment, unsure if I should knock or slip away. But I had nowhere else to go. I rapped gently.

Aagot, my aunt's maid, opened the door and quickly smiled. "What a surprise, Miss Nora," she said, then led me through to the parlor.

My aunt rose from her chair. "Why, Nora! You've finally come to visit!"

"For a bit, Aunt. If you don't mind." I kissed her powdered cheek.

"Of course. But where are the children? Certainly Ivar's old enough to travel with you."

"Ivar's in school, Aunt. I thought it best to come by myself."

She motioned toward a chair, then opened the front of the stove to let out the heat, a show of civility. "Please, sit. Supper will be in soon. Tell me why you're here."

I sank into an ancient brocaded chair and looked around. The familiar finery hung heavy with wear; the stale air reeked of rose water and dust. How little had changed since my father's death. I could feel him there, as if he might appear and put his hand on my hair.

A wave of dizziness swept over me. I leaned back and closed my eyes. It had been a long time since I'd thought about my father.

"You seem a bit faint, dear," said my aunt.

I sighed and looked at her, tightly laced into her high-necked dress. Age had diminished her. She perched on the edge of her chair.

"Perhaps more hungry than faint," I said.

"Of course." She rang the bell, and Aagot appeared with bowls of parsnip soup. My aunt watched me as I ate.

"Is something wrong, Nora?" she finally said. "Something between you and Torvald?"

"Why would you say that, Aunt? Aren't you pleased to see me?"

She gave me a puzzled look. "But no one travels in midwinter unless they must."

"Well, I, I just . . ." The room started to spin. I had no idea how to explain it to her.

"Please, Nora. Tell me what has happened."

I hesitated for a long moment, old feelings and resentments swirling in my mind. "Marriage isn't easy," I finally said. It was deeply humiliating to admit this to her, this woman who had so often judged me more than loved me.

"But I would think now that Torvald has been promoted to bank manager, now that money needn't be so tight . . ."

I put my napkin down. "It's a long story, Aunt. I will tell you in the morning."

She pursed her lips. "You've come for help, Nora, and I won't sleep until I know what you want."

I sighed. There was no way to pretend—I would have to tell her the truth. "Torvald and I cannot live together anymore, Aunt. I've left him."

She sucked in a breath. "What are you talking about?"

"He was . . . he was disrespectful to me."

"Nora, Nora!" Her hands flew to her face. "What do you mean? Was he cruel? Sometimes husbands are a bit rough with their wives, I know that, but just go back and tell him you won't stand for it!"

"No, not that."

"Then what do you mean?"

"He said cruel things, Aunt. Unforgivable things." I could only look down at my hands.

"Nora, dear—I understand if you need a break. But please don't say you've left Torvald. No one leaves their husband, especially young mothers. It would be a terrible scandal!"

Of course it was scandalous, but, in a flash, I saw that I didn't care. Scandal was better than throwing myself into the fjord. "We had a terrible fight, about a loan."

She sat back. "You know I have no money, Nora."

"I'm not here to ask for money," I said, reddening. "I paid it off myself, taking in sewing and copying. But Torvald doesn't believe in borrowing, so we fought."

My aunt let out a small huff of despair. "Oh, Nora . . . How could you two let something like that come between you?" Her face grew stern. "There's only one thing to do. Go back tomorrow morning and beg his forgiveness."

"But, Aunt, he was the one who said I should never have borrowed, that such a thing made me unfit to be a mother!"

"It doesn't matter what he said! Go home where you belong, first thing, and then behave yourself. Be a better mother!" She jumped up, as if to get my coat. "Quick, before word gets out that you've left!"

But I sat frozen to my chair. If I stood up, I would be blown back to Kristiania by the winter wind. "I cannot go back, Aunt. I cannot."

"Nora, your children need you. There's no other question."

"Oh, Aunt, I'm not sure what being a mother means right now. Their nurse has done a better job mothering the children than I ever could—." My voice broke. The thought that I had made a serious mistake leaving the children behind surfaced in my addled brain, but I couldn't tell her that.

She paced about, wiping her forehead with her handkerchief. "Nora, I would think you, of all people, would understand how important a mother is." She reached for a chair, then sat back down. "This is so worrisome, Nora; I feel a bit faint."

"I don't mean to abandon the children, Aunt. I just need time to decide what to do."

She dabbed at her face, then called for Aagot to bring her salts. "And my Bible, too, please," she said, when Aagot appeared. "I swear, Nora, you will be the death of me."

"Forgive me, Aunt, but I am family." Something in me hardened. "Would you rather I slept on the street?"

She shot me a piercing look, furious I had trapped her this way.

I stood. "Perhaps it's best we both go to bed. We can discuss it in the morning."

"No, Nora, stay. We must pray."

It was only after we petitioned God for my salvation that I was allowed to escape upstairs to my old room.

LATER, I huddled by the stove in the narrow room of my childhood, shivering with exhaustion and chilled by my aunt's opposition. If my father were alive, things might be different. Or if I'd been a better niece, a small voice said in my head. If I had visited my aunt a few times, surely she would have received me better now.

I gazed about the room. My drawings still hung from the walls and my schoolbooks stood on the shelf, but the room felt empty, as if the schoolgirl had died.

And there, up near the ceiling as if watching from heaven, was the picture of the angel my father had given me when I was very small.

He brought the drawing to me one day and told me it was my mother. She had died two days after my birth, and so I never knew her.

"She will fly down at night to kiss your cheek, Nora," he said, hammering in a nail and hanging the picture.

"If I stay awake will she talk to me?"

"No, child. You know that angels come only when you're asleep."

Sometimes I lay very still with my eyes barely open, hoping to catch my angel mother flitting around the bed. It never worked. I knew by the time I was six that no one came down to kiss my cheek.

Now I undressed and washed, memories rising around me as I stood over the familiar china basin.

Had I been happy here? I couldn't say. Without a mother, the only life I knew as a girl was the attention of my father and the care of my nurse. My sole purpose was to bring light and laughter into this house. My father loved me dearly, particularly when I spun through the house like a gleeful sprite. But he ignored me when I was quiet or—God forbid—unhappy. He bought fancy dresses and ribbons to set off my flaxen beauty and refused to talk about anything sad or difficult, including my mother.

But the more he urged me to forget my morbid thoughts, the more I wanted to know.

As I matured, he grew anxious, as if he couldn't bear for me to grow up. He kept me in braids and pinafores well past the appropriate age, and when I turned into a graceful young woman despite him, he struggled to keep me at his side, insisting I stay home to entertain him rather than visiting friends.

I would wait until his afternoon nap, then slip out of the house to walk with my beaux among the stones of the old cathedral. He never knew. By then my nurse, Anne-Marie, who understood what a girl needed, was keeping my secrets for me.

My father always said we were happy, and so I made myself lighthearted and bent to his whims. At night, though, I begged God to send him a wife, to relieve his intense consideration of me. But God has never listened to my prayers.

When I was fourteen, my father invested in a line of steamships on the lake, but the business soon failed, and he sank into debt. Still, he insisted on sending me to an exclusive ladies' academy, where I learned French, English, and German, as if I might marry a Danish count.

Torvald, when he appeared, was not what my father had imagined, but in some dark way they understood each other. Torvald, by then a young lawyer, salvaged my father's reputation. My father, beholden, offered Torvald my hand.

It didn't occur to me to say no. I was already attracted by Torvald's dark eyes and his adoration of me. Indeed, I thought he would be easy to manage, he was so besotted. I thought marrying would free me.

It all might have turned out differently if my mother had lived. She might have sensed Torvald's flaws and discouraged me from marrying him, or steered me to marry someone else. She could have advised me, guided me. Perhaps she would have raised me to be a different young woman—one that Torvald Helmer wouldn't have wanted, or who wouldn't have wanted Torvald Helmer.

But she did not live, and there was no one else to caution me. So I married, and we moved to Kristiania, settling into a good apartment on the second floor of a new building close to the center of town.

I soon discovered, however, that instead of being liberated, I had been passed from one man to the next, like a horse groomed for the parade grounds. Once we settled, Torvald forbade me to do anything utilitarian; he even brought my old nurse, Anne-Marie, to tend our babies so he could show me off in the parlors of the well-to-do.

Torvald also loved the girl in me, so I dressed below my years, danced the silly peasant dances he found so bewitching, and pretended to accept his rules. Torvald said we were happy, and so I made myself lighthearted, laughing when he caught me in a lie, slipping from his grasp when he lectured. If he chastised me for eating sweets, I kissed him and denied it, even as I fingered the package in my pocket. And when he called me scatter-brains and scolded me for running through money, I told myself it didn't hurt—and then counted up what I had for my lender, the hateful Mr. Krogstad, the next time I met him on a darkened street.

In the end, it caught up with me. All the playacting, all the cheerful, frenzied effort to make everything right. The truth had its own desires, a lust to be known.

I looked at myself now in the mirror. Who would I have become if Torvald hadn't gotten sick, if I had never taken on that terrible debt? I would have been trapped forever as the girl he married. Instead, my troubles had given me a backbone, something I was not allowed before. When I saw what I could do, the girl bride fell away like a husk.

THE NEXT MORNING I woke up angry. Angry that Torvald had allowed me so little freedom in our life together, angry that I was given so little authority over anything that mattered. As if he never trusted me, as if he never understood all I had done for him. And now I was the one who had to crawl back to my childhood home and beg for a bed.

I splashed my face with cold water from the pitcher, but it did little to calm the anger burning in my cheeks. I dressed quickly and went downstairs to confront my aunt.

When I came into the dining room, she was nervously tying a small box with string.

"I hope you've changed your mind, Nora," she said, unable to meet my eyes. "There's a train at nine-thirty, but you'll have to hurry." She pushed the box toward me. "Your lunch."

"Aunt, I am sorry, but I'm not going back to Torvald."

"But the gossips will be talking, Nora! There's no time to lose." She glared at me for an instant, an angry crow ready to chase me away.

I took some toast, poured myself coffee, and sat down.

She came over to sit beside me, bustling her skirts about as if that gave her more authority. "Nora, listen to me. You'll be tarnished, my dear; tarnished for life. People will think the worst, and it's difficult to recover from that. Don't you understand?"

I flushed deeply. "I understand that gossips will say whatever distasteful thoughts come into their minds, but I cannot let that keep me entombed in a miserable marriage."

She gave me a chastising look. "I hardly think you were entombed, Nora."

"You weren't there, Aunt." Bitterness welled up inside me, making me tremble so that I could scarcely keep from spilling my coffee.

She held her breath for a long moment, then sighed and pushed the boxed lunch away. "I don't know why I bothered," she muttered.

I closed my eyes for a moment to calm myself, then looked up and reached for her hands. "Aunt, please, I know how uncomfortable this must be for you, but I have no one else. Please let me stay until I find work and a place of my own."

She held my gaze, her eyes glittering.

"Let me stay so that I need not resort to anything we would both regret."

At that, she looked away.

"I'll help with expenses," I said. "I know coal is dear."

"You've no idea what it means to be alone in the world, Nora."

"I'm grateful to have you, Aunt. Truly."

She stood up and sniffed into her handkerchief, then looked back at me with defiance. "You may stay a few weeks, but first you must answer one question and answer it honestly."

"Of course, Aunt."

"Swear to me there's no other man involved."

Heat rose in my face again. "Is that what you think?"

"Honestly, Nora, I have no idea what to think. Swear to me."

I tried to breathe evenly. I had never liked having to swear to anything, but I had little choice. "No, Aunt. I swear; I have always been faithful to Torvald."

"Most women couldn't afford to leave their husbands unless they had a promise from someone else. I daresay you couldn't either."

"But I do not have a promise, or anyone else, Aunt. I have no one, except you."

"That's a sad state of affairs, Nora. But, as you are my niece, I must accept your word." She stood up, taking the boxed lunch with her. "Just remember one thing: I've little stomach for gossip. For your sake, I hope it stays in Kristiania."

LATER THAT DAY my chest arrived. I dragged it upstairs eagerly, but when I opened the lid my heart sank. It was only half full. On top was a note.

> *Dear Nora: Torvald pulled out most of your dresses and books, saying you don't deserve anything but the barest necessities. He's furious that you took your pearls, yet he expects you to return any minute. Your friend, Kristine*

I pawed through the meager piles. Three faded dresses I'd put aside for the maid, a pair of scuffed shoes, a handful of underwear. None of my favorite gowns, none of my music or novels. A chill settled over me. The only respectable things I had were those I wore the night I left—my better traveling dress, my winter boots and good coat, my rabbit-fur hat.

I pulled out the dresses to examine them, and there, tucked between the skirts, was a single book, my confirmation Bible. Inside it—sticking out so I would notice—was a photograph of us as a family. Me in gray, the boys in their sailor suits, Emma in lace, and Torvald towering over us. I lifted the picture to the fading afternoon light, thinking of the day it was taken. How excited the children were to be together on an outing to the photographer's studio. We looked like the perfect family, which explained the victorious expression on Torvald's face.

I pressed the photograph to my cheek, squinting back tears. What were the children doing now? Playing in the park, no doubt. Soon they would return for their supper and get ready for bed. It was the hour I loved best. Anne-Marie would bathe Emma first, then hand her to me for nursery rhymes while Nurse pushed the rowdy boys through the tub. Once the boys were in bed, handsome in their pajamas and slicked-back hair, I would tell them a story. Outside the nursery Torvald paced, hurrying me along so he could have his supper.

It was true that Anne-Marie handled most of the children's care, but I was the one who understood their hearts. Torvald called Ivar "little man," but I knew Ivar hid a tender nature behind this facade and would feel his father's shame as much as the loss of me. Bob, my elf, often spun through the apartment only to fall in my lap and twist his fingers in my hair. If any of them kicked and cried over my disappearance, it would be poor Bobby. And then there was little Emma, too young to be much more than a mystery. My only consolation was that she preferred Nurse and so would miss me least.

I tucked the photograph away and took one last look in the trunk. Ah, my bag of embroidery, stuffed in the bottom. I pulled it out and released the clasp, and it was only then that my life came surging back in a wave of despair. All so familiar, the tangle of silk thread, the little wooden hoops. And there, beneath a knot of ribbon, was a small linen cap for Emma I'd been stitching with a border of flowers.

I sank onto the bed, overcome. How could I leave these children? How would I live without them? We shared things no one else knew—silly songs and games, secrets they whispered in my ear. I could still feel their arms around my neck. And poor Emma, my little daughter, just two years old. I wept into the pillow so my aunt wouldn't hear.

Yet, at the same time, I knew I could not go back, not even for them. I felt this more than understood it, like bedrock beneath everything. I could not live the lie that was my marriage anymore—pretending not to care when Torvald teased and belittled me, pretending I was just tatting lace when I was saving the family from ruin. I could not.

I washed my face and went downstairs to supper.

THE NEXT MORNING dawned cloudy and cold. I rose, brushed my dark blond hair until it gleamed, and swept it into a knot. As I did, I studied my image in the mirror—the broad brow, the deeply set blue eyes, the angled Norwegian cheekbones and strong chin. Familiar yet different, more serious.

I smiled to reassure myself and raised my chin.

The snow whirled in flurries as I walked through town. At first I just eyed the shops, but soon I began stopping wherever a lady might work. To afford my own room, I would need a salaried position, not the piecemeal copying and bookkeeping I had done to pay off Krogstad.

I asked first at several solicitors' offices, unleashing my finest smile. The managers greeted me politely but offered little. Perhaps if I had a letter of introduction, they said.

"I can give you references," I told them, ashamed I hadn't thought to bring a letter from someone in Kristiania. They looked at each other and cleared their throats. If I found nothing better, they said, I could stop back for piecework.

I soon began sizing up the shops, but the girls behind the counters appeared far below my station. I walked across the square to the hotel, thinking it more respectable, and was encouraged when the matron at the desk recognized me. But when I asked for a job, her smile faded.

"Don't you have children, Mrs. Helmer?" she said, her voice tight.

"Yes, but they're mostly in school now. I've come back to help my aunt for a while. Her health, you know."

"I'm sorry, Mrs. Helmer," she said, shaking her head as if there was something strange about me. "Give my best to your aunt. Good day."

I returned to one of the solicitors for copying work, then waded home through the snow. Later that evening, when I had finally finished the tedious documents, I took out Emma's cap and stitched tiny flowers until the candle guttered. Don't be discouraged, I told myself. You are safe tonight, and your stomach is full. Tomorrow will be better. Perhaps working in a shop would be fine.

OVER THE NEXT FEW DAYS I visited nearly every business in Hamar. No one had a salaried position for *a lady such as yourself*, as they put it. This covered all my sins: bred too high, overeducated, married but not wearing a ring. One gentleman inquired hopefully whether I was a widow, but when I said no, he shook his head. At the end of each disappointing day, I would stop at the solicitor's office for copying work, then stay up late taxing my eyes and burning precious candles. But it earned me enough to help pay for coal and food.

On Sunday my aunt insisted we walk to the Lutheran church, slipping quietly into a pew in the back. That didn't stop people from staring. The pastor, alerted by my aunt, spoke of the sanctity of the family, the mother as the keel and ballast of the family ship while the husband, at the helm, steered through storms and troubles. When we thanked him after the service, he gave my hand a meaningful squeeze.

In time I ran into old friends, including Sigrid Rorlund, a schoolmate who invited me to dinner. I remembered her more as rival than friend, but accepted anyway. Her husband, a local merchant, might know of work, I reasoned. Besides, I longed to escape my aunt's thinning patience, if just for an evening.

The night of the dinner I wore my only presentable dress, a simple blue wool gown. Sigrid appeared in an elegant taffeta with a bustle of Belgian lace; next to her I looked like the governess. Still, she greeted me with warmth and took me around her parlor, showing off all she had ordered from Copenhagen, then boasting about her sons, bright boys picked by the dean of the parish for an academy in Kristiania.

When we gathered at the table with her husband, however, he gave me an odd look, as if he had heard something.

"Nora, I understand you're looking for work in Hamar," Mr. Rorlund said, handing me a glass of claret while the maid served. "Are you planning to stay for a while?"

"Oh, I just want a bit of office work to keep me busy while I'm visiting my aunt, which may be some months. She's not well, you know. "

"I'm sorry to hear that," Sigrid said. "But do you work in Kristiania?" She couldn't keep the surprise out of her voice.

"When I can. I enjoy simple bookkeeping and copying. It's much more interesting that sitting around the house caring for the potted plants."

Mr. Rorlund looked up from his beef. "I wonder that Mr. Helmer allows it."

"He's very forward thinking," I rattled on, taking another sip of wine. It was the first I'd had since Christmas and tasted like God's own nectar. "Things in Kristiania are different. Women are finding more to do outside the home."

"Then what happens *inside* the home?" Mr. Rorlund asked.

"The servants do a fine job running most households," I said. "Our nurse raised me, so I trust her with the children."

"Indeed," Mr. Rorlund said, exchanging a glance with Sigrid. They thought Torvald and I were in debt. Fine—it might make them more likely to help me.

"Mr. Rorlund, perhaps you know someone who needs an office clerk."

He coughed in surprise. "There are few office jobs in Hamar, Mrs. Helmer, and there are always honest men ready to take them. Young men, hoping to start a family—those are the best people to hire."

"I thought all the honest young men had gone to America."

He grunted. "It can be difficult, what with the overblown optimism from abroad, but I hardly think that means we should employ our wives."

"Some honest women don't have husbands to rely on, Mr. Rorlund. What of them?"

He gave me a sharp look. "The definition of an honest woman is one with a husband, is it not, Mrs. Helmer?"

I gave him a faint smile and turned away.

Sigrid coughed, then called for Mr. Rorlund's coffee to be served in his study. He bowed stiffly and fled.

I spent the rest of the evening nodding as Sigrid boasted about her sons.

TWO DAYS LATER my aunt returned from visiting and called me into the parlor. "Nora, I'm sorry I must say this, but I'm angry with you."

"I'm sorry too. What have I done?"

"You've compromised Torvald's reputation by telling the Rorlunds you've been working."

"I don't understand."

"The only reason a gentleman would let his wife work would be to save him from financial ruin," she said, frowning. "I also hear you are visiting because I'm in ill health."

I blushed. "I'm sorry, Aunt. That came out before I could stop it. I suppose I felt I had to say something."

"I don't mean to criticize, Nora, but you struggle with the truth."

"I didn't think you wanted me to tell the truth, Aunt."

Her brow knotted. "Which is why you should return to Torvald before it gets any worse! I doubt anyone will have you in for Sunday dinner once this gets around. No more gay evenings drinking other people's wine."

"I don't need their wine. If I had a job, I could buy my own."

"That would be a sad life, Nora, drinking alone at your solitary table." Then her eyes filled. "I don't understand why that's better than dining with your family. I pray every night you'll come to your senses and go home. It breaks my heart."

I looked at her, scarcely able to breathe. It broke my heart, too, but I could not tell her that.

THE NEXT MORNING Sigrid Rorlund appeared in our parlor. My aunt nodded happily, then slipped into the kitchen to gather coffee and cake.

I was surprised but pleased. "Sigrid! Come in. Please sit."

She sat on the edge of a chair but didn't take off her gloves. "I don't have long, Nora. I just wanted to talk to you for a moment."

"Of course." My aunt appeared in the doorway, but I waved her away. "What is it?"

"I wanted to tell you I thought it quite interesting that you work, in Kristiania, I mean."

I sighed. This couldn't be why she came.

"Nora, I thought I should warn you." She leaned forward, as if we were children who must whisper secrets. "I heard the most awful rumor yesterday, and I prayed about it last night and resolved to tell you."

"What was it? That I've grown donkey ears?"

"No, worse," she said, shaking her head. "There's a story that you've abandoned your family. That you've left your husband."

I could only look at her.

"I mean," she said, wringing her hands, "I'm sure it can't be true, but I thought you should know. I can't imagine why someone would spread such a story."

"Well, perhaps it is true."

Her eyes grew large. "What do you mean?"

"I did leave Torvald. He was cruel to me, and I decided I couldn't stay with such a man."

She pulled away. "That's astonishing, Nora," she finally said. "That must have taken courage."

"I wouldn't call it courage. I just couldn't be his wife anymore."

Her face darkened. "But what of your children?"

"I'm hoping he'll let me see them. Thankfully, they're very attached to their nurse."

"Well, I had no idea. So I suppose, then, you must work."

"Yes. You might be so kind as to explain it to your husband. I'm sure he would know if a job opened up."

She gave me a nervous glance, then stood. "I'm so sorry, Nora, but he told me that if the rumor was true, I shouldn't see you again."

I went cold. "Is that what you want, Sigrid?"

She kissed me on the cheek ever so lightly. "Good luck, Nora. I hope you find what you're looking for."

And then she was gone.

My aunt appeared with the coffee tray, but her face fell when she saw me alone.

"My truth is out," I said.

"Oh, Nora!" She shot me a stricken look, turned, and took the tray back to the kitchen. It wasn't meant for me.

AFTER SIGRID'S VISIT, I sent notes to other childhood friends in Hamar, hoping I was wrong, but they were soon returned with regrets. All I did was leave my husband, and I knew—from years of chatting over the tea cakes—that other women had reason to do the same. But no, they would stand at the water's edge and watch me slip under the ice, then straighten their hats and walk away.

A WEEK LATER, on a cold Sunday afternoon, my aunt and I were sewing in the parlor when I heard harness bells. My aunt put down her needle and turned her head, listening.

A horse snorted. I glanced outside—a sleigh had stopped in front of the house. Then someone stamped on the doorstep and knocked, hard. My aunt gave me a timid smile and called to her maid. "Aagot, get the door. Nora's husband is here."

I threw aside my sewing. "No. You didn't." I jumped to my feet, but before I could flee Torvald appeared in the doorway. And there, next to him, was Ivar.

My beautiful boy. He stared at me, wide-eyed, as if I were a ghost.

"Darling!" I said, sweeping him into a hug. He fell against me, and I pressed my face to his hair, filling my lungs with him. I glanced at Torvald over Ivar's head. Such clever cruelty, to bring the boy.

Torvald smiled and took off his coat, as if he'd come for dinner. He wasn't a big man, but his body seemed to fill the room. He embraced my aunt. "I cannot tell you how grateful I am for your letter." Then he stepped over to me, gripping my shoulders and leaning in to kiss my cheek.

I went stiff. His touch and smell, so familiar, so unwelcome.

"How are you, Nora?" he said. "Are you better?"

I glanced at Ivar, who looked up at me with a worried brow. "Yes, somewhat, but the fevers persist." I leaned over, took Ivar's hand, and pressed it to my forehead. "Here, darling. You can feel the heat, can't you?"

He nodded solemnly.

"But don't worry. I'll get better in time. Aunt's been taking good care of me."

Torvald watched this pantomime. "It's good to see you, Nora," he said pleasantly, playacting himself. "We've missed you." He settled into a chair and began to chat about the weather, as if nothing had happened. I sat with Ivar, drinking him in, nodding and listening to them both, but I could scarcely breathe.

My aunt fidgeted, then leaped up and called for Aagot to bring the soup, though it was still early. She bustled about laying the tablecloth and silver, avoiding my eye.

"So, Nora, do you think you're well enough to return?" Torvald said. "The doctors in Kristiania are prepared for you. Ivar and I would be happy to take you home tonight."

Ivar looked at me hopefully.

I gazed at him. Can one weigh love, balance it against other needs? And, if so, why did I feel my refusal of Torvald more than my love for my children?

I smiled sadly at Ivar. "Well, this is all rather sudden, Torvald. I'm not sure I have the strength. Why don't we have supper, and then perhaps you and I can talk."

"Then let's eat," Torvald said. "Ivar and I are hungry!"

We sat down—my aunt had ordered a rich fish stew, and Aagot brought out the best cheeses—but I just nibbled at the bread, my throat tight as a vice. Torvald talked of the years he worked in Hamar, glancing and smiling at me as the story unfolded. Is this how he thought it would be, that I just needed a short holiday and life would soon be back to normal? I watched him warily.

"Eat, Nora." He passed me the butter. "You must build yourself up if you're to recover."

I turned to Ivar, who chattered away. He told me he had taught Emma to draw but had to lock away his drum, as she was making too much noise. Bob was starting to read a few words but still needed a lot of help. The family downstairs got a little dog.

My eyes filled. The comforting familiarity of Ivar and his world beckoned like a glimpse of paradise. I had to stand up to break the spell.

"Aagot, would you please take Ivar out for a walk? He needs a run before getting back on the train."

She glanced at my aunt, who nodded. I helped Ivar with his coat, then gave him a hug. "Have her show you the church. It has big brass doors!"

As soon as they left, I turned to Torvald. "I never thought you would use the children this way."

He cocked his head. "Whatever do you mean, Nora?"

"Bringing Ivar, using him as bait."

"Nora, we're just trying to do what's best for you!"

"How can you be so cruel to him?"

"Nora," he said, moving toward me, "calm yourself. Your aunt wrote and told me how hard things are for you, and as you can see, the children miss you terribly. So now your little vacation is over. It's time to come home and fulfill your responsibilities to them even if you cannot fulfill them to me. I'm prepared to wait for that day."

"Torvald, I'm not going home. If I could go home, I never would have left."

"Please, Nora. None of your dramatics now. This is too serious."

"Yes, this is serious. I am serious."

"Nora, if you persist in this it will be a tragedy for the children," he said. "You must think of them!"

"I cannot return to our life together, Torvald. I know that's painful for everyone, but I cannot."

Torvald leaned toward me. "But how will Ivar feel if you don't come home with us tonight?" he said in a hush, as if I'd gone mad. "How can they survive this? How am I to raise them in the shadow of this?"

In the shadow of a crazy mother, he meant.

Tears welled in my eyes. "I'm sorry for the children, for Ivar, but you should have thought of that before you brought him," I cried. "I can't believe you would be so selfish, to use him for your purpose!"

"Selfish? To bring my son to see his dear mama? He's brokenhearted— as is Bob. If you're truly sorry for them, Nora, you'll realize it's you who are selfish and come home, where you belong."

"I can't, Torvald. If I do, I'll . . . I'll die!"

He flinched, and in that moment I saw the pain I had inflicted. It made my knees weak. "Was it that bad, Nora," he said softly, "our life together?"

"I've changed, Torvald. That's the problem. I'm not your little . . . your little squirrel anymore. I'm not your anything! I told you that night, we're free from each other now. You must divorce me and let me live my life."

"Divorce you?" Then he laughed. "You have no idea what you're talking about. The king rarely grants divorce, Nora. And even if he did, I would never divorce you. I wouldn't give you that satisfaction."

I caught my breath. "You cannot hold on to me, Torvald!"

"Yes, I can. I can make you come home. I can get the police."

"Then send for the police."

My aunt stepped forward. "Torvald, really. Not the police."

He glared at me, imposing and stern. I could scarcely remember loving him.

"Did she tell you, Aunt, what she did?"

"Do you mean borrowing the money?"

"Yes, but did she tell you how she got the money? That she forged her father's signature? I'll bet she didn't tell you that."

My aunt gasped. "Nora!"

"After he died," Torvald said, his eyes never leaving my face.

"But that's a crime!" My aunt turned to me. "Nora, did you know that?"

"I did it to save your life, Torvald. Doesn't that count for anything?"

"That's what you tell yourself," Torvald said, "but you and I know how many cunning lies you spin. You . . ."

I stepped back. "Enough. I'm going to bed. Bring Ivar up to say good-bye. He needs to see that I'm too sick to travel."

"I refuse to participate in your little dramas, Nora," Torvald spat. "You're healthy as a horse; anyone can see that."

I turned to my aunt. "Bring me my son. You owe me that much."

She twisted her handkerchief but nodded. I swept through the room and up the stairs. I put on my nightgown and climbed into bed, though it was barely dusk. I was so angry, heat rose off me as if I really did have a fever.

Soon my aunt appeared with Ivar, who came and knelt by the bed.

"Mama! Papa says you're too sick to travel."

"Yes, darling. I'm sorry." I tried to smile. "But I'll see you again soon, I promise."

"When you come back home?"

"If I can, darling. But even if I cannot, I will see you."

He looked at me, perplexed. This made little sense to him, but I could not pretend otherwise.

"Here," I said, sitting up and taking one of my childhood drawings off the wall—a scene of mountain meadows, with cows and birds. "This is for you. Someday I will take you and Bob and Emmie to this valley. My father took me there when I was your age."

He looked at it in awe. "You drew this? For me?"

"Well, I didn't know I would have a handsome boy like you back then, but I drew it so I would never forget the place. When you see it, you'll never forget it either."

He kissed me. "Thank you, Mama. I'll show it to Bob and Emma."

"Go now," I whispered. "Your train is waiting!"

My aunt pulled him away, and after the door closed, the walls of the room seemed to fold in on me. I clutched my pillow to keep from howling. If Torvald came all the way to Hamar to hound me, would I ever be free of him? Did he really think I would bend to his will and obey him again, after all this?

But even worse was his face at the end, so stern and unyielding. As if he didn't love me anymore.

And then I understood—he didn't love me anymore. I would never have thought it possible, but it was true. And with that, a great void opened inside me. Because we had loved each other, in our tangled way, a love that obscured everything else. But I saw it in his eyes. He would never let himself love me again.

And if he didn't love me, he would never forgive me. And without that forgiveness, he would never let me see the children.

Somehow I imagined that when love died, the connections would die as well, all the old obligations and promises. How naive! Torvald and I were still bound tight together, like overgrown trees in a neglected garden. And all those old, knotted memories—the slights and misunderstandings, the secret pleasures as well as the games and falsehoods—were still twisted around me. Love didn't just fade away. It died and then rotted, but the roots held fast.

THE NEXT MORNING my aunt called me into the parlor. "I cannot allow you to stay any longer, Nora. I fear I've made it too easy for you."

I had anticipated this but not so soon. "Please, Aunt, just a few more months? It takes time to find good work, and . . ."

"Enough, Nora. I told you I had no stomach for gossip, and I have even less for those who flout the law. It's time to return to your husband and children. It was agonizing to see how much Ivar misses you. By Friday, I think. That gives you time to prepare." And then she turned her back and left the room.

I was surprised how much it hurt.

THE NEXT DAY, I got schedules for the trains to Trondheim and Bergen. I would be damned if I was going to do my aunt's bidding and return to Kristiania. I needed a place with more opportunity and where I wouldn't be known.

As I walked back from the train station, there was a lightness in my step. I had no idea how I would manage, but I was relieved to be escaping Hamar.

A few days later a letter arrived, from Torvald.

Dear Nora, You've been gone now eight weeks. If you do not return in a month's time, I will have to tell the children you have died. I do not enjoy these lies, but it's too much to ask these innocent children to understand what you've done. Ivar's had a very difficult time since he saw you and is holding on to hope uselessly. I cannot allow you to torture him anymore. If you're ready to return, I will take you back with the understanding that you'll live in the maid's room and keep away from the children until I'm convinced you mean to stay. If you return to your senses and come home without fuss, I will permit you to see the children briefly on Sunday afternoons, perhaps more in the future. Your Husband, Torvald Helmer

The world went dark. I had to grab for a chair, I was so overcome. He would tell them I had died? If he did that, they would never try to find me. If he did that, it would rob me of the chance to know them in the future, when they were grown.

Suddenly, I saw that I had no choice: I had to return to Kristiania. I must speak to my boys, Torvald be damned. They had to know that I was alive.

TO PREPARE FOR MY RETURN, I bought two mourning gowns and traded my rabbit-fur hat for a plain one with a veil. The night I left Torvald, I demanded we give our rings back to each other. I considered selling his ring, but now I took it to the jeweler and had it refitted for my own finger. No widow would be seen without a wedding ring, after all.

The last morning I packed my trunk, snatching up everything useful— writing paper, pens, novels, and schoolbooks. They had once been mine, after all.

My aunt appeared in the doorway of my room holding a wooden box. "This was your mother's, Nora," she said.

I placed the box on the bed and unlocked the clasp. Inside was a delicate china tea set painted with exquisite red flowers. I wondered that I had never seen it before, but thanked her anyway. As I examined one of the pretty cups, I felt a faint premonition of death, as if this was my aunt's last obligation to me. And in that moment I understood I would never be welcomed in her home again.

When I appeared downstairs in my widow's weeds, she squinted at me in confusion. "What is this, Nora, another deception? You've hardly earned the respect we pay to those who mourn."

"I mourn, Aunt. Every day."

"But, Nora, you've chosen this sad path," she said, pressing her hand for a moment against my cheek. "Someday I hope you'll learn to live without lies and costumes, for the sake of your soul."

Her touch brought tears to my eyes. I kissed her farewell, then rode to the station cradling the wooden box in my arms.

AS THE TRAIN HURTLED SOUTH, my aunt's last words echoed in my head. I was not proud of my fabrications; indeed, over the years I had vowed again and again to stick to the truth. But when I was married to Torvald, I concocted so many little deceptions, I could barely keep them straight. If I had news that would anger him, I pretended I didn't know. If I spent money on something he would disapprove, I hid it in the house. I did these things, I told myself, to keep the peace, but at the same time I knew I shouldn't. It was a relief to speak honestly to him the night I left, though it turned out he couldn't bear to hear what I had to say.

Perhaps that was the problem: no one ever wanted to hear what was true for me.

Now I smoothed the black crepe of my gown. Who would suspect this humble lady in mourning, hiding behind her veil, was the notorious Nora Helmer? If this was deception, so be it. Because how else could women live honestly in the world? We had so little authority, so few choices, how could we manage without a bit of fibbing?

As far as I could see, those with little power had to use what they could find.

CHAPTER FOUR

SOLVI

November 1918 ■ *Kristiania, Norway*

It was late afternoon when Solvi stepped from the train into the commotion of Kristiania. So many people, all in a hurry. She checked the address of the women's study house, then looked around. Before this day, she had always known where she was going, always had friends or family waiting for her. Now there was no one.

She asked an older gentleman for directions, and he pointed her to a tram; she climbed aboard. It bumped up a grand avenue between granite buildings lit up like ships in the dark. Solvi eyed the crowd. So much more sophistication than Bergen. Even in her lovely cape, she felt like she'd come from some upland farm.

She stepped off at a quiet corner in a residential area. The study house, when she found it, was larger than Solvi had imagined and reassuringly tidy. She knocked.

A plump woman in a yellowed cap opened the door. "Lord help me, another girl with a bag," the woman said. "You should have written first."

"Well, I, ah, I didn't know," Solvi said. "I've come to take my matriculation exams. My teacher in Bergen said I could room here." She pulled out an envelope. "I've a letter from her."

"Might as well come in out of the cold," the matron said.

Inside there were coat racks, a potted fern, and a front desk, like a hotel. "Solveig Lange," Solvi said, sticking out her hand. "My grandfather was a banker in Bergen, and my father was a famous Danish botanist."

"Were they now," the woman muttered, scanning Solvi's letter. "Well, I suppose we can give you a room. There's space because some of the girls got the influenza." She gave Solvi a sharp look. "Some of them died. Too much traipsing around."

"I'm so sorry," Solvi said. "It's been terrible."

The matron pushed a ledger across the counter. "It's forty crowns a month, due on the first. That covers your room, board, linens, and a tutor for the matriculation exams. See that you pay up, Miss Lange."

"Of course," Solvi said, uneasy now as she pulled the bills from her purse. She hadn't expected it to cost that much. But she had enough for several months, so she signed the ledger.

"And see that you study hard," the matron said. "If you fail the exams, you must leave. Many girls fail."

"Yes, Matron." Failure and death, Solvi thought. But surely, there must be other endings; her Papa would believe in other endings.

The matron reviewed Solvi's entry. "Curfew's at nine; I lock the door after that. And I expect proper decorum at all times. No cigarette smoking or sneaking out."

"I won't give you any trouble."

"Well, you'd be the first," Matron said. She led Solvi upstairs to a tight little room that had no more than a bed, a desk by the window, and a dresser with a washbowl. "Dinner's at six; don't be late."

Solvi closed her door. What if those poor girls hadn't gotten sick? It made her dizzy to think there might not have been a place for her. She looked around. *The wallpaper's faded, and the curtains need washing*—she could just hear what her mother would say. But Solvi didn't care. It was safe, and her first toehold in the great world.

A drumbeat of excitement trilled in her chest as she unpacked. She felt as if she was someone else, not Solvi Lange, the spoiled girl who lived in a fine town house. She felt ready to surprise herself.

When she was done, she pulled out the photograph of her mother's family and slipped it in the corner of the mirror. Maybe they would be surprising, too. Different from what she knew, what she might expect. But first, she needed to find them.

Solvi tidied herself for dinner, wondering what the other girls would think of her. She knew she was not a beauty like her mother, sleek as a lioness, but then beauty could cut both ways. Solvi had the same blond hair, but her curls defied styling, and her clothes hung on her tall, thin frame. She did have her mother's deep-set blue eyes, though, and her Viking cheekbones.

Her mother. Guilt rose again, like bile, and Solvi had to sit down until it passed. She knew it was cruel, what she'd done; indeed, her mother might never speak to her again. But if she had stayed, her mother would have found another Stefan, and another after that, until Solvi's resolve crumbled and she stood in a flouncy dress promising herself to a lifetime of stultifying dinners, talking about nothing.

She stared at herself in the mirror. She had broken with her mother, hadn't she? Motherless girls didn't worry about what their mothers would think.

She pulled herself up to her full height and lifted her chin, like her grandmother in the photograph.

The dinner bell rang.

IN THE DINING ROOM, several girls circled around Solvi in welcome. Some were already students, while others were more recent arrivals preparing for the entrance exams in January. They all struck Solvi as modest and serious, with their serge skirts and sturdy shoes.

Except one.

Solvi noticed her the minute she walked in. She was small and lithe, with scandalously bobbed chocolate hair and dark eyes. Her slender skirt fell just to her knees. She had a bundled energy about her, but also an air of remove.

The girl watched Solvi out of the corner of her eye but didn't come to greet her. Arrogance, Solvi thought, and she turned to talk with the others, asking about their studies, their homes, their families. When Solvi looked up from her coffee, the interesting girl was gone.

After supper most of the girls gathered in the parlor to talk and read, but Solvi went back upstairs. If she didn't write to her mother, she wouldn't be able to sleep.

> *Dear Mama: I wanted to let you know I've taken a room at the women's study house. The matron has strict rules and locks the door after nine. The older girls serve as tutors, which will help me prepare for the matriculation exams.*
>
> *I know you're angry that I left, and without a good-bye kiss. I'm sorry; it seemed the only way. I hope someday you can forgive me.*
>
> *Your Solvi*

THE NEXT MORNING Solvi met with her assigned tutor, Marit, a tense, older girl who wore her hair in a severe knot and seemed to have forgotten how to smile.

Marit flipped dismissively through Solvi's textbooks. "These are too rudimentary," she scowled. "Where on earth did you go to school?"

"The best ladies' academy in Bergen," Solvi said, trying to keep her chin high. It was only noon, but Solvi has already received a bewildering list of exam topics: mathematics, science, languages, history, and literature.

"Well, there are better references in the library. You'd better use those."

"Library?"

Marit pointed down the hall. "At the end. That's where the serious girls work."

Solvi took her books and stepped quietly to the library door. It was a somber place, lined with bookshelves and crowded with small desks. The interesting girl sat with her back to the door and a large tome before her—anatomical drawings, it appeared. Several girls looked up at Solvi and smiled, but not the interesting girl. Solvi chose a desk near a window, opened her Latin grammar, and lowered her head. No one said a word.

A few hours later, the interesting girl pushed her book aside and left. Solvi, her mind muddled with declensions, did the same, though the interesting girl had already disappeared by the time Solvi stepped into the hallway.

Solvi glanced out the window. The sun was dropping—her favorite light. She retrieved her camera and cape and at the last moment snatched up the family photograph, then headed out the door.

She had hoped to spot the interesting girl, but there was no one about. Still, the sprawling city glowed in the angled afternoon sun, so Solvi descended the hill and took a few shots capturing the hubbub down Karl Johans Gate, the busy main thoroughfare. She surreptitiously photographed two women in stylish clothes and short hair pointing at something in a store window, then spoke to a little girl who posed in her new felt hat. Before long, Solvi had run out of plates.

She pulled out the photograph and looked at the address on the back. *365 Mollergata.*

It took her a while to find it, but finally she stopped before a broad glass storefront. *Stenberg's Photography Atelier* was lettered across the window case. Inside, an older man in a knitted vest sorted photographs at a counter.

Solvi peered through the window, and her pulse quickened. This was where her family had come. Her mother as a baby, her grandmother in her gray silk. Those two little boys.

Solvi opened the door, setting off a bell, and stepped hesitantly inside. A painted backdrop of Germany's Brandenburg Gate hung to one side, an oriental rug in front and a box of props beside it—parasols, toys, guns. Other rolled backdrops stood in the corner.

"May I help you?" The man pushed his glasses up his nose.

"Yes, please. I . . ." Solvi hesitated. "I need, ah, an album."

He pulled out several and spread them on the counter. "That looks like a fine piece," he said kindly, nodding at the camera around Solvi's neck. "May I?"

She smiled and handed it to him.

He snapped it open, then peered through the viewfinder and adjusted the lens. "I hate to admit it, but the Germans do make such fine equipment."

"My father gave it to me. He used it to photograph rare plants. He was a botanist, but he died." Solvi faltered, embarrassed to have shared this with a stranger.

But the man just nodded at her with sympathy and respect and handed the camera back. "It's always nice to meet another photographer."

Solvi picked out an album, then asked for plates.

"Is there anything else?" the man asked.

"Well, yes," Solvi said, pulling out the photograph of her mother's family. "This was taken here many years ago. It's rather a mystery. I was hoping you could identify it."

He studied the picture, ran his finger down the burned edge, and then looked at the back. "But this was taken forty years ago."

"Yes, I know. It's my mother's family—she's the baby. But I never knew she had brothers until recently. Would you have a record of this sitting, maybe the names of the boys?"

He scratched his head. "Perhaps. My father ran the studio then. I'll have to look in the basement."

"I don't want to put you to any trouble."

"Oh, I love a mystery," he said. "Come back Thursday; I'll know by then." He took out a notepad. "Your name?"

"Solvi Lange. My grandfather was Torvald Fallesen."

"Fine. I'll need this," he said, clipping the photograph to the note.

She hesitated. "It's the only picture I have of them."

"You can trust me," he said, bowing. "My name is Anton Stenberg. I'm always here."

THE NEXT MORNING, Marit leaned over Solvi's biology test, checking her answers. "Well, at least you know something."

"My father was a botanist," said Solvi, relieved to get a scrap of approval. She had tried to make a friend of Marit, but the few times Solvi said something funny or clever, Marit only frowned in response.

"Tomorrow, I'll test you on European history," Marit said. "See that you're ready."

Solvi sighed, then went to her desk in the library. She hadn't seen the interesting girl for several days; perhaps she'd gone home for a visit. It would be a dull life here in Kristiania, Solvi thought, if this was what university was like. Perhaps Grandfather was right.

SOLVI WORKED until the afternoon light began to slant again, then fetched her camera. As she came downstairs, she stopped and pulled back. The interesting girl was heading out the door in a nursing uniform, carrying a medical bag.

How odd. Solvi waited a few minutes, then followed her down the sidewalk, keeping just far enough behind that she wouldn't be noticed. The girl, strange in her costume, was easy to track among the crowd.

For some reason Solvi couldn't quite fathom, she followed the girl, past the palace on the hill, through the commercial section, and down toward the harbor. The neighborhood coarsened. The interesting girl marched past pawnshops and neglected storefronts, then finally turned into a maze of rough, weathered cottages—Kristiania's slum.

Solvi stopped. Barefoot children huddled on doorsteps, rodents scurried openly along the gutters, and garbage lay banked like snow against the decrepit buildings. The interesting girl spoke to a woman selling apples, then turned down a muddy lane.

Solvi walked to the corner, unwilling to go farther, but the neighborhood didn't seem to bother the interesting girl. Solvi took a picture of her walking away between the listing shacks, like a figure from another century.

Solvi turned back into town and took more pictures of the city, but none of them haunted her like the girl in her nursing clothes, walking toward some mysterious fate.

IN THE MIDDLE OF THE NIGHT, Solvi started awake. There was something amiss; she heard it again. Pebbles rattling against her window. She looked out. Down below, at the foot of a spruce up against the house, a figure waved a handkerchief. The interesting girl.

Solvi raised the sash, the cold night air billowing her nightdress. The girl didn't say anything, just hiked up her skirt and climbed the tree as if it were a ladder, pulling herself onto Solvi's window ledge.

"Are you crazy?" Solvi whispered. "We'll get kicked out!"

"Don't be a prig—help me in before I fall," the girl said.

"I'm not a prig!" Solvi hissed, but at the same time, against her better judgment, she grabbed the girl by the elbows and pulled her over the sill.

The girl scrambled to her feet, yanked her skirt back into place, and grinned at Solvi. "Thank God it was you up here. I was pretty sure Matron gave you this room. I'm Rikka Toft, by the way."

"I'm not a prig, Rikka Toft. I just can't afford to get kicked out."

"Don't worry. Matron has no idea that tree is so easy to climb."

"Do you do this often? Stay out late, then wake up some hardworking student and drag her into trouble?"

Rikka laughed. "Oh, yes. I've been friends with every girl who stayed in this room."

Solvi folded her arms over her nightdress. "You may find it harder this time."

Rikka cocked her head to one side. "Do you really think so? You seem so promising."

"We're supposed to be asleep! I swear, if I get kicked out because of you . . ."

Rikka went to the door. "My apologies, then, ah, what is your name?"

"Solvi Lange."

"Thanks, Solvi Lange." Rikka hesitated, then gave her a sly smile. "And, by the way, I know you were following me earlier."

With that, she slipped out the door.

RIKKA was not at breakfast the next day, nor in the library, nor at lunch. Solvi was both relieved and disappointed. She couldn't help but wonder what Rikka meant when she called her promising.

After lunch, Solvi returned to the photography studio, eager to learn if Mr. Stenberg had found the names of her uncles. She also brought her new album, which she had filled with pictures of the housemaids, arranged so that each girl's formal portrait was paired with a photo of her working. When Solvi did that, the working pictures—full of movement and feeling—seemed to jump off the page. She hoped Mr. Stenberg would be impressed.

"Ah, Miss Lange," he said when she entered. "I have an interesting answer for you."

Solvi sucked in a sharp breath. "What did you find?"

He patted a frayed account book on the counter. "I had to rummage around a bit, but, fortunately, my father kept good records." He opened the book and pointed to an entry in October 1879. "I think this might be your family."

Solvi peered at the faded handwriting. *Portrait, Torvald Helmer and family, five crowns, paid in full.* "But that's not their name. Their name is Fallesen."

"Yes, I understand. But is it possible your grandfather changed his name later?"

"What do you mean?"

"According to this account book, nobody by the name of Fallesen came to the studio in 1879. There were only three family portraits recorded in October, and as this entry is for a Torvald, I think this might be your family."

"But Torvald is not an uncommon name," Solvi said, dismayed. She had wanted something definitive, a clue to light her way. "Why would someone change their name?"

Mr. Stenberg looked at her with sympathy. "To escape something, usually—financial ruin, scandal."

Solvi stepped back. "But my grandfather was a fine citizen. He managed a bank in Bergen." Her voice cracked. "He just died a few months ago."

"I'm very sorry, Miss Lange. I didn't mean to upset you." He handed back the photograph.

Solvi tried to pull herself together. "I guess when you set out to solve a mystery, you have to expect surprises." She opened her satchel and tucked the photo away.

"Is that an album of your work?" Mr. Stenberg said, pointing at her bag.

She nodded, then shyly pulled it out. "If you have a moment," she said, "I'd like to know if they're any good."

"Of course." He laid it on the counter and turned a few pages.

Solvi watched, nervous. What if he didn't like them? What if he didn't understand?

After a few minutes, he looked up. "These are lovely, Miss Lange, and quite interesting."

"Can you see what I'm trying to do?"

"Well, you're developing your technique and your eye, but you're also making a statement—rather a revolutionary one, I think."

"I'm trying to show their dignity and dedication, how hard they work under difficult conditions."

"I especially like this one," he said, tapping a picture of a maid washing dishes stacked high to one side, her back to the camera, her single brown braid fraying in the steam of the scullery. "She almost looks like a Chinese laborer. Very nice. Few people can see like this, Miss Lange."

"Thank you," Solvi said, blushing.

"You've quite a talent. You must keep shooting."

"I do need more plates."

He pulled out several boxes and rang them up. "Please feel free to stop by anytime."

Solvi smiled. "I will."

TWO DAYS LATER Solvi set out through an icy drizzle to find a cemetery.

Examining the photograph of her lost family the night before, she started thinking of ways to test her mother's statements. If her uncles and grandmother had truly died, the first step would be to find their graves. If they lived in Kristiania, they should be buried here.

She asked Matron, who told her that most of the gentry of that time were buried at Our Saviour Cemetery, out past St. Olav's Church. Solvi grabbed her cape and headed out.

When she found the graveyard, however, it seemed an impossible task. Hundreds of tombstones marched in all directions, and the rain blew between the old stone walls and hedges. She felt a bit like Death herself, stalking around in the mist.

She pulled her cape tight and started scanning stones, checking for Fallesen and Helmer. Could there have been a scandal? It seemed unlikely, given that her grandfather was so contemptuous of those with low morals, but she was sure something had fractured the family. Death would be more likely.

She walked up and down the rows a long time, scraping away moss when she couldn't read the inscription. Her hands soon ached with cold. Then, just as she was about to give up, she spotted something: *Johanna Helmer, beloved wife of Torvald Helmer, 1864–1889.*

Was this the Torvald Helmer who had his family photographed at Stenberg's in 1879? Or could the woman in the photograph be Johanna Helmer instead of her grandmother Solveig Fallesen? Solvi's stomach clenched. Please, no, not death. She looked at the stone again.

Johanna had been born in 1864. But if Johanna was the woman in the photograph, she was only fifteen when the photo was taken, and a fifteen-year-old could hardly have been the mother to three children. Besides, the woman in the photograph was almost thirty, if a day, and she looked too much like Solvi's mother to be unrelated. No, this dead Johanna could not possibly be her grandmother.

She took out her camera and crouched down to shoot the low headstone. Poor Johanna. She was only twenty-five when she died, most likely in childbirth.

Before standing, Solvi paused. If her mother had been telling the truth and Solvi's grandmother lay in another grave somewhere, how would such a place have appeared to a little girl brought to her mother's grave site to say good-bye? Solvi knelt, looking through the lens from the vantage point of a child, then took another shot of the misty cemetery, the stones looming in the frame, the trees bending and reaching in the wind. It would have looked to her something like that, Solvi thought. Little wonder she had wanted to forget.

RIKKA WAS NOT AT SUPPER the evening Solvi returned from the cemetery, but that was no surprise, as she didn't seem to live in the study house like the other girls. She must have a life outside these dull walls, Solvi thought with a stab of jealousy.

She studied until late, and then, as she was about to turn off her light, someone tapped on her door. Solvi opened it a crack.

"What are you doing?" said Rikka, standing there as if they'd been friends forever.

"Going to bed, Rikka. What are you doing?"

Rikka gave her a grin. "Taking a break. May I come in and try again? You weren't very hospitable the other night when I came through the window."

Solvi hesitated. Something about Rikka unsettled her.

"Besides," said Rikka, "I wanted to know what you were doing at Our Saviour Cemetery this afternoon."

Solvi's mouth dropped open.

"Yes, I followed you. Now you know how it feels."

"I'm sorry I followed you the other day, Rikka," Solvi said. "I, well, I just wondered, you looked so, um, unusual in that nursing uniform, I was just curious . . ."

"Look, Solvi Lange, I'm not angry. I just don't like being followed." Rikka elbowed the door open. "Let me in, and we can start over. If you tell me why you were at the cemetery, I'll tell you what I was doing in Vika."

Solvi pulled the door wide and offered her the chair. Then she took the photograph of her mother's family from her bag and handed it to Rikka. "I was looking for them."

Rikka ran her finger over the burned edge. "Are these your grandparents?"

"Probably, but I'm not sure. What makes you say that?"

"The woman looks like you."

"Do you think so? She's very beautiful, not like me at all."

"Well, your hair's different, but look at her face—that's you, all right. Who are the others?"

"The baby's my mother, I believe, and this is my grandfather," Solvi said. "My parents and I lived with him. He died last month of heart failure. We only found this photograph then."

"Are these your uncles?"

"Yes, but I've never met them. I'm not even sure they're alive." Solvi sighed. "I'm trying to figure it out."

Rikka looked at the photograph more closely. "Who tried to burn it?"

"My grandfather, just before he collapsed. The maids found it under the stove. I was surprised—my mother had told me her mother died in childbirth, and she'd never mentioned any brothers."

Rikka's eyes widened. "Did you show it to her?"

"Yes, but by then she was sick with the influenza. I had no choice; I thought she was dying. She admitted this was her family but said she didn't know if they were alive. I got the strong feeling they were. Later, though, after she recovered, she said her mother and brothers died shortly after this photograph was taken."

"So if they're dead, what's the mystery?"

"I don't think they're dead; I think my mother is lying. She claimed she couldn't remember the boys' names, which can't be true. These were her brothers."

"Did you find them at Our Saviour?"

"No, but there's confusion about the last name." Solvi flipped the photograph over to show her the stamp on the back, then told her about Mr. Stenberg, his ledger, the different name, and the possibility of scandal.

Rikka whistled. "Oh, boy. This is getting better and better."

"Rikka, this is my family."

"I'm sorry." Rikka bit her lip. "Can I help?"

"I need to find them, but I'm not sure where to start."

"Well, let's ask around. If your uncles are here, they're likely working and have families. You could even talk with the police. They might have records of who lives in Kristiania."

Solvi smiled. "Thanks. It's a relief to tell someone."

"So, would you like to know why I went to Vika?"

"Only if you want to tell me."

"It's hardly a secret. I'm a nurse; I help find poor women with tuberculosis, then try to get them to the sanitarium before they die."

Solvi nodded, then looked away. "I have a confession, Rikka. I took a picture of you walking down the lane. I think it will be quite haunting. I'll show it to you when it's developed."

Rikka cocked her head. "Is that why you were following me?"

"Probably. To be honest, I don't know why I follow people. Sometimes I just do."

"And then take their pictures when they aren't looking?"

"Yes. I take pictures whenever I see something unusual or revealing."

Rikka considered this. "I should be angry, but I'll forgive you if we can be friends."

"That would be wonderful," Solvi heard herself say. "I've tried to make friends with Marit, but she's hopeless."

Rikka laughed, then reached out and tugged one of Solvi's blond curls. "You look like Isolde with your hair down. You should cut it."

Solvi laughed. "Is this how you make friends?"

"Yes," Rikka said, stepping to the door. "I'm impossible; everyone will tell you that. See you at breakfast." Then she slipped out, quick as a ferret.

Solvi turned to the mirror, pulling her hair back to see what it would look like short. No, she couldn't possibly cut her curls; her mother would be scandalized. She'd never be able to go home again.

CHAPTER FIVE

NORA
Spring 1919 ■ *Spokane, Washington*

I waited until Anders left for town with the children, both mules pulling the load. With Jens and Katrin's family living with us in the orchard, it was difficult to find a moment of quiet. As much as I adored them, I sighed with relief as they disappeared down the track.

Once again, I pulled the newspaper advertisement from my apron pocket, where I kept it. It felt like carrying around a stick of dynamite.

If anyone has information about the woman in this photograph, please send a letter to box 143 at the central post office, Kristiania, Norway.

Twice already I had tried to write a response, but after a few sentences I tossed the paper into the stove. I had asked Anders once before to make a painful choice and was afraid now to bring that unhappiness back into our lives. In that heart-stopping moment, he chose to believe me rather than give me up to the whims of justice. He did it, he said, because he had already chosen me—for better or for worse—before God. In his eyes, he had no alternative; he was bound to me and loved me, even as flawed as I was. His decision moved me deeply in ways I still could scarcely explain.

Later he told me he didn't understand why God had made it so, but that he would be patient and pray the mystery would be revealed. This problem seemed to be his only argument with God, and in that I was jealous, as I had a thousand arguments with God.

I looked out the kitchen window across to the apple orchard that grew below the house. The trees were in full bloom, each one a pale beauty quivering gently in the breeze. Such an unholy pleasure, this view. I ached with the fullness of it. For me, such natural loveliness was one of the great mysteries of the world. That and our life here together—the dirt and the labor and the smell of the apple barn and the grandchildren climbing the trees for the topmost fruit. These have proved to me that Anders's choice was for the best.

But I knew Anders still waited for his revelation and, with it, forgiveness. Sometimes I found him on his knees in the barn. Otherwise, he didn't trouble me over his struggle with God. His argument was never my argument, which we both understood.

I considered the appeal in the advertisement again. *Please send a letter* ... How desperately I longed to do so, but how could I without jeopardizing my marriage, my life, my entire world?

NORA
March 1880 ■ *Kristiania, Norway*

When I arrived in Kristiania from Hamar, I left my baggage at the station and headed up Karl Johans Gate. It felt strange to walk my old haunt as a widow behind a veil, but the anonymity was comforting. With my honeyed hair and graceful figure, I had attracted too much attention in the past. Now I was ignored. No one notices those of limited circumstance.

I took a room in a run-down neighborhood filled with factory workers and forgotten elders. The widow who opened the door took in my mourning dress and nodded to me in kinship. The tiny apartment—in the back looking out on the alley—was dingy and shabbily furnished, but it had all I needed: a stove, table and chair, and a lumpy rope bed. I could afford it for a few months, though I would need steady work to keep it.

I sent a man for my trunk, then bought a few groceries and set up housekeeping—fetched wood, built a fire, cooked my supper—fumbling through these unfamiliar chores. Until that evening, I had always had a servant, someone working quietly in the next room for my comfort. Now I was alone as never before.

I had always tried to be kind to our maids, but I could see now how much I had taken for granted. My nurse, Anne-Marie, had to send her own daughter away to be raised by strangers so that she could care for me. I was just an infant when that decision was made, but, still, had I ever acknowledged her sacrifice? I blushed to remember how I hung on her as a child, then grew bossy as a young lady. And now I had left my own children in her care, without asking her permission or considering her age or health. I simply assumed she would step into her role once again: the dependable nurse selflessly caring for the motherless children.

Perhaps Kristine was right. Perhaps I *was* selfish.

I took out my mother's tea set and washed it gently, then brewed a few leaves. How different my life might have been if my mother had lived. Sipping from the cup, I imagined my mother's mouth on the very spot and tried to conjure her.

Who was she? She must have been beautiful, knowing my father, but what else? Was she independent and courageous or obedient and fearful? I wondered if she clung to me after my birth, desperate as her life ebbed away. My first few days with each newborn child were some of my happiest, examining their darling little features and imagining the fun we would have together. How sad for that to be the moment of death.

I could only imagine what my angel mother would think of me now, here in this crabbed room instead of home with my children. She would think me mad to give up what she was denied—a life with her child.

I finished my tea and washed the little cup, then climbed into bed and tried to sleep.

If she swept down from heaven now, it wouldn't be to console me but to beat me about the ears with her angel wings.

THE NEXT MORNING, I stopped by the office of the solicitors who had given me work before, anticipating a warm welcome. But instead, the senior partner went pale when he recognized me.

He seemed befuddled, especially by my widow's gown. Everyone knew Torvald, after all. At first, he could only hem and haw, peering over his glasses. Finally, he found the words. "We cannot take you here, Mrs. Helmer; it wouldn't do."

I blinked, then turned away. My reputation, or some gossiped version of it, must have preceded me. I tried to compose myself. "Given all the hard work I've done for your firm in the past, would you be willing to write me a letter of recommendation? You only need comment on the quality of my work. As I'm sure you recall, I always returned everything on time and neatly done."

More consternation. "I wish I could, Mrs. Helmer, but that is also impossible." Then he reached for my hand and gave it a squeeze. "You are welcome to take more copying work, to be done at home if you would like. But as for a letter, well . . . I'm sure you understand."

I didn't understand, but thanked him as best I could and retreated with my head held high. Outside, however, I lowered my veil in shame. These had been friends! I thought they would offer something, even if just to save a good woman from an uncertain future.

I walked for a long time behind my veil. How could these reasonable men—people who knew me—treat me like a common criminal? It wasn't a crime for a wife to leave her husband; husbands didn't own their wives, after all. And as long as the wife didn't abscond with someone else's husband, where was the moral crime? Countless women lost husbands, to illness or abandonment, and no one banished them.

Was I too dangerous to let into their offices and parlors? If I were old or plain, maybe I wouldn't be so threatening. Maybe the women thought I was out to steal their husbands. Or perhaps the fear was on the other side: the husbands worried I would incite envy, inspire other wives to do the same.

It was as if I were a wild beast, roaming the streets.

I BEGAN TO CAST ABOUT for lesser jobs, work usually left to women. I did not relish teaching, having disliked my spinster teachers when I was young, but now it felt like the only respectable line of work left to try. Women in my circumstances often taught in the small private academies held in the homes of respectable widows.

But when I knocked on their doors, I met similar resistance. I used my maiden name, Solberg, but ours was such a small society here in Kristiania that I was soon recognized. I tried at three schools before I gave up, shamed by the abrupt response of the elderly matrons.

"We could hardly have someone such as you teaching young ladies," the last widow sputtered at me. "Surely, Mrs. Helmer, even you can understand that."

"I'm not sure I do," I said peevishly. "Perhaps you could explain it to me."

But she just sniffed with impatience and slammed the door.

PERHAPS I COULD WORK as a companion to someone, I thought, or even a governess if the children were well behaved. But to do that, I would need a letter of recommendation. And so I went to see my friend Kristine.

I stopped by during the hour that visitors could expect coffee and cake. She had written to me before I left Hamar, saying she had just married into a better life and giving me the address of her new apartment. *I have a marriage of equals, as I've always wanted,* she said.

When I read that, I felt as if she had reached out with one of her knitting needles and pricked my soul. But now I swallowed that down, along with my pride. Maybe her new perfect husband would offer me help, given that I was one of her oldest friends.

A maid answered the door, then ushered me into a parlor with streaming sunlight, padded chairs, respectability. It felt as if the world had tipped and Kristine and I had exchanged roles.

Kristine glided into the room, clad in a soft green dress trimmed with lace. "Nora, you're back," she said, but her thin smile gave her away. I was not a happy surprise. She kissed my cheek but did not invite me to sit.

"Well, there was nothing for me in Hamar," I said, taking off my gloves. "It was foolish to think it would be easier there. The gossip got around, and people can be so malicious."

"Well, Hamar has always been like that." She paused. "I would offer you coffee, but I have an appointment."

"Of course," I said, my heart sinking. "It's good to see you doing so well, Kristine."

"Yes, we're quite comfortable. Torvald kindly helped my husband get his new job."

Clever Torvald. By helping them, he had made them beholden to him. "How good of him," I said, my voice tight. "I came today because I need something now, something I thought you could help me with."

Instead of responding, she rang a little bell. Her maid stepped into the room. "My coat, please," Kristine said, as if she had bossed around servants her entire life.

Then she turned back to me. "What do you want, Nora?"

"Do you know anyone who might help me find work? You've had to do it. Who should I ask?"

"Work?" She took her coat from her maid, then held it against her chest, like a shield. "No, I wouldn't know where to direct you. I can't help you with that."

"I mean, as I'm on my own now."

Her eyes narrowed. "Nora, I never suggested you leave Torvald."

"No, but you did insist I tell Torvald the truth or we would never have an equal marriage. And now I'm alone, unable to find a job. Apparently, I'm tainted."

She put her coat on, buttoning it slowly and fussing with her scarf so as not to look at me. "Nora, you made your own bed."

Bile rose in my throat. "Kristine, when you needed me as a friend, you said you understood what I was going through. You encouraged me!"

She looked up with a wooden face. "What do you want, Nora?"

"I need work, and salaried positions are impossible without a letter of introduction. Perhaps your husband could write a letter for me."

"Based on what? He has never worked with you."

"Based on our friendship, Kristine."

She cocked her head, and a strange expression spread across her face, pity mixed with a strained patience. "I wouldn't want to impose on him for that."

"But if you have a marriage of equals, Kristine, I would think you could ask."

Now she pulled on her gloves, carefully snapping each one. They were fine lambskin, with mother-of-pearl clasps. "I don't know, Nora. We wouldn't want to risk it."

"Risk what?"

"Torvald's displeasure, Nora!" Her eyes glittered with anger. "He's a powerful man now that he's manager of the bank, despite your scandal. Don't you understand anything? We can't afford to help you!"

I stood there, stunned, then looked down in shame. How scuffed my boots had gotten with no one to shine them for me. Was I becoming the poor widow I pretended to be? I wasn't particularly fond of Kristine, but as we had grown up together, and because I had helped her find work when she was a desperate widow, I had expected support rather than this rude rebuff.

"What would you have me do, Kristine?"

"I would have you go home, Nora. No one imagined you'd do something this extreme. So go back to Torvald, back to your precious children. How can you possibly make a life for yourself? The gossip will get around, just as it did in Hamar." Her voice dropped. "In truth, it already has."

"And what are people saying?"

"Well, no one can quite believe it, Nora. Torvald adored you; everyone could see that as plain as the midsummer sun, and he gave you a comfortable home and a piano—everything you wanted! It all looks rather ungrateful. And then there are your children . . ." She paused. "No one understands how you could walk away from your children. Some have even wondered if you're in your right mind."

"I'm not walking away from my children," I said, my voice catching. "I've come back to Kristiania so as not to lose them. Surely Torvald will understand they need me in their lives."

"He's a stubborn man, Nora." She put on her hat. "I'll see you out."

"Just a minute," I said, pulling out a card with my address. "If there's anything you can do, I trust you'll let me know."

She looked at the address. "Oh, Nora . . ."

"It's fine. Perfectly serviceable."

"Perhaps you should go see that Dr. Rank of yours," she said.

"Dr. Rank? But he's dying."

"Yes, but not yet. Perhaps he can help you. People tell me you were quite close."

I raised my chin. "Torvald and I, together, were close to Dr. Rank. If people knew the truth, they wouldn't need to cast judgments." I bid her a curt farewell and swept from the room.

IN MY RIGHT MIND—Kristine's words gnawed at me as I walked to the corner. The minute a woman made trouble, everyone leaped to that. Kristiania felt as narrow and claustrophobic as Hamar.

I stopped and gazed down the street, a route I used to take home when I lived with Torvald. Since returning to Kristiania, I had longed to sneak past his apartment in hopes of a glimpse of the children. Now something desperate in me turned my feet in that direction.

When I got to Torvald's corner, I lowered my veil and approached the building cautiously. When no one was about, I slipped through the entry into the inner courtyard. From there, I looked up. A lamp burned in the nursery window; I could see shadows behind the lace curtains. I watched, willing a small face to appear, but no one came.

Instead, the door at the bottom of the servants' stair swung open. Torvald's maid, with the garbage.

I darted forward and pulled the veil from my face.

She gasped when she saw it was me.

I grabbed her arm. "Helene, please. I must speak to you!"

She shook her head and tried to pull free. "No, go away! Mr. Helmer said we're not to say anything to you, under any circumstance!"

"Helene, calm down. I just want to see Ivar for a moment, or Bobby. Ask Nurse."

"Oh, Mrs. Helmer, I can't do that. Mr. Helmer made us swear!"

"It's still me, Helene." Tears filled my eyes. "Wasn't I always kind to you? Please, get Nurse. Let her decide."

Helene hesitated, then softened and turned back inside.

I waited, aching with anticipation. Finally, Helene opened the door and thrust a bundle into my hands—something wrapped in a tea towel. "This is all I can do, Mrs. Helmer. I'll lose my job!" She slammed the door.

I peered through the glass at the empty stairwell, still hoping, but no one was coming. My chest tightened. To be here but not free to race up the stairs and hug my children—it was almost more than I could bear.

I stumbled into the street, then hurried back to my room, bursting into tears as the door shut behind me.

I shouldn't have gone; it was easier not to remember. I gulped air to stop the sobs. I was just hungry and cold, I told myself. I stoked the stove, set the kettle, got my supper from the cupboard. Then I remembered the bundle.

I picked it up—hunks of bread and cheese tumbled out. Helene thought I needed food. She was probably telling the others that I came begging.

I doubled over in humiliation, blackness surging over me as if I might faint. Did I look like a beggar? Was I not wearing a fine dress, even if it was crepe? Was I not still a lady?

I sat very still for a long time. Who was I, now that I had been stripped of my position in society? Was I lower than a housemaid, lower than the lowest clerk? Was I truly unfit to see my children?

Finally, I made myself eat. I took a bite of the bread, then grew curious and tugged on the tea towel again. Out dropped some dried fruit and finally, with a clink, five pieces from my familiar silver service—the pickle forks we never used. Helene thought I needed money.

I nibbled the bread and cheese, turning the little forks in the lamplight. How I had taken for granted the comfort of such pretty things. Was this what I wanted when I walked away? A dreary, coin-pinching future, dressed in black, grieving the loss of my children, and skittering about on the fringes of society?

Maybe this was how women went mad.

THE NEXT MORNING I rose with fresh resolve. I wasn't a crone, and I shouldn't need to beg for crumbs. I had every right to see my children, and so I would.

It was Sunday. I knew that, after church, Torvald would be home relaxing with his precious newspapers. I shined my shoes and brushed the mud from the hem of my best dress. Then, at precisely two o'clock, I returned to Torvald's building, but this time I went in the front door, up the stairs, and stood before our apartment door. The nameplate still said Torvald and Nora Helmer, which made me want to walk right in, but instead I knocked. No more blundering.

Helene answered. "Mrs. Helmer!" she huffed. "Not again!"

"Helene, just tell Mr. Helmer I'm here. I know he's home."

"No, please go away!"

I heard Bob say something behind her, and my heart leaped.

"Helene, I'm not leaving. Do as you're told."

She shut the door and I waited, listening.

Torvald finally opened it, pushing his shoulders into the entrance. "Nora. Have you come back?"

"No, Torvald, but I need to speak with you."

"Why are you in mourning?"

"I thought it appropriate."

He regarded me for a moment. "If you're not returning to your obligations, I've nothing to say to you, Nora."

"Please, Torvald. Unless you prefer everyone in the building hears me."

At that he grunted and closed the door. Inside, he asked Nurse to take the children out. I heard their boots clattering down the back staircase.

Finally, Torvald reappeared. "Go straight to my study."

I stepped inside. It was all still there, as if nothing had changed—the wine-colored drapes, the cozy lamps, the toys scattered on the floor. A rush of longing overwhelmed me. I moved into Torvald's office and sat down to steady myself.

He stepped behind his desk. "What have you come for, Nora? Money? Or perhaps your evening dresses and silk shawls? If you're hoping to get back into society, I can assure you that's impossible."

"Torvald, I know I've hurt you, and I am sorry for that. That wasn't my purpose."

He blinked at me. "I'm, well, I'm glad to hear you acknowledge that, Nora."

"I do. But now that I am an independent person, I hope we can talk reasonably, for the children's sake."

"What do you want, Nora?"

"Two things, Torvald. First, you must promise not to lie to the children by telling them I have died."

His jaw stiffened. "I cannot promise that. You have abandoned them, leaving me to provide everything: the roof over their heads, their education and care, the parental love they desperately need. I think I'm free to say whatever I like to the children."

"But Torvald, you always said children who grew up with parents who lied would turn out to be evil! Yet you are planning to tell them the worst lie of all! What will they think?"

"Think? What will they *think*? They will think that their mother is gone, and once they can grieve and get over you, their lives will get easier. Right now they're in hell. They need resolution, Nora. I've spoken with the pastor, and he agrees."

"But what if they see me again?"

"They cannot see you again, ever. It would be devastating."

My stomach knotted. "But, Torvald, wouldn't it be better for them to see me occasionally? Perhaps on Sundays, and a few weeks every summer? Just enough for them to know I love them?"

He pulled back. "That would be torture for them, Nora. How would I explain that you're alive but don't want to live with them or care for them?"

"Tell them I'm too sick. Then, when they're older, we'll explain the trouble was between us, not with them."

"Nora, they're already being ostracized, as everyone's quite shocked by your behavior. Your actions, if connected with the children, will drag them down. I cannot allow that."

"Torvald, please, I beg you, do not tell them this lie! You may have them now, but give me a future to hope for, a time—when they're grown—that they can choose to know me if they want!"

He gazed at me down the length of his nose. "You look hungry, Nora." He fished in his pocket and pulled out several bills. "Here, buy yourself a good meal."

"Torvald, please let me see them Sunday afternoons. I could take them to the park . . ."

"Nora, it's time to go. Take the money. I could even have the kitchen make you a basket." So he had heard of my foray to the back door. "But I must tell you that if you come to the house again, or anywhere near the children, I will have you locked up."

"Locked up? It's not against the law for a mother to speak to her children."

"And it's not against the law for a husband to commit his wife to an asylum if she behaves hysterically. Frankly, Nora, all Kristiania thinks you quite insane."

The blood began to pound in my ears. I stood, willing myself to stay calm so he wouldn't see how this frightened me. I walked slowly into the living room, drinking it in for one last dizzying moment. Suddenly, I wanted something, something to help me remember. I crossed to the piano and snatched my book of Chopin's Mazurkas.

"May I have this, Torvald?"

He hesitated, then acquiesced with a sweep of his hand. "Of course— your favorite. Though I don't know where you think you'll find a piano."

I forced a smile. "Something to hope for."

He grunted again, then slammed the door behind me.

I RETREATED TO MY ROOM and spent the rest of that day by my stove knitting furiously, trying to quell my fears. Kristine might betray me, give Torvald my address so that he could send the police. I had little doubt he would discuss it with her.

That night I tossed in bed, unable to sleep. All I could think of was the asylum. I had never been to Kristiania's home for the insane, but I could just imagine a hospital filled with jabbering old men rotted by aquavit and syphilis. Did they have wards for women? Probably, though good families usually kept their mad women at home.

The next morning I looked in the mirror. Pale skin and disheveled hair, but no spittle on my chin, no outward insanity. Could they confine someone like me, lucid and polite? Perhaps. Norwegian laws were written by men; perhaps husbands had such power. I sat by the fire and tried to sew, but Torvald's threat gnawed at me.

For several days I stayed inside, my world darkening as a great argument raged in my soul. Perhaps I was mad—if not, why couldn't I return to Torvald and the children? I thought of the familiar minuet that had been my marriage, the coming together and pulling apart. Happy moments, sometimes, but so many admonishments, like the flick of a whip overhead, little wounds followed by regret and the requisite forgiving. So childish— his belittling endearments, my flirting to get what I wanted. But couldn't I bear it, to live with my children? If I went back, I might spend the summer shut in the maid's bedroom, but soon Torvald would long to dress me up again and show me off, the rebellious wife brought to heel. All I would have to do is beg his forgiveness, and I could return to my children, my comfortable life, my feather bed.

But then I thought about that bed. If I returned, that was where I would end up, as that was the central purpose of our marriage. And Torvald would be master in a way he wasn't before, now that I was disgraced. He would call me squirrel and scatterbrains again, make up new rules, and lecture me on moral behavior. All to keep me dependent and weak.

It made my skin crawl.

And I wouldn't survive it; I knew that now. That was why.

A KNOCK CAME ONE EVENING, making me jump, but it was only my landlady. "Are you all right, dear?" she asked. "I haven't heard you go out recently."

"I'm fine," I said, trying to smooth my hair. I needed to bathe.

"If you care to, I have supper on the table. Might do you good." She stood there, not to be refused.

And so I joined her for warm mutton with potatoes and gravy. She talked of her garden, and I told her of the farm in the Østerdalen where my father and I summered. We smiled; she poured coffee. It was an astonishing consolation just to sit with someone.

OVER THE NEXT FEW WEEKS, I pulled myself together. I walked in the brightening spring light, then found another firm that gave me copying work, which allowed me to eat a little better. As I got my strength back, Torvald's threat receded. He was angry, yes, but I no longer feared he would send the police for the mother of his children. It would be unbearably scandalous, and if there was anything that drove his decisions, it was avoiding the taint of scandal. He was probably hoping everyone would forget about me.

Before long I stood outside his apartment again, stalking the children.

I WENT IN THE MORNING, when I knew they would be headed to school. I stood at the corner across the street, my veil down. After a bit, the boys burst from the door of the building with Anne-Marie behind them. They seemed to be just as they always were—their bodies all elbow and knee, the familiar tug and pull between them. They filled me with happiness.

Soon, I was spying on them every morning. Usually the boys seemed fine, but one day Ivar was scowling and Bobby dragged along, pouting and kicking rocks. Yet Nurse marched on ahead. And there, in the space between them, I could see the wound I'd left behind.

The next day I found Nurse alone, waiting for me.

"Anne-Marie!" I reached out to hug her, but she stepped back, nervous as a finch.

"No, Nora. No good will come of it." She squared her shoulders. "If you don't stop spying, I'll have to tell Mr. Helmer. The boys are beginning to heal. Leave them be."

"I'm sorry. I just needed to see that they walk and breathe."

"Aye, they do. But it hasn't been easy for them."

"Has Mr. Helmer told them I died?"

"Not yet. He says you're in the South, recuperating. The boys write you letters, but I throw them away."

"Throw them away?" I could not hide my dismay.

"I say you're too ill to write back."

"Send them to me, please!" I scribbled my address on a card and handed it to her. "But be careful. Mr. Helmer mustn't know where I'm living."

She looked at the card, then back at me, sadness tugging at her thin mouth. "Dear Nora, please come home! It's too hard, watching them lose you. It's as bad as when I gave my daughter away so I could be your nurse."

I winced. "I am sorry, Anne-Marie. I'm sure it's a burden to you, and I regret that. But I can't come home; it's just impossible with Torvald. I've been thinking, though, that the children don't need to lose me. If you're willing to help."

Her brow creased. How I knew that look.

"Anne-Marie, please let me write to you. In case I must get a message to the children."

She sighed, then pulled out her own card. "Write to this address, as Mr. Helmer is so careful with the mail. My daughter's house."

"She's back in Kristiania?"

"Aye, to be near me."

"I'm so glad to hear that. And how is Emma?"

"She's fine. Mr. Helmer has made quite a pet of her. He's changed—become a better father. Someone had to fill the gap."

"Can he, Anne-Marie?"

"No," she said. "No one can replace you, Miss Nora."

TWO DAYS LATER an envelope came from Anne-Marie, and inside was a letter from the children! Someone, Bob probably, had drawn a figure with yellow hair and a white gown sitting in a chair with wheels, beneath a window. Outside was a glimpse of beach and sea. Emma had put a crazy sun in the corner, pink pastel circles. Down at the bottom Ivar had written: *Dear Mama, please get better and come home soon. We miss you.* Ivar and Bobby signed their names, and Emma scribbled illegibly with her pink crayon.

I slipped the letter inside my blouse, but it didn't stop the ache.

I STOPPED BY MORE OFTEN, trying to keep myself hidden but lingering longer. I knew I shouldn't, but I couldn't stop myself. When I finally saw Emma, I was stunned by how much she had changed. She was playing on the pavement with a ball, her golden curls pinned up with ribbons, laughing and tormenting Bob.

Ah, sly girl, I thought, and then my throat knotted. How much had I already missed. For her brother's sake, I hoped she would learn to be kind.

Bob finally grabbed the ball and kicked it to Ivar, waiting in the street. Then the ball flew into the entry, where I was hiding, followed by Ivar, who scooped it up and turned around. It happened quickly, before I could lower my veil.

He recognized me instantly. "Mama!" Then he looked around and dropped his voice. "Papa said you were in Italy! Are you better?"

I held out my arms to him. "Darling, quick, before Anne-Marie sees you!"

He fell into my embrace for a precious moment, then pulled away. "Why are you here? Are you coming back?"

"I'm back in Kristiania, but I'm not well yet, and it's best I don't come home right now. I just wanted to see my little monkeys."

"Papa says you're never coming back."

"Ivar!" Anne-Marie suspected something; I could hear it in her voice.

"Go, darling. Don't tell anyone you've seen me. I'll be back next week."

"Papa will be angry." He looked around nervously.

"Our secret, then, yes? Now go, quickly."

He gave me one last anguished look, then ducked his head and ran back.

"Where did you go?" Anne-Marie said.

"I had to get the ball. Bobby, here," then the thwack of his kick.

Anne-Marie was rattled, though, and herded them inside.

My children slipped from my grasp.

I WAITED A WEEK before resuming my surveillance, but they didn't appear again. Had Torvald taken the boys out of school? I wrote to Anne-Marie, asking what had happened. I heard nothing for days, and then finally received a short note. Torvald had sent the boys to cousins in Sandefjord, she said. Until Easter, perhaps longer.

Ivar must have told his father. The thought of the boys being shipped off to Torvald's relatives, stiff and judgmental people, made me sick with worry. For one long afternoon I considered going to Sandefjord myself, then thought better of it. The family would surely shield them from me. The boys would have to suffer on their own.

LONELINESS TOOK OVER MY LIFE, the quiet consuming me. More and more, I longed to sit with a friend, and now that Kristine was in Torvald's pocket, the only person I could think of was Dr. Rank.

After Torvald's bout with tuberculosis, Dr. Rank had visited our apartment daily, sitting by the stove and chatting with me most mornings. He seemed hungry for companionship and, over time, became my confidant. Unlike Torvald, Dr. Rank let me gossip and chatter about the little interests of my life. We shared jokes and stories, and because he was a doctor, I could ask about things that made other men blush. And sometimes— especially on dreary winter days—I flirted with him. Gently, properly. To entertain him and pass the time.

He came to see me, I was sure of it, but he befriended Torvald as well. The two men often retreated to Torvald's study in the afternoon, sharing port and talking of business and politics, things I was not expected to understand. I often pulled up a chair and listened through the door.

Our little triangle stood solid as a three-legged stool until the day my blackmailer threatened to tell Torvald about my forged loan. Desperate, I decided to ask Dr. Rank for help. To soften him up, I showed him my silk stockings and joked about oysters. It was cruel of me, playing on his affections that way, and it backfired. He seized my hand and told me he loved me, and that was when everything crumbled. I couldn't ask for his help after that, so I punished him with coldness. It sickened me now to think of it.

I knew he was dying of tuberculosis, so I hadn't wanted to bother him since my return to Kristiania. But perhaps Kristine was right. I should go, to apologize and say a true good-bye.

THE NEXT MORNING I pinned my hair back severely. No coquetting anymore.

At Dr. Rank's door, his maid Nancy welcomed me with a smile of relief. "Hello, Mrs. Helmer. Thank you for coming."

In the parlor, Dr. Rank sat slumped in a wheeled chair, the newspaper sliding from his lap. Nancy shook him awake.

"You have a visitor, Doctor." She helped him sit up.

"Nora," he said, his eyes widening. "How good to see you! But you're in mourning. Did something happen?"

I gave him a polite kiss. "No. I wear this to fade into the background."

"Ah, my poor Nora! You look quite the schoolmarm. No longer our society lark." He patted a chair.

"Let's not talk about me, Dr. Rank. I came to see how you are."

"Oh, not well," he said. "The illness is eating away at my spine."

"I'm very sorry to hear that."

He peered at me. "You don't look well yourself, my dear. Where are you living now?"

"In town, a nice flat," I lied. He didn't need to know how low I'd slipped. "Dr. Rank, does Torvald come to see you?"

"Torvald? No. He sent a note last month, but that's all. I won't see him again until my funeral."

"Oh, Dr. Rank, is it that bad?"

"Let's hope it's that bad, as the pain is growing worse. But, come now, Nora. Tell me how you're getting on."

"Well, I do some copying for solicitors, but I've had a hard time finding something more dependable. Do you know anyone you could recommend me to? Perhaps a doctor who needs help with his books?"

Dr. Rank studied me for a long time, then sighed. "It's hard to imagine our Nora earning her own keep and living in some dreary room. Clove cheese and eggs most nights, no doubt. You're pale."

"It's not bad. I have a stove and a bed."

"This is hardly the Nora who hid macaroons all over the house."

"Ah! I've forgotten. Are they delicious?"

He laughed. "Oh, yes. I'll show you." He rang, and when Nancy brought the coffee he whispered in her ear. She soon returned with a plate of sweets.

"Please," he said. "Be the old Nora. Put some in your pockets."

I took one and nibbled, the sugar dissolving deliciously on my tongue. I smiled to hide my sadness.

"Nora, come stay here with me and be my companion until I die. I will pay you well."

"Live with you in your house? But I'm a married woman."

"Oh, Nora, let's not get tangled in laws."

"But, Dr. Rank, I couldn't. People would talk. Surely you understand!"

"Let them talk, the buzzards! I don't care, and I would think you wouldn't care either, not anymore."

My face fell. He meant that I no longer had a reputation to defend.

He reached for my hand. "My apologies. I'm being a selfish old man. But, come, we can make it respectable. You stay where you are living, but every morning, you visit and read to me. My eyesight is failing; my doctor can attest to that." He gave me an encouraging smile. "Think of it as a mission of mercy on both sides."

I felt brittle as an autumn leaf. How desperately I needed the comfort of him.

"Perhaps I could visit."

He patted my hand with his palsied one. "Good. Come tomorrow at ten, and sit with me until evening. I'll give you dinner and a bit of supper later. We need to fatten you up. Bring your embroidery. I always loved watching you embroider."

"I mostly knit now."

"How dull, but if that is what we are reduced to, we will soldier through."

I smiled and kissed his brow. "Tomorrow, then. And thank you."

OVER THE NEXT MONTH spring eased into the city, sunlight widening the day. I tried to make myself useful to Dr. Rank, reading him the papers in the morning, then playing the piano and entertaining him until twilight. He still enjoyed conversation, and that, more than anything, began to restore me.

As my cheeks filled out, however, he grew thinner and more forgetful by the day. I tried to distract him, chattering about politics, labor issues, and women's rights. On his better days, he would tease me, calling me his parlor radical. I was particularly fond of Aasta Hansteen, an advocate for women's suffrage, and read him her articles with dramatic flair.

One day I noticed a column titled "The Woman Question," written by a man we knew, a professor. It started as a diatribe about women's suffrage in England but then shifted. *These revolutionary ideas are beginning to spread their poison through Norway. Recently, a woman of quality and comfort, well cared for by her loving husband, walked away from her marriage, leaving behind a houseful of inconsolable children. If that is what the newfangled "feminism" is bringing us, the abandonment of children, then I propose we legislate to keep women from stealing jobs from worthy young men. Women will stay with their husbands, where they belong, if they cannot find work to support themselves.*

"My God," I gasped. "He's talking about me!"

"Where? Read it to me, Nora. It can't be."

"He says I've left a houseful of inconsolable children!" I read it out loud, choking near the end.

Dr. Rank let out a soft whistle. "He must mean you, Nora, or you've started a revolution and women across Kristiania are walking out on their churlish husbands."

"But why does anyone care, beyond my own family? It's just malicious gossip!"

"They care because you've done something many women long to do. Bourgeois ladies often fantasize about independence, but only from the comfort of their drawing rooms. Few have your courage."

"I don't feel courageous, now that I cannot show my face in public."

"Well, I'm not sure you've lost much. You're a rebel, my dear, and in that way you've stepped outside your class." He pulled up the blanket across his lap. "Truly, Nora, I don't know quite what to make of you. Since you left Torvald, you've grown full of opinions."

"Well, I was never as naive as you and Torvald thought. I didn't say much because Torvald scoffed at my ideas, but I read the papers and listened through the door when you two talked politics."

"I knew you did, but I thought it was because you were lonely." He looked at me thoughtfully. "Maybe you should go to America, Nora."

"America? I may have been cast out of society, Dr. Rank, but I'm hardly a peasant. There's nothing but farmwork in America."

"There's opportunity in America. Especially for people like you, who have, shall we say, liberated themselves from their past."

"Really," I said. "I'm surprised you would encourage me in that way."

"I cannot rest until I find a future for you, Nora. This is all very enjoyable, but we both know it won't last long."

I smiled sadly and patted his hand. "I don't like to think of it, Dr. Rank. But you are right. If you write me a letter of recommendation, that would help."

He gave me a sly look. "I will, but I'm working on something better. I'll tell you soon."

SUMMER CAME, and the weeks whispered past. Dr. Rank worsened, and I feared he had forgotten his promise to give me a letter, but I didn't want to ask him again.

One morning, inevitably, I found the household in disarray, a doctor passing through the rooms with his medical bag.

"What's happened, Nancy?"

"Dr. Rank had an attack last night; it was terrible to see."

The doctor approached me. "Hello, Mrs. Helmer. Dr. Rank has been asking for you. Would you like to see him?"

"Yes, please," I said, then followed him into the sickroom.

My friend lay motionless in a massive mahogany bed, staring at the ceiling. It made me ache to think of losing him.

"Oh, Dr. Rank," I said, taking the chair beside the bed and reaching for his hand.

His eyes shifted toward me. "Nora." He said it so sadly.

"I'm so sorry! The doctor says I must say good-bye!" I felt like I was being hollowed out, as if I could not hold on to anyone.

"Ach, maybe not yet. Only God knows." He tried to sit up, then called for his maid. "Nancy, fetch the letter from Mr. Lyngstrand, the one on my desk."

He turned to me with a weak smile. "I have something for you."

Nancy handed me the letter, and I opened it up. *Dear Dr. Rank: I would be happy to meet your friend Mrs. Helmer. Tell her to come by the Kristiania Theater. Konrad Lyngstrand*

"The Kristiania? What is this, Dr. Rank?"

"This is the solution," he said, pulling himself up against the pillows. "The thing for you, Nora, is the stage."

I opened my mouth to protest, but he squeezed my hand. "I don't have much strength, so listen to me. You're a born actress. You're beautiful, musical, and talented at . . . well, let's call it the art of dissembling."

I flushed red.

"Oh, Nora, you know you're good at it. I've watched you for years in Torvald's parlor. You're a genius at it." He held my gaze.

I had daydreamed about the stage when I was a girl, but pursuing it now, when I was already disgraced, would be a leap into the abyss.

"Dr. Rank, I can't do that."

"Of course you can, especially with this connection. Mr. Lyngstrand is the director."

"But Torvald might take offense. He would use it to block me from the children."

Dr. Rank smiled gently. "Nora, dear. Torvald will block you from the children anyway." He took my hand. "Think of it. You go onstage, travel abroad with the new Norwegian plays, conquer Europe, and return the pride of Kristiania. You would never want for anything again."

I could only look at him, speechless.

Then he grimaced, shifting uncomfortably. The doctor stepped forward. "It's time for his medicine."

Dr. Rank squeezed my hand again. "Thank you for our time together. You can't imagine what it's meant to me."

Tears slid down my face. "You've been so kind. No one else understands me."

"Mustn't cry, Nora."

"No," I said, taking out my handkerchief. "I'm sorry."

"We're kindred spirits, you and I," he said. "That's why I loved you."

I kissed Dr. Rank's cheek and whispered into his ear. "I'll always remember you."

He smiled at me one last time. "And I will remember you. I promise."

NANCY FOLLOWED ME TO THE DOOR and handed me an envelope fat with bills. I hesitated, but she insisted. "Dr. Rank's orders, ma'am," she said.

When I got home I took Mr. Lyngstrand's note and tucked it in the mirror. Each time I brushed my hair or put on my hat, I thought about Dr. Rank's proposition. It was tempting, certainly, but it also felt like crossing into a dark forest, into a netherworld that would swallow me whole.

Actresses, no matter how famous they were, lived lives beyond the pale. None that I ever heard of had children who would admit to knowing them.

It was impossible.

A FEW WEEKS LATER, I stood in a dress shop, weeping.

"I'm sorry, Mrs. Helmer, but I cannot put you behind the counter," said the manager. "But if you're clever with a needle, I need fancywork. It pays better than basting shirts."

I fingered the lace collar at my neck.

"Good. Bring me twenty like it, and I'll give you forty crowns."

THE LINDENS HAD TURNED, and the summer twilight was fading fast. If I had hoped lacework would pay for my room, tatting all day proved an odious task—all needle pricks and aching eyes. It also gave me too much time to think.

By the time I finished the collars, I snatched Mr. Lyngstrand's letter from the mirror and tucked it in my purse. Something inside me had flipped, like a coin tossed a second time. I could not live like this, eating porridge hunched by the drafty stove and squinting at my sewing in the gloomy flicker of the gaslight.

I took the collars back to the store and, instead of taking cash, traded them for a stylish black skirt and fresh linen blouse. The widow emerging from her sorrow. I would meet with Mr. Lyngstrand and change my fate— one way or another.

THE NEXT DAY I stood before the big doors of the Kristiania Theater. How many times had I come here, dressed in my best silk and nodding to the people I knew, entering happily on Torvald's arm. He didn't like theater as much as I did, but it was the place to be seen, even if we had to give up beef for the month to afford it.

Now, however, I found the doors locked, forbidding as a troll's cave. I slipped into the side alley, not wanting anyone to see me waiting out front. I wasn't sure what to do, but then I heard laughter.

Down toward the back of the theater a couple of stagehands stood around an open door, smoking. I walked over to them and asked for Mr. Lyngstrand.

They raised their eyebrows, appraising me. "His office is backstage, ma'am," the tallest one said, pointing through the door. "You best go on in."

I stepped hesitantly into the dusky interior. Giant painted screens, cobwebbed from disuse, stood against the wall. Dust floated through the light from the doorway, and I could just make out stacks of props and tawdry furniture heaped in the shadows. Bits of costumes—odd hats, an old shawl, even a wig—lay about, as if the company had flung them aside after the last performance. Then I spotted a small lighted room, with an open door.

A wiry young man in shirtsleeves sat counting money at a desk strewn with programs.

"Good day," I said, smiling. "I've come to see the director, Mr. Lyngstrand. Is he in?"

The young man looked me up and down. "For you he could be in."

Heat rose in my face. No one had ever spoken to me that way before. I gave him a steely look.

"Forgive me, ma'am." He jumped from his chair. "Mrs. Helmer, you say? I'll find him." He disappeared.

A few minutes later a well-dressed, trimly bearded man came through the door. He appeared to be in his late forties and seemed boldly confident, a man who knew himself. He took my hand, scanning my face and my burnished hair, which I had knotted behind. His eyes sparkled with intelligence.

"Ah, Mrs. Helmer. I've been expecting you." His assistant brought chairs. "Yes, as lovely as Dr. Rank said. What can I do for you?"

I sat as primly as possible. "Dr. Rank suggested that I might, well, I might be able to find employment here, in the theater." I stuttered a bit; I didn't really know what I wanted from this man. "How does one get a role in a play? Are there openings, auditions?"

Mr. Lyngstrand laughed. "Yes, there are always openings for people with talent and beauty. But acting is becoming a profession. Perhaps you have some training?"

"Oh, yes. I see what you mean. I've studied singing, piano, dancing, and elocution. I was often asked to sing or dance in the homes of Hamar, where I grew up."

"In Hamar, you say?"

He had measured me a provincial. "Yes, and then here in Kristiania," I quickly added. "Once I married and moved here."

"Yes, I heard about your, ah, situation. You live on your own now, Dr. Rank said."

"Yes."

"Well, Mrs. Helmer. Perhaps we can talk about it over supper. Are you free tomorrow evening? I could pick you up if you just tell me where you live." He gave me a look rich with meaning.

My mind tumbled. I hadn't expected to be invited to dinner.

"I thought you might enjoy a dinner out, and we could talk about how the theater works and how you could perhaps get more, ah, advanced training."

"Does advanced training cost money?"

He squeezed my hand. "Come now, Mrs. Helmer. I'll explain at dinner. I need to get back to my work, but I look forward to tomorrow night. Would eight o'clock do?"

I finally nodded. "Yes, but no need to pick me up. I'll meet you at the restaurant." I didn't want him to see how I lived.

"Eight o'clock, then, at the Einhorn," he said bowing politely.

I shook his hand, sensing the warmth of his grip. "Thank you."

BACK IN MY ROOM, I turned to the mirror to remove my hat and barely recognized myself. My eyes glittered; my skin glowed. Life had been poured back into me. I thought of his hand around mine, his appreciative gaze on my face.

It had been a long time since someone saw me anew.

But how could I possibly go to dinner with him? I didn't have an evening dress and could scarcely afford one. I sat down, stumped. Then I thought of my landlady.

I knocked on her door, and when she opened I explained my dilemma. She listened, smug as a cat. She went to look through her closet and then returned with an old black taffeta stinking of camphor and fifteen years out of fashion. But it was made of a rich fabric and well preserved.

"It's lovely," I said. "Can I give you five crowns?"

She sighed happily. "I didn't know you moved in such circles," she said, handing me the dress with a nod of respect.

IT TOOK ALL NIGHT, but by morning I had managed to remove the high collar and much of the trimming, then lowered the neckline and cut off the sleeves. I could do little to subdue the cascading layers of the skirt, though I managed to pull them back into a presentable bustle. I sprinkled it with cologne and hung it in the window to air.

When I dressed that evening, I brushed my hair until it fell in glossy folds and pinned it loosely. Then I pulled on the dress. If anyone looked closely, they would see it for what it was, but I hoped Mr. Lyngstrand wouldn't notice. I fastened my pearls around my throat, then walked to the restaurant through a dense fog. I felt like a character in a masquerade.

Mr. Lyngstrand greeted me at the door and squired me to a corner table beneath a painting of a unicorn. The room was lit only with candles, more romantic than I expected. A waiter poured wine; I could only imagine what the other diners thought.

Mr. Lyngstrand raised his glass. "You look stunning tonight, Mrs. Helmer. Or should I say, Nora."

I sucked in a breath, startled to hear him use my Christian name but didn't protest. Instead, I smiled. I didn't know where the evening would lead, but I would never know if I refused to follow.

"So tell me," he said, "have you seen many of our plays at the Kristiania?"

"In the past, yes, but not recently, not since I live on my own." I coughed. "Tickets are quite dear, after all."

He smiled. His eyes were deep blue, like the sky on a summer night. "I'm sure it's not easy being independent, Nora. Enviable, perhaps, but it must take courage."

I swallowed. "It's harder than you can imagine."

"Was it a long time coming? The split, I mean."

"Yes and no. The split was sudden, like a thunderclap, but things had . . ." I sipped my wine to steady myself. "It's difficult to explain."

"I would like to understand, Nora," he said. "You intrigue me."

"But you barely know me."

"I know more than you might think. Dr. Rank was quite full of you and concerned for your future. He had me stop by so we could discuss it. He was very fond of you, Nora."

I blushed deeply. "Yes, but it wasn't like that," I said. "He was always a gentleman, and a good friend to my husband."

"Oh, well, I didn't mean to suggest—forgive me." Then he leaned in. "It's hardly your fault if men fall in love with you."

The waiter appeared beside us, trying to look as if he hadn't overheard. I busied myself with my small bag while Mr. Lyngstrand ordered our supper—goose liver and venison, pudding and figs.

When Mr. Lyngstrand turned back to me, I was ready for him. "I assume you're a gentleman as well, sir. Most likely a married one."

"I was married, Nora," he said smoothly, "but my wife died two years ago, of sepsis. She was never able to have children and was always weak."

"Oh, I am sorry. I'm sure that's been very difficult."

He sighed, his eyes searching my face for something. "Can I tell you a secret? I feel like I can tell you secrets."

I could only nod.

"My wife's death was not as difficult as it should have been," he said softly. "Our marriage was unhappy from the start. When she died, I didn't know what to feel. At long last, there were no more arguments, no more recriminations. It was impossible not to be relieved." He shook his head. "So few of us marry the right person, don't you think?"

"I don't know why others marry as they do," I said. "In my case, I was young and naive. Torvald seemed to adore me, and my father insisted I marry him. I was seventeen; how could I have resisted them both? I fell in love with Torvald because it was the only way to make everyone happy."

"So you did love him."

"Oh, yes."

"Do you love him still?"

I looked away, to regain my composure. "No. He turned out not to be the man I thought he was, and I doubt he loves me anymore. He couldn't forgive me for becoming complicated, for trying to do things."

"But complicated people are so much more interesting! My wife was too simple to make a good partner; her horizons barely extended past the windowsills."

"Many women prefer the life of the parlor. I suppose it's safe. But it wasn't for me."

"Are you happier now, on your own?"

"I, I don't know about happiness. Happiness is a luxury; I've little money for luxuries."

"I thought independence was doing whatever you pleased."

He wanted me to laugh, but my throat went tight. "Perhaps for wealthy men, but not for me," I said. "Apparently, it's some sort of crime for a woman to choose to live alone." I stopped. I didn't want to sound bitter. "And it's very difficult to find respectable work."

"Which is why you've turned to the theater." He lifted his eyebrows at me.

"I apologize, Mr. Lyngstrand."

"Konrad," he said, with a smile. "Let's not argue, Nora. It's rare that I get such an interesting woman all to myself."

I sat, tongue-tied. We were like lovers, in this dark corner, so close our knees knocked, and I couldn't help but look into his eyes. But maybe that was what I wanted, a step into the unknown.

Our food came, and Mr. Lyngstrand turned professional again, telling me about the new theater and how it had shifted away from the familiar symbolic dramas of the past. A good play, he said, was one that made the audience feel like they were peering into intimate spaces, someone's home or marriage. And the best actors were those who could tap their inner knowledge to illuminate their roles.

"But how do they do that?" I asked. "Aren't they pretending to be a particular character?"

"It's less about pretending and more about feeling." He looked at me over his fork. "Demons are helpful. I suspect you have demons, Nora."

"We all have demons," I said. Then I thought of my chilly room, my somber widow's weeds. Perhaps obscurity was my demon. "How do demons help?"

"To understand our characters, we dig into our own most difficult experiences—the things that frighten or upset us, the things that have destroyed bits of our soul. Spoiled young women don't understand this, but for someone like you," he said, "this would all come quite naturally."

It was both flattering and unnerving to feel him unwrapping me in this way. "You presume, Mr. Lyngstrand, yet you are right."

He reached out and tipped my chin up; our eyes locked. "Heartbreak and sorrow give a woman depth, Nora. It makes you beautiful in a way no others can touch. Why, someone might even write a play about a woman like you."

I smiled but pulled away, taking up my wineglass again. "To interest others, Mr. Lyngstrand, my story would have to be idealized, and then it would no longer be true."

"But that's just it, Nora! Audiences are tired of the ideal; they want real people, with flaws and problems. You, with your charms and contradictions, you could be quite the heroine."

I looked at him for a long moment. What I would give to go onstage as myself, just as I was. I had always felt too big for the life I was handed; perhaps this was what I was made for. "So how would I get the training you require?"

He leaned in. "You would need someone to guide you, set you up. I would be happy to do that for you, Nora. I like your intelligence and you're quite lovely—even in that dress."

I reddened. "Perhaps you're unaware how little women own in this world."

"But you have a string of pearls." He reached out, as if he wanted to run his hand along the sweep of them where they lay, just above my breasts.

I shielded the pearls protectively. "These are my insurance, Mr. Lyngstrand. We take what we can."

"And you're a rebel. That makes you even more interesting." He sighed and smiled at me. "But if I'm to help, you need to be willing."

"Willing?" I knew what he meant, but pretended otherwise. Propriety was my lifeboat.

"Willing to venture away from here, away from the prying eyes of Kristiania society. I'd think that might be acceptable to someone in your position."

"What, exactly, would be the terms of this arrangement?"

Now he took my hand again, holding it firmly. "Nora, come with me to Copenhagen. We'll have a little holiday together, and I'll set you up in a nice apartment, then find someone to give you lessons. If you do well, we'll feature you in a play." Now he turned my hand over, exposing the vulnerable inside of my arm, and quickly, before I could pull away, ran a finger up to the sensitive spot inside my elbow, which he gently squeezed. A jolt shot through me. He registered my reaction and raised my hand to his lips. "If you're willing."

I slid my hand from his grasp and pulled back to collect myself. "Why Copenhagen? Is it impossible for me to start here in Kristiania?"

"Why, Mrs. Helmer, I cannot put you onstage here."

"Why ever not?"

"You're too controversial a figure."

"Me?"

"I assumed you knew."

"Well, I had some idea, but too controversial to go onstage?"

"It could disrupt the production; people might boycott the play." He nodded at my disbelief. "Kristiania's a hard town, Nora. What was it the poet Bjørnson called it? The City of Tigers. All those teeth and claws." Now he shook his head. "Trust me—the only respectable way to do this is to set you up in Copenhagen. The Danish are so indulgent."

Respectable. We both knew better. "I will have to think it over."

"Certainly, my dear. Take your time. I understand it's a serious decision."

"You see, my, my children," I stammered, despair washing over me. "I'm not sure I can leave my children."

"I thought you left your children."

Such bitter words! "I'm hoping my husband will let me see them occasionally. That might be difficult if I'm living in Copenhagen."

"Well, if you return to Norway a darling of the stage, I've no doubt Mr. Helmer would allow his children to visit with their famous mother. Better to come back the toast of Kristiania than to languish here in obscurity, Nora." He looked at me as if he saw right through me. "If I may be so bold, you'll find it hard with only your integrity to keep you warm at night."

And with those words, a deep crevasse opened before me.

I stood up. "Thank you for your advice, Mr. Lyngstrand," I said, as formally as possible. "I will let you know."

He turned businesslike. "When you've made your decision, write to me at the theater. I keep my theatrical obligations separate from my personal life."

"Yes, your theatrical obligations." I smoothed my dress. "Thank you for supper," I said, then slipped away through the crowded room.

OUTSIDE I THREW MY COAT ABOUT ME and bolted into the fog, walking faster and faster. When I got home I slammed the door, horrified by both the power of Mr. Lyngstrand's offer and the fear that I would give in to it. His touch on the inside of my arm had awakened a dragon. What would it be like to be loved again, to be the center of attention and acclaim? What I would give for recognition and the elevated life that would come with it.

Yet how could I even consider such a thing? How could I have simpered at him, encouraged him? After all my fine dreams of independence! After all that had happened and all it had cost!

No. I jumped up and yanked the evening dress from my shoulders, then grabbed my scissors and stabbed at the elegant fabric, tearing it in long gashes. I could not. I would not. I stabbed and ripped in a frenzy, reducing the dress to a mound of black ribbon heaped about my ankles. I kicked it aside, then sat down and wrote a terse note to Mr. Lyngstrand. I would not be going to Copenhagen. I could no more sell myself in such a fashion than I could return to Torvald as his concubine.

The next morning I posted the note before I could reconsider. No doubt Mr. Lyngstrand would be offended by such a quick decision, but I didn't care. I had always been able to look myself in the eye and could not bear to lose that. Torvald was wrong—I was not immoral. I had my own code, whether it was condoned by church and society or not. I just wished there was a place for me in Norwegian society, a safe place, an accepted place.

Perhaps Dr. Rank was right. Perhaps America was the place for me.

I RETURNED TO THE LIFE OF A SEAMSTRESS, tatting lace collars by the dozen. On the warmer autumn afternoons, I often took my sewing outside to work in the natural light, sometimes on a bench up near the Akershus Fortress, looking out over the fjord. I thought about Mr. Lyngstrand, who seemed drawn to my mind and my body but showed little interest in winning my heart. I wondered if I would ever love anyone again.

A few weeks later, as fall crept in from the north, Dr. Rank's maid wrote that he had passed away. His death left me bereft. I could not attend his funeral, as both Torvald and Mr. Lyngstrand would be there. Instead, I went down to the fjord, broke off a branch of maple leaves just beginning to turn, and tossed them into the water as the bell tolled for my old friend.

I felt like I'd been cast adrift on a windswept sea. How would I ever be happy again? Perhaps happiness was for others—children and those too coddled to know about life. Or maybe happiness was the private purview of men; they seemed happy in the world, striving in business and bossing others around. But for a woman, happiness felt impossible. If her spirit expanded, it cracked her world apart, and who could be happy then?

If happiness came, it would arrive like a stranger, in a form I did not know.

CHAPTER SIX

SOLVI

December 1918 ■ *Kristiania, Norway*

Rikka dropped into the empty chair beside Solvi at lunch a few days later. "Are you studying this afternoon?"

"Of course, aren't you?"

"No. I'm taking you on Rikka's grand tour of Kristiania."

Solvi froze. Something about Rikka made her feel like she was being dragged down the street by a wild pony. "I don't know, Rikka. I'm behind on my Latin. Besides, you might take me to a den of iniquity."

"Exactly! But we'll see the sights first."

Solvi glanced at the other girls, all mesmerized by their soup bowls. She stood up.

"Great," Rikka said. "Get your cape. It's snowing."

"THE PROMISED DEN," Rikka said, opening the door of a brightly lit café. Her grand tour—a dash past the palace and the parliament building—was cursory at best, but that wasn't the point. Inside the café, a fog of cigarette smoke and chatter enveloped them. The girls shook the snow from their wraps and looked about the room. Young men sat at nearly every table. This was the point, Solvi thought.

Rikka pushed confidently through the crowd at the counter, greeting people but steering Solvi to a spot in back so they could talk. Solvi could feel the boys looking at her.

Once they were seated, Rikka waved to a waiter, then pulled out a battered tin cigarette case. "My father's," she said. "Care for one?"

"No, thanks. My mother would die if I smoked a cigarette. In fact, my mother would die just to see me here with all these strangers."

"Isn't she back in Bergen?"

"Yes, but she could always tell when I was up to something. She's probably getting that tingly feeling right now."

"All the more reason," Rikka said.

Solvi glanced about. Everyone was smoking, even the young ladies. And didn't she decide she was motherless? "Okay," she said, letting Rikka light her a cigarette. Solvi took little ladylike puffs, coughing delicately, pretending this wasn't her first time.

The waiter brought coffee and a plate of pastries. Rikka snatched an almond roll and relaxed back into her chair. "You'll have to inhale if you want to be my friend."

Solvi drew more deeply. "What makes you think I want to be your friend?" she said, trying to hold in the smoke. But her lungs refused; her breath exploded with a loud cough.

"Because you're smoking!" Rikka hooted, and then they were both laughing.

"You know everyone," Solvi said, once she had regained her composure. She didn't even try to hide her envy.

"I grew up in Kristiania."

"So why do you live at the study house?"

"Because both my parents are gone." Rikka glanced up from buttering her roll, sad and defiant at the same time.

"I'm so sorry, Rikka. What happened to them?"

"My mother died when I was seven. She was sick for a long time, and then she was gone."

Solvi felt another prick of envy. It wasn't the first time she'd wished it was her mother who died, rather than her father.

"I'd give anything to have her here, worried about me," Rikka said.

Solvi blushed, ashamed of herself. "My father died some years ago, as well. Then my mother got the influenza, and I was terrified I'd lose her, even though she's hardly been the mother I needed. I couldn't imagine being orphaned. What happened to your father?"

"He died in the war, just last year."

"I'm sorry to hear that, as well," Solvi said. "Was he on a ship?"

"No, he was a doctor, working behind the British lines in France. He volunteered as soon as the war started. I'd always been his assistant, so I went with him."

Solvi drew back. "You went to the war? Is that where you learned to nurse?"

"Yes," Rikka said. "I stupidly believed that if I watched over him, nothing would happen. Then one day, while I was away picking up medical supplies, a shell hit our dressing station."

Solvi stared at her for a long moment. "That's the most extraordinary story I've ever heard." She thought of how she had tormented her mother by threatening to run off to nurse the troops. Instead, she had stayed in Bergen in her comfortable house, grumbling about coal rationing. "That must have been awful. I'm so sorry."

Rikka sighed. "After he died, I had to come back to Norway. I wasn't brave anymore."

"You seem brave to me, climbing in second-story windows in the middle of the night."

Rikka smiled sadly. "Or reckless. I'm never sure which."

"So you'll study medicine?"

Rikka nodded. "What about you?"

"History or literature, though right now I'm just trying to pass the matriculation exams. My mother hopes I'll fail so I'll return home and marry Stefan Vinter."

Rikka leaned forward. "I knew there was something interesting about you. What was wrong with Stefan Vinter?"

Solvi smiled, then thought for a moment. "Stefan was perfect—handsome, from an excellent family, employed in his father's shipyard. He scared me to death. When I realized I couldn't live the life my mother wanted for me, I had to leave. I didn't even say good-bye."

"You ran away?"

"Yes. I expect her to show up at the study house any day now."

"Did you always want to go to university?" Rikka asked.

"My father wanted me to go. He was a botanist—alpine plants. He wasn't conventional like my mother, but he was often away in the mountains or the Far North."

"What did he die of?"

"Stomach cancer," Solvi said. "The war had just started. It felt to me like he was the first casualty."

Rikka's face clouded over. "Our own losses always feel like the first casualties." She lit another cigarette. "At the front I saw young men die every day, but I didn't really feel it until Nigel died."

"Who was Nigel?"

"A young British officer. I nursed him after he took some shrapnel in the legs. We talked at night while the others slept. When his unit moved north, he promised to find me after the war was over, but a few weeks later I heard he'd been killed." She gave Solvi another dark look. "We don't see it here in Norway because we've been so protected from most of this war, but terrible things have happened. Sometimes I can't sleep for remembering."

Solvi sensed it again, Rikka's haunted remove from the world. How safe Solvi's life had been; it made her feel a bit stupid and inconsequential. "What kind of doctor would you be?"

"An interesting question, Solvi Lange," Rikka said. "I want to treat women, to help them understand their own bodies and manage their pregnancies. So many die young out of sheer exhaustion or complications from childbirth. Tuberculosis, pneumonia—most could be avoided if women had better nutrition and living conditions, and had fewer children. It's a crime how women are enslaved by childbearing."

"That sounds rather radical. How do you do that?"

Now Rikka squinted, sizing her up. "Sometimes, when I'm checking them for tuberculosis, I talk to them about controlling their pregnancies."

Solvi raised an eyebrow. "I want to know, but I don't think I should ask."

Rikka shook her head. "It's not pornography, Solvi. It's information women need."

"My mother will get pains in her stomach, all the way back in Bergen."

Rikka smiled. "Good. She'll have to get used to it."

WHEN THEY RETURNED to the study house, Matron handed Solvi a letter, from her mother. Almost as if she had overheard Solvi's conversation with Rikka in the café. Solvi took it upstairs to read in private, her hands shaking.

Dear Solveig: I don't know quite what to say to you. Indeed, I considered not responding, but you are my daughter and my only kin in the world. So I might as well start with the truth. I don't understand why you would leave me without a farewell and under cover of darkness, and so soon after Grandfather's death. I almost think you were waiting for him to die and me to be weakened, as I am. I can scarcely face the world. The scandal of your running off like this, well, I've had to talk very sternly to Cook and Mathilde so they don't gossip about your behavior. Lisanne came looking for you. She was quite hurt you left without a word.

*If I felt better, I would come to Kristiania, but in my present con-
dition I must rely on you to use your best judgment and keep out of
trouble. I am concerned about the study house and hope you are not
tramping all over the city. It's a big, dangerous place, Solvi. I can only
hope you are taking care where you are seen and with whom. If I
thought otherwise, I would not be able to sleep. If you need money, just
ask. I would rather support you than have you looking for employment
in some common shop.*

Your Mother

Solvi stared at the last line. Employment in some common shop. She
should have thought of that herself.

WHEN SOLVI got to the photography studio the next day, she spotted a
problem even before she entered. Through the window she saw five young
boys in leather hiking shorts posing before a backdrop of snowy peaks, but
each time Mr. Stenberg ducked behind the camera, they started fidgeting.

Solvi went into the shop and stepped to Mr. Stenberg's side. "Now, you
little hooligans, stay very still and watch me." She put her thumbs in her
ears and made a face.

The children laughed; the shutter clicked. A few more tricks, and then
they were done.

Mr. Stenberg herded the children outside to their waiting nurse. "Thank
you, Miss Lange. The young ones can be the devil to shoot. Did you come
for your prints?"

"Yes, but I also have a question."

"I especially liked your picture of the nurse," Mr. Stenberg said, handing
her the photographs.

Solvi looked through them. The one of Rikka was just as she thought—
wistful and mysterious. She looked up at him. "Mr. Stenberg, I'd like to
learn to develop photos, and I need a job. Could I work for you? Maybe as
an apprentice?"

He looked at her for a long moment and nodded thoughtfully. "Things
have gotten busier, with the war over. You could be a big help, especially
with the developing and the portraits. Can you work hard?"

"Oh, yes, and I'm quick. You'll see."

"I'm sure you are," he said. "Shall we say three afternoons a week?"

Solvi nodded, smiling. The thought of working in the studio—with someone who understood her—felt like finding a home. "Thank you, Mr. Stenberg. I'll start tomorrow."

BACK AT THE STUDY HOUSE THAT EVENING, Solvi went by Rikka's room; she found her sitting in the open window wearing her coat, smoking.

"Rikka, Matron will kick you out!"

"No, she won't," Rikka said, throwing the cigarette out into the freezing rain. "Because she'll never know." She shut the window and squirted cologne in the air. "See? Nothing to worry about. So where have you been?"

"I got a job. My mother said it would make me common, so I had to do it."

Rikka's eyes widened. "Don't tell me you're selling men's underwear . . ."

"No," Solvi laughed. "The man at the photography shop hired me, to develop photos and help with portraits." She took out the photograph of Rikka in her nursing costume and handed it to her. "He especially liked this one."

Rikka fell silent, then finally cleared her throat. "I had no idea I looked like that, as if I just stepped off the battlefield."

"Would you like to keep it?"

"Yes, thank you," Rikka said. Then she cocked her head, as if seeing Solvi for the first time. "Do you have others?"

Solvi pulled out her album of the housemaids and put it in her lap.

Rikka opened it. After a few pages, she looked up. "Is this what you do, then?"

"I suppose. I take photographs because I see things I'm not sure others see."

"So these are the girls working, and these are their portraits."

"Yes," Solvi said. "I love the contrast, first the girls in dirty aprons, then the same girls in their church clothes. You can see who they'd be if they weren't housemaids."

Rikka turned more pages. "Why did you take these pictures?"

"I'm not sure. The girls wanted portraits, but I was more interested in photographing them at work. I felt sorry for them, working and living in those conditions."

Rikka looked at her. "You're going to have to meet Petra."

THE DAYS SHORTENED and the cold descended, but for Solvi life started to blossom. Mr. Stenberg taught her how to frame and balance a photo, how to control the mood with light, and how to make people relax so they would open to the camera. She particularly enjoyed the darkroom, moving photographs from one chemical bath to another as the images slowly emerged. During portrait sessions, he let Solvi take several of her own shots, and later they compared their work, discussing the finer points of exposure and character. She loved that he took her seriously.

Back at the study house, Rikka wormed her way into Solvi's life, saving her a spot at meals, moving to the desk next to her in the library, coming by late at night for tea and gossip.

Within weeks, Solvi found herself dressed in a white sheet, like an Athenian goddess, swaying and bending with Rikka and nine other girls in a dusty ballroom. An aging ballerina played Chopin on a piano and called out the movements. Solvi, tripping over her feet, wished she could take photographs instead of dancing, but soon she was breathless from the exercise and laughter.

"I knew you'd like it," Rikka said, as they changed afterward. "Now, next on the Solvi modernization program: we need to do something about those braids of yours."

"You have a whole program for me?"

"Of course. Why not just wear your hair loose? I mean, if you aren't going to chop it off. And after that, new outfits. A couple of narrow skirts, a jacket or sweater, and some pale hose."

"But, Rikka, I won't know myself."

"That's the idea." Rikka glanced at her watch. "I told Petra we'd come by tonight. Do you have your photo album?"

"Yes," Solvi said. "I've been carrying it around because I thought we might run into her. Will she be at the café?"

"No—too many spoiled students at the café for her. We're going to her flat."

AFTER A LONG TRAMP through an old section of town, Solvi and Rikka stopped before a rickety tenement.

"She lives here, in this sad place?" Solvi said, glancing around with apprehension. It was evening, long since dark. Rikka had told her little about Petra or why Solvi needed to meet her. Solvi suspected it was some sort of test.

Rikka checked the street number. "Come on. She's waiting for us."

They entered the dim hallway, climbed to the top floor, then knocked on a door. A tall auburn-haired young woman in a plain blouse and black skirt opened. She had the bearing of a queen, imposing and cool. Her hair was braided and crossed over her head.

"Hello, Rikka," Petra said, her mouth tight. "Is this your new friend?"

"Nice to meet you, Petra," said Solvi.

Petra took in Solvi's fur-trimmed cape and gave her a brief nod.

"We'd love some tea," Rikka said, nudging the door open. "Is it too late to warm the kettle?"

"No, I suppose not," Petra said, turning to the counter that served as her kitchen. Rikka pushed Solvi inside.

So this was what her mother had meant by a dank little room, Solvi thought. The apartment was no more than a tight sitting room with a narrow bed in an alcove. The wallpaper, hazy from a scrim of coal smoke, was peeling in places. But there was a small sofa with a shawl over it, curtains in the window, and a cast-iron stove that emitted a bit of warmth. An open book lay on the sofa.

"How long have you been in Kristiania, Solvi?" said Petra, spooning tea into a pot.

"Just a month, but Rikka's already taken over my life."

Petra grunted. "No doubt. She says you're a photographer."

"Yes, though I'm studying for the matriculation exams right now."

Petra brought a tray of mismatched cups. "Rikka says you have some photographs of housemaids."

Something gave Solvi pause, but Rikka elbowed her, so she pulled out her album and handed it over.

Petra started paging through it slowly. After a few minutes, she glanced at Solvi, her eyes narrowing. "Who are these girls? How did you get these pictures?"

"They're maids at the homes of friends back in Bergen."

"Who let you in?"

"My friends. Usually when their mothers were out."

"Do their parents know you photographed their maids working?"

"No. They might have stopped me," Solvi said.

Petra leafed through the album again, then handed it back to her. "Those are remarkable." She turned to Rikka. "We could use those."

"I thought so," said Rikka.

"Excuse me," Solvi said, holding the album to her chest. "Use them for what?"

"I'm writing a newspaper article about the need for housemaid reforms," said Petra. "Your photographs could illustrate it."

"Do you mean publish my photographs in the newspaper?"

"Yes, but first we need an editor who's interested," Petra said. "Your album might do the trick."

Solvi could just hear her mother. *If Lisanne's parents recognize their maids, they'll fire them all. What were you thinking?* "I don't have permission to publish these in a newspaper," Solvi said. "What about their privacy?"

"The housemaids' privacy? I'm sure they'd be happy to help the reform movement," said Petra. "You could write your friends, ask for permission from their parents and their maids."

"If my friends' parents saw these photos, they might fire their maids," Solvi said. She put her album back in her satchel and buckled it tight.

"No progress without risk," Petra said.

Solvi looked helplessly at Rikka.

Rikka drained her cup. "Listen, perhaps we could get other photographs here in Kristiania, through people you know, Petra. I mean, if Solvi can't get permission to use these."

Petra just looked at Solvi. "Rikka, you have friends who write for the newspapers," she said. "Can you introduce me?"

"Sure. I'll ask around."

"And Solvi, when I'm ready to talk with an editor," Petra said, "I'll need to borrow your album."

"I go where it goes," Solvi heard herself say. "I don't lend it."

Petra gave Rikka a scowl.

Rikka rose. "Well, I'm glad you two met." She pushed Solvi toward the door. "Thanks for the tea, Petra."

Outside, Solvi turned to Rikka. "She doesn't like me."

"She doesn't know you yet," Rikka said. "She doesn't like the gentry much and probably doesn't know what to make of you. Most well-bred girls don't go around taking photographs of housemaids."

A FEW DAYS LATER, Solvi found herself telling a bemused police officer that her grandmother, and perhaps several uncles, had disappeared.

"They are named Helmer or Fallesen, I'm not sure which," she said. "My grandmother's husband would be Torvald, who might have been in some sort of trouble, legal or financial, perhaps in the, ah, 1880s?"

The officer laughed. "I guess we're not talking about anything recent, eh?"

"No, but it's still important," Rikka piped up. "People are missing."

"People alive now, or people from history?" The officer couldn't keep the smirk off his face.

"Possibly alive now," Rikka said, frowning. "We won't know for sure until we find them."

Solvi elbowed Rikka out of the way and gave the officer her sweetest smile. "Perhaps you could check the police records from 1879 or 1880 or 1881?" She slid a few coins across the counter. "Please?"

"I'd be happy to, miss. But are you certain they were in trouble with the law?"

The girls glanced at each other. "Absolutely," Solvi said. "Notorious criminals."

"Well, leave your address, young lady. If I find anything, I'll let you know."

IT WAS BLOWING SNOW as Solvi and Rikka left the police station, so they hurried to the café. Inside, Rikka pulled Solvi toward two young men who were talking intently.

"They look busy," Solvi said, feeling shy for a moment but then pushing back her hood and shaking out her curls. Rikka was right, wearing her hair down made her braver.

"Nonsense. Trust me."

One boy stood as they approached, then gave Rikka a weak smile and moved away.

The other young man, fair skinned with unruly blond hair, turned. "Rikka! I haven't seen you in weeks. Come. Sit," he said, reaching for extra chairs. "Why, now you've frightened Andre away!" Then he noticed Solvi. "And who's this?"

Solvi smiled hesitantly. "Solveig Lange," she said, holding out her hand.

"Dominik Engstrom," he said, taking her hand. But instead of giving it a shake, he grabbed her other hand and held them tight between his own.

"Good Lord, you're cold," he said, rubbing them vigorously. "Can't let you get frostbite."

Solvi blushed. He was quite handsome, with a big smile and mischievous brown eyes.

Rikka watched Andre head toward the door. "I'll be back in a minute."

"Can I get you a coffee, Miss Lange?" asked Dominik, finally letting go of her.

"I'll get my own, thank you," she said. At the counter she tried to steady herself, but when she returned Dominik gallantly pulled out her chair, making her blush again. "I realize many young women prefer to do for themselves these days, but I can't retrain myself," he said. "Tell me if it bothers you."

"No, of course not," said Solvi. "I come from an old Bergen family, and my grandfather would have pegged you a barbarian if you hadn't done that." Then she stopped. "Actually, I thought I came from an old Bergen family, but I've recently discovered that may not be true."

"It's difficult to tell these days who people are and where they're from," Dominik said. "All kinds of barbarians are showing up in people's parlors, the skeptics with the religious, the harmless with the snakes. I think it's wonderful, but I know some find it threatening."

"My mother would be shocked to see me here, drinking coffee with someone I hadn't been formally introduced to."

"You're safe, Miss Lange. I'm one of the harmless skeptics."

"Then you must be a university student."

Dominik laughed. "Yes. How about you?"

"I take the admission exams in January, but I may not pass. I had no idea how much my ladies' academy was keeping from me. It's like a conspiracy to block young women from qualifying for university," Solvi rattled on. "I wish they would make you boys learn to draw and embroider. It would level the field a bit."

Dominik leaned toward her. "There *is* a conspiracy, Miss Lange!" he whispered. "They want you all to go back to your knitting needles. If you're a true rebel, you'll work day and night to deny them victory."

Solvi laughed. "So what are you studying?"

"Philosophy and politics," Dominik said as he motioned to a waiter. "The young lady here would like some rolls and butter. With jam, I think."

"Yes, jam, please," Solvi said. "How did you know I was hungry?"

"The look in your eye," he said, gazing at her. "So what made you doubt your old Bergen family?"

"A photograph my grandfather tried to burn just before he died," Solvi said.

"Burning photographs?" He leaned forward again. "How mysterious! Who is in this photograph?"

She hesitated. It was all so personal, but there was something about this boy that made her want to talk. She told him about the family portrait and then, before she could stop herself, about her mother lying about it. "She seemed to be hiding something," Solvi said. "I'm hoping the people in the portrait are still alive."

The waiter brought their rolls. Solvi took one and spread it with jam, a thick raspberry that reminded her of Cook back home stirring the copper pot.

"Do you think they might be here, in Kristiania?" Dominik asked.

"Maybe, but I've little to go on."

Rikka returned, but not with Andre. With someone new—a tall young man with dark hair, a trim beard, and kind eyes behind wire-rimmed glasses.

"Solvi, this is Magnus Clemmensen," Rikka said. "I found him outside, looking in the window at you."

Solvi could only blush again.

"Welcome to Kristiania, Solvi," Magnus said, blushing a bit himself and extending his hand. "Rikka says you've only recently arrived."

Solvi smiled and shook his hand. His eyes were gray as the winter sea.

Then Magnus laughed. "Dominik, hello. I didn't see you there."

"I guess you all know one another," Solvi said, as Magnus pulled up a chair.

"Yes," Dominik said. "We met in Latin review before our exams, is that right?"

Magnus nodded. "As I recall, I finally beat you out for the highest score."

"You did not!" said Dominik. "You're just showing off. You know I was best."

"Well," said Rikka, reaching for a roll and smearing it with butter. "Solvi could use a little help with her Latin review."

Solvi kicked Rikka under the table. "Really, must you tell all my shameful secrets right off?"

"Many people struggle with Latin," said Magnus. "It's hardly shameful."

"It seems so useless, a language nobody speaks," Solvi said.

"The Latin exam's easy," said Dominik. "Just practice translating the most famous bits of Cicero."

"It's a bit more complicated than that," said Magnus. "I'd be happy to tutor you."

"I think I should tutor her," Dominik said, putting his elbows on the table. "Since I got the highest score." He grinned at Magnus, but there was defiance in his smile.

Solvi looked from one to the other, then glanced at Rikka, who lifted her eyebrows. "Thank you both," Solvi said, "but I have a tutor. She's not much fun but quite thorough."

"Solvi would do fine if she wasn't running around taking photographs," Rikka said.

"I'm too busy running around with you, Rikka," Solvi said.

Dominik cocked his head. "You're a photographer?"

"I suppose, though I'm not very good yet."

"You should see her work; she's quite the social critic," Rikka said. "At the moment she's criticizing how we treat our housemaids."

Magnus looked at her with interest. "How do you do that with photography?"

"I take pictures of housemaids working," Solvi said. "I'm sure you can imagine. They're usually surrounded by heaps of dirty laundry or standing over steaming kettles. I try to show how hard their labor is, often alone in hot kitchens or dank basements."

Dominik laughed. "Well, of course their work is hard, but I can assure you it isn't as bad as the farms most of them came from."

"That's no excuse for overworking housemaids," Magnus said, an edge to his voice.

Rikka abruptly turned to him. "Magnus, you write for *Dagbladet*."

"Yes. Why?"

"Solvi and I have been talking with Petra Jeppesen, the maid pushing for housemaid reforms. She needs an introduction to the editor. She wants to write an article and use Solvi's photographs to illustrate it."

Dominik glanced at his watch and jumped to his feet. "Sorry—late for class. It was lovely to meet you, Miss Lange. I hope I'll see you here again."

Solvi smiled at him. "Rikka drags me here nearly every day, so I'm sure you will."

He tipped his cap, then strode away.

Magnus turned to Rikka. "I'd be happy to introduce Petra to the editor." Then he looked at Solvi. "And I'd love to see your photographs. Are you helping Petra with the article?"

"I, ah, I don't know. I only just met her." Solvi glanced at Rikka. "We need to be concentrating on our exams right now."

"I'm sure the editor, Mr. Blehr, would be interested in your photographs."

"Perfect," Rikka said.

"That's very kind, Magnus," Solvi said, "but I'm not sure I want to publish my photographs in a newspaper."

"No progress without risk," said Rikka.

"Don't push her," Magnus said. "Solvi, when you're ready, just let me know." He put a few coins on the table, then stood. "Rikka, I'll talk to Mr. Blehr, and, Solvi, it's been a pleasure." He gave her a warm smile as he turned away.

Rikka laughed.

"What?"

"You're right," Rikka said. "You should keep your Isolde hair."

LATER THAT NIGHT, Rikka peeked around Solvi's door, then slipped in and curled up on her bed like an otter. Solvi sighed, pushed her books aside, and sat down beside her.

"Who is Andre, Rikka, and why are his manners so bad?"

"Just a student, like all of us. His manners are usually fine; he's just angry with me."

"You spurned him, didn't you?"

Rikka sighed. "I told him not to fall in love with me."

"Because you're not in love with him?"

"No, I am not," Rikka said, then paused for a long moment. "Honestly, Solvi, love did not serve me well. I think now I'm immune."

"You can't believe that, Rikka. Don't worry, you will fall in love again. Maybe an Arctic explorer or a famous surgeon. Someone bold, someone brave enough to approach you."

Rikka laughed. "I do seem to scare men. That's why I don't have a Dominik in my life."

"I don't have a Dominik in my life."

"Just you wait. He was quite taken with you."

Solvi got up and poured her a cup of tea, turning away to hide a smile. "What do you know about him?"

"Dominik?" Rikka shook her head. "He's, well, he's Dominik. He's brilliant, with a million ideas, but he can drive you mad. He'll contradict everything you say and is usually right. His family is old Kristiania gentry. He grew up debating his father, who's a lawyer."

"And what do you know of Magnus? Is he from a good family?"

"Ask me a better question."

"Sorry. Is he intelligent?"

"Certainly, though I suspect Dominik got the better Latin score. Magnus writes columns for *Dagbladet* about society and politics. He's quite thoughtful; he's studying history, I think. His father's in the parliament."

"The Storting? You're joking."

"No, it's true; he's one of the labor leaders. I think he was a shipwright."

A laborer, Solvi thought. The kind of man who might have organized workers in the Vinters' shipyard, a man her grandfather would have ridiculed. Solvi could just see him, railing about Bolsheviks and shaking the newspaper in disgust.

"Do you like Magnus?" Solvi asked, glancing at Rikka.

"I like Magnus very much, but I'm not in love with him, if that's what you mean," Rikka said. "I refuse to fall in love, because I refuse to marry."

"Don't you want a husband?"

"A husband might be fine, but unfortunately they come dragging marriage along with them."

"Why are you set against marriage?"

"I don't want to marry because—from what I can see—marriage keeps women from becoming powerful. I'd rather be powerful."

"But don't you want a family?"

Rikka shook her head. "Not really. I worry about another war. I couldn't raise a son and send him to fight, not after what I've seen."

Solvi picked at a hole in her shawl. "I've always dreamed of a string of children. My family would've been happier if there'd been more of us. That's why I want to find my grandmother and my uncles. I long for more family."

"Don't you want to be powerful, do something for the world?"

"Perhaps, but I want to be loved, too."

"Oh, no," Rikka said, laughing sadly. "You don't get both—you have to choose."

"I'll never be the rebel you are, Rikka, even if we cut my hair. Can we still be friends?"

"Of course. I'm sorry. Sometimes I feel rather black inside; just ignore me."

"You're impossible to ignore, Rikka."

"Well, then don't take me seriously."

CHAPTER SEVEN

NORA

Spring 1919 ■ *Spokane, Washington*

I pulled the advertisement out of my apron pocket and examined it again. Torvald must have died. That was the only way to explain it—the ad, the photo, the plea.

I was tidying up after supper when this thought came to me. Anders sat nearby repairing a boot, hammering in nails with quick taps.

I imagined the hammering as someone nailing down the lid of Torvald's coffin. But maybe that was just my desire speaking.

If so, it wasn't the first time.

I had wished Torvald would die during those frantic days in Kristiania, when he was blocking me from seeing the children. I wished he would die when he threatened to drag me to the insane asylum. And years later, when I finally returned to Norway, I harbored a guilty hope that I would find him gone.

But, as I've said before, God has never listened to my prayers.

I put the ad back in my pocket, then dried the pots and stacked them on a shelf. The Church fathers would be shocked if they knew I had prayed for someone else's death, even if it might mean my liberation.

Maybe now, though, it had finally happened. Torvald had died, and the children found something in his papers—a letter or a secret will. I thought of Torvald in the photograph, so proud of his family, so sure of his place in the world. He was still like that when I last saw him thirty years ago. Only death could silence that resolute arrogance of his.

But if he had died, what would that mean? Had he left me a legacy? No, all his wealth would go to the children. Maybe he left me a note, one last scorching message. Or perhaps he left a letter begging my forgiveness. Given his life, he might have feared God's judgment.

I considered these alternatives but concluded they were equally unlikely. He would go to his grave without lifting a finger to communicate with me.

I took the wash basin outside to dump behind the garden. Years of avoiding church had hardened my heart, I could see that. I hung the basin on a nail and then walked down to Katrin's to help put the grandchildren to bed. Anything to redeem my wicked soul.

NORA
October 1880 ■ Kristiania, Norway

Fall brought rain, and my life narrowed again to my drab room. An envelope from Kristine arrived with a note from Torvald inside, as if she had resisted giving him my address.

> DEAR WIFE (apparently I was no longer Nora to him): *I heard from friends concerned for your welfare that you recently dined with the director of the Kristiania Theater. I also know that you've been working as a companion to Dr. Rank. Such behavior is deeply damaging to your reputation and has served to confirm everyone's suspicions. All I can think is that you are suffering from a perverse hysteria—indeed, that you've been suffering since Mr. Krogstad began blackmailing you. Therefore, for your own safety, I'm moving forward to have you committed. If you return to my protection, perhaps we can care for you at home. Your Husband, Torvald Helmer*

My pulse hammered. I crept down the hall of the widow's house and peered out the front door. Had Torvald already sent his men? No, not yet, but they would come.

Back in my room, I paced. My instincts said hide, but where could I go? North to some windswept fishing village above the Arctic Circle? No; strangers and outsiders were quick to attract attention in such places, and there would be little work. America? Copenhagen? I couldn't afford passage to either, and how would I manage alone in such a place? How would I live without seeing the children occasionally, even if just from the street corner? No, I must stay in Kristiania.

So I would hide here, in plain sight.

I put aside a simple widow's dress to wear the next day and then took my bustle and better dresses—everything that signaled my class—and rolled them into a bundle. I then sewed my pearls into the seam of my chemise for safekeeping. I spent the evening knitting a rough shawl, then threw it to the floor and ground it under my heel to make it look old and dirty.

The next morning I covered my head with the shawl and tossed the bundle over my shoulder. Everything disappeared beneath a shawl—hair, carriage, class. I hunched my way down to the pawnbrokers' alley.

I picked the first store I found and dropped my bundle on the counter. A weasel-faced man in a grimy jacket tested the fabrics and the hoops, then counted out a fistful of coins. I thought for a moment, then took off my fashionable coat and put it on the counter.

"Won't you need that this winter, ma'am?"

"Something lighter will do," I said. He brought me an old tweed misshapen with use. I examined a seam, checking for lice. It smelled of mold but seemed free of bugs. "This is fine," I said. "What else do you take?"

He looked me up and down. "Those are lovely buttons, ma'am."

I glanced down at my dress, which was plain but well made, with buttons of horn. I flushed with humiliation—would nothing be left to me?

"I suppose you have pins," I croaked.

He pulled them from a drawer and snapped open his pocket knife, as if this happened every day. I turned away to cut off the buttons and pin my bodice closed, embarrassed to be so proud, angry to be so embarrassed. I wrapped my new coat around my mutilated dress and pocketed the money.

Out on the street the damp came straight through the thin tweed, and in that instant I was transformed into one of Kristiania's poor, stoop shouldered and sullen. Was this a disguise or my fate? I wasn't sure anymore.

I walked a few blocks just to get away from the odious pawnbroker, then turned a corner. I had come to the edge of the slum.

Vika, the retreat of the shameless and the dispossessed. The quarter was a maze of tumble-down buildings, dirty taverns, and humble huts. Fishermen watched me from beneath their caps; children in tattered clothes stared. I pulled my purse close but didn't shy away.

Few in Kristiania society ever uttered its name, yet Vika was the secret nightmare of all who perched precariously on the ladder of civility. Looking about, though, it just seemed forgotten. Was it truly a breeding ground for labor unrest and political radicals, as the police often claimed? I noticed a few students in shabby coats and some factory workers in overalls waiting for the horse-drawn tram. On the corner, an elderly woman in a shawl stood beside a small cart hawking apples. Perhaps it was more of a refuge, a place for those who had nothing.

Either way, I knew one thing: Torvald would never look for me here. He couldn't imagine me here.

At a small market I found notices for rooms and soon stood before a two-story house with wooden clapboards gone gray from the salt air. Several young men turned out the door, tipped their hats at me with puzzled smiles, and headed up the lane.

I took a deep breath and went in.

A pinched-faced woman in a cap sat at one of several tables in the large front room, making notes in a ledger. Men and boys bent over books or slouched in chairs, reading or writing. A fire smoldered in an open hearth, but otherwise there was little comfort—no rug or curtains, just benches and a few rough chairs.

Everyone looked up, caution in their gaze. I felt like I had stumbled into a wolf's lair.

The landlady stood, eyeing me with the same mild suspicion as everyone in Vika. "May I help you?"

"I, well, I need a room," I said. "I saw the posting—you let to students."

"You're not a student, I daresay."

"No, but, well, it seems a nice house." I could not keep a touch of irony out of my voice.

Someone coughed to cover a laugh.

The landlady frowned, then looked me up and down, from my boots to the blond knot at the back of my head, seeing right past my battered pawn-shop coat. "If you don't mind my asking, can't a lady like yourself do better than this, ma'am? I rarely accept women; they attract the police."

My face went hot. Is that what she thought? "Since my husband died, I've had to sew for my living," I said, offering my hand and my maiden name. "Nora Solberg."

She eyed me warily. "The boys are noisy, and some don't have the best manners."

"Perhaps I'll have a civilizing effect."

She laughed at that, then softened enough to take my hand. "I'm Mrs. Blum. I've got a room the maid used, back when I could afford a maid." She led me to a closet off the kitchen, stacked with broken furniture. The walls were stuffed with rags, but the cold still found its way in. A narrow window faced into the alley.

"I'll clean it out. You get a bed, a washing stand, and a chair. The privies are out back."

Privies. "Is this your best room?" I asked, faltering.

"I can't have you upstairs with the boys, ma'am." She told me the rent, then watched to see how desperate I was.

I nodded, thinking. I could stay here indefinitely on what I earned sewing. "I'll move in tomorrow morning."

When I got back to my room, I wrote to Anne-Marie. She would be the only one who would know where I had gone.

AT THE ROOMING HOUSE in Vika the next day, I unpacked my few possessions. It was strange to consider how much had been stripped from my life. When I finished, I pinned the drawing from my children to the wall, but there was no hiding the crudeness of this place, this living among strangers. The boots of the students sounded overhead. I sat down to my lacework, nervously waiting for the dinner bell.

When it rang, the young men thundered down the stairs. I hesitated, shy in a way I couldn't name, but their animated voices soon pulled me from my chair.

When I stepped into the crowded front room, the chatter subsided. Some were truly boys, with thin shoulders and smooth faces, but others were older, bearded—closer to my age. Everyone stared.

"My God, Queen Sofia has come to live among us!" someone said.

Laughter. I flushed with embarrassment. There was no space for me. Then a young man at the end of a bench shoved the others down and stood up. "We can fit you here, ma'am," he said, sticking out his hand. "Tobias. Whatever you need, just let me know."

"Mrs. Solberg," I said, smiling my gratitude. The landlady brought a bowl of vegetable soup, and someone passed me bread and *nøkkelost*, the cheese so common and cheap. Another boy fetched me a glass of water. The chatter resumed, but softly. They watched me over their spoons; not all of them seemed friendly.

"Mrs. Solberg, we're honored to have you with us," said Tobias, warming to his role. He had a moon face, dark curly hair, and spectacles. "Are you matriculating as well?"

That brought more laughter, as women could not attend university.

Tobias turned to them. "Perhaps she's the first!"

"Judging from my performance in school, I would prove a poor student,"

I said. "But maybe university is different. For your sakes, I hope so. Are you all students?"

"Students or hopefuls," Tobias said. "Some still need to pass their matriculation exams."

"What do you study?"

"The usual—philosophy, Latin, Greek, history," he said. "After that, I will read the law."

"A fine profession, I suppose," I said, then heard myself add something that would have shocked Torvald: "As long as the law protects all citizens."

"Careful there, Mrs. Solberg," said a young man across from me. He was taller than Tobias, with a thick beard and intense dark eyes. "You could be taken for some kind of revolutionary, saying such things." He extended his hand. "Erlend, also at your service."

"No. Just a humble seamstress looking for respectable work."

"Then you couldn't have come to a better quarter," Erlend said. "Vika, well known as a capital of commerce. Why, you could scrape pigskins down at the yard, or sort old fish in the market, or . . ."

"Shush, Erlend, or you'll frighten Mrs. Solberg, and she'll go back to wherever she came from," said Tobias. He turned to me. "Where did you come from, if I may?"

"North, on Lake Mjøsa. I lost my husband and now must provide for myself."

They nodded, though I could tell nobody believed that was the full story. I bent to my soup, and before long the debates resumed—arguments and joking about all things political, from parliamentary systems to class reforms. It was both intimidating and exciting.

Tobias noticed me assessing the conversation. "We're not always so highbrow, Mrs. Solberg. They're just showing off."

I smiled and helped clear the bowls, then returned to my chilly room, too shy to sit with them into the evening. Not all the young men seemed happy I was there, but for the first time in days I had laughed.

THE NEXT MORNING I shared porridge with the students, then brought my sewing to sit by the fire, as I could barely thread a needle in my frigid room.

Most of the boys left for classes, but a few stayed behind, reading or scribbling out essays with pencil nubs. Some of them watched me out of the corners of their eyes, unsettled that such a strange person had entered their world. Newspapers lay about; most were unionist sheets.

Perhaps I had stumbled into a nest of radicals, the kind the police watched and sometimes arrested. I fidgeted, feeling out of place and wondering if I was safe.

But then Tobias appeared. "Ah, Mrs. Solberg, I'm glad to see you didn't flee in the night. I've needed a friend with a sewing bag. Could I borrow a bit of thread?"

"What needs mending?"

He spread his arms wide. "Everything!"

I smiled and gave him a needle, and he started on his coat sleeve, torn at the elbow. After a few minutes I handed him a patch, a bit from a fine old jacket of Torvald's. He examined it, then gave me a puzzled glance.

"You'd be surprised what people throw away," I said. "So, tell me about your studies. If I can't go to university, perhaps I can learn something from you."

He began tacking down the patch with awkward stitches. "Yes, well, I'm reading an interesting German philosopher at the moment. He says God is nothing more than a manifestation of man's own nature."

I thought about that for a minute. "That might explain why God seems so much like men, domineering and easily offended. Is your philosopher one of those atheists?"

Tobias chuckled, though he also seemed wary. "Maybe you're on to something. As for my philosopher, he's not an atheist, but he dislikes the Church and its trappings—the sacraments and such. He says they lead to superstition."

I bit off a thread. "Yes. There seems to be either a mysterious God or an intimate God, but in my experience both ignore the pleas of women."

He cocked his head to one side. "Perhaps you're right. I have three grown sisters, and only one has married, despite many prayers. I worry about the financial burden on my parents, but they insist I continue my studies."

"Do you think the law will make you happy?"

"I don't know. Right now I only want to read philosophy."

"I knew a man who trained for the law but couldn't bear to defend those who had done wrong. He became a banker. Do you think that made him a better man?"

Tobias shrugged. "Maybe it would be better to defend the worst sinner rather than a pile of money. I hope to use the law to—how did you put it last night—defend the rights of all citizens, including women and workers."

"So what do you think of the Woman Question? Should we be allowed to vote?"

He put down his work and looked at me. "I must say, Mrs. Solberg, you are a conundrum. Everyone's quite perplexed by you."

"I had no idea I was a conundrum. In what way?"

"Everyone wants to know why you're here."

My breathing grew shallow. "It's quite simple: I'm a poor widow down on my luck. Vika was the only place I could afford. Living with students seemed safer than the alternatives."

"Some are puzzled that you have no widow's pension."

"Unfortunately, my husband lost his company, and then he, well, he . . ." I looked away, so Tobias wouldn't see how poorly I was fabricating this story.

"It's just that you're obviously a lady, Mrs. Solberg. Everything about you is, forgive me, of a class most of us only aspire to—your language, your posture, even your skin. Surely you have family or friends who could take you in."

I gave him a sad smile. "Not everyone has such good fortune, Tobias."

He nodded, but I could see he was not satisfied. "Let me just warn you, some of the others are threatening to complain to Mrs. Blum. They are worried you might be a plant."

"What do you mean by a plant?"

"Someone planted by the police."

I stared at him, then shook my head with dismay and looked up to control the tears rising in my eyes. Last night this place felt like a refuge, a place where I might be accepted, where I could make friends. Now that was slipping away.

"Why is it so difficult for women deprived of family to find a place in this world?" I couldn't keep the disappointment out of my voice. "I'm beginning to understand why so many women turn to the streets."

Tobias put down his sewing. "Forgive me, Mrs. Solberg. I didn't mean to upset you. You're right. There are few easy paths for women in your situation."

"If I can't stay here, I don't know where I will go." We looked at each other for a long moment. "To be honest, Tobias, I'm trying to not be found. That is why I am here, in Vika."

He blinked.

"And I don't want to see the police any more than anyone else in this rooming house," I said. "I swear to that."

He nodded slowly. "I'm sorry, Mrs. Solberg. I'm beginning to understand."

"But please keep my secret, Tobias. I can't afford to have anyone talking about me."

His eyes glittered with interest. "Don't worry, Mrs. Solberg. I will talk with the others without giving you away."

OVER THE NEXT FEW WEEKS, I did little more than keep up with my lacework and adjust to the rooming house. If it had not been for the company of the boys, it would have been a dismal existence. The mist rolled in at night, sliding through chinks and under the doors, and the privies out back proved a misery and humiliation. My hands bloomed with chilblains; my clothes soon smelled of poverty.

But despite everything, my life opened like an alpine plant warming to a new season. Tobias shared his books and escorted me through the rough streets. Erlend became my tutor, lecturing me on politics and badgering me to sharpen my opinions. In return, I patched their clothes and knit them socks and mittens. It hardly seemed a fair exchange.

At first I just listened when the students argued, fascinated by their revolutionary rhetoric. The authorities would have been interested to know a volume of Marx was being passed around, along with other banned material. Some of the boys kept their distance, like sailors who distrust having a woman on board ship. But many of the boys soon came to welcome my company. We stayed up late most nights, huddled around the fire philosophizing.

It was a relief, at long last, to hear others asking the questions that troubled me—why society was organized for the benefit of wealthy men, why the law treated workers and women like children, why so many were blocked from university or better jobs simply because of their class or sex. Tobias lent me a novel written by a woman, *The District Governor's Daughters*, that captured a bleak, confined world that was painfully familiar. It made me weep into my pillow.

Even outside the rooming house I grew more comfortable, often walking about behind my crude veil or taking the air down by the docks. One blustery day I stopped to talk with a woman selling cakes to passersby. She and her children had been left behind when her husband immigrated three years earlier to Nebraska in America, promising to send for them when he could. The cold wind whipped about us as we talked, and on an impulse I offered her my muffler in exchange for one of her cakes.

After that I stopped to chat whenever I saw her, sometimes bringing knitted caps or socks for her children. She showed me letters from her husband, who was struggling to wring enough cash from his homestead to pay passage for his family. The letters, a crabbed hand on rough paper, brimmed with both hope and failure—the promising wheat crop ravaged by hail, the shanty built in summer that proved inadequate for the frigid winter. I told her that when she joined her husband, she could make their farm better. She just nodded and tucked the letters back into her pocket.

Tobias told me she was an "America widow." There were many like her in Vika, he said, waiting for passage. Their husbands rarely sent for them.

ONE AFTERNOON Tobias suggested we walk to the wharf where the emigrant ships were loading. "Just to look at the crowd," he said, but I knew it was more than that. Living in Vika, I now understood why Norway's poor dreamed of crossing the ocean for something better. I, too, stopped to gaze at the posters of rippling wheat on Dakota land and listened as shipping agents hawked fares from the sidewalks.

All the boys in the rooming house knew what it cost; most had secret America plans.

"I'll bet you would go pan gold in California," I teased, as Tobias and I walked along the seawall. The wind was up—it would be an uncomfortable trip out the fjord that day.

Tobias laughed. "Good Lord, no. Prospecting's too dangerous. No, I'd go to Chicago. There's a Norwegian community there and plenty of opportunity. I might teach, or write for a newspaper."

"Is your English that good?"

"No, but it wouldn't matter. They have Norwegian papers and Norwegian schools."

"Now you're teasing me."

"I swear. Before long, half of Norway will be living in America. We don't see it here in Kristiania, but the mountain regions are emptying out. In some places only the old people are left." Then he glanced at me. "Maybe you have an America plan of your own, Mrs. Solberg."

"Tobias, how did you know? Aasta Hansteen is leaving for New York next spring, and she has asked me to go with her."

"I'm serious. You don't belong in Vika. You must be plotting an escape."

I looked down the fjord. "I can't leave Norway, Tobias. I have ties here I cannot sever." Then I smiled at him. "But, I'll admit, sometimes I wish I could."

We approached the steamship wharf where a restive crowd waited to board.

"My God, how young they are," I said, glancing about.

"Yes, it seems true for every boatload," Tobias said, pointing out boys no older than ten and several pairs of sturdy girls traveling without husbands. Even the families seemed young, newlyweds and couples with small children. Everyone had a heap of bags, and the mothers, often clutching an infant, perched on their red wedding chests, many apprehensive and sad. It made my heart ache to think that these chests—decorated with the rosemaling of their districts—might soon be the only links back to their Oppland farms.

I noticed a girl standing by herself. "Look at that one there, in the brown coat. Do you think she's going to America alone? Why, she can't be fifteen!"

He watched her. "They say some girls leave Norway because they are with child. They take their secret with them to America and bear their children away from Norwegian eyes."

"The poor thing, to be alone at a time like that! What will become of her?"

"There are few unmarried women on the frontier, so she may be able to find a husband, even with a child. Perhaps she'll be fine. She'll certainly be better off than if she stays here."

We watched the passengers move slowly up the gangway.

"Do you think they'll miss Norway?" I asked.

"Norway's done little for them," Tobias said, an edge to his voice. "These are the courageous ones. How exciting it must be to leave this narrow, fog-bound country for the freedom of America. I think about it all the time."

"I considered going to Copenhagen once."

"Why Copenhagen?"

"Because people who go to Copenhagen don't write home complaining about grasshoppers."

He laughed. "The grasshopper plagues are mostly gone, as are the Indians, who've been pushed west by the army."

"Then I don't know why we aren't all packing our traveling chests."

"The emigration bug might catch you yet, Mrs. Solberg. As soon as I finish my studies, I might go."

"How would you afford passage?"

"That's the trick," he said, eyeing the ship. "That's the trick."

ASIDE FROM AMERICA DREAMS, the popular topic that fall in the rooming house was the election of the new Storting and whether Norway would adopt universal suffrage for all men. Feeling bold one evening, I asked if suffrage could be called universal if it didn't include women.

Some of the boys shifted uneasily in their seats. Tobias and Erlend were as freethinking as I was on the Woman Question, but others were not. Henrik, a newcomer who seemed to resent my presence, started making fun of my heroine, Miss Hansteen, joking about her wearing men's boots beneath her skirts and threatening politicians with her umbrella.

I put down my sewing and frowned at him.

"Careful there," said Erlend. "Mrs. Solberg considers herself one of Hansteen's lieutenants."

"I think Hansteen is dangerous," Henrik said. "She wants the rights of women improved before the rights of working men."

"That's because women don't have the most basic human rights," I said. "Even poor farmers have more rights than women of any class."

"But you can't let women take jobs from men. Women already get most of the factory work because they'll work for less and are afraid to strike."

"Because they must feed their children," I said hotly.

"That's the problem with women," said Henrik. "They're weak and their concerns are narrow. They shouldn't be part of the labor debate."

"Not part of the debate? Have you any idea how imprisoned women feel because they cannot . . ."

"Watch out, Henrik," Erlend laughed. "She's got an umbrella!"

I opened my mouth again, but Tobias pulled me away.

"Mrs. Solberg and I are going out for some sea air," he said with his usual gallantry, handing me my coat. Outside he slipped his arm through mine.

"Don't bother with Henrik—he's a prig. But he's right: the Woman Question is not simple."

"But nothing is simple, Tobias. Surely you understand that. Sometimes I get impatient hearing all these grand theories because they seem to ignore what is actually happening to people. And why women should be cut out, time after time, just because their situation is complicated—it just keeps us bottled up in our parlors with our knitting, as if we are no good for anything else," I said bitterly. "I've lived that life, and I'm not going back there."

Tobias was silent for a long moment before he spoke again. "Mrs. Solberg, if you don't mind my asking, what happened to your husband?"

I stopped and looked at him. A vague story formed on my tongue, but I could not lie to Tobias. I just shook my head.

"I'm sorry," he said. "I shouldn't have asked."

"It's all right," I murmured. I wanted to tell him the truth, because he would have understood, but I did not dare.

A FEW WEEKS LATER we celebrated Christmas at the rooming house over a bowl of lamb stew, a special treat from our landlady. Tobias brought me a bit of holly tied with red yarn he pulled from a sock. I hung the holly in my room.

The next day I walked to the fjord in the late afternoon. A year had passed since I came down here in the inky dark after my fight with Torvald. I looked down at the heaving sea. For some reason, I had been pulled back to this spot, back from Hamar to Kristiania, then here to Vika. Now I lived at the harbor's very edge, the damp in my sheets and foghorns in my dreams.

If I took one more step, I'd be in the water. Or on a ship.

AFTER THE HOLIDAY, the Arctic winds bore down from the north. The cold stiffened my hands, making it harder to sew. One evening I asked the boys if I should try to get a job at one of the factories. They listened with interest, and then several exchanged glances.

"We could send you in as our spy," said Nikolai.

"Your spy?"

"We need evidence of poor working conditions and injuries. You could be very helpful."

"Good Lord, Nikolai, do you want Mrs. Solberg to end up in prison?" Tobias said. He turned to me. "Don't listen to him. Standing at a loom is backbreaking work."

"But I don't seem useful for anything, Tobias."

"Don't worry. We'll find you something."

THE FOLLOWING WEEK, Tobias burst into the rooming house waving a newspaper. "I've found you a job, Mrs. Solberg. Look here." He pointed at a small notice. *The agent for the White Star Line needs a secretary for his office in Bjørvika. English required.*

"Clerk for a shipping agent?" I wrinkled my nose.

"Yes, why not?"

"Well, you know what they say, that the shipping agents go through the countryside swindling poor emigrants."

"Mrs. Solberg, have we taught you nothing?" Tobias said. "The authorities spread those tales to discourage farmers from leaving. Just go talk to the agent. See what he's like."

I CHANGED INTO MY BLACK DRESS, fumbling nervously with the buttons, and then walked quickly to Bjørvika, where the shipping lines kept their offices. I wasn't sure what to think. I'd heard many stories of unscrupulous shipping agents and doubted they were all lies.

When I entered the office, the agent was leaning over a counter in his shirtsleeves and vest, explaining a contract to a young family. He was tall, with thinning hair, dark sideburns, and a stern face. Commanding, but not a gentleman.

He didn't look up, so I took off my hat and coughed.

He glanced at me, taking in my golden hair, then straightened up. "You've come about the job."

"Yes. I have my academy credentials, I've done copying and bookkeeping for several law offices in town, and I speak English and some German."

"Can you now." He looked me up and down. "Mrs.—"

"Mrs. Solberg."

He gave my hand a quick shake. "Fredrik Nielsen," he said. "A widow, I see."

I didn't correct him.

"Well, now, let's test you out." He pushed a document toward me. "Here's the standard contract for passage to America in steerage. Review it with the next family. In a nutshell, they take a Wilson Line ship across the North Sea to Hull, on the eastern coast of England, then the train to Liverpool. They sail from Liverpool on one of the White Star ships."

I scanned the contract. "Does it cover lodging in Liverpool?"

"No, but there are rooming houses near the docks. Have them sign two copies. Then I'll sign them." He leaned over and whispered in my ear.

"Don't read the whole damn thing; it only confuses them. Just the first page will do."

I slid behind the counter and faced a farmer with two daughters. I smiled. "Are you traveling steerage?"

He gave me a tight nod, so I read the contract slowly. His daughters kept stopping me, asking questions about everything from washing to cooking onboard.

"Mr. Nielsen, do they serve meals, or can they cook their own?" I said, turning to him.

"Good God, no! These are steamships, not broken-down whalers." Mr. Nielsen leaned over and stabbed at the contract with a long, bony finger. "Right there: two meals a day, no cooking allowed."

"Of course." I blushed at his rudeness. The poor farmer finally signed, and another family pushed forward. With each party Mr. Nielsen checked and signed the documents while I took the money, nearly two hundred crowns per person for steerage, more for staterooms. A fortune, it seemed to me.

Near closing time, a family of cotters approached, the wife pushing her husband toward me. "Ma'am," he said, his mouth working with anxiety, "how often do the ships wreck?"

"Wreck?" I instantly thought of the SS *Atlantic*, which went down off Nova Scotia ten years earlier. Over five hundred people drowned, including all the women and children. A White Star ship. "Not often," I stammered.

"There are terms for shipwreck," he said, pointing to a page. "So it must happen."

Mr. Nielsen appeared behind me. "The White Star ships have a 99.9 percent rate of safe completion. The terms are there in the rare case something goes wrong, and when it does, the lifeboats are more than adequate." He shooed the couple away, then glared at me. "Mrs. Solberg, if you want to keep this job, you'll refrain from discussing such matters."

I felt my back stiffen. "But what if they lose their nerve? What if they decide not to go and need to get out of their contract? Do they get their money back?"

"Rarely. Now, Mrs. Solberg, I trust you're not going to create more problems than you solve. If you cannot think of an appropriate answer, refer them to me."

After clearing a few more parties, Mr. Nielsen closed the office for the day, then turned to me. "Well, Mrs. Solberg, do you have a letter of recommendation?"

"No, but I've worked for the solicitors Meier and Dahlberg. You could ask them for a reference." All of a sudden I wanted this job. I didn't like Mr. Nielsen, but at least I was out in the world rather than huddled by the fire with my knitting.

He regarded me for a moment, then sighed. "I suppose you'll do—just promise me you won't ever talk of shipwrecks. The office is open Monday through Saturday, eight to five. I pay twenty crowns a week."

It was less than factory work, but I was in no position to complain. "Tomorrow, then, Mr. Nielsen. Thank you."

WHEN I STEPPED into the shipping office the next morning, Mr. Nielsen looked up with surprise. "Good day, Mrs. Solberg. I wasn't sure you'd return. I figured your brother, or whoever cares for you, would forbid you to take the position. With a shipping agent, I mean."

"I decide for myself, Mr. Nielsen. No one forbids me."

"Because there's no one looking after you."

"Mr. Nielsen, there are people waiting. Shall we open?"

"So you have no family." It wasn't a question.

"I do have a family, Mr. Nielsen, if that is what you wish to know."

He stroked his sideburns. "But there's something mysterious about you, Mrs. Solberg. You wear black, yet you don't carry yourself like a widow."

"There are many losses to mourn, Mr. Nielsen."

"Perhaps you were unhappy in marriage, and God answered your prayers. Tuberculosis, was it? Or chest fever?"

I flushed with anger. "Sir, if I'm required to divulge my personal history, then perhaps you should hire someone else."

"No need for a fuss, Mrs. Solberg," he said, turning away. "Didn't mean to offend."

AND SO THE WINTER PASSED. At the shipping office, I managed the correspondence and helped with the contracts. It was what I had always wanted—a job where my intelligence and skill were put to good use—except for Mr. Nielsen.

I quickly grew to dislike him, and it was hard to believe he didn't mean to offend. He was often brusque and demeaning, and when we worked late in the office, he liked to read over my shoulder so he could lean against me or squeeze my arm. When he did this, I pulled away and told him to refrain, but my words carried little weight. I hated the smell of him.

Mr. Nielsen soon assigned me to the steerage passengers so he wouldn't have to dirty his hands tending to the lower classes. He meant this as a social slight, as a way of elevating himself over me, but I didn't care. I came to enjoy helping these neediest emigrants.

I was particularly interested in the women. Most seemed to be emigrating reluctantly, leaving behind children buried in churchyards and elderly parents they would never see again. It was as if the women carried the sadness for the entire family. I told them what I could to ease their passage—bring vinegar in case of lice and dried apples to keep the children happy—but it never seemed enough to quiet their worries. Still, I went home at the end of the day knowing I had done what I could.

AT NIGHT, curled in bed against the cold, I sometimes imagined what I would be doing if I had gone to Copenhagen with Mr. Lyngstrand. Starring in the latest play, or waiting in my apartment for a lover who had moved on to someone else? I did not regret my choice, though sometimes I despaired that anyone would ever love me again. Because who on earth would it be? Mr. Nielsen made my skin crawl, and Tobias, though very dear, was far too green. Sometimes I watched Erlend across the table and wondered if he thought about me in the dark of night. He was older than Tobias and world-weary in a way I recognized. Yet I was his senior and different because I'd had a family. He knew nothing of this but sometimes glimpsed this other Nora.

"You're too good at darning socks," he said one day, giving me a knowing look. I reddened and turned away, feeling like an old lady.

In time I came to envy the families shipping out, as Tobias had predicted. What I would have given to escape Torvald, to get out from under Mr. Nielsen's unwanted attentions, to leave Norway so I could be myself again rather than posing as a poor widow with a murky past.

But at the end of the day I would return to my room and stand before the drawing from my children. It was faded but still my altar. As long as they were in Norway, I could not leave.

ONE FRIDAY EVENING I returned to the rooming house and sank gratefully into a chair by the fire, hungry for supper.

But Erlend approached, with other plans. "Get your coat, Mrs. Solberg!"

"Oh, Erlend, I've been out on the wharf all day, in the sleet."

"Aasta Hansteen is giving a farewell address. She leaves for America next month. Tobias told me to bring you."

I looked at him, eyes wide.

"Come. The talk starts soon."

THE HALL where Miss Hansteen was appearing proved to be little more than a crowded warehouse with a crude stage at one end. The audience was mostly men, but I also spotted several society girls, a few maids and shop clerks, and a knot of women factory workers. In the back were several constables.

We found Tobias and squeezed in next to him. Before long a broad-shouldered woman in a traveling dress and men's boots, with her dark hair pinned up behind, stepped onto the stage, an umbrella over her arm.

"Welcome," Miss Hansteen said. "Even if you've come only out of curiosity, to see this strange phenomenon of a woman speaking in public, I hope my words will fall on receptive ears. As you may know, I'm leaving for New York in a few weeks. The American suffragettes have extended a kind welcome to me, and I hope to learn from their excellent work fighting for women's natural rights of equality and prosperity."

This seemed inoffensive enough and made me wonder why the constables were necessary. But in the next moment Miss Hansteen gave the crowd a fierce look and launched into a tirade against Norway, condemning the government and the Church for undermining efforts by women to organize and improve their lives. She shouted; she stamped her feet. She praised the American system and harangued the audience about Norway's patriarchal laws and mores.

"The rights women need are personal as well," she cried, shaking her umbrella. "Women should be allowed to keep their own property after they marry, and women cast aside by their husbands should have the right to care for their children if they can!"

There were a few derisive shouts, but she waved them to silence. "Why, here in Kristiania, a woman who left her husband to live on her own has been blocked from seeing her children!"

I took a sharp breath. Erlend turned toward me, but I dared not catch his eye.

"Women shouldn't have to stay with husbands who beat them or keep them locked up at home. Yet if they leave, they're cut off without support or access to their children. I ask you, is this fair?"

There was a momentary hush, and then a man in the back yelled, "But that lady abandoned her children. That's unnatural!"

With that, the crowd erupted, everyone shouting at once. My knees buckled; the room spun. Erlend grabbed my elbow. "Mrs. Solberg, are you all right?"

"Yes," I said, though I leaned heavily on his arm. Several men were heckling Hansteen, who banged on the lectern to regain control.

A factory woman in a skirt powdered with lint strode onstage. "And what about us who work long hours to feed our children? I don't need rights—I need a fair wage!"

"Careful, or the government will be at your neck, like they are with labor!" someone else cried out.

The constables started for the front of the room.

"Let's go," Erlend said. He and Tobias pulled me through the crowd to a side door that opened into an alley. Once outside, we heard shouting from the front, so the boys dragged me the other direction. We ran through the freezing rain, turned a few more corners, emerged on an empty street, and stopped to catch our breath under an overhang.

Erlend peered into my face. "Are you all right?"

"Yes, but what about Miss Hansteen? Are they arresting her?"

"Maybe," said Tobias. "But they'll let her leave. It's what the authorities want."

"Did you find it interesting?" Erlend said, watching me.

"It's inspiring what Miss Hansteen says about America," I said, still breathing hard. "And I'd like to hear more about her theology of equality."

"What do you think of the case of Nora Helmer?" Erlend asked.

My blood went cold. "Nora who?"

"Nora Helmer, the lady she spoke of—who left her family."

"I guess I did hear of it."

"She was a society lady. Did you know her?" asked Tobias.

I glanced at him for a moment, then shrugged. "I probably met her once or twice. I don't remember. I've met her husband. I believe he's manager of a bank."

"That's right," said Erlend. "I wonder if he was awful to her."

"He must have been, or she wouldn't have been able to leave her children," I said, my voice breaking. "What kind of mother would leave three small children?"

"What kind indeed," said Tobias.

"I mean, it must have broken her heart," I said, choking on the words.

"Why, Mrs. Solberg, you're shivering," said Erlend. "That thin coat! Here . . ." He wrapped his scarf around my neck. "Let's get you home."

BACK AT THE ROOMING HOUSE, Erlend seated me by the fire, and then he and Tobias disappeared into the kitchen to brew a pot of tea. I stared into the flames. They had figured me out.

When they came back, they sat in front of me.

"We must ask you something, for your own protection," Tobias said.

I gazed at them, then nodded. "Yes."

They glanced at each other.

"You're Nora Helmer?" whispered Tobias.

"Yes. I would have told you, but I'm hiding from my husband. You cannot tell anyone."

"Look, Mrs. Solberg, I mean, Mrs. Helmer—," said Tobias.

"Please, Solberg. It's my maiden name."

"Fine, but listen. You may not know this, but some women find you inspiring, and everyone wants to know what's happened to you. The talk is that you left for Bergen or Trondheim, or have gone home to Hamar, where you're from, I believe."

"Good Lord, everyone knows all about me."

"You're quite the cause célèbre," said Erlend. "Even the Church is preaching against you. Several pastors have suggested you be officially shunned."

I went still. "What does that mean?"

"You couldn't attend services or be given the sacraments."

I turned away so they wouldn't see my shock. Church meant little to me, but this felt like being banished.

Tobias tugged on my hand. "But we can help you."

"Listen, boys, please. I'm not a heroine. I'm just trying to survive."

They nodded, but it didn't dim their excitement. Their eyes glittered with eagerness.

"I am serious," I said. "The most important thing is that my husband not find me, because he intends to have me committed to an asylum."

Erlend sucked in a breath. "Could he do that?"

"He believes so. He's angry because I tried to speak to my children. He threatened to tell them I died, and I couldn't let them believe that. He says that's evidence of hysteria."

Tobias stared at me, then took my hand. "Mrs. Solberg, you should go to America. Escape this brute of a husband."

"He's not a brute, just a man who thought his wife should obey him," I said, shaking my head. "We disagreed on many things, but he loved me, in his way."

"Then why did you leave him?" said Erlend.

I sighed. That question again. Perhaps I would never escape it. "I did something outside the law, in order to save my husband's life and keep my family from financial ruin. It hurt no one, and I earned the money to make it right. Yet when my husband discovered my misdeed, he condemned me as a criminal. I realized then I could never love him again, and so I left."

They looked at me, blinking.

"So much sophistication in a simple seamstress," Erlend said quietly.

"Then go to America," said Tobias. "You'll be safe there!"

"But if I go to America I'll never see my children again, Tobias! I couldn't bear it."

They nodded, solemn now. Tobias squeezed my hand again. "Don't worry, Mrs. Solberg. We'll keep your confidence and do what we can to help you."

CONFESSING MY IDENTITY rescued me from the isolation of my secret but hampered my freedom. Erlend said no more public lectures for me, and Tobias insisted on escorting me to work each morning.

One day a letter arrived, from Anne-Marie.

The boys are home from Sandefjord and heartily glad, if a bit subdued. They haven't asked for you, and perhaps that's best. They are to be enrolled at the cathedral school next week. Bobby is reading, and Ivar seems very much a young man. Mr. Helmer told me he heard you had moved to Bergen. Emma's doing well. Anne-Marie

Bergen! Perhaps Torvald was lying and hoping Anne-Marie would relay the message to me so I would let down my guard. As for the boys, a plan formed in my head. If Bobby could read, it was time to answer their letter.

I WAITED FOR THEM IN THE PARK near their school. I knew they would walk past, since the path linked to the street that led to Torvald's apartment. I dressed so they would know me, in one of my old skirts and my hair styled as I used to wear it. A letter for them sat in my pocket—cheerful, loving, explaining that I couldn't be with them but that I missed them and would see them again when they were older. Ivar might understand and be able to explain things to Bobby.

The thin March sun illuminated the barren trees. An hour passed, and then the school bell rang. Boys began trickling past on the street outside. Finally, I saw my two approach.

I waited until they were close, then took off my hat and stepped forward. "Ivar! Bobby!"

They stopped dead. Ivar recognized me first, but instead of rushing into my open arms, he stood his ground, his eyes burning into me.

Bobby squinted. "Mama!" he cried and started toward me.

"Bobby, no! You mustn't!" Ivar yelled, grabbing him by the coat. Bob pulled and twisted as Ivar held him back. Ivar grew frantic and smacked his brother with his open hand. "Bobby, stop! You know what Father said!"

"Ivar, darling, it's me," I said, more gently now, moving slowly toward them. I didn't want them to bolt. "It's all right."

They stood in the middle of the path, Ivar blocking his brother, Bobby struggling and beginning to cry. "Go away!" Ivar yelled.

"Sweetheart, it's all right," I said, but I stopped.

"No, it isn't!" Ivar screamed. Now Bobby was sobbing. "Do you see what this does? Go away!" he cried. "Go away!"

I took the letter from my pocket. "I have something for you, an answer to the letter you wrote me." I held it out, like bait.

"We don't want your letter now!" Ivar yelled again, tears streaming down his face. "We don't want you now!" Then he backed up, still holding onto his brother, and looked wildly around. Suddenly, he bent down and grabbed a rock. And then he cocked his arm.

"Ivar, darling—"

With a mighty sob, he hurled the stone.

I didn't even duck. It hit my cheekbone, stunning me. Ivar pushed Bobby down the path away from me, still yelling over his shoulder, then dragged him out the gate.

I stood there in the path, and my heart split in two. I sank to my knees. At my feet lay the stone, Ivar's stone, smooth and round. I felt the welt on my cheek. Dear God, how had it come to this? A knot of pain swelled in my chest. I picked up the stone, feeling its weight in my palm. Oh, Ivar, sweet Ivar!

I looked up now, remembering my surroundings. I didn't want to catch the attention of a constable, so I stood, put on my hat, and pulled down my veil. My tears stung the wound. I slid Ivar's stone into my pocket, along with the undelivered letter, and hurried home to Vika.

BACK IN MY ROOM, I lay on my bed, turning Ivar's stone over and over in my hand. I felt as if someone had cut the cord that held me to everything dear. A terrible truth loomed before me: I must let go of my children and allow them grow up without me. And to do that, I would need an ocean between us. Otherwise, I wouldn't be strong enough. Torvald had won for now, but if I could find a way to leave, I could find a way back—when they were old enough to decide for themselves.

I heard footsteps, then a knock. "Mrs. Solberg! Are you in there?" It was Tobias.

I cracked the door.

"Mrs. Solberg! What happened?" He peered in anxiously. "Are you all right?"

"Yes, just a small accident. What is it, Tobias?"

"An elderly woman is here to see you. She says her name is Anne-Marie."

My stomach flipped—I had gotten her in trouble. "Of course. I'll be right there." I splashed water on my face and dabbed at the cut, purple now as it bruised up, then went out into the front room. Anne-Marie sat by the fire, looking old and sad.

"Oh, Anne-Marie, I'm so sorry!" I sank down next to her. She reached up gently to touch my cheek.

"He said he hit you with a rock," she whispered. "I didn't believe it, but he was crying so!"

"It's all my fault. I should never have tried to see them!"

"There, there, Miss Nora. No one can blame you for wanting to see your boys."

"They were so upset," I said. "It was quite shocking, Ivar's fear."

"Yes," she nodded. "They were crying when they got home. They told me everything, and then I had them take baths and go to bed. I was hoping to keep it from their father, but Ivar couldn't hold it in his heart—it was too much for him."

"What did Torvald say?"

"I don't know what he said to the boys. Whatever it was, it quieted them. But then he came into the kitchen and told me I had to leave. He knew I'd written you, and when I wouldn't give him your address . . ." Her voice trailed off.

"He let you go? But that's impossible! You're their nurse! You're part of the family!"

"Aye, Miss Nora, but perhaps it's for the best. I can't take the unhappiness in that house anymore. Forgive me."

"No, Anne-Marie, I should beg you for forgiveness! I'm the one who put you in this impossible position. I thought it would be all right. That you could raise them the way you raised me, but I see how selfish that was!" I could scarcely look at her. I was the one to blame, for everything; I had frightened my children, and now I had gotten Anne-Marie fired.

And so I must take responsibility for what I had done. "I'll go tomorrow and speak to Torvald at the bank, Anne-Marie. I'll convince him to take you back."

"Oh, Miss Nora, you can't do that! He means to have you committed! If you walk into the bank, he'll have you taken away. He's hiring men to find you!"

I grabbed her hands. "Did anyone follow you here? Does Torvald know where I live?"

"No, I don't think anyone followed me tonight. It was so late, I'm sure he assumed I was going home to my daughter's." She looked at me sadly. "You must leave Kristiania as soon as possible, Miss Nora, because Mr. Helmer will find you. He pretends he's gotten over you, but he hasn't. He's consumed with what you've done and talks it over endlessly with his new friend, a solicitor—he's not very nice."

Panic swelled in my chest. "Yes, I'll go, for the children's sake, perhaps to Copenhagen."

"That might be best. I'm sure there's a better place for you somewhere."

I nodded, understanding at that moment that this was good-bye. If only I had some way to thank Anne-Marie for all she had been to me—mother, nurse, bedrock. And then I remembered my mother's tea set. "Wait here, Anne-Marie; I have something for you."

I ran to my room and got the small wooden box, then put it in her lap. "These were my mother's. Please take them. It's all I have to thank you."

She looked inside, then shook her head. "They're beautiful. Shouldn't Emma have them?"

"No, they are yours," I said. "I'll be leaving Kristiania soon, but I'll write and tell you where I am going. And when the children are old enough, please let them know I love them and desperately want to hear from them."

"I promise." She kissed my cheek. "Good-bye, dear Nora."

I could scarcely imagine my world without Anne-Marie standing steadfast at its core. "Good-bye," I whispered.

She slipped out into the night.

I SAT UP LATE wrapped in a quilt. If I left Kristiania, I would have to go far enough that no one would know my name or my story, and only then would I have the freedom to build a new life. I couldn't do it hiding here in Norway, clinging like a castaway to the flotsam of what I had known before. Even Copenhagen might not be far enough.

But Chicago, big, crowded Chicago—chaotic with immigrants from many different countries, if Tobias was right. I needed a place where I could make myself anew, unfettered by the old Nora. Where I could walk the streets unveiled, live by my word and deed, grow into a better person. I was sure I could find work in Chicago, and with any luck, Tobias might follow me one day.

I took my scissors and opened the seam of my shift that held my pearls. Tomorrow I would find out how far they could take me.

CHAPTER EIGHT

SOLVI

December 1918 ■ *Kristiania, Norway*

December ground past—a haze of snow, Latin, reading, and review. Before Christmas, Solvi and Rikka vowed they would do nothing but study until the January exams, breaking only long enough to toast the holiday with a bottle of champagne Rikka smuggled into her room.

It worked; they passed their exams. Rikka smuggled in another bottle, and Solvi sent her mother a telegram.

Accepted to university. Start next week. Solveig

"I DO BELIEVE HELL HAS FROZEN OVER," Rikka said, a few days later. She and Solvi stood at the university gates for the first day of classes, their breath billowing about them. "Must be because we were admitted."

Solvi laughed with a shiver, then looked across the broad quadrangle. Only men and boys as far as she could see. "Where are the other women students?"

"There's just a handful each year," Rikka said. "I may be the first in medicine; I'm worried the boys will give me trouble."

"If they do, just crack them over the head with your anatomy book."

"Solvi Lange, honestly. Advocating violence so early in the war with men."

"Is it a war?"

"Of course it is," Rikka said, turning toward the science laboratory. "Good luck!"

Without Rikka, Solvi suddenly felt very alone. She crossed to the history building and stepped inside, bumping into a crowd of young men. She seemed to be the only girl. She took the staircase and found her classroom, but a knot of boys blocked the doorway.

"Excuse me," Solvi murmured, hoping they would let her pass without notice. Instead, they fell silent and backed away.

"Thank you," she said.

At that, one of them dropped into a deep, mocking bow, then hopped to a desk and pulled out a chair. "At your service, miss," he said. Several boys laughed.

Solvi raised her chin. "No need to be at my service." She chose a different seat farther in and dropped her books with a smack.

"There's no pleasing them these days," the boy said in a stage whisper. "I use my best manners and . . ."

"Good morning, students," bellowed an older man pushing his way through the door. The professor. He wore spectacles and had curly gray hair around a bald spot. He scanned the room, pausing for a moment when he spotted Solvi, then smiled at her. The students scattered to their seats.

A young man slipped in next to her. "Don't mind Gregor. He's rude to everyone," he said.

She looked up and her mouth dropped open. "Magnus! What are you doing here?"

"Taking a history class," he said with a grin. "I couldn't believe it when you came through the door."

The professor knocked on the lectern. "Welcome to Norwegian History. I'm Professor Wolff. We'll start with the Vikings." He stopped. "What, no groans?"

The class laughed and Solvi relaxed. At least he had a sense of humor.

"After that," he said, "we'll move quickly toward the modern era. We'll examine the forces that forged present-day Norway: emigration, the separation from Denmark and Sweden, the rise of the working class, the rise of women, the war. Any questions?"

With that, he launched into his lecture, talking of recent archaeological finds that challenged romantic notions of Viking hegemony. Solvi took notes, thinking for the first time about Viking women, those who managed the farms after the warriors sailed away in their sleek boats. It seemed odd to her that women rarely figured in the legends. Professor Wolff raised so many interesting questions, the time passed in a snap. Before she knew it, he told them to start thinking of essay topics, then grabbed his papers and strode from the room.

Magnus turned to her. "Nothing like starting the day with the history of pillaging. Do you have time for coffee before your next class?"

She hesitated, not sure if she should encourage him.

"Come," he said, undeterred. "We can celebrate your matriculation."

As they walked to a coffee shop, chatting comfortably, Solvi wondered why her mother had shielded her from talking with boys. Weren't young women safer when they had male friends they could rely on? Solvi had always longed for a brother, someone who could have escorted her places and pushed out her narrow boundaries. It thrilled her now to have both a boy she was interested in, Dominik, and a boy like Magnus, someone trustworthy, someone she could talk to about all that seemed challenging at university. Someone like a brother who would defend her from the boys who weren't so nice.

But she would have to be careful and not lead him on. She didn't want to be the kind of girl who broke men's hearts.

"Don't you think so, Solvi?" Magnus said, turning to her as he opened the door to the coffee shop.

"Oh, yes," she said, not wanting to confess she hadn't been listening. If she was going to be his friend, she would have to pay better attention.

Inside, they bought coffee and a packet of sweets, then claimed a table in a sunny window, their knees bumping as they sat down.

He raised his coffee cup in a toast. "Congratulations on passing your exams, Solvi Lange. You are now, certifiably, one of the best-educated young women in Norway, and I trust you'll make the most of it and stay in university. No running off and marrying the first charming lad you meet."

Solvi clinked her cup against his. "I've already refused one boy, so I think I can resist that temptation. I promise—academics above all else!"

"You already refused someone?" Magnus said, his brow crinkling. "Did you break his heart?"

"I doubt it. Our parents arranged it, and I knew instantly I couldn't marry him."

"So you did not love him."

"No. He mostly talked about his rifle and hiking club."

Magnus pulled a small notebook from his pocket and scribbled something. "Get rid of rifle and hiking boots," he muttered. He put the notebook away and looked at her with mock innocence.

Solvi laughed nervously. Perhaps she shouldn't have come here with him. "I didn't know you were studying history. Do you hope to teach, like Professor Wolff?"

"No, I want to be a journalist, and history seems important. I hope to travel and write about world events. So far I've only written about Norway, but the world is wide."

"Where would you go first?"

"Well, I should probably visit the capitals of Europe, but that's not what I really want. What I really want is to go to South America."

"South America! Why not North America? New York, San Francisco, the Wild West?"

"Fewer Norwegians in South America," he said. "I want to write home about things most Norwegians have never seen. As a people and a government, Norwegians need to look out into the world more. I think this war has proved that."

"I think you're right, Magnus," she said, nodding. Then something occurred to her. "So if you're a journalist, you must know how to investigate things for your articles, yes?"

"Of course. Why do you ask?"

Solvi pulled out the photo of her mother's family and handed it to him. "This was taken here in Kristiania, in 1879. I first saw it just a few months ago." He took it and examined the figures and the burned edge as Solvi explained the contradictory history of her grandmother and uncles and how her mother probably lied about what happened to them.

"How strange," Magnus said.

"I'm convinced my mother's hiding something. I desperately want to find them, alive, hopefully. It's possible they're here in Kristiania."

"What do you know so far?" Magnus took out his notebook again.

Solvi told him of Mr. Stenberg's records at the photography studio and the different name, along with the shadow of scandal. Then she told him about the headstone for Johanna Helmer and her visit with Rikka to the police station.

He spun his pencil, thinking. "I'll ask my editor; he knows everyone."

"Thank you, Magnus."

"At your service, Miss Lange."

Solvi leaned back. "My mother would faint if she knew I'd had coffee with a journalist."

"I always wanted to make a lady faint," said Magnus. "But I imagined someone younger, a girl of my own generation."

Solvi felt the heat rise in her face. Had she been flirting? It wasn't what she meant to do. "I, ah, I have literature class now, but thank you, Magnus.

You're so kind to listen and help . . ." She faltered. She wasn't sure what to say.

"May I sit with you in class again?"

Solvi nodded, tongue-tied, then grabbed her books and fled.

"YOU, ME, AND ALL THE AGING SUFFRAGETTES," Rikka whispered. She and Solvi stood at the entrance of a large salon, another stop on Rikka's plan to modernize her.

They looked around—older women, yes, but hardly ones Solvi's mother would have invited for tea. Most wore modern outfits, and there were even several women dressed in men's suits. Solvi regretted leaving her camera behind.

The girls found seats, smiling as the women greeted them. *So nice to see fresh faces. So good of you to come.*

"Why are we the only young ones here?" Solvi asked.

"The feminists are struggling to attract younger women, so they're hosting lectures about the heroic days," Rikka said. "I thought that, as a budding historian, you might find it interesting."

Before long a tall, businesslike woman called the meeting to order and then introduced the speaker, who turned out to be a shriveled older lady in a lace bonnet seated on a divan. With her widow's gown settled around her, she looked like a black swan bedded down for the night.

But then she started speaking.

"To understand the story I tell tonight, you must imagine Norway in the 1880s. Society was still divided into strict classes, yet social unrest had bubbled for a decade. Labor leaders were jailed and frequent demonstrations called for universal suffrage for men, and better factory conditions. Women had few opportunities for employment and few legal rights. And the only serious voice advocating for Norwegian women, the painter Aasta Hansteen, was leaving for New York to seek the help of the American feminists.

"And then, one woman—a genteel lady—did something unthinkable. She walked out one night, leaving behind her husband and young children. By all accounts her husband was a fine, upstanding man. No one had any suspicion that there were problems in the marriage. She just walked away and never went back.

"At first, most people assumed she was having an affair. This had happened before and, while providing amusing gossip, did little to upset the social order. But this case was different; no other man could be identi-fied, and the lady was soon spotted looking for work. People concluded that she left her family—some said she had seven children—to live on her own, which outraged them. It didn't matter that the children had a trusted nurse and were well cared for by their father. The very idea of a mother abandoning them was scandalous.

"At the same time, though, a handful of people understood. There were many reasons a woman might strike off on her own. The first, of course, would be if her husband had done something unforgivable, but we don't know if that was true in this case. We also do not know if she suffered from melancholy or some other mental anguish that made her think it better to leave her children until she recovered. Perhaps she was in trou-ble; perhaps she was driven by something inexplicable, even to herself. As we can now acknowledge, marriage and motherhood cannot contain every woman.

"Over time, society moved on to fresh gossip, and her story went blank. Most likely, she left Kristiania for a life somewhere else and died poor and forgotten.

"What she never knew was that her bold action, so personal and pri-vate, spread like a rumble of thunder. Other wives started speaking up, pushing their husbands to treat them better, and many took courage from her example to start fighting for women's rights. The early feminists argued that her tragedy could have been prevented if she'd had the same human rights as men: to care for her children, to secure honorable work, to own property, and to keep her wealth. When Aasta Hansteen returned to Nor-way some years later, women were ready to fight for those rights."

The speaker stopped for a long moment and looked around the room. "I wish we knew what became of her. I also wish she knew how important she was. This woman, the Forgotten One, was the first woman in Norway who said no. And her 'no' started everything."

She dropped her hands into her lap and smiled. The gathered group clapped politely.

Solvi sat unmoving for a long moment.

Rikka elbowed her. "They have punch. Would you like some?"

Solvi could barely breathe. She looked at Rikka. "That's an interesting story. Had you heard it before?"

"No, I hadn't." Rikka stood. "I'll bring you a cup."

Solvi jumped up and pushed through the crowd to meet the speaker.

"Thank you for a wonderful talk. It was, ah, quite interesting. Did you know her, the Forgotten One?"

The woman blinked at her with watery eyes. "No, but I heard the gossip. I always suspected other women were a bit envious, that some wished they had the courage to leave their difficult husbands."

"Do you remember her name?"

She shook her head sadly. "I wish I did. No one I know seems to remember."

"Are any of the people who knew her still alive?"

"Possibly, but I doubt they know what happened to her. She was not allowed to see her children and was excluded from polite society. Besides, it was a long time ago, forty years." She shook her head again. "I believe she was also shunned by the Church."

"Shunned? Because she left her husband?"

"Well, it was like that, back then. If a grown woman was not living with a husband or a male relative, she was assumed to be an adulterer. Unless, of course, she was a widow."

Solvi gulped. "That would be enough to make one wear black."

"Yes," the woman said, looking at Solvi more closely. "It would."

AFTER THE LECTURE, Solvi stumbled along the sidewalk, wrapped in thought.

"What do you think happened to her?" Rikka asked.

"The Forgotten One? Oh, I don't know. Probably she died poor and alone, as they said." Unmourned too, Solvi thought, with a pang of sorrow.

"Well, I disagree," said Rikka. "I say she married a sea captain and traveled the world."

"But she wasn't divorced; she couldn't have married again."

"Maybe she pretended to be someone else or changed her name."

Solvi glanced at her friend. She loved how Rikka never accepted the simple answers. "You're right. It's got to be better than a solitary death. Maybe she went to America as a stowaway, hiding in the hold until they reached Boston."

"Okay, she can be a stowaway, but she didn't go to America," said Rikka. "Only farmers and dairymaids went to America. No, she must have done something grand with her life—maybe she immigrated to Africa to hunt lions. That would explain why she didn't take her children."

"Maybe she went to South America," said Solvi, starting to laugh. "Maybe she went to China as a missionary!"

"Or maybe she stayed in Kristiania and lived in the basements of her sympathizers as their clandestine leader," said Rikka. "Maybe she was there tonight, one of those wizened owls in the back!"

"No," Solvi said, her smile fading. "She must have left Kristiania. It would have been too hard for her to stay here, watching her children grow up without her."

Rikka sighed. "The truth is, she probably isn't real."

Solvi stopped in her tracks. "What do you mean?" For some reason this bothered her. "The speaker remembered her. Why would you say that?"

"Well, such figures are often jumbled together from the experiences of several people, and then the story gets embellished over time. She became iconic, I suspect, because there was more than one woman who said no."

Solvi shook her head. "No, it's not that long ago, just forty years. There must be people who remember her."

"Well, even if she was real, I doubt she had seven children. That just sounds exaggerated."

"A lot of people had big families back then," Solvi muttered. The Forgotten One must be real, Solvi thought. How could such a tale start if there wasn't someone real at the heart of it?

They soon reached the study house and just in time. Matron locked the door behind them.

"Are you angry with me?" Rikka asked.

"Sorry—just tired, I guess."

Rikka gave her a hug, and Solvi shut her door. Why did it matter whether the Forgotten One was real? Solvi undressed and started brushing out her hair. After a few minutes, she stopped.

Because if a woman had the courage to do all that, then she shouldn't be forgotten.

A FEW DAYS LATER, Matron handed Solvi another letter from her mother.

It cut like broken glass.

Dear Solvi, I have waited for weeks now—no, months—hoping for a letter from you, but apparently you are too busy to remember me. I, personally, don't like telegrams, as they always make me think someone

*has died. There is little to report here. Life is quite dull now, without you
and Grandfather. Lisanne came by again, mystified that you haven't
written to her. At least send something to her if you don't have time to
write to me.*

Your Mother

Solvi, chastened, sat down at her desk.

*Dear Mama: I'm sorry I haven't written. How are you doing, and how
are Cook and Mathilde? I hope you are all well. I must tell you that
many exciting things are happening for me. First, university is going
well. I think my course of study will be history, although I also enjoy
literature.*

*I have good friends here at the study house, and we go to cafés some-
times and, yes, talk with boys. I've also been learning to do some rhyth-
mic dancing, like Isadora Duncan. But don't worry, there are no boys in
that class—just girls.*

*Despite what you might think, I'm being good and working hard. Life
in the study house is fine, though I miss Cook's dinners. Please tell her
that. And I will write Lisanne soon, I promise.*

Love, Solvi

She looked it over, then quickly added a postscript.

*P.S. Is it possible that Grandfather's name was originally Helmer? I've
found some evidence that he changed it to Fallesen later, after you were
born.*

She mailed it first thing the next morning, before she could reconsider.

TWO DAYS LATER Rikka peeked in the library door. "Solvi! There's someone to see you."

Solvi looked up. Not her mother; please, not that. "Who is it, Rikka?"

"You'll just have to come see."

Solvi followed, raking her fingers through her hair, praying.

There in the lobby was the last person she would have expected:
Dominik. Her stomach fluttered.

He swept his cap off his head. "Hello, Solvi. I thought you might like to
get some air."

Solvi had gone to the café several times hoping to run into him but with no luck. She turned to Rikka. "Want to come?"

"Heavens, no. I've a million pages to read," Rikka said, edging toward the stairs and giving Solvi a stiff smile. "Have fun."

Solvi fetched her cape and put her camera around her neck. She felt lightheaded with happiness.

SOLVI AND DOMINIK first walked around the curve of the harbor, then found a bench on a hill near the Akershus Fortress. Below them, the passenger steamers to England and Bremerhaven were lined up along the wharf. Farther away, trawlers and merchant ships unloaded their wares. The early spring day was mild, but the ground still held the cold. A few brave crocuses had pushed up and were starting to bloom.

Solvi took a picture of the harbor, then put in a fresh plate, swung around, and took one of Dominik gazing at her with a quizzical expression.

"Hey, don't you warn a fellow? I have a better side." He twisted around and mocked a profile, nose high in the air. "Take one quick, before I fall off this bench."

"Oops, completely out of plates," Solvi laughed. "I think I'll like the one I got."

"Are you going to put it under your pillow?"

She flushed red. "We don't know each other well enough to discuss my pillow, Dominik."

He grinned, unabashed. "When did you start taking photographs?"

"As a girl; my father got this camera to record rare flowers. I was his photographer."

"So doesn't he need it anymore? Or perhaps you stole it when you left for university."

Solvi looked at him. "He gave it to me before he died."

Dominik ran his hands through his hair. "Oh, Lord, I apologize. Sometimes I speak without thinking."

"It's all right," she said, though she wondered at his manners.

"Do you always bring it along? I need to know if I'm going to be taking you places."

She snapped the camera closed and put it away. "Not necessarily. I bring it when I need to feel braver; it helps me forget myself."

"No need to be brave today," he said, patting the bench next to him. "I won't bite."

She sat down. "I'm not used to walking out with boys like this."

He laughed. "Well, this is hardly a date, sitting up here on a spring day. Perhaps I should arrange something more interesting, something you could dress up for, like dinner or a dance."

"Ah, maybe," she said, trying not to sound eager. "But I'd have to know you better."

"Which is why we are here." He pulled a sleeve of biscuits from his pocket. "And I brought a little something in case we get hungry."

"That's very thoughtful," she said, taking one.

"So, tell me more about your missing relatives," he said. "Have you found any clues?"

"Not really. I'm not even sure I've got the right family name." She told him about Mr. Stenberg's ledgers as well as Helmer and Fallesen. "I searched a cemetery one afternoon, but could only find a stone for a Johanna Helmer, who was too young to be my grandmother. I don't think she was related to me."

He took a few biscuits. "I'm impressed that you're looking for them, Solvi. Most young women come to university to escape their families."

"What do you mean?"

"Many girls say they want to study, but they really just want to leave home."

She laughed nervously. "Are you mocking me?"

"No. It's just that sometimes I wonder how serious these girls are about their studies. It's a lot of work if they're only going to marry and have children."

"But women like knowing things, just as men do," Solvi said. "And some of us will go into professions, like you university boys. Rikka's studying to be a doctor."

"Yes, and I wish her luck fighting her way into that field." He leaned his shoulder against Solvi for a moment. "But let's not argue; I can see you're serious. Which class do you like best?"

"Norwegian History. It's taught by Professor Wolff—maybe you know him?"

"I do. A bit radical for my taste, but a fine scholar, or so they say. Do you have an essay topic yet?"

"Maybe. Have you ever heard about the Forgotten One?"

"Let me guess, some old agitator languishing in a dungeon. Sounds boring."

"No, it's a woman, a genteel lady who left her family in 1880 because she wanted to be independent. One of the first feminists. Rikka and I heard a lecture about her last week."

"Independent? She must have run off with another man."

"She didn't; that's why she's interesting," Solvi said. "She tried to find work in Kristiania and live on her own, but it proved impossible. Leaving her husband cost her everything—her children, her position, her wealth, her protection. Eventually, she disappeared. I thought I might try to find out what happened to her."

"If she didn't have a man to support her, she probably became a prostitute."

Solvi frowned. "Oh, I don't think so. She was a respected society lady, a mother."

"But she did leave," Dominik said. "She probably had little money, unless someone gave her some. Without money, she would have had to turn to prostitution."

"I don't know why you would insist on that, Dominik," Solvi said, growing irritated. "Maybe she found other work."

"But, Solvi, that's what happened to women then. I agree, it's not a pretty picture, but it's realistic. Prostitution exploded in the 1870s and '80s because so many men left the country for America and there were few jobs for the women left behind. Some men abandoned their families right there on the docks because they couldn't afford passage for them. They were called America widows. After a few months on the streets, they often turned to prostitution to feed their children. The government actually built public brothels where the women could find men looking for their services."

"That's terrible," Solvi said, pulling away from him. How had they stumbled into a discussion of prostitution? "That couldn't have happened to the Forgotten One. She was a lady . . ."

"I've got a book for you—*Albertine*, published in the 1880s. It's the story of a young woman who gets tricked into prostitution. It caused quite an uproar when it came out and was banned by the government. If you're going to write your essay about this Forgotten One, you should read it."

"But she was one of the first feminists," Solvi said, her face red.

Dominik stood, as if he hadn't heard her. "Let's get some cocoa." He took her arm and steered her down the hill. "Would you like to have supper with me next week?"

"But we're arguing."

He squeezed her elbow. "That just means I like you, Solvi. I only argue with people I take seriously. You want to be taken seriously, don't you?"

Her stomach fluttered again. "Well, I suppose so."

"How about Wednesday? Wear something nice. I'll pick you up."

"Okay," she murmured. She was still a bit angry with him for dismissing the Forgotten One as a common prostitute, but as they walked to the café she tried to let that go. He knew more, had read more, she thought.

And perhaps that was how love worked—no one was perfect; no one was quite who you wanted them to be.

"THEY CALL HER THE FORGOTTEN ONE, the woman who first said no," Solvi said. "Do you think Professor Wolff would approve that as my essay topic?"

Magnus handed her the sugar bowl. They had come to the pastry shop every week now after history class, though Solvi told herself it meant nothing.

Magnus cocked his head. "Today it would be easier for a woman to strike out on her own, obviously," he said. "But in the 1880s? Maybe she could have worked as a maid or found a job in the factories, but if she was from the upper class, she would hardly have been suited for such work. I think Professor Wolff would be interested. Tell him you want to write about the Woman Question—that's what they called it back then."

"It's time someone wrote about that era, isn't it? I mean, now that we've progressed to an answer."

"An answer to the Woman Question?" Magnus said, pulling back in surprise. "Good Lord, what is it?"

She laughed. "It's quite simple: let women have everything men have."

"Are you suggesting men share their power and authority?"

"Yes, but there will be advantages," Solvi said. "Perhaps there'll be no need for war. If women are leaders, calmer heads might prevail, and all the men could stay home, safely farming and fishing or going to their offices."

"Put that in your essay," Magnus said. "If you do a good job, you might sell it to the newspaper. That reminds me, did you bring your photographs of the housemaids? I've wanted to see what the fuss is all about."

She nodded, pulling out her album and sliding it toward him. Then she jumped to her feet, too nervous to watch. "I'll get more coffee."

When she returned, he gave her a piercing look, then looked back at the pages, leafing through them slowly.

Finally he spoke. "These are wonderful, Solvi. You've got an artist's eye, but they're also intelligent."

She smiled with relief. She desperately wanted her friends to understand her work.

"I'm sure the editor will be interested," Magnus said. "Can I take this to show him?"

Solvi thought about that for a moment, then nodded. "But only because I trust you, Magnus. Don't leave it with him."

"I'll guard it with my life."

RIKKA NUDGED SOLVI at supper that night. "Have you written to your friends for permission to use the housemaid photographs? Petra asked me today."

Solvi just looked at her.

"You haven't, have you?" Rikka said, with an admonishing scowl.

"I'm afraid, Rikka."

"Afraid of what?"

Solvi started to say she was afraid it would get back to her mother, but then she realized it wasn't about her mother. "I'm afraid my friend Lisanne will never speak to me again."

Rikka started to speak, but Solvi stopped her. "Please don't say no progress without risk. That doesn't help me when I'm betraying people I care about."

Rikka looked down. "I was just going to say that if Lisanne is worthy of your friendship, either she'll try to get permission, or if she can't, she'll forgive you for asking."

UPSTAIRS, SOLVI WROTE LISANNE a long, chatty letter. She imagined them sitting together in their favorite Bergen coffee shop, sharing secrets again. She told her about life in Kristiania, working at the photo shop, studying with the young men at the university. At the end, in a postscript, Solvi asked, as politely as she could, if Lisanne might get permission from the maids and her family so that Solvi could publish the pictures.

The next morning, sorry and sad, she stuffed it in the post.

WHEN WEDNESDAY CAME, Solvi put on her nicest outfit and waited nervously for Dominik in the lobby of the study house. She wasn't sure why, but she didn't want Rikka to know she was going out with him.

When he arrived, she bustled him back out the door before he could get his cap off.

"You're happy to see me, Solvi," Dominik said.

She just smiled.

THE RESTAURANT was all candlelight and luminous shadow, fancier than Solvi had expected. Dominik ordered wine and raised his glass. "To Solvi and her Forgotten One."

Her brow knit. "Let's not start the conversation there, Dominik."

He gave her a mischievous smile. "But it's a great topic, Solvi, and I was just getting going the other day!"

"Thank you very much, but I'll research it myself," she said.

"I'm trying to find a copy of *Albertine* for you," he said, gulping down half his glass and smiling at her over the candles. "Most were burned by the government, but a few survived."

She watched him. Something about him made her think of a fox—quick, sharp eyed, liable to nip if you didn't watch out. "Tell me about your family, Dominik. We didn't get to them the other day."

"They're boring," he said, pouring himself more wine.

"Indulge me," Solvi said.

"Well, all right. Let's see, my father's a lawyer who works for the mining companies, my brother's reading the law, my mother shops in Copenhagen. Old Kristiania money, I'm afraid."

"Have you always lived here?"

"My father came to Kristiania from Røros as a young man to make his fortune, then later built a house in Homans Byen, which is where I grew up."

"You're lucky to have a brother."

"I suppose, though he's not much fun now that he studies all the time. It's rather clipped his wings."

"I wish I had siblings," Solvi said. "It's hard to be your mother's only child."

"She must be fairly open-minded, allowing you to come to university."

"She tried to forbid me, but I came anyway."

Dominik gave her a sidelong look. "A rebel. My favorite type."

Solvi looked away so he wouldn't see how this pleased her. "No, Rikka's the rebel, not me."

"Rikka is, hmm, how should I put this? Rikka's tough and brittle, too hard."

"She nursed soldiers in France. That would make anyone hard."

"No, I like a girl with a little give," Dominik said, reaching out and tugging a lock of Solvi's hair. "A bit of feminine softness."

Solvi blushed again.

"But honestly, Solvi, don't you have a more stylish dress?"

Solvi looked down at her silk, chosen by her mother. It was lovely but demure. "Is something wrong with this one?"

"It's okay, I guess; I just mean one you can dance in. You know, sleeveless, where your knees show when you kick."

"Dominik, why are you asking me this?"

"My club is hosting a dance next Saturday night. I'd like you to come."

"Oh," Solvi said. She had never been asked to a dance before. "What kind of club is it?"

"You're sounding like a very proper young lady, Solvi," he teased. "It's my residence club. Most of the male students live in one; mine just happens to be the best."

"What makes it the best?"

He leaned across the table, his eyes twinkling at her. "We're the smartest and handsomest, and if your mother would like to know, the boys come from the best families."

"Well," Solvi said, "I'll just have to see for myself."

CHAPTER NINE

NORA

Spring 1919 ■ *Spokane, Washington*

Anders brought me a cup of tea. He was normally a traditional man, expecting me to keep the house and manage the kitchen, but every evening, in this way, he treated me like royalty.

I had not deserved him, this steadfast and tender man. Some back in Norway would have said he didn't deserve me, a lady raised and educated for the life of the parlor. But he rescued me, three times over, and I would always be grateful. At the end of the day, our different breeding meant nothing.

Because what was marriage, really, beyond a web of small gestures and kindnesses? It was not the promise we made at the altar; it was the living of that promise, however many compromises must be made. It was like pouring wine into a glass. A drop meant nothing; it was the fullness that mattered.

Maybe that was what went wrong with my marriage to Torvald, though at the time I could not have named it. There was little kindness between us. Instead, there was electricity, but it burned my fingers as often as it excited or illuminated my life. And it didn't last.

I sat beside Anders and watched him slowly whittle away at a tiny block of wood. He was famous in town for his carving and recently had been making little toy animals to sell. Now he was carving a goose, a little bird with its beak tucked under a wing. But then I looked more closely. It was two geese, nestled together. A mated pair.

"That's a bit odd for a child's toy," I said. "Don't horses and sheep sell better?"

"This is not a toy," he said, taking up a bit of sandpaper and polishing the backs of the geese. He examined it, fussed at it with the knife for another moment, buffed it with a cloth, then handed it to me. "This is for you."

NORA
May 1881 ■ *Kristiania, Norway*

The next morning I took my pearls and went to the shipping office early, filing contracts while I waited for Mr. Nielsen. When he arrived, he greeted me with an approving nod.

"Good to see you working industriously, Mrs. Solberg," he said, taking off his coat. "I think the weather may lift soon. It seems to be warming."

"Mr. Nielsen, I need to ask you something."

He looked up sharply, as if he'd been waiting for this moment. "Mrs. Solberg?"

I pulled my pearls out of the little bag at my waist. "I'd like to purchase a ticket to America. I don't know what these pearls are worth, but perhaps— as reward for my hard work—you could accept them as payment." I held them up to the light so he could see how fine they were.

He leaned back with a sigh, ignoring the pearls. "You would leave, now that I've finally trained you to be of some use? And ask for my help to do so?"

"I'm sorry, Mr. Nielsen, but I cannot stay in Norway any longer."

"Why? Has the law finally caught up with you?"

I flushed—with guilt, anger, dismay. "Whatever do you mean, Mr. Nielsen?"

"Come now, Mrs. Solberg. You're a refined, well-educated widow living in a squalid rooming house in Vika. Yes, I've followed you. I don't know what you're hiding, but you're hiding something."

I stared at him, then shook the pearls. "Please, have some kindness, Mr. Nielsen. Help me do this."

"Why should I?" he said, standing up.

"Perhaps I could earn the fare working extra hours."

He barked a laugh. "It would take you years to earn your passage, my dear. Besides, why America? Have you any idea what it's like over there for single women?"

"Many single women make the journey. I've seen them."

"Yes, rough peasant girls, willing to marry some dull farmer and work in the fields the rest of their lives. I hardly think that's the life for you."

Now he leaned toward me, his unwelcome breath and thick cologne filling my nose. "The hard truth, Mrs. Solberg, is that you cannot afford passage, pearls or no pearls, so give up this foolish notion. I'm sure you can work out your little problem so you can stay in Kristiania."

He turned and picked up some papers. "In time, if you perform well, I might consider taking you on as my business partner. With your help I could expand, represent other steamship lines." He cleared his throat. "We might even marry someday."

I flinched.

He glanced at me. "I could restore you to respectability, Mrs. Solberg."

All I could do was stare at him, mute.

Someone tapped on the window. "Is the office open today?"

Mr. Nielsen went to the door. "I'm not promising anything, Mrs. Solberg, but consider it. When you think of the rigors of life in America—and it can be brutal over there—I'm sure you'll come to your senses." With that he swung the door open, and the anxious emigrants pushed into the room. I spent the rest of the morning reading over contracts, avoiding his eye.

LATER THAT DAY, just before closing, a dark-haired man in a worn but well-made coat stepped up to my counter. His face radiated both intelligence and grief, and his muscular shoulders fell forward in a stoop. He gave me a tense nod, then pulled out a sheaf of papers and searched through them. I noticed his hands were calloused, like those of a tradesman. A cooper or carpenter most likely, probably of some education. He had five tickets.

He handed one to me, issued to an Inge Eriksen. "My wife," he said in a hoarse whisper. "She's passed away and therefore has no use for it. I would like to have my money refunded."

I looked into his deep-set eyes, pools of sorrow. "I am very sorry for your loss, sir. Let me ask the agent."

Mr. Nielsen slid over and peered at the ticket. "Your contract, sir," Mr. Nielsen demanded.

"My children and I sail on the *Angelo* Friday, but as my wife has unfortunately died, I'd like a refund," the man said. "I understand I cannot sell the ticket to someone else."

"That is correct," Mr. Nielsen said, scanning the contract. "Ah, here it is: *The White Star Line is not required to reimburse you for an unused ticket, but you may petition the court, which will order restitution if it is deemed valid.*" He tapped the paper. "It's right there, in the contract you signed."

"Petition the court? That could take months! How am I to argue my case from America?"

"I don't know, sir. Perhaps you can file your petition before you leave and hope for a settlement sometime in the following year." The agent folded his arms across his chest. "They do have mail in America."

The tradesman glared at Mr. Nielsen for a long moment. "How would I file such a petition?"

"I don't know. You could speak to a solicitor." Mr. Nielsen sighed. "Is there anything else we can do for you, Mr. Eriksen?"

"No. You've done nothing and apparently will do nothing." He gathered his papers and turned to leave, then glanced back at me and tipped his cap. "Thank you, ma'am."

I stood behind the counter, paralyzed. My mind had suddenly filled with an astonishing thought, and all I could do was hold it in wonder. I could not speak, could not move. And then I realized I must speak and move, or Mr. Nielsen would think of it, too. I helped the last customer of the day, then stacked papers and tidied up. Mr. Nielsen put the "Closed" notice in the window and pulled the shades.

I grabbed my coat and hat.

"Off early? We've files to tend to."

"I'm sorry, Mr. Nielsen. I need to take care of some business before the shops close. That's why I came in early." I slowed down and looked around the office for a moment so he wouldn't get suspicious.

He scowled. "I'd prefer you ask permission to leave early."

"Yes, well, I'll come in early tomorrow. Just leave the files for me."

I slammed the door before he could respond.

EXCITEMENT DRUMMED IN MY CHEST as I scanned the wharf. Where had the man gone? I walked quickly toward the emigrant rooming houses. His children must be waiting. I began to worry that I had lost him, then saw him staring in a market window.

"Mr. Eriksen!"

He turned with a start. "Why, ma'am . . ."

"Mrs. Solberg," I said, holding out my hand. "I apologize for the shipping agent. He has little sympathy for passengers." I pushed a strand of hair off my face. "Emigrating is such an anxious time for most families."

"You're very kind, ma'am," Mr. Eriksen said. "I'm not sure what I expected. I've heard the agents are often difficult."

"Well, I followed you because I wanted to say, ah, that . . . ," I hesitated, caution getting hold of my tongue, "that I know a few solicitors in Kristiania, if you'd like a reference."

He shook his head. "I don't know what to do. I was counting on selling Inge's ticket, as it will cost us nearly all we have to reach Minnesota."

"Where in Minnesota are you going?"

"The western prairie. My brother is there and doing fairly well, now that the grasshoppers have retreated."

"I admire you, Mr. Eriksen, emigrating with three children after losing your wife."

"I've little choice. We sold everything so have nothing to go back to." He looked down at his hands. "The baby is just two months old, but I have a strong girl, Birgitte. She'll be mother to him now."

"And the third?"

"Another boy, my right hand, though still a child. Jens."

A plan was gathering in my head. "Perhaps I could persuade the agent to make some accommodation. Where are you staying in case I need to find you?"

"That's very kind, ma'am, but I doubt you'd know it. The White Gull, in Vika."

"Yes, I know it. I live in Vika."

"You do?" He looked at me, puzzled. "I would hardly have imagined . . ."

"Yes, well, life moves in mysterious ways."

"Most would say God moves in mysterious ways."

"I don't know where God has gone," I said.

He stared at me for a moment. "Thank you, Mrs. Solberg. Good night."

I headed home, my mind turning.

THE NEXT DAY I put on a simple skirt, then threw my old shawl over my head. I felt like an actor again, as if my own self was dissolving away. Instead of going to the shipping office, I went to the White Gull in search of Mr. Eriksen.

At the emigrant inn, families were already stacking their bags alongside the wagons that would take them to the wharf. Inside, travelers at rough tables bent over their porridge.

Mr. Eriksen and his children were bunched in a corner. The girl was tall, perhaps twelve or thirteen, almost a young woman. She held the infant on her lap as she tried to eat, but the baby fretted and squirmed. Her brother

Jens seemed about Ivar's age; he was poking the baby to distract him. They were dark haired and blue eyed, all of them.

"Mr. Eriksen," I said. "Good morning."

He spun around. "Why, Mrs. Solberg! Good morning. Have you an answer already?"

I hesitated, then shook my head. "No, not an answer but possibly a solution. Is there somewhere we can talk?"

He studied me for a long moment, then turned and whispered to his children. Birgitte shot me a piercing look.

Mr. Eriksen followed me outside. "Mrs. Solberg, please explain."

"It's quite simple, Mr. Eriksen. You have a ticket to America you cannot use and an infant. I've been a mother three times over, and I need to go to America."

He stared at me. "What do you mean?"

"You have a ticket, and I need passage."

He choked out a hoarse laugh. "Don't play with me, Mrs. Solberg."

"Please, Mr. Eriksen. I thought we might reach some agreement. I will accompany your family and care for the baby as long as you think appropriate in exchange for passage to America."

"But you heard the agent. I can't sell the ticket. They won't even let me give it to you."

"Yes, but I've thought of a way," I said, looking about to make sure no one was listening. "I hope this won't offend you, but if I, well, if I posed as your wife, Mr. Eriksen. Just for the voyage."

"Posed as . . ." He stepped back and ran his hands through his hair. "Wouldn't that be illegal?"

I lowered my voice. "Perhaps, but no one will think to question us. The agents just want to get one ship loaded so they can turn to the next. If we travel as a family, we'll blend in with the others."

"They know you; they'll recognize you."

"Not the Wilson Line agents, who register us the morning of departure. Mr. Nielsen works for the White Star Line only. He doesn't like the Wilson Line agents, so he has as little to do with them as possible. If I keep my head down, I should be able to get aboard without being spotted. If I carry the baby, no one will question that I am your wife."

"But you don't look like my wife!" He waved at my attire. "It's all wrong, and anyone would spot it. You're too fine. Yesterday you didn't wear a blanket as a shawl."

"I'll change what I wear. I'll wear your wife's clothes—surely you have them."

"Your face and hair, your language . . ."

"I'll roughen my face, and I won't speak. You'll talk for us."

He considered me for so long, I was sure he would refuse. "Where is your family, if I may ask?"

I looked down for a moment to compose my face. "I lost them, all of them," I said. "Some years ago."

"I am sorry to hear that," he said, with a stiff nod. "I'm sure that's been quite difficult for you. Is that why you want to leave Norway now, in this sudden way? I've a right to know."

"Of course, but it's complicated," I said. "The shipping agent, just yesterday, started pressuring me to marry him, and he's threatening to fire me if I refuse. But I can't bear the thought of him—you saw how he is!" I paused, breathless that this was what I had chosen to say. "Norway has been a place of great sorrow for me, Mr. Eriksen. I started dreaming of America as a way of forgetting what happened here, but it will take me years to earn my passage."

He listened to this with an inscrutable face.

"If I lose my job in the shipping office, there's little else I can do here in Kristiania. I know, because I've tried everything. But in America there would be better opportunities."

"But we're going to farm. You couldn't possibly know what that will be like."

"Don't underestimate me, Mr. Eriksen. Tell me your plans, and I'll judge what I can do."

He gave me a steely look. "It's a homestead outside a small village in far western Minnesota, near the Dakota border. The county, Lac qui Parle, was only recently settled, though there were trappers and missionaries earlier, before the Indian Wars."

"But those wars were twenty years ago," I said. "Surely Minnesota is safe."

"Yes, but where we're settling has only recently been abandoned by the Indians. There's a lake filled with duck and geese, with wood around it, my brother says."

"How long have they worked their homestead?"

"Several years. We'll stay with them to start, then find a farm nearby to buy. I need a homestead with a dwelling, as I won't have time to build one myself before the snow comes. The winters in Minnesota are very cold, even worse than Gudbrandsdalen, where we're from."

I nodded. Gudbrandsdalen, surrounded by Norway's highest peaks. Lush in summer but forbidding in winter. I thought of his calloused hands. "Are you a wood carver? My father traveled to Gudbrandsdalen once and brought back the most exquisite carved mirror."

"Yes. My father owned a large dairy farm, which was left to my older brother. I was apprenticed to a local carver, who also educated me. When I married, my brother leased me a house and enough pasture to keep a few cows, but I could no longer make a living carving, as so many have emigrated. My younger brother, Gustaf, managed the farm for our brother, but it chafed at his pride. After watching friends leave for America, he went too. They have a boy now, born in Minnesota."

We fell silent. Finally, something in him began to yield. "What would be the terms of your employment?"

"I would care for the infant and, with Birgitte's help, manage the housework. I know nothing of farming, but I could teach the children."

"They already read and write but need more schooling. What education do you have?"

"I graduated from a private academy in Hamar. I speak some English."

"Why don't you teach? I would think that sensible for a woman in your position."

"I did, for a time," I lied. "The pay was poor and the girls quite spoiled."

He accepted that, and then I knew he would agree.

"But you and I cannot live together, after we move to our own farm," he said. "I wouldn't want to pose as man and wife in America."

"No, of course not," I said, shaking my head. "Only for the voyage."

"You could stay with my brother's family and help in both households. I believe his wife will soon have another confinement."

"That would be fine. Do you think a year of work would be appropriate?"

He nodded. "I suppose we'll provide your board. What of your clothes?"

"I have what I need."

We quickly talked out the details. I would dress as his wife and travel with her emigration papers, issued before her death. Inge Eriksen, exhausted from the birth and preparations for the trip, died of a fever just days into their journey out of the mountains, he told me. They stopped only to bury her in Lillehammer, fearful of missing the ship. He said he would give me one of his wife's woven skirts and her shawl, so that I would look like part of the family. "Birgitte will wear a skirt like it," he said.

Then he cocked his head. "You were wealthy once."

"Never wealthy, Mr. Eriksen," I said, reddening. "I was comfortable, but I didn't marry well, and we struggled to make ends meet."

"I don't mean to offend, Mrs. Solberg. I just need to understand the person I'm hiring." He looked away. "I do need help with the child, as Birgitte is not yet adept. I believe the baby misses his mother as much as the rest of us. He cries so."

"I'll do what I can for him, Mr. Eriksen."

With that we shook hands, and I promised to stop by the next day for Inge's clothes.

"What will you do when you're done working for us?" he asked.

"I'd like to find a job in Chicago," I said. "There are neighborhoods where they speak Norwegian. I hope to serve as governess for a family."

"You've thought this out," he said.

I nodded—another fabrication—then said good-bye.

LATER, I huddled with Tobias beside the fire at the rooming house. "I've something important to tell you—I'm going to America! We leave this Friday."

He opened his mouth, but I quickly squeezed his hand. "Shhh. It's a secret."

He nodded, eyes wide. "I can scarcely believe it!" he whispered. "I had no idea you'd saved enough for a ticket! Did you sell a secret stash of jewelry?"

I blushed. Perhaps I was more transparent than I thought. "No, I'm earning my way across. I'm going with a family to care for an infant."

"As a nurse? As their maid?"

"Like a member of the family." I told him the story of Mr. Eriksen, the baby, the wife buried in Lillehammer, and the farm in Minnesota.

He listened intently, but when I was finished he sat back in dismay. "Mrs. Solberg, you can't do this!"

"I know it sounds like madness, but I must leave Norway, and it's the only way possible."

"But it could be dangerous. You don't know this man; he could be a brute! Does he expect you to live in the same house with him? It's lonely on the prairie, Nora."

"No. His brother and wife are nearby," I said. "The baby and I will live with them."

He just shook his head.

I leaned forward. "Listen, Tobias, I understand how it looks, going with a stranger, but he's a good man. I've seen how he speaks to his family, and he clearly loved his wife. There are years of hard work in his hands and shoulders. He wants me to teach his children, Tobias. He trusts me with the baby. And if it turns out I've misjudged him, I'll walk away once I'm over there."

Tobias just looked at me. "But Mrs. Solberg, the prairie is so isolated, and you've no idea what it will be like living with his relatives. It may be a very poor farm—some of them barely scrape out a living—and you will be trapped for a year of labor. What do you know of farmwork?"

"Please, Tobias. I must believe I can do this, because I've little choice." He was right—I had no idea what it would be like working for this family, but it didn't matter. I was confident I could find my way to what I needed.

He reached out and took my hands. "Maybe you need another choice, Mrs. Solberg. Or, if I may, Nora—." His eyes blazed at me.

I stared at him in wonder. "Tobias, no, please . . ."

"I know I'm young, and I can't offer you anything now, but if you'll wait for me, until I finish my degree, maybe we could go to America together."

"Oh, Tobias," I said. "You've been so kind to me, but I am far too old for you! You need someone young and interesting, someone with her life before her. Not a compromised woman like me, running from her husband. And he is coming for me, Tobias, maybe not today, but soon. I need to go far away to be safe. The American prairie is so distant, so distant . . ." I choked and my eyes filled. A vast gulf would open between me and Torvald, yes, but also between me and my children and my dear friend Tobias.

He gazed at me, disappointment in his eyes. Finally, he nodded, resigned. "Perhaps you can write to me when you get to America, so I'll know where to find you."

"Of course."

"Is there anything I can do?"

"Just keep my secret, Tobias, always and forever. Don't even tell Erlend. No one can ever know."

He looked at me, solemn now. "Of course. I promise."

I NEVER RETURNED to the shipping office, as I dared not face Mr. Niel-sen again. Instead, I took my mourning gowns, corset, and veiled hat the next morning and gave them to my friend the America widow, with a fond farewell.

"I'm off to Minnesota," I said, handing her my widow's wear. How glad I was to get rid of it. "I won't need these any longer," I said.

She took the things gratefully, but I could see the envy in her eyes.

"I wish you could go with me," I told her.

"Aye, as do I." She put on the hat. "I suppose I'm a true widow now, Mrs. Solberg."

"Good-bye, dear friend. I hope to see you in America someday."

She gave me several cakes, which I put in my pocket. Then I walked to the White Gull.

AS ARRANGED, Mr. Eriksen met me outside and led me upstairs to a cramped room. Birgitte sat with her brothers on a cot, knitting a small shirt. Jens entertained the baby with a carved wooden horse. They looked up wordlessly when I said hello.

"I've brought you a treat," I said, handing them the little cakes.

"Thank you, ma'am," said Jens. "May we eat them, Papa?"

"Yes, as soon as your sister says thank you to Mrs. Solberg."

"Thank you," Birgitte said, with a sullen look, though her mouth regis-tered grief more than anger.

The children unwrapped their cakes and ate them in the awkward silence. I suddenly saw how much I was intruding on their privacy. It had only been two weeks since their mother's death.

"Let me see what we can find for you to wear," Mr. Eriksen said, jump-ing up and bustling about nervously. He cleared some space, then opened the rosemaled chest his wife, Inge, had packed before they left. He sorted through stacks of clothes, finally handing me one of his wife's woven skirts and a black rose-embroidered shawl to wear on the ship.

They must have been a family of some wealth, because at the bottom of the trunk were heirlooms—silver spoons, carved wooden candlesticks, the thick blue skirt and flowered vest of a traditional Gudbrandsdalen *bunad*. Everything was beautifully crafted.

There was also a small wooden box. "My woodworking tools," Mr. Erik-sen said. Then he pulled out a sewing bag of embroidered felt. "Women's tools. You should carry it as part of your disguise."

Birgitte put down her knitting.

I opened the sewing bag; everything was so neatly kept. My own jumbled sewing kit would fit inside.

"Shouldn't I have Mama's sewing bag?" Birgitte said.

"Yes, of course," I said, handing it to her. "I didn't mean . . ."

"No," said Mr. Eriksen, putting it in my pile. "For now. For the voyage. We have to be as faithful to the truth as we can be, or no one will believe us."

"To the truth?" Birgitte squeaked, in disbelief. She'd only known me a few minutes and had already drawn her battle lines.

"To the truth we want them to believe," her father said. "This is no time to quibble with me, Birgitte."

The girl turned away, her jaw working.

I sighed. Would we be safe with this fuming girl in our midst?

Mr. Eriksen just pushed ahead. Ignoring his daughter, he handed me the baby, so I could get to know him a little. The child gazed up at me from his swaddling. The familiar weight in my arms nearly brought me to tears. He reminded me of Bobby, with his silken curls and observant blue eyes.

Then he began to fuss.

"He doesn't like her," Birgitte said.

"He's hungry, Birgitte," Mr. Eriksen said. "Get his flask."

Birgitte prepared the suckling flask, then passed it to me with a challenging look, as if she doubted I'd ever fed an infant before. Fortunately, I knew how the flask worked, and Tomas sucked eagerly. Birgitte took up her knitting again, pulling angrily at a row of loops.

"We will also need food for the train travel," I said. "We may not have time to get it in New York. Dried apples, cheeses and sausages, and crackers. And, of course, cans of milk for Tomas."

"Yes, I will get it this afternoon," Mr. Eriksen said. "We can restock in Minnesota when we get the wagon."

I looked up at him. "I didn't imagine we'd be traveling by wagon."

"There's no railroad yet to Lac qui Parle. We'll get a wagon and oxen at the end of the rail line and walk from there. It will only take a couple of days."

Walk across the prairie? I handed Tomas back to his sister. Would I be able to do this? Would I be expected to carry the child on such a journey?

"Thank you, Mr. Eriksen," I said, picking up the bundle of things he set aside for me. "If there isn't anything else, I will meet you on the wharf tomorrow morning." I bid good-bye to Birgitte and Jens and left them to themselves.

BACK AT THE ROOMING HOUSE, the immensity of what I was doing began to fill me with dread. Would I ever return to Norway, ever see my children again? There would be many dangers on the prairie—snakes, cyclones, men of little decency. And Tobias was right—I knew nothing of Mr. Eriksen. I tried to imagine living in his brother's house, a primitive cabin with few comforts. But there would be a stove, no doubt, and maybe a rocking chair. I could see myself feeding Tomas, helping with meals. At least there would be another woman, and they appeared honest folk. Small things were reassuring—the fine *bunad* and silver spoons packed in the chest, Jens entertaining Tomas with the toy horse. How could malice be harbored in such a family? Birgitte might be difficult at first, but that was understandable.

What they carried was sorrow rather than malice, I thought, and sorrow I could handle. Sorrow I knew.

Tobias knocked to see if I needed anything, so I asked him to trade my wooden chest for his old valise. He agreed reluctantly.

"Please be happy for me, Tobias. You're the one who told me to go to America!"

"But not like this, like stepping off a cliff! You're a lady, Mrs. Solberg!"

"Tobias, I'm stronger than I look." I stopped, thinking how to explain. "I'm like those pregnant girls on the wharf, Tobias, carrying something in my womb, something only partly formed but important. It cannot grow here in Kristiania—even if I were restored to my class. I see that now. It needs space and freedom, or it will never flourish. And so, I too must go to America."

He gazed at me, solemn and sad, then left me alone so I could pack.

I TUCKED MY VALUABLES inside my drawstring bag: my money and the silver pickle forks; the letter from my children, Emma's cap, and the picture of my family; then my own certificate of baptism and Ivar's stone—strangely precious to me. I tested the bag around my waist, then sewed my pearls back into my shift. In the valise I packed Chopin's Mazurkas, my English grammar and other books, then the few clothes I had left. On the ship, I would wear my plainest dress beneath Inge's woven skirt, with her shawl over my head.

Later, Tobias and I slipped out for one last walk. He offered me his arm and chatted to ease my mind. Soon we stood in front of Torvald's apartment. Lamps flickered in the parlor—Torvald would be reading beside the tiled stove. We crept into the courtyard so I could gaze up at the darkened nursery window. They were in there, so close. I imagined myself moving about that familiar room, leaning over each bed. Good-bye, Ivar, and forgive me. Good-bye, my Bobby. Good-bye, sweet Emma. I'll come back for you someday—I promise.

Tobias, concerned someone would hear me weeping, finally led me out.

WHEN WE GOT BACK to the rooming house, the boys were celebrating a visit from a well-known Danish intellectual, toasting him with bottles of beer. I could not share their mood, so said good night and retired.

My sadness felt like a deep well in my heart, and I stood beside it, bucket in hand. But I didn't dare lower the bucket, for fear that it would pull me in.

I washed, then let down my hair and brushed it long and hard—suspended between all that was familiar and all that was unknown. When the brushing was done, I braided my locks into two thick ropes, then pinned them across my head like a dairymaid.

I climbed into bed and tried to sleep.

THE HAMMERING came deep in the night, waking me with a start. Then the sound of boots, many boots, entering the rooming house and moving up the stairs.

Had the day started, this day of days? Suddenly, there were voices as well. Angry voices. I jumped up and threw on my dress, tossed my bag under my mattress, then peeked out the window. It was blacker than midnight outside.

I crept from my room into the kitchen. I could see the glimmer of torchlight under the door that led to the parlor. Now I heard shouting, then furniture crashing and footsteps tumbling down the stairwell. I cracked the door.

Police were everywhere, sticks swinging, boys fighting, boys on the floor. Some being kicked.

I retreated into the shadows. No, not on this night.

Then, two policemen, with a lantern, looking for me. "Nora Helmer?"

"My name is Solberg."

One pulled out a rope. "Turn around."

I stepped back and tried to look as imperious as possible. "What are you doing? Are you arresting *me*?"

"If you cooperate, you have nothing to worry about," the older one said. "Everyone in this house is under arrest, for sedition."

Then, before I could think about the consequences, I lied. "I am not one of them."

The policemen looked at me and laughed.

"But I've never done anything seditious," I protested. "I'm a simple seamstress; I wouldn't know how!"

"That's not what I heard, Mrs. Helmer," the other one said. He grabbed my arm and dragged me toward the front door. He had the strength of a bulldog.

In the parlor students and police still scuffled, though the police were getting the upper hand. Through the fray I spotted Tobias, his hands bound. He rose from a bench. "Mrs. Solberg!"

A policeman whirled about and clubbed him on the head; Tobias sank to the ground. The shock jolted me fully awake. My friend, my truest friend in the world, lay limp. Blood started to pool beside his head.

Shame shot through me. How could I have denied that I was one of them? I tried to jerk away, to go to Tobias, but the officer pushed me through the crowd and out the front door.

On the street, they were loading the boys into a wagon, but they hustled me into a small carriage. There were two men inside. One was a policeman, but the other wore a dark coat and a hat pulled low so I couldn't see his face.

"Good evening, Mrs. Helmer," he said.

"My name is Nora Solberg. If you're looking for a Mrs. Helmer, you've made a grave mistake."

The man laughed gently. "Solberg, Helmer, it doesn't matter. We know who you are."

I couldn't help but shiver. "Where are you taking me?"

"To the police station."

"Why?"

"We'll explain when we get there."

Then I understood. Torvald must have sent them. The police were rounding up the boys as cover. If it wasn't for me, they never would have come to this rooming house. These students weren't any more seditious than anyone else in Vika.

No, they came for me, and now Tobias was hurt, possibly worse. I turned away so they couldn't see my face. Why had I said I wasn't one of them? Of course I was. When I had nowhere else to hide, the students had accepted and sheltered me. Tobias, in particular, had counseled me, listened to me, protected me. And now he lay injured, because of me.

Here I was again, in trouble and trying to slip the trap by denying my truth. No, I am not a wife; I am not a mother; I am not a friend. That was the root of the shame, right there.

WHEN THE CARRIAGE FINALLY STOPPED, the men bundled me into the police station and then into a small room. A senior officer, possibly the commissioner, shouldered his way in and tossed my drawstring bag on a table. They had searched my room.

"Well, well, Mrs. Helmer. We looked all over town for you. Your husband insisted you wouldn't be in Vika, but there you were. It makes sense to me now."

I flushed. "I hid in Vika because I knew my honor would protect me. No one would suspect it."

"Until we questioned your honor," he said.

"I am not a prostitute, if that is what you are implying. And my name is Solberg."

He pulled a folded paper from his coat. "You were baptized Solberg, but your married name is Helmer." He had my marriage certificate; Torvald must have sent them.

"Since you've been lying, let's see what we have here," the commissioner said, dumping the contents of my bag on the table. "An interesting collection, Mrs. Helmer." He picked up the small cloth bundle that held the little pickle forks and untied it. The shimmer of the silver seemed strange in the starkness of the interrogation room.

"Did you steal these?"

"No, they're mine," I said. "They were . . . my mother's."

"You do know, Mrs. Helmer, that because you are still married, everything belongs to your husband. Even if they were your mother's. That's the law."

"I apologize. I didn't know the silver belonged to my husband. He may have them."

The commissioner harrumphed, then picked up the stone, Ivar's stone. "An odd thing to carry in your purse," he said. "Ammunition? To throw at the police?"

"No, of course not. One stone wouldn't get me far, now, would it? It's just a favorite, a gift from someone I love."

He leaned over, as if speaking to a child. "It's not wise to lie to us, Mrs. Helmer."

"That isn't a lie," I said evenly. "And I am Nora Solberg, now that I no longer live with Mr. Helmer. As that is not a crime, I'd like to know why I've been arrested."

"We have plenty to arrest you for. Be smart, Mrs. Helmer; tell us about these students. Did you know that a Danish radical was meeting with them this evening? The police in Copenhagen are looking for him."

I stiffened. Where was there room for truth in a place like this? "No. I retired early."

"If you tell us what they're planning, we'll take you home."

I thought of Tobias on the floor, bleeding. "I don't know of any plans."

"What books do they read? Do they have any weapons? You must know something. How could you live with those scum and not know their plans?"

"They aren't scum, or radicals. They are university students, all of them."

"As I said, scum, radicals." He watched me for a moment. "I'll give you one last chance to tell us the truth."

I raised my chin but said nothing.

He reached for my head. I pulled back but could not escape him. His fingers burrowed in under my braids and pulled out first one pin, then the other. The heavy braids flopped down.

He tugged on one. "What beautiful golden hair you have, Mrs. Helmer." Then he dropped it and wiped his hand on his trousers. "Pity you have lice."

"I do not have lice, sir."

"You must, Mrs. Helmer. You cannot lie with vermin without picking up vermin."

Then he turned to one of the guards. "Take her to the courtyard and cut it off."

"No, please—!"

"Then tell us their plans."

But I couldn't, I wouldn't, give the boys away, even if it cost me everything. I would not deny them again.

The commissioner grunted, and a policeman dragged me down the hall and outside to the courtyard. They used scissors first, cutting close to my head, then brought a basin of water and a razor.

When it was over, I was as bald as a baby bird.

SEVERAL HOURS LATER, when I ached with cold, they dragged me to an empty cell. It had little more than a bucket to relieve myself, a blanket, and a filthy pallet. I thought about lice and sat on the frigid stone floor, my arms around my knees.

In one stroke, they had rendered me ugly for the first time in my life. I ran my hand over my scalp, stopping at the tender places where the razor had nicked the skin. How often had I used my blond hair to my advantage, asking for an extra slice of ham at the butcher's or charming some poor man to do my bidding? It almost felt like divine retribution. I wondered if it made it easier for the police to lock me up, disarming me in this way and making me hideous. I told myself my hair would grow back, but still—it felt as if they had branded me.

WHEN THE POLICE finally let me out of the cell near dawn, Torvald was there waiting. My heart flared with anger at the sight of him, but also something else—relief to see a familiar face.

He caught his breath. "Why did you shave her head?"

"She had lice, and a bad case of refusal."

Torvald gazed at me, and his face filled with pain. "You scarcely look like Nora without your lion's mane." Then he did the last thing I expected— he unbuttoned his coat and threw it over my shoulders. I could not look at him, but gratefulness flooded through me.

"I'll take her home," Torvald said. "Thank you for bringing her in. We need to work on cooperation."

A policeman untied my hands.

I turned to the commissioner. "Am I being released?"

"For now. Into your husband's care."

"Then I want my bag."

He retrieved my drawstring purse and handed it to me. Everything was there, Ivar's stone and Torvald's silver forks, everything except my coin purse. The only thing I truly needed.

"You've taken my money."

"Expenses, ma'am."

Torvald tugged at my arm. "Come, Nora. You don't need money now. I'll take care of you." He edged me toward the door.

"And Mrs. Helmer, if your memory improves, the law requires you tell us anything you know about these young men." The commissioner gave me a stern look.

Torvald whispered in my ear. "Just come, Nora. Let's get away from here."

Outside, we climbed into a hansom cab. It was like old times—the intimacy of the coach, his coat around me. Yet I was changed, irrevocably. My hair was the least of it.

He gave the driver the address of his apartment.

"No, Torvald. Take me back to Vika. The police have released me."

"They only released you into my care, Nora, which means you're no longer free to wander the city alone. A judge has deemed you a danger to yourself, and for that reason you must either stay at home or, if you do not comply, go to the asylum. I'd be happy to take you there, if that is what you prefer, or we can go home. With a bath and a good night's sleep, things might look different in the morning."

"Torvald, please listen. I'm leaving Norway, this very day. I need to go back to Vika to get my things."

"Leaving Norway? You bluff, Nora. How could you afford to go anywhere?"

"I'm not bluffing. I'm leaving for America."

"Nora, don't lie to me—ever again. Or I'll take you straight to the asylum and never look back."

"It's not a lie, I swear! I'm leaving today on the SS *Angelo*, bound for England and then from Liverpool to New York."

Torvald looked at me, then abruptly laughed. "You? To America? I can't think of anything more absurd. How will you live in America?" He laughed again, though nervously this time. He could see my resolve.

"I'm going to Chicago. I'll find a job in a dress shop or something. Be a governess to a wealthy family."

His laughter faded. "You can't be serious."

"Torvald, I made a grave error trying to see the children. I see that now. I will not interfere with them again until they're grown. For their sakes."

Something passed over his face. "I am—." His voice snagged. "I am very relieved to hear you say that. It's been quite difficult for the boys."

"I know, and I am sorry. Hopefully, in America I can build a new life. But if I'm to do this, you must agree to several things."

"You're in no position to dictate to me, Nora."

I hesitated. My life and my children's lives hung precariously in that moment. As difficult as it was for me to touch him, I took hold of Torvald's hands. "It will be a great sorrow for me to be so far away from the children,

Torvald, but it's the only way to give you your freedom, to release all of you. For this sacrifice, I beg you to consider what I ask."

He did not reply, but he did not look away.

"First, please take Anne-Marie back. The children need her."

"She lied to me, Nora."

"She won't lie to you again once I am gone."

He looked at me for a long moment, then finally nodded. "They miss her terribly, almost as much as they miss you. What else?"

"You must promise not to tell the children I have died, because I need to know I can see them when they're grown."

"What would you have me tell them?"

"The truth—that we couldn't be married anymore, and I had to go away."

"I don't know, Nora. They need this to be over."

"Please, Torvald. The world is small. They will see me again, when they are older."

"What are you talking about?"

"When they reach their maturity, they should be allowed to choose whether they want to know me."

"I doubt they'll come to America to find you, Nora. They're forgetting you as best they can."

I glanced out the window; we were turning into our old neighborhood. "If they won't come to America, I'll come back to Norway, but not for many years, I promise. As long as you tell them the truth."

He grunted. "Is there anything else?"

"Yes. You must divorce me."

"Are you going to America with a man?"

"That's not for you to know. I want to be free, and you should be free. It will be better for both of us."

"I cannot make you any promises, Nora. Divorce would be scandalous. It would harm the children."

"But what if you want to marry again? Surely you would . . ."

He cut me off. "I don't know if I could trust a woman again, Nora. I'm not sure I trust you now."

The cab stopped outside our old apartment, the familiar doorway looming like a prison gate. I knew that if I went inside, I would never get away. And there was no point in running—Torvald would just send them after me again. I needed his permission.

"Think of it, Torvald! If you take me to Vika tonight, I promise you'll neither see nor hear of me again for many years."

He looked at me for a long, searing moment, and then his face crumbled. "How did it come to this, Nora? You're thin; you smell. Is this how you want to live? Why can't you come home and let me restore you to society, to civility? Let me help you . . ." His voice cracked again.

"You're not the one to help me, Torvald, as you weren't the one to teach me how to live in the world. I must work that out for myself. Please, take me back to Vika, and your troubles will be over. I'll vanish, and you can make of that what you will."

He considered this, finally reaching out and stroking my bare head. "You're so cold."

"Let me go, Torvald. Let me go so that we may both find peace."

He hesitated, then banged on the window of the cab. "Take us to Vika."

"Vika?" The driver shouted, incredulous.

"Yes, Vika, damn it. Quick, before I change my mind!"

The driver pulled away, the apartment building growing smaller behind us. The cab turned the corner, and soon we were wending our way toward the harbor.

"Thank you, Torvald."

"Just keep your promise this time, Nora."

When we got to the rooming house, Torvald stepped out and bowed stiffly. "Good-bye, Nora," he said, pressing money into my hand. "This should help you get started. Did you say Chicago? Dirty, windy place, I hear."

I lingered, momentarily overcome with sadness. "Torvald, I—."

He cut me off. "Just make sure you get on that ship. The *Angelo*, you said?"

"Yes, this morning."

"Bon voyage."

I watched him go, then knocked on the door of the rooming house. The landlady appeared, her eyes widening when she saw my bald head. The house was silent, as I was the only one released. In my room everything had been flung about. I repacked my bag, then tied a kerchief around my scalp and a shawl over the kerchief, hoping no one would notice.

When it was light, I walked to the wharf.

IF I HADN'T FELT LIKE A CRIMINAL BEFORE, I did by the time I stood waiting at the foot of the gangplank with another woman's child on my hip. Tomas was a beautiful baby, plump and just old enough to straighten his back. Every few minutes he would pull away and stare at me, then collapse against my chest again, as if it was all right I held him. My arms ached, but I didn't care. I clutched him like a life ring, the only thing holding my head above water.

Beside me, Mr. Eriksen seemed agitated, scanning the crowded pier for the police. The baby whimpered. It was spring, but the sea breeze was cold. I pulled Tomas's knit blanket over his head to protect him from the wind and turned my shoulder to the officials. But I couldn't keep my heart from hammering. If the police found me here, trying to board the ship with another woman's papers, there would be no escape: it would be jail or the asylum.

How had I ended up here, ready to break the law again? Why was there no other way for me to live in this world? Nothing felt right, except the baby in my arms. Birgitte, still furious, stood apart from us, refusing to acknowledge me. It was bad enough that her mother was gone, but to have me wearing her mother's woven skirt and familiar shawl was too much to bear. Mr. Eriksen whispered in Birgitte's ear at one point, but she turned and hissed in his, so it did no good.

When the official finally reached for our papers, I shifted the baby to the other hip, nodded at Birgitte as if I had always commanded her, then took Jens by the hand. Birgitte bristled as I rose to the role of mother, and for a sinking moment, I feared she would give us away. But Mr. Eriksen put his arm around her and gently pushed her forward. The official looked through our papers, then studied us for a long moment. I didn't smile as I might have in my former life; charm was no use to me anymore. Instead, I gave him a world-weary gaze—the exhausted mother of a newborn enduring the upheaval of emigrating. He waved us up the gangplank.

None of us could look at each other. Overcome with relief, I faltered as I stepped down onto the deck. Mr. Eriksen took my elbow to steady me.

Onboard, it was a different world. Sailors strode across the decks, passing crates into the hold and pulling on ropes. Smoke from the steam engines eddied about in the shifting wind. The steadying sails flapped on short lines, waiting to be set after the ship cast off.

A porter urged us down the ladders, to stow our luggage. We hurried, happy to disappear belowdecks, but the steerage compartment proved a rude shock. This small steamer, which would take us across the North Sea to England, had only an open hold for the lowest class of travelers. It was dank and crowded, and it reeked of the unwashed. There were two levels of sleeping shelves on each side, with a narrow passageway between. Lanterns and empty buckets hung from hooks, rolling with the swell. It seemed all of Norway's poor—cottars, laborers, housemaids—elbowed for space. We found a spot for our things, then went topside again to breathe.

Now that we were safely aboard and obscured by the crowd, Birgitte snatched the baby from my arms. Freed for the moment, I edged to the rail and scanned the wharf below. The people on the pier waved good-bye, but there was no one there for me. I wondered for a moment if Tobias was there, but I couldn't find him. He was probably still in jail.

Then my stomach dropped. There, off to one side, was Torvald, looking straight at me. We stared at each other for a moment, and then he lifted his hand in farewell.

I backed up, disappearing into the mob. The gangplank was pulled aboard, the ship's engines ground in earnest, and finally the sailors tossed the lines ashore. With a blast of her horn, the SS *Angelo* fell away from the pier.

Only when we were well out in the harbor did I return to the ship's rail. All of Kristiania spread before me, my entire world. At the head of the bay was Vika, with its jumbled rooftops and smudge of smoke. Beyond Vika, the commercial center and green promenade where I often walked. Behind that, the neighborhoods climbed the hills. And in that maze of streets were those who had pushed me to this—Torvald and the police; the blackmailing Mr. Krogstad; Mr. Lyngstrand, who would have sealed my fate; and the hateful shipping agent. I had escaped, slipped from their grasp.

But to do it I had to leave my own children behind. They, too, were out there, probably playing in a park. Unknowing, innocent, and now motherless.

CHAPTER TEN

SOLVI

February 1919 ■ *Kristiania, Norway*

Magnus slipped into his seat next to Solvi with a smile, then leaned over. "I've got something for you."

"What is it?"

He pulled a yellowed scrap of newspaper from his jacket pocket. "I was looking through the archives at the newspaper yesterday for references to the Forgotten One. Back then they kept files on various topics, and there was one on the Woman Question. I found this."

It was a letter to the editor titled "An Answer to the Woman Question," apparently written by a professor at the university. It was dated July 1880.

Solvi scanned the article, then sucked in a breath. "This is it! This is her story!"

"Yes, it must be," he said, pointing. "Look at this part—*Recently a woman of quality and comfort, well cared for by her loving husband, walked away from her marriage, leaving behind a houseful of inconsolable children.*"

Solvi read it through. "The writer isn't very sympathetic, is he? And he doesn't give her name. I need her name."

"I didn't have time to read everything in the file, but when you meet the editor, Mr. Blehr, you can ask permission to look through it."

"Did you show him my photographs?"

"Yes. He wants you to come by tomorrow morning. We could meet at the pastry shop, say, ten o'clock?"

Solvi nodded but hesitantly. What was she getting herself into?

"I did one other thing for you at the newspaper. I looked through a register of professionals here in Kristiania, and I couldn't find anyone named either Helmer or Fallesen."

"Does that mean my uncles are not working here in Kristiania?"

"Well, not as professional men. Given that their father was a banker, they must have been educated for a profession."

Solvi shook her head. "Perhaps my mother wasn't lying."

"But it doesn't mean they don't exist, Solvi. They could be somewhere else in Norway, or they may have emigrated."

Professor Wolff entered, dropping a pile of books on the lectern.

"Thank you, Magnus," Solvi whispered.

"HAVE YOU EVER BEEN IN A NEWSPAPER OFFICE?" Magnus said, as he pulled open the door of a tall brick building the next morning.

"Heavens, no," Solvi said. "I was brought up to be a lady."

"Well, let's fix that," he said. Inside, they climbed a flight of stairs to a bustling space crowded with desks heaped with newspapers. Everyone worked in shirtsleeves, and many were drumming away on typewriters. A man in a rumpled suit saw them and broke from a conversation to walk over.

"Is this your photographer, Magnus?" said the man, shaking Solvi's hand. He was small in stature but had sharp, observant eyes and a mop of black hair. "Stanislas Blehr."

"Solvi Lange, sir."

"Pleasure to meet you. Let's talk." They followed him into a private office, Magnus giving her an encouraging smile as they sat down.

"Miss Lange, I must say, your photographs are very interesting. Few people take pictures that have so much movement and grace. Did you take them here in Kristiania?"

"No, in Bergen, where I grew up."

"I'd like to publish a few with the article Petra Jeppesen is preparing, but I'd also like some photos of housemaids here. Are you willing to take more? I'm sure Petra could get you into some houses."

"Yes," Solvi said, though the idea made her nervous. "I'll talk to her."

"Good. When you've got some to show me, bring them by." He smiled. "If we publish your photos, Miss Lange, you would be the first woman to sell us pictures. That would be something to write home about, eh?"

"Yes," Solvi murmured, imagining her mother reading such a letter.

Mr. Blehr stood. "Get to work on the housemaid story, and if you think of other interesting stories to tell, take some pictures and I'll look at them. Magnus says you're studying at the university."

"Yes. I've just started."

Mr. Blehr gave her a slight bow of respect. "I failed the matriculation exams myself, yet here I sit, editor of a newspaper. Just remember, there's a bigger world than the one at university."

"I'm not sure I understand, sir."

"If you have the mettle you seem to, Miss Lange, you don't need a university degree. You could start working as a journalist today."

Solvi just looked at him, unable to speak.

Magnus leaned forward. "Miss Lange has a request. Could she look through the archives? She's doing an essay on women's rights."

"Yes, of course. Whatever she needs, Magnus."

"Thank you, Mr. Blehr," Solvi said, finding her voice again.

He held her gaze for a long moment, then turned to Magnus. "You and your friends better watch out. These young ladies are going to take over the world."

Magnus laughed. "Yes, sir. I'm already worried."

MAGNUS SHOWED SOLVI to a room full of old newspapers, then pulled a fat file from a drawer and handed it to her. It was labeled "The Woman Question."

He started to go but turned back. "One other thing, Solvi. Mr. Blehr suggested we go look through the parish records to find your family."

"Parish records? Like, marriages and baptisms?"

"Yes, and deaths. The Church has been keeping these records for hundreds of years. I'm sure we'd find something."

Deaths, Solvi thought. At least it would be definitive.

"Come find me in the newsroom when you're done," he said.

SOLVI PICKED THROUGH THE ARTICLES. Several were written by the early feminist Aasta Hansteen, and several were written about Hansteen, most of them derisive. There were accounts of various talks about the Woman Question, some attended by hostile all-male audiences, and letters from various luminaries arguing over whether women should be accorded human rights or whether those were the exclusive territory of men. And on and on.

Then she found this curious report: "Hansteen Talk Turns to Riot over Case of Runaway Mother." Solvi leaned forward to decipher the tiny print:

Miss Hansteen praised the American suffragettes and called for more rights for women. The crowd became unruly when Miss Hansteen referenced the Kristiania woman who recently abandoned her marriage, saying the law shouldn't block her from seeing her children and that she should have the right to care for them if she can. Constables were called. Miss Hansteen is to leave for America in the near future, which should allow the social order to be restored.

Solvi sat back. Another reference to the Forgotten One! Could Miss Hansteen still be alive? Professor Wolff might know.

She copied the article and made notes on others. Several referred to a mother who abandoned her children, but no one named her, almost as if everyone knew who she was but was unwilling to put her name in print.

At the bottom of the pile she found a death notice—Aasta Hansteen's. She died in 1908. The obituary hardly did her justice.

After several hours Magnus stuck his head in the door. "Lunch?"

"Please," Solvi said, blinking at him as if she were coming up for air. She had never been so absorbed, never felt so alive.

LATER THAT AFTERNOON, Solvi was reading her history assignment when someone tapped on her door.

It was Rikka, in her nursing uniform. "I need you to go with me to Vika. Change into something that won't draw attention and bring your camera."

"I wish you would give me some warning, Rikka, really . . . ," Solvi said, but she stepped out of her nice skirt nonetheless.

"Do you have a plain blouse?"

"No. My mother always insisted on lace."

"Then put this over your head." Rikka handed Solvi her shawl.

"Like a peasant?"

"Solvi, buck up. You don't want to stand out, believe me. And keep your camera hidden."

Out in the street Solvi felt as if she had dressed for a part in a play, but as they made their way down to the poorer sections she began to understand. When they crossed into Vika, she recognized the area—it was the place Rikka went the day Solvi followed her. Today, amid the usual trash and unkempt children, she noticed several women sitting at windows in low-cut gowns, almost as if they were on display.

"Rikka, are those prostitutes?"

"Yes. Do not judge them, Solvi."

"No, I, but . . . prostitutes? I've never seen one."

"We may be talking to some."

Solvi caught her breath. "Rikka, I, I don't know . . ."

Rikka spun around. "Listen, Solvi, they get sick too. They need medicine as much as anyone. They do what they do because they have nothing."

"Of course, I'm sorry. I'm fine."

"Good." Rikka gave her a quick smile. "Not everyone can come down here with me, so I appreciate it." She glanced at a slip of paper. "This way," she said, turning down a narrow lane. Solvi could see racks of drying fish at the bottom of the street, the fjord just beyond. The air was heavy with salt, and damp. Perhaps the Forgotten One lived here once, Solvi thought. Perhaps she lived here still.

They stopped at a dilapidated shack with its door split at the bottom, as if someone had tried to kick it in. Rikka knocked; a thin woman peered out. Rikka explained who she was, and the woman let them inside. The room was chilly and dark, with only a dim oil lamp. An oppressive stench enveloped them—sweat, dirty clothing, rotten vegetables. As Solvi's eyes adjusted she noticed several children sitting on a rumpled pallet in the corner, watching them.

The woman offered Rikka and Solvi the only chairs. Solvi sat, but Rikka just put her medical bag on the table and opened it up.

"Here, ma'am, you sit, and I'll check you," she said in a soft voice, so unlike her usual self. The woman unbuttoned the top of her blouse so Rikka could listen to her lungs. Rikka glanced at Solvi. "Talk to the children. Maybe they'll let you take their picture."

Solvi looked at them. There were five, the youngest barely old enough to speak. "Good day," she said.

They stared at her like a row of owls.

She untied the ridiculous shawl, revealing the camera.

The eldest, a boy, stood up. "What is that, miss?"

"A camera. It can take pictures of people. Have you seen pictures, like the advertisements in store windows?"

They nodded.

"Would you like to see how it works?"

The baby struggled to her feet and tottered over. Solvi unbuttoned the case, and they crowded around. She let them touch it and look through the viewfinder.

"Can you take our picture, miss?" said one.

"If your mama agrees."

The mother glanced at Solvi. "Outside," she said. Solvi looked at Rikka, who nodded.

The children followed Solvi into the street. She sat them in the doorway, the baby in the lap of the eldest girl and the smallest boy on his brother's shoulders. For a moment she heard her mother's voice—*Don't touch them, Solvi, you'll get disease*—but she ignored it. Once the children were settled, Solvi knelt in the dirt so she could shoot them straight on. No one smiled. She took two pictures, then one more down the lane toward the water. A man bent over a wagon several blocks down straightened up and looked at her, then shouted something she could not hear.

The children jumped up. "That's our *Far*," said the older girl. "He doesn't like strangers."

The man started walking toward them.

"When can we see the pictures, miss?" asked the older boy.

"Soon. When Miss Toft and I come back."

Rikka came out with her bag and handed Solvi her shawl.

"Their *Far*," Solvi said. He had stopped but watched them.

"We'd better go," said Rikka, quickly turning up the street. "The fathers, when there are fathers, are protective; they don't like us talking to their wives."

THEY VISITED THREE MORE HOMES, each sad in the same way—the same dank smells, the same pale children.

In one house the mother was dressed only in a soiled shift, a bundled baby with crusty eyes squalling in her arms.

"This is why we do not judge," Rikka whispered. The poor woman looked so miserable, so humiliated, Solvi kept her camera under her shawl.

But at the next house a pair of brothers led Solvi to a stall so she could take their picture with their father's draft horse. And in the last home seven children were bickering over a heel of bread, so Solvi herded them outside for a portrait. She was taken by their scuffed wooden shoes and scabbed ankles. After getting a picture of the children together, she had them stick out their feet and shot from above. They shouted with glee.

THAT EVENING Matron handed Solvi a letter, this one from Lisanne. She took it into the library.

Dear Solvi: Thank you for your letter. I was glad to finally hear from you. I was quite saddened to find you had left Bergen, though I guess I understand why you went without fanfare. Congratulations on passing the matriculation exams. I hope you've written to our teachers back at our academy. They'll be as thrilled as I am to hear of your success.

I am doing well, as is my family. I will admit I was taken aback by your request to get permission to publish those photographs. Is that what you planned when you took them? If so, you should have told me. I'll be honest—I cannot speak to my parents about it, as they would feel quite betrayed. And it doesn't feel right to ask the maids. We lost Marte to the influenza, and I wouldn't want to do anything that might jeopardize the others. I'm sorry I cannot help you.

There is one other thing I must tell you, and I hope it will not be hurtful. Stefan Vinter and I are to be married in July.

I wish you well with your endeavors.

Love, Lisanne

For a moment, Solvi couldn't breathe. How could Lisanne marry Stefan Vinter? How would Solvi ever be able to sit again with her and talk as they used to? She folded the letter and tucked it in her pocket. Her old life in Bergen felt so distant—her grandfather, her mother, Lisanne—all receding into the past, as if Solvi was on a train traveling swiftly, inexorably, away from them.

The next morning Solvi sent Lisanne her congratulations, but she couldn't help feeling as if someone had died.

WHEN SOLVI DEVELOPED HER PHOTOGRAPHS of the Vika children, she was surprised by what she had caught. In the photo of the boys with the horse, the scraggly nag hung her head between the two brothers, her eyes closed in rapture as they scratched her ears. In the next, the seven siblings jostled for the crust of bread, the eldest holding it just out of reach as they looked up at the camera. But it was the shot of their feet—with their dirty ankles and bruised legs—that brought tears to her eyes. They were too poor to have socks. She thought of them laughing as she clicked the shutter. How silly; how painfully revealing.

When she came out of the darkroom, she showed them to Mr. Stenberg.

"Excellent work, Miss Lange," he said. "So many contrasts in such a small world."

A DRIVING RAIN blew across Kristiania the morning Solvi was to meet with Professor Wolff. She arrived at his office damp and bedraggled.

"Good morning, Professor. I'm Miss Lange, from your Norwegian History class."

"Of course, come in. Goodness, you're wet." He helped her shake off her cape and invited her to sit, then squinted at her for a long moment. "Miss Lange, if I may, where are you from?"

"Bergen."

"Ah," he said, studying her from behind his wire-rimmed glasses. "You remind me of a long-lost friend, someone I knew many years ago. How very odd." Then he smiled. "Forgive me. You've come to discuss your essay."

"Yes," Solvi said, opening her notebook. "I'd like to write about the roots of the campaign for women's rights. Who the leaders were here in Norway, how they came to their convictions, how they rallied support. For my generation it feels like the dramatic victories are over—we can vote, we can work—yet most of us know little of what our mothers and grandmothers did to get us here."

"That's quite interesting," he said, leaning back in his chair. "I've been waiting for someone to propose such an essay, but, well, it hasn't appealed to any of the young men."

"I understand you knew some of the early feminists."

"I did."

"There are two figures from the 1880s that particularly interest me. One is Aasta Hansteen. Did you know her?"

"Oh, yes. I went to some of her talks before she left for America, and I worked with her when she returned later."

"You went to her talks? I read in an old newspaper clipping about a riot at one of them, in 1881, I believe. The constables had to break it up. Were you there that night?"

Professor Wolff blinked in surprise, then looked away. "I scarcely remember. The constables were often busy when Miss Hansteen spoke, as hecklers followed wherever she went. She left Norway, she said, because 'the ground was burning beneath her feet.'"

Solvi scribbled notes. "I asked about that riot because I'm interested in the case of a woman who walked away from her family in the 1880s and caused an uproar. I first heard about her in a lecture at the Women's Rights Association. The riot reported in the newspaper seemed to have been triggered by Miss Hansteen talking about this woman, saying that it was unfair she had no right to property or access to her children. Do you know anything about this woman, perhaps her name? They call her the Forgotten One."

Professor Wolff coughed. "Yes, I, ah, heard about such a case, but I don't remember a name."

Solvi sat up with excitement. "So she was real?"

He pressed his fingertips together. "Hmm, an important question." He took his glasses off and cleaned them with his handkerchief. "Are you suggesting someone made her up?"

"Well, perhaps not deliberately. More that there was some kernel of truth that got exaggerated over time. Sometimes iconic figures turn out to be more myth than substance. Or so I understand."

"That's true, Miss Lange, and as a historian it's your job to try to separate truth from myth. But what makes you curious about this woman?"

Curious? It was much more than curiosity, Solvi thought, gathering her thoughts. "My grandmother also disappeared and probably died in this period," Solvi said. "It just seems like a tragic time for women—so many restrictions and limitations, so few legal rights, and so few opportunities, just as they were beginning to want more. The story of the Forgotten One captures all of that, as well as the painful consequences. She lost everything—perhaps even her life—trying to follow a principle of individual freedom."

Solvi stopped to think for a moment. "But she's also interesting because there's so much mystery about her, where she went, how or whether she survived, whether she's even real. I hope to find some of the answers."

He blinked at her again. "Your grandmother died at this time?"

"Well, my mother has heard nothing from her since she was a child, so she must be gone. I think she died in some unsavory way because my family has tried to shield me from it."

He stared at her. "How, ah, unfortunate, Miss Lange." He pulled himself straight in his chair. "So, as for your essay, you're right, the case of the Forgotten One is iconic for a reason. It would be interesting to juxtapose the myth with the reality, as far as it can be discovered. Even if she wasn't real, perhaps you can find the origin of the story."

Solvi put down her pen. "One thing I don't understand is why it would have been considered such a radical step for a woman to leave her husband. Hadn't women done that before?"

He sighed. "Well, a lot has changed in forty years, but in the 1880s society ladies who left their families invariably ran off with other men to live in sin. But this woman, as I recall the story, was a mother of small children and did not have a lover. That's what made her so controversial."

"Forgive me if this is a rude question," Solvi said, with a faint blush, "but how could anyone know whether she had a lover?"

"When you are examining the facts, there are no rude questions, Miss Lange. Norway was an even smaller place back then, with a limited bourgeois class. Everyone knew everyone else, at least here in Kristiania. I wasn't of their class, but I heard the gossip. I remember how scandalized people were that this woman left her children just for the sake of independence. Passion they could understand; to leave for freedom sounded like lunacy."

"What would her alternatives have been if she no longer loved her husband?"

"Well, that is what I want you to explore in your research," Professor Wolff said. "What were her rights, her opportunities? What did it mean to leave her husband's care and protection?" He put his hands together, thinking. "This woman was interesting because she refused to stay in a broken marriage. What she experienced, though, may have been much worse."

"Why would she have been blocked from seeing her children?"

"Most women could afford to leave their husbands only by attaching themselves to another man. Under the law, then, a woman who left her husband was assumed to be an adulterer. Whether they were or not didn't matter. They were treated as a moral threat to their children."

"That's hardly fair," Solvi said, offended. "How could it not matter whether she actually was an adulterer? One's moral code is, well, it's everything!"

"You're right to be angry. Everything bad was assumed about her when, in fact, we don't really know."

"Do you have any idea what might have happened to her?"

He gazed at Solvi for a very long moment. "If she was real, she probably left Kristiania to escape the gossip and found a job somewhere in Norway where she wasn't known," he said, his voice growing hoarse. "Most likely she died cold and forgotten in some drafty garret."

Solvi nodded and put down her pen. "I hope I can solve the mystery. It would be wonderful to know the truth."

"Well, I'm glad you've caught the historian's bug," he said. He squinted at Solvi again. "It's uncanny how much you remind me of my old friend."

"Who was she?"

"A remarkable woman; we were friends at a time when we both needed friends." He laughed softly. "We lived in a rooming house in Vika back then, if you can believe it. We were both quite poor; I was still just a student."

"Was she, a, um, a . . ." Solvi hesitated, but hadn't he said there were no rude questions? "Was she a prostitute?"

"No. She was quite charming, well educated, and mannered. She ended up there through unusual circumstances. She taught me to sew; I taught her labor politics."

Solvi smiled. "I guess that's a fair trade. What became of her?"

"I think she immigrated to America. I still miss her." He looked at Solvi, his head cocked to one side. "Did your grandparents live in Bergen?"

"I don't really know. They may have been from Kristiania earlier, but they moved to Bergen before I was born. I've got fog in my veins. I'm surprised it doesn't come out my ears."

He nodded thoughtfully. "Good day, Miss Lange."

LATER THAT NIGHT, Solvi sat at her desk, a blank paper before her. The chasm between her and her mother had become an abyss, something capable of swallowing them both if Solvi didn't tread carefully. The only way she could think to bridge it was to be honest.

Dear Mama: I hope you are well and feel your strength returning. I am doing fine and happy for the spring rains, as Kristiania has been very cold this winter. So far I love university, though there are not many women students and I'm often the only one in the room. It feels strange, but doesn't seem to bother the professors, who are kind and helpful despite my being "just a girl," as some of the boys say. I'm quite excited about my Norwegian History class and am working on an essay about the roots of the movement for women's rights, particularly the early feminists from the 1880s. You might have heard of Aasta Hansteen, who was a famous portrait painter and early advocate for women. Apparently, she wore men's boots and once threatened to hit a member of the Storting over the head with her umbrella! She went to America to learn from the American suffragettes and even traveled out to Chicago and Minnesota to talk about women's rights.

I must also tell you that I am working at a photography shop, clerking at the counter and developing photographs. I take pictures all over the city but am always careful where I go and take a friend with me.

Much love, Solvi

P.S. I'm still curious to know if there is any chance Grandfather changed his name from Helmer to Fallesen.

Maybe in the next letter she would have the courage to tell her about Rikka.

CHAPTER ELEVEN

NORA

Spring 1919 ■ *Spokane, Washington*

I got up in the middle of the night to write a response to the notice from the newspaper. I could not sleep for fretting over the mystery of the advertisement and realized I would have no peace until I knew who was searching for me.

But I wrote only a few sentences before fear stopped my hand.

What if my response brought something unwanted? Something that would be difficult for Anders, something that would drive us out again or even worse? I crept back to bed, moving in close to Anders's warm back.

The next morning, though, I was more agitated than ever. My old hunger to see my children gnawed at my heart, but so did a thousand doubts. What would we do if we lost this place? What if someone brought the authorities?

I was feeding the chickens, and in the distance I could see Anders and Jens driving slowly through the orchard picking up windfall. In this calm pastoral, I was the snake in the grass.

I thought of the Mormons, driven out of Ohio those many years ago. Their houses burned and their leader killed. My darling flock scurried about my skirts, and I remembered the awful smell of charred meat and feathers.

I could not bear that again.

NORA

May 1881 ■ *At Sea*

Supper on board the *Angelo* the first night of our voyage was peasant fare—tea, bread, salt herring. We gulped it quickly, then made our way topside again.

Up on deck people had gathered in the lingering May twilight. The green hills of the Oslofjord glowed in the dusky haze as the ship made its way south toward the North Sea. Norway at its most beguiling. Those who had hungered to emigrate were now nostalgic for the land they were leaving behind.

Mr. Eriksen stood at the rail, Birgitte next to him, Jens slouched against his legs. I knew Mr. Eriksen was thinking of his wife but doubted he would speak of such things. He carried his grief like a burden on his back, heavy and private.

Tomas slumbered in the shawl I wore tied around my neck as a sling. How strange, to be on this ship with this motherless child in my arms. I was leaving Norway, and my own children, to journey to an unknown country, bound as a servant to a family of strangers beneath my station. Yet what bubbled inside me was the elixir of freedom I felt the night I left Torvald. I had finally escaped him; I never needed to fear him or the vortex of my marriage again.

The light ebbed from the sky. Tomas began to fret, so I took him below for his nighttime flask, glad to have a purpose.

ONCE THE SHIP left the sheltering fjord and headed out across the North Sea, it started to pitch. Soon, nearly everyone was groaning with seasickness. Mr. Eriksen, the only one who seemed impervious, took Tomas for safekeeping while the rest of us rolled about on the sleeping shelves in agony, reaching for the buckets time and again.

At dawn Mr. Eriksen gave us hard crackers to nibble, then took us on deck for fresh air. The wind howled and seawater sluiced across the deck, but we felt better, even if chilled to the bone.

We spent the rest of the crossing to England huddled topside during the day, then confined to the wretchedness below at night. If we worried someone would discover our secret, that was forgotten in the chaos of the journey. Birgitte broke down the third day and sobbed in her father's arms for her lost mother. Though she had treated me with disdain and sullenness, it softened my feelings toward her.

WE STUMBLED ASHORE in Hull on the east coast of England three days later, then endured the long train ride to Liverpool and a nasty night at an emigrant inn that smelled of cabbage and the foul privies down the hall.

Liverpool, with its bands of feral children and dismal tenements, seemed a labyrinth of human misery. It made me worry that America, perhaps Chicago, would be like this—foreign and threatening. Vika had been poor, but it was a poverty I understood. Liverpool was overwhelming.

The next morning we rose early, irritable with exhaustion but anxious to get to the quay to board the oceangoing White Star Line ship to America.

As the others packed up, I fed Tomas his milk, then put him against my shoulder to pat his back. Suddenly, as babies will, he yanked off my kerchief—revealing my bald head.

Birgitte noticed first, yelping with surprise.

Mr. Eriksen turned, then stared. "What is this!" he whispered, his eyes wide with anger. "What in God's name is this?"

I put the baby on the bed and retied the kerchief. I couldn't look at Mr. Eriksen.

He grabbed my shoulders. "Tell me!"

I swallowed hard. "The police raided my rooming house the night before we sailed. They arrested me and the students who lived there."

"The police did this?"

"They wanted me to inform on the students. I refused, so they punished me."

"Christ, I knew there had to be something," he said, turning away. "So you're running from the police."

"No, they let me go because I wasn't their target, but they meant to question me again. I was lucky to be leaving with you."

At this, he swore softly. "Good God, Mrs. Solberg, they could have notified the shipping lines! I'm surprised we weren't arrested on the dock in Kristiania! Don't you think you should have told me?"

Tomas began to howl.

"Mr. Eriksen, the authorities have no reason to think I've left Norway. You must trust me on this."

"How can I trust you when you haven't been honest with me?" He walked away from me, then swung back. "If your problem with the authorities threatens my family, Mrs. Solberg, I will disown you completely."

My chest tightened. What would he think if he knew the truth?

"And I thought you were just the simple clerk you claimed to be . . ."

"I am who I claim to be. Please believe me!" I sank onto the bed. I was a simple clerk, but I also carried a complicated past I couldn't begin to explain. He would disown me the minute I did.

I dropped my head into my hands and sobbed.

That unnerved him. He yelled at Birgitte to tend to Tomas, then paced about the room. Finally, he crouched before me. "Please, Mrs. Solberg, please. I'm sorry. Since my wife died, I've become a desperate man; I fear it will unravel me."

I finally looked at him. "I'm sorry I didn't tell you. It's . . . it's a terrible humiliation."

"Yes, I'm sure it is. I am sorry for you."

"She needn't come with us, Papa," Birgitte said. "I can manage the baby."

"Shush, Birgitte!"

"But if she puts us in danger . . ."

"Enough!"

AFTER A BREAKFAST OF COLD GRUEL, which did little to lift our gloom, we loaded our baggage onto a wagon and followed it down to the vast waterway. I had heard about Liverpool's famous harbor but was still stunned to see it in all its ambitious glory. Clippers and steamers lined the waterfront as far as the eye could see, and many more swung at anchor offshore. Scores of small boats—tugs, ferries, and fishing sloops—plied the Mersey River. Mr. Eriksen took his children by the hand as we crossed the broad esplanade so they wouldn't get swept away in the crowd. I followed like a sheepdog.

At the gangplank, we waited several hours to board, our anxiety building with every minute. Mr. Eriksen stood with his back to me, too angry to acknowledge my presence. Birgitte whispered to Jens. Worry, and the burden of carrying Tomas, left me faint.

But when it was finally our turn, we were quickly waved aboard, like everyone else. Apparently, the officials only cared about filling the ship as efficiently as possible. I wondered how many others in the crowd were traveling with secrets to hide.

A steward led us to a tiny cabin with two tight bunks. We were still in steerage, but on this bigger ship, even the lowest class was afforded a bit of privacy. We crowded in and closed the door.

"I think we're safe," I whispered.

"They could still come for you," said Mr. Eriksen. "Stay here with Tomas, and the rest of us will go topside. If they ask to check your papers, say your husband has them. Perhaps they won't pursue it."

I could only nod, my throat dry. As soon as they were gone, I lay down and pulled the baby close. To come this far only to be put back ashore—I couldn't bear it. I would have to sell my pearls just to get home to Norway, and then I'd have to crawl back to Torvald because I'd have nothing.

And the thought of leaving Tomas now, just as he was getting used to me, made me ache. Why did it feel as if everything good got snatched away from me? How had I blundered into this state, traveling on my wits with a family who barely knew me, who did not trust me?

I lay as still as possible beside the sleeping baby so I could listen to the creaks and banging of the enormous steamship as it prepared to sail. Please, I begged: haul in the gangplank; toss away the lines. Please, before the police knock on the door.

In time, the turbines began to churn, and there were shouts on deck as the sailors cast off. More commotion and banging, then the distinctive blaring of the steam whistle that signaled our departure.

I sat up, still listening, my nerves straining. The ship began to move; I could feel it. I straightened my kerchief.

Next stop, New York.

THE GALLEY OF THE SHIP buzzed that evening with a babble of strange tongues. I recognized Swedes, Germans, and Irish, but there were also people from more distant parts of Europe, Romanians and Hungarians, perhaps.

There was little space on the benches, so Birgitte and I ate first, then gave our seats to Mr. Eriksen and Jens while we escaped back to the cabin with Tomas.

Birgitte, uncomfortable alone with me, insisted on feeding the baby herself, though she was clumsy and had to stop often to mop up the mess.

After a few minutes watching, I spoke up. "This may surprise you, Birgitte, but I also grew up without a mother."

Birgitte didn't look up.

"I'm sorry circumstances have made my intrusion on your family necessary. I know this must be hard for you, losing your mother and your home at the same time."

Birgitte's lower lip began to shake, but she pulled it between her teeth and patted her brother's chin with a rag.

"How old were you when your mother died?" she finally said, still not looking at me.

"An infant—a few days old. I never knew her."

"So you don't know what you lost. I know what I've lost." A tear ran down her cheek, but she rubbed it away, anger radiating from her like heat. "And did you have a servant that moved in with your family and pretended to be your mother?"

"I am not a servant, Birgitte," I said, offended. I wondered if her father had said that to her. Perhaps he thought of me as a servant. "I had a kind nurse who raised me, but she never pretended to be my mother. And I will not pretend to be your mother."

"But you want to be Tomas's mother," Birgitte said. "You talk to him and kiss him, as if he were your own."

"I need to act like his mother while we're on the ship, as your father explained, but I don't think of him as mine. I had my own children, Birgitte. I know the difference."

"How many did you have?"

"How many children? Two boys and a girl."

"What happened to them?"

"I lost them."

Birgitte looked up at me, her nose wrinkling as if she had caught a whiff of something rotten. "What do you mean you lost them? How does a mother lose all her children?"

I took a breath before answering. "You know how easy it is to lose people you love, Birgitte."

She opened her mouth to say more but stopped and looked away.

"It was a terrible shock and a lasting sorrow," I said. Was that a lie? Not really; it was a shock and a sorrow. "I don't like to talk of it."

Birgitte looked down at her brother and patted his chin several more times. "Just promise me you won't try to be Tomas's mother."

"Birgitte, I will be helping your father for one year, and that's not very long. I am sure that when Tomas grows up, he'll think of you as his mother. He won't even remember me."

"I don't like it when you carry him."

"Once we get off this ship, Birgitte, you may carry him all you like."

She hugged him possessively. "I will. He's mine, not yours."

AFTER SUPPER, Birgitte and Jens went off to explore. I meant to follow them topside, but Mr. Eriksen put his hand on my arm. My stomach tightened.

"I need to speak to you." He sat down on the bunk next to Tomas and twisted his hands.

"I am very sorry I did not tell you . . ." I started.

He held up his hand and shook his head. "I just can't quite make you out, Mrs. Solberg. You don't make sense to me, now that I know you a little. Your manners, your poise, your language; it's hard for me to believe you lived in Vika with a bunch of anarchists. You look as if you were wealthy once, maybe recently, but for some reason fell on hard times. You say you lost your family and you wore black in Kristiania, but one would think that kind of loss would strangle a person. To lose your husband and all your children? Yet you move through the world as if you know exactly what you are doing."

The deck seemed to dip beneath me, as if I might slide down a perilous slope and be dumped into the sea. Mr. Eriksen was my only lifeline. If he did not believe me, no one else would.

I leaned toward him. "I swear to you, Mr. Eriksen, I have no idea what I'm doing. I don't know anything about where we are headed, and I don't know how to be of help on a farm, beyond cooking, cleaning, and caring for Tomas. I pray I'll carry my weight rather than become a burden to you, but I don't really know. I did lose my family, all of them, but that was several years ago. And yes, I still grieve, Mr. Eriksen. It's just that it changes. One must find a new life."

He watched me impassively. "It occurred to me you might be one of those America widows. Perhaps you're planning to join your husband once we get to New York."

"I do not have a husband waiting for me in America, Mr. Eriksen. I swear to you. I have no one in America."

We held each other's gaze for a long moment.

"We must trust each other, Mr. Eriksen, mustn't we?" I finally said. "I don't know anything about you, either. I am trusting you are a good man and that what you need from me is honest work. I swear to you that everything I have told you is true. I lost my family; my circumstances in Norway became untenable, and I desperately wanted to go to America to start over."

He looked down at the baby and sighed. "All right, Mrs. Solberg, I will accept your word, for now. I realize we are both taking risks." Then he met my gaze again. "But there are lies of omission that can be just as damaging as what is falsely said. If there is anything else I should know, please do not keep it from me."

I nodded, my throat too tight to speak.

He grunted, then jumped up and banged out the cabin door.

I SAT ON THE BUNK, my head swimming. How could I bear to live with this family for a full year, especially if Mr. Eriksen and Birgitte simmered with resentment the entire time? The trouble with having run away before was that I knew I could do it again. Sometimes I ran and things were worse, sometimes they were better—but they were always different. I didn't want to run away this time, though, now that there was a little child who needed me. And God knew I had nowhere to run. I had been honest about that, at least—there was no one for me in America.

If this was my fresh start, I needed to do better. Tomas stirred, and I tucked another blanket around him. I needed to be true to my word, to do my share and earn my keep. More than anything, I wanted to keep little Tomas safe and fed, warm and loved.

Because if I couldn't care for my own motherless children, I could care for this one. Perhaps this one could redeem me.

THE ATLANTIC proved kinder than the North Sea, the passage easy, the skies clear. When Jens wasn't off exploring with his sister, he often stayed with me and the baby on deck. He desperately wanted to see an iceberg and sat watching for one for hours. I entertained him with folktales and funny stories about three children who lived in a fancy Kristiania town house. Tomas grew rosy in the sun and salt air and soon smiled when I spoke to him. Jens and I spotted seabirds and, one day, porpoises racing alongside, but no icebergs.

Down below, the realities of life traveled with us. Steerage proved crowded and fetid but protected me from discovery. No one cared whether I was the real Mrs. Eriksen. No one seemed to care about anything other than keeping their own family alive.

Supper was a thin soup with bits of pork fat floating on top and break-fast never more than a herring and dry biscuit. I spent hours in a stinking laundry closet that hung out over the side of the ship, washing out Tomas's linens in buckets of seawater. Maybe I was a servant after all.

The baby's diapers did not dry well, and poor Tomas soon developed an alarming rash. Desperate, I asked Mr. Eriksen to do something. He soon returned with a small cup of lard.

"I begged the cook, and he took pity on us," Mr. Eriksen said. He told me the shipping officials worried about the infants on board. "It's an embarrassment to the White Star officials when the children don't survive the voyage," he said.

I flinched at that but quickly removed Tomas's diaper and gently dabbed the grease on his red bottom. It made him smell like a roasted piglet, but I didn't care. Anything to keep him healthy. Then I rubbed a bit into my own chapped hands.

The next night a Polish child sickened and died—of a fever, someone said. In the morning the family gathered by the rail to bury him at sea. The child's body lay on a board, wrapped in sailcloth. The ship's chaplain, his robes blowing in the wind, read the service for the dead while the mother keened. At the end, they tipped the board, and the little bundle slid off into the deep.

I crept to the side of the ship. He was gone, swallowed up by the indifferent ocean.

ALL THE WAY across the wide Atlantic, I watched Birgitte and Jens. Thinking of my own children, I had a hungry curiosity to see how these two would adjust to the loss of their mother. For Birgitte, the journey away from Norway and everything she had known was deeply troubling, each day a raw awakening and more proof of all she had lost when her mother died. Birgitte and I shared a narrow bunk with the baby between us, and at night I could feel the mattress shake with her noiseless sobs. By day, she took sanctuary in her anger, talking little except to her brother and funneling her resentment at me. It was exhausting for all of us.

Jens was different. Though just a young boy, he seemed powered by some deep sense of survival. He often chattered to me about the wondrous voyage and strange people on board. He was buoyed by his love of adventure and found every day a new revelation. He reminded me so much of Ivar sometimes, it brought tears to my eyes.

AFTER NINE DAYS AT SEA, Jens noticed sea grass floating on the swells, and different birds appeared overhead. The children, hoping to spot land, stood at the rail watching the horizon. Mr. Eriksen, however, just stayed in the cabin, sorting through his things as if he was afraid something was missing.

When I went to check on him, he handed me Inge's papers.

"When we get to the immigration authorities, you will need to answer questions as if you were my wife," he said. "Go over these so that you know the answers."

I looked through them, but there was little information to learn. If only I could have talked to Inge, I would have asked a million questions. But Inge was like my mother—a silent, ghostlike figure that shared little about herself. I memorized her place and date of birth, her middle and maiden names. There wasn't much else.

Then Mr. Eriksen handed me a small stack of *Amerikabrev*—letters sent back home by earlier emigrants. Nearly everyone in Norway had relatives who had gone before, and their letters were often passed from family to family in villages back home.

I opened the first letter, releasing a scent of grass and dust. It was from Mr. Eriksen's younger brother, Gustaf, who had immigrated with his wife, Kari, six years earlier to far western Minnesota. The couple we were going to meet.

July 20, 1875: Dear Family, We arrived in Lac qui Parle four months ago. We've taken a claim north of the village on prairie land not far from a lake. We live in a sod house, but as soon as possible I'll build Kari a proper home. We've planted wheat and corn and a large garden. When the wheat comes in, I'll buy a cow and a pig. Kari says hello. Gustaf

Then the next, two years later. *August 1877. Dear Family, We would have written sooner but waited till we had good news. We lost most of our wheat the last two summers to insects and blackbirds, but with corn and fishing we have gotten through the winters. The sod house is warm, and we have a cow. We are very happy that Anders and Inge may join us. We should have a proper house by next year. Kari is with child. Gustaf*

I scanned the others. *We have a son, Hans, born last winter, strong and healthy. A cyclone last month destroyed three houses and killed a woman who ran to save her horse. Sometimes the blizzards last for days and leave chest-deep snow. Kari was pregnant again but lost the child two weeks ago.*

The last letter came with specifics. *Anders, I've saved enough for lumber and will build our house after the spring thaw. You and your family may use the sod house the first winter if you cannot find a farm to buy. We wish you a safe voyage.*

I looked up at Mr. Eriksen. "Does Gustaf know about your wife?"

"I wrote from Lillehammer."

"Will you live in the sod house this winter?"

"Yes, most likely."

I thought of a cottar's hut I visited as a child. A crude hovel, with a fire pit in the middle and a smoke hole open to the wind. Primitive, dark, rimmed with soot. Little more than furs laid on rough benches and a dirt floor underfoot. Is that what a sod house would be like in America?

When I asked Mr. Eriksen about their home in Gudbrandsdalen, he described a comfortable stone farmhouse, with a big hearth and turf roof. They hadn't been poor, just landless after the farm went to his eldest brother.

"Do you worry about living in a dirt house, how it might affect the children?"

He squinted at me. "What do you mean?"

"Well, surely not everyone in the village lives in a dirt house. They might feel ashamed."

He huffed, just once, as if he'd taken my measure. "You're the one who will care, Mrs. Solberg, but you can live with my brother so as to have planks beneath your toes. Maybe even a rag rug."

My face went hot; I had offended him. "Forgive me. I'm sure we'll all have compromises to make." I folded the letters and tucked them back in their envelopes. "How long before we get to Lac qui Parle?"

"The train to Chicago and on to St. Paul will take a week or more, then another day to Montevideo, where we must find a wagon and team. It will take several days from there to walk to Lac qui Parle. I hope my brother will have the wheat planted."

"I fear I won't be the help you need, on the farm, I mean."

"You're quite capable with Tomas, Mrs. Solberg. That is the help I need."

I lowered my head. He had forgiven me.

LATER THAT DAY we sailed into New York Harbor and moored near a looming brick fortress on the tip of Manhattan Island—Castle Garden, the immigration station. We debarked in long lines and were herded into the vast registration room, which teemed with foreigners of every stripe—Poles, Germans, Greeks, and Italians. People napped on benches rolled in blankets like sausages, while others brewed tea on big stoves clustered in the center of the waiting room. Mr. Eriksen went to change his crowns to dollars, and then we queued up for the Scandinavia desk.

When it was our turn, I pinched Tomas to make him fuss, then answered the questions as if I were Inge Eriksen. The official stamped our papers, and within minutes it was done; we had immigrated. Or rather, Inge Eriksen had immigrated.

We were soon ferried across the Hudson River to a vast train depot in New Jersey. A crushing crowd waited for the Chicago train. We had to fight our way on board, Mr. Eriksen and Birgitte elbowing and squeezing through until we found space. I sank down and looked about. Instead of plush seats, there were only wooden benches, as uncomfortable as church pews, and just a rough wash closet at one end of the car. Bags and people were piled everywhere; we could scarcely move. Tomas cried for his milk, and I spilled half a precious can struggling with the suckling flask in the crowded car.

Mr. Eriksen hovered. "I'm worried about the chest. When I asked about it, they did not understand me."

The train lurched forward; the whistle shrieked.

"They lost our chest?" Jens looked up anxiously.

"Don't worry," I said. "I saw them loading the chests in the last car. There were none left on the platform, so ours must be with the others."

"Thank you," Mr. Eriksen said, finally sitting down. "I had not anticipated these difficulties with the language." He shook his head. The things he could not manage chafed at his pride. "As we go west, you must teach us some English, Mrs. Solberg. I just hope Minnesota is thick with Norwegians."

After I fed the baby, I looked out the window. Nothing but dreary marshland, no green mountains anywhere in sight. I felt lightheaded. Would I ever be Nora again? Perhaps she died at sea and was dropped over the rail in a winding sheet. I felt like I was being stripped of all that was familiar—my country, my language, my identity.

Then again, maybe that was the adventure; maybe that was what it took to escape. In the wide-open spaces of America, perhaps I could become the woman I wanted to be—someone valued, someone trusted, someone loved. Someone who belonged to somebody else.

All I had to do was tuck my own children away in my heart and turn my attention to those in front of me.

I gazed at Tomas, my special charge. How grateful I was for him.

ON THE THIRD NIGHT of our journey, the train rattled to a stop somewhere in Ohio. People shifted about on the benches, groaning with frustration. Tomas woke and started to cry. I unwrapped him from the shawl slung across my breast and held him up to look about.

Mr. Eriksen stirred and sat up, then reached a finger out to the child, who took it firmly. "Where are we?" he said, peering out into the blackness. "Is there a town? A station?"

"No. Nothing—just another siding." I could smell pig manure on the warm breeze, though there were only trees out the window.

Birgitte rose, pushed her loose hair from her eyes, and immediately reached for the baby. She often took him from me.

"Thank you," I said, as sweetly as I could. "I'll get his flask, and you can feed him."

We had been trapped on this dilapidated train since leaving New York, cinders and smoke seeping in through windows cracked for air, our bones aching from the hard benches. Several times a day the train stopped inexplicably, often for hours at a time, then just as mysteriously chugged to life and rumbled on. No one explained anything, and we never stopped at stations—just to fill up at the occasional watering tank. I had heard about the trains at the shipping office in Kristiania but never imagined they could be this bad. They had one purpose: to carry the stream of foreigners from the docks of New York straight through to Chicago. On board, the toilets reeked, and the water reservoirs went stale. At night the Eriksens and I lay down as best we could, Birgitte and I each on a bench, Jens and Mr. Eriksen curled on the floor between us. No one slept much, except the baby.

During the day the journey was easier to bear, but only because we could watch the countryside change, as if unwrapping a gift from a stranger. The marshes of New Jersey gave way to the forests and rocky outcroppings of New York State. The mountain areas looked more like Norway, but the towns were surprisingly poor. Shoddily built shanties and dirty villages popped up along the tracks, only to vanish as the train swept past. We rumbled through several small cities, with granite buildings and nicer houses, but mostly the landscape was dotted with poor farms.

Now that we were out in the great American middle, cultivated fields stretched like a lumpy quilt to the horizon. The farms began to appear more prosperous; probably the soil was better. Jens pointed out engineering marvels—canals, bridges, telegraph wires—and asked for the English words for everything he saw. I tried to teach the family some rudimentary phrases, though my vocabulary was limited. Birgitte grumbled through the first few lessons but took to it nonetheless. Mr. Eriksen found it much harder. The little English he knew failed him when he needed it most. I was the only one who could speak for us.

AFTER OUR NIGHT on the siding in Ohio, the gentle hillocks disappeared and the land flattened, though there were still occasional stands of trees.

"Is this the prairie?" I asked. We were all weary and eager to get to Minnesota.

Mr. Eriksen looked out. "No. The prairie is flat like this, but there's only grass. No trees."

"No trees?" I couldn't imagine a world without trees.

"Only in the river bottoms and along the lakes, where the roots can find water."

"But your brother's house is near a lake, yes?"

Mr. Eriksen nodded. "And there will be some trees—as long as the other settlers haven't chopped them all down to build their huts."

Birgitte heard this and started whispering to Jens. This bothered me, but I didn't complain, as Mr. Eriksen never seemed to notice how often she did it. He was deeply preoccupied by the challenges to come and watched the landscape with a furrowed brow.

Two more days, and we still hadn't made it to Chicago. America must be vast beyond imagining, I said to Jens, who nodded solemnly. Traveling through this immense land stretched my bond back to Norway almost to breaking. I felt like an explorer going over the horizon. Would anything ever feel like home again? Would I ever see my children again, or even hear of them? Would I ever hear of poor Tobias or Erlend? I tried not to think about all of them back in Kristiania, though the boredom of the trip left my mind with little else to do.

My scalp itched as a stubble of hair began to grow in. Tomas fretted; our clothes soured. We divided our last bit of sausage as if performing a sacred ritual.

FINALLY—when it felt as if America would never end—the train pulled into Chicago, a huge depot choked with trains and enormous piles of coal and lumber. The Eriksens and I stepped off, stiff as old people, and Mr. Eriksen went to find our chest. I looked around. There was something new here, something I had never felt before—a hot wind blowing through, as if the Wild West crouched just beyond. I said this to Birgitte, but the girl turned away, tears in her eyes. She had come too far from Gudbrandsdalen and her mother's grave.

A horse cart carried us through the city to the western depot, the start of the rail line to Minnesota. The streets were thick with people—clerks and ladies in city dress picking their way past ragged street children, laborers in overalls, and uniformed maids out on errands. Jens and Birgitte watched, transfixed. To my relief, it felt different from Liverpool, brighter, with a breeze blowing in off the lake. We crossed the Chicago River, past blocks of rickety tenements, and then came to a more civilized section— brick houses, stone office buildings, shops. The city stretched forever in each direction, a beehive of people and industry.

When we got to the western train station, we had two hours before our train, so I offered to go find a market.

"You're not afraid?" Mr. Eriksen said.

"No." My pulse quickened with excitement at the thought of walking about on my own. But I didn't tell him that. "I'll be fine."

He handed me a few coins. "Bread, some fresh cheese, a sausage, milk."

And then I walked out into the swirling crowd and under the wide blue sky. Chicago! I stood on the corner for a long moment, soaking in the strangeness of the city and wishing Tobias were here to see it. The city felt as if it had no roof, as if anything could happen.

I remembered Tobias telling me the Norwegian community was on the west side of the city. I looked around. Perhaps it was nearby.

I crossed the street and headed out, dodging wagons and buggies. I soon found a market and was pleased to see signs in German and Danish. I asked the butcher if there was a Norwegian quarter nearby.

"Go over to Halsted," he said, pointing. "Then up to Milwaukee Avenue. About five blocks."

I paid for my groceries, then stepped out onto the sidewalk. Did I dare?

There was time, and Mr. Eriksen need not know, I reasoned. I walked a few blocks, passing a tavern where I heard a man shouting in Norwegian. In a few more blocks, all the signs were in Norwegian.

I stepped into a dress shop. The woman behind the counter was talking with a customer in my own tongue.

I listened, trying to place her. From Telemark, probably, yet she seemed remarkably worldly. When her customer left, she turned to me.

"Newly immigrated?"

"Yes, from Kristiania," I replied. She glanced at my homespun skirt. No one in Chicago, not even the Norwegians, wore anything like it. They were city folk, with city fashions.

She smiled anyway. "Welcome." Then she handed me a newspaper, the *Skandinaven*—in Norwegian. "Free to newcomers."

"Thank you." I nodded politely, then turned away. I longed to chat, but if I did I was afraid I wouldn't return to the Eriksens.

Back outside, however, I couldn't resist walking up Milwaukee Avenue, peeking in shop windows and reading postings for rooms and jobs. A plan flickered inside me. When my obligation to the Eriksens was done, I would return to Chicago and get work in a shop, like the woman from Telemark. I'd save money, rebuild my life, and then return to Norway for my children—when they were old enough to choose for themselves.

All of a sudden, I noticed the sun had dropped. I had to hurry or I would miss the train. And if I did? Possibilities crowded into my head, but I shook myself. I had given Mr. Eriksen my word. I hadn't come to America to degrade into something worse than I was in Norway. I would not abandon them.

I rushed back to the station, anxiety mounting as I neared the platform. With relief I spotted them, Mr. Eriksen pacing about and Birgitte struggling with Tomas, who wailed with hunger.

I ran up, smiling as if everything was fine.

But Mr. Eriksen wasn't fooled. "Where did you go? I gave you money, and you vanished!"

"I'm back now, Mr. Eriksen. I'm sorry I worried you."

"You've been gone more than an hour!"

"Look!" I held up the bag. "I found the market, and I found the Norwegian quarter. Here—a newspaper, in Norwegian!"

Mr. Eriksen ignored the paper and instead looked deep into my eyes. "You mean to stay in Chicago."

I reddened. "No. I will not run from my obligation, Mr. Eriksen. I'm not that kind of person." I paused to breathe. "I just wanted to see if there really was a Norwegian neighborhood."

"The problem, Nora, is I don't know who you are or why you've agreed to our bargain. I can see now I've been expecting something like this."

"Well, you needn't worry. I won't do that." I sounded surer than I felt, but I had to convince him. "Please forgive me."

The conductor unlocked the compartment doors. Mr. Eriksen handed me the baby.

He had called me Nora.

THE GREAT NORTHERN RAILCAR had padded seats and fresh water, which made the next two days easier. We pulled into St. Paul late in the afternoon. Like Chicago, the city bustled with construction projects, buildings of brick and granite rising on every corner. Yet St. Paul felt more civilized, with tree-lined streets and gentle hills above the Mississippi River. Norwegians and Swedes walked among the Americans as if they owned the place.

We found a room for the night and collapsed into real beds. The next morning we boarded yet another train, passing through land that grew flatter and drier, with fewer towns and farms. The trees soon disappeared, except those growing in the sunken trace of the Minnesota River. Then I began seeing mounds of turf, widely spaced; with a start I realized some had doors and windows—they must be sod houses. They looked like animal burrows.

Mr. Eriksen watched the landscape unfold. When the train raced along the river, we could see that the water ran high—rain, perhaps, or heavy snowmelt. Beyond the river, the prairie stretched away to tomorrow, flooded sloughs twinkling in the sun.

FINALLY, Montevideo, the end of the line. We climbed down and headed out to find a store and livery. The town felt strangely empty, as if we had traveled to the very edge of civilization. A tall Swede with a red beard greeted us in Norwegian at the livery, a relief for Mr. Eriksen, who sent the rest of us across to the general store to get provisions.

The store also felt empty. The shelves were mostly bare, and the shopkeeper was thin and pale. I smiled and asked what she could offer.

The shopkeeper put cornmeal, salt pork, and beans on the counter. "We usually carry more things, but we've barely restocked since winter. The trains are only now getting through."

"The winter was hard?"

She stared at me. "You must be new."

"Yes, we're going to, to homestead?" I wasn't sure of the word.

The woman nodded, then sighed.

"Near Lac qui Parle," I said.

"Well, you're brave folk. Some people are heading back east."

That gave me pause. "But it's beautiful land," I said, watching her face.

"Looks can be deceiving." She glanced at the children. "But I don't want to discourage you. A winter like we've had probably won't happen again for a hundred years." She reached for a bag of seed potatoes. "You'll be wanting to plant these. There's still time to get them in the ground."

I opened my mouth to ask what she meant about the winter, but Mr. Eriksen called from the door. "Come! The oxen won't stand still for long."

"Oxen!" Jens yipped, then shot out the door.

I paid and gathered our things.

"There's something odd about this town," Mr. Eriksen said, taking the groceries from me. "It's as if no one lives here."

"Apparently they had a rough winter."

"The Swede had several teams for me to choose from, since some families sold theirs back to him when they left after a bad blizzard in October."

We stepped outside, and my heart stopped. There was Jens, standing in front of a pair of horned beasts as big as mountain trolls, tugging at their halters and rubbing their noses. I grabbed for the boy, afraid the oxen would step on him.

But Mr. Eriksen just laughed. "Cattle love Jens, and this team seems fairly well trained." He helped me onto the seat, handed me the baby, and climbed up beside me. Jens and Birgitte clambered onto a buckboard behind. "Let's see if this team understands Norwegian," he said, and with a smack of the reins we jolted forward.

MONTEVIDEO soon dropped behind us, and the road faded to a rutted track. The wagon clattered slowly along; the tall grass undulated in the breeze, like waves.

Birgitte surveyed the endless plain and sighed. "I never thought there would be no mountains at all," she said. "There aren't even any trees, except those by the river. It doesn't look anything like Norway."

I didn't know what to tell her. The prairie had a strange, ethereal beauty—with its bright-green grass, distant horizon, and enormous sky, brushed now with vermillion as the sun sank. But there was also a silence as deep, vast, and indifferent as the sea.

One could not help feeling very small in such a place.

THAT NIGHT we camped near the river so that Jens and Mr. Eriksen could catch fish for our supper. Birgitte cut prairie grass, which I stuffed into the two bed ticks. We spread the ticks on the ground under the wagon, then topped them with blankets. I spotted a small snake in the brush, which made me jump. Birgitte chased it away, laughing at me, then pointed out other holes in the sod. Who knew what might come out at night to sniff our hair?

Mr. Eriksen and Jens returned with several small trout. We built a fire, made porridge, fried the fish, and ate them with our fingers, like savages. No one cared. We were all lost in the immensity of the prairie and the task before us—to learn how to live in this new world. After night fell, I fed Tomas his milk, crept under the wagon with him, and tried to settle on the rough mattress. I had never slept outside in my life and could barely face the prairie in the dark. I curled tight around the baby and tried to imagine myself back in Vika.

THE NEXT MORNING we pushed off again into the sea of grass. Jens asked to drive the team, so he sat on the wagon seat with me, telling me about the animals at their farm in Norway and how he hoped we might soon get cows and pigs here, in America. Birgitte, walking with her father, turned several times to glare at him. She didn't like it when Jens talked to me about their life in Gudbrandsdalen.

As we trundled farther west, the prairie began to fill me with a mysterious weight, like a stone set gently on my chest. The emptiness, the crudeness of the life; I wondered if I would be able to bear it. In my America dream, I had always imagined a city life, not unlike my life in Kristiania. Snug apartments or little houses, with warm rugs on the floors and pianos in every parlor. Educated people, modern conveniences. I might have to work as a governess or companion, but it would be in gentle circumstances.

But there didn't seem to be any evidence of a life like that out here.

LATE THE SECOND DAY a small wooden sign appeared just off the edge of the track. There was no other sign of life around. It pointed to the right, to Lac qui Parle village. Mr. Eriksen climbed up onto the wagon seat, taking the reins from Jens with trembling hands. "Soon," he said. "We're almost there."

The track dipped toward a line of low trees, and then we could see the lake in the distance, bulrushes at one end. We rounded a bend, and a town appeared: a short main street, just two blocks long, flanked by wooden buildings. We passed a bank and general store and could see up ahead a livery, two saloons, and a hotel. Some had Norwegian names.

Like Montevideo, the town seemed unusually quiet. Perhaps the men were out in the fields. We stopped in front of the hotel, and Mr. Eriksen asked me to accompany him inside, in case I must translate.

The man behind the desk looked up and greeted us in Norwegian.

Mr. Eriksen nodded politely. "We're looking for Gustaf Eriksen's place," he said. "We understand it is northwest of town."

The man peered at us. "Will you be buying the place, then?"

"No," Mr. Eriksen said, puzzled. "He's my brother."

There was a long silence. "Yes," the man finally said. "We heard you were coming."

"What is it?" said Mr. Eriksen. "What's wrong? Is he ill?"

The man shook his head. "No, not ill. Your brother is dead, I am sorry to tell you. He and his family starved to death last winter. They were found in April."

My breath caught in my throat. Mr. Eriksen clutched the edge of the counter.

"They weren't the only ones who died around here," the man continued. "We had terrible cold, unrelenting. James Renville, the Indian that lives down near the old mission, he found them. He was their friend—took them food sometimes."

"No, you must be mistaken," Mr. Eriksen stammered. "We have a letter from him!"

"I'm sorry, sir. We're coming out of the worst winter anyone's ever seen. The blizzards started early and never let up. The snow drifted twenty feet in places, and the trains couldn't get through to resupply the towns. The lucky ones left before Christmas. Some families survived on nothing but turnips; others didn't even have that." He stopped to let us absorb this news, then shook his head again. "They're buried in a small plot near their soddie, toward the lake, in a stand of trees."

Mr. Eriksen's face hardened. "Please tell us how to get there."

The hotel keeper pulled out a map and showed us which track to follow. "It's not much of a place. The sod house sits where the tableland breaks toward the lake."

"There's no frame house?"

"No. Most of these farmers had such a tough time with the drought and grasshoppers a few years back, they still can't afford lumber. You'll see the fields first, not that there's anything in them."

Mr. Eriksen nodded.

"If you want to take over his claim, you'll have to talk to the land surveyor in Montevideo. You might want to check with Mr. Pearsall—that's the law office across the street."

Mr. Eriksen thanked him, and then we stepped outside.

"I cannot believe it," he said. "I hope they're mistaken. We must go see."

"What is it, Papa?" Birgitte asked. "What's the matter?"

"Silence, Birgitte. Nora, take the baby."

MR. ERIKSEN led the oxen so I couldn't see his face. My mind skittered about like a frightened rabbit—a family freezing and starving to death in their own home? How could Mr. Eriksen bring his family to such a place? Then, crowding in quickly, the complications for me. If Gustaf and Kari were gone, I would have nowhere to live. It was one thing to pretend to be Mr. Eriksen's wife on the ship, but I could not live with him in his house, sod or not.

We bumped over the faint track; few had come this way. The land sloped toward the lake, broken by small creeks and exposed banks. The track turned; the oxen stopped. There, stretching out before us, were several fields of broken ground, with a low sod house tucked against a bank beyond. Mr. Eriksen walked out into the first field and kicked at the dirt. "Just weeds," he said grimly.

He turned to the children. "Stay here until I call for you."

"What is it?" Birgitte said, panic in her voice.

"I don't know yet," he said. I handed her the baby and then walked with Mr. Eriksen down the track toward the small, oddly shaped house. The back half appeared to be a dugout built into the hillside. Sod bricks extended the little house in front, with a roof of branches covered by more sod bricks. A stovepipe stuck through the roof at one end. In front was a crude wooden door beside a window opening covered with dirty parchment. A few yards down the trail where the hill deepened, another sod building—rougher, windowless—stood out from the bank. Perhaps the barn.

Mr. Eriksen called a *hallo*, but we both knew there was no one inside. Between the house and the barn the trail was thick with hay underfoot, as if someone had brought a haystack inside. Mr. Eriksen looked at me and cleared his throat. Then he opened the door.

Inside it was so dim we could barely see anything at first, and then Mr. Eriksen pulled a fold of blanket away from the parchment window. Yellow light seeped in.

"Dear God," he whispered.

It looked like the scene of a crime and smelled of the grave. Crockery lay tumbled on the floor, and a filthy hay tick slouched against the wall, dry grass spilling from a rent down the middle. Grit covered everything, as if the place had been long abandoned. There was little furniture beyond the rusted stove and a rosemaled wedding chest, which stood beneath the window. An open Bible lay on top, facedown.

Mr. Eriksen picked it up. "Gustaf's—here's his confirmation name and date."

If this was all the family had when they died, it was precious little. Newspaper pages had been pinned to one wall, as if to serve as wallpaper, but they did little to hide the ugly sod. The grass of the bricks had dried to a pale yellow sandwiched between the darker dirt. I suddenly started shivering. The chill and closeness of the soddie, the primitive quality of it all. To the left of the door was a pile of tins and pans. Yet other things they should have had were missing—there was no wooden counter, no butter churn or spinning wheel, no flour barrel. The house must have been stripped by someone, yet they had taken only, only . . . My mind reeled.

Mr. Eriksen pulled back the faded calico cloth that separated the front room from the bedroom. "They even burned the bedstead," he said, his voice hoarse with emotion.

"What do you mean?"

"Can't you see it? Nearly everything that would burn—that was not precious to them, like the chest and Bible—is gone. No table, no chairs, no shelves." He pointed out grooves in the dirt floor where furniture once stood. "Gustaf was a gifted carpenter. Surely he built what they needed." He opened the stove, then pulled out bits of charred grass. "In the end they were burning hay. It couldn't have given much heat."

A few clothes, black with grime, hung from a nail. I could see why the sod house felt like a grave—the back wall was solid dirt and smelled of fungus and melting snow.

Mr. Eriksen picked up a leather jerkin with Norwegian tooling on the front, a woman's stained skirt, and a child's knitted cap. Then he buried his face in them and began to weep. He fell to his knees.

I desperately wanted to touch his shoulder or reassure him somehow, but I didn't dare interrupt his private grief. I stepped back around the curtain and over to the corner with the tins and pots. As quietly as possible, I looked through them. Nothing, not a seed. A large spider scuttled along the wall and backed into a crevice.

I couldn't breathe. I plunged through the door and ran several steps, gulping air. Gentle afternoon light poured down around me, and a warm breeze bathed my face. I burst into tears. I could hardly bear the contradiction between the loveliness of the land and the squalid life of this family. I could scarcely imagine their last months, the snow piled as high as the roof, the stove going cold, their strength ebbing. I wondered who died first, then pushed the thought from my mind. It made no difference. They were gone, and our life out on this prairie was going to be very different from what we had imagined.

After a time Mr. Eriksen came out, his face grim. "We must tell the children."

Birgitte and Jens stood nervously beside the wagon. "Papa, what is it?" Birgitte shrieked when she saw his face.

"Quiet, Birgitte," he said. "Your uncle and aunt died this past winter. I am sorry."

Birgitte stiffened and pulled away. "How? How could that happen? And what of little Hans?" Jens looked at his sister's panicked face and began to cry.

"Hans died as well. They starved to death during the hard winter."

"Then why did you bring us here?" Birgitte screamed, backing away from her father's consoling hands. "First Mama and now them! We'll all die! We'll all starve!" She flailed at him with her fists.

He caught her hands and held her. "Gentle, child, gentle!"

She broke into heaving sobs.

"These are terrible misfortunes, I grant you that, Birgitte," he said. "But it doesn't mean we will starve. The past winter was very severe. People died because the trains couldn't get through the snowdrifts to bring food. That won't happen most winters."

I stood to the side, touched by the care their father gave them. He sat on the ground and took them into his lap, stroking their hair until they stopped weeping.

Tomas, kicking on a blanket in the grass, started to fuss, pulling me back to the day before me. I prepared his flask; the Eriksens finally stood.

"I must find their graves," Mr. Eriksen said. "Nora, children, prepare a camp, and do not go near the sod house."

"Why not?" asked Birgitte, wiping her eyes.

"Do as I say." He walked off.

He had called me Nora again.

CHAPTER TWELVE

SOLVI

March 1919 ■ *Kristiania, Norway*

"No," said Rikka. "That's hideous. You look consumptive."

Solvi had already tried on five dresses, none of them to Rikka's liking. She turned back to the dressing room.

"Try the one with flounces," Rikka called.

But when Solvi came out, Rikka wrinkled her nose. "Makes you look like a child's toy, all dolled up."

Solvi went to the rack and pulled out a pale-green gown trimmed with satin ribbon, sheer at the top with a heavier drape below. "I like this one."

"Only witches wear green," Rikka said.

"Well, I'm trying it." Solvi disappeared into the dressing room.

When Solvi emerged again, the shop clerk stepped over. "Lovely, miss. Just a string of pearls, and that's all you need."

"Thank you. I think I'll take it," Solvi said. She slipped back into the dressing room, then reemerged in her street clothes. The clerk took the gown to wrap.

"Just a string of pearls," Rikka said, mocking the woman's nasal tones.

"Rikka, what's the matter with you?"

"You must have pearls," Rikka said. "All well-bred girls from Bergen have a string of pearls."

Solvi thought of her mother trying to bribe her to marry Stefan. "I do not have pearls, Rikka."

"Well, too bad. The other girls at the club dance will, I can assure you."

"Rikka, what is this about?"

Rikka puffed out her cheeks, then sighed. "I just don't understand why you think you'll enjoy this dance at Dominik's club. The only people there will be his rich friends and their stupid girlfriends."

"That's open-minded of you," Solvi said. "You sound jealous."

Rikka gave her a dry laugh. "Hardly."

"Then why are you angry with me?"

"Because you're going off to a dance with the bourgeoisie, Solvi. Only the boys from the best families live at Dominik's club. People like Magnus are not allowed."

"That's hard to believe. His father's a legislator."

"His father was a shipwright; he represents labor. Magnus could never join Dominik's club and would never want to."

"I'm just going to a dance, Rikka. Nothing more; it hardly matters."

"But it all matters, Solvi," Rikka said. "Every time you go someplace where your other friends aren't invited, you escape into the comfort of your class."

Solvi paid for her new dress and tucked the package under her arm. "Well, if it makes you feel any better, I'm poor again now."

"What I don't understand, Solvi, is why you're going out with Dominik while leading Magnus along."

Solvi spun around. "Who says I'm leading Magnus along? We're just friends. He's helping me, he's . . ."

"Exactly," Rikka said. "He would be quite hurt if he heard you were going to this club dance with Dominik."

"Why does he need to know?"

Rikka nodded. "See? This is the problem—hiding and keeping secrets from people."

"Are you suggesting I tell Magnus?"

"Yes. If you're seeing Dominik, tell Magnus, before he hears it from someone else."

Solvi felt her face redden. "Rikka, don't. Please don't. It would only hurt him."

"If you knew it would hurt Magnus, then maybe you should have thought twice before letting Dominik sweep you off your feet."

"No one has swept me off my feet. I'm standing right here."

Rikka just harrumphed and headed out the door.

SOLVI SPENT ANOTHER MORNING in the newspaper archives, and then she and Magnus got fish sandwiches from a stand and found a park bench for their picnic. The day was blustery, and Solvi's curls flew about her head in the wind.

"What did Mr. Blehr mean when he said I could start work as a journalist right away?" Solvi asked. "I don't know nearly enough about the world, and I'm just learning how to take pictures. Does he say that to you?"

Magnus nodded. "Every day. He gets very annoyed when I waste my time in lectures, as he puts it, but I'm determined to finish my degree. It helps me over the class barrier. Education obscures those lines."

"I was thinking the other day, Magnus, how little you talk about yourself," Solvi said. "Tell me about your family."

"Well, my mother and younger siblings are back in Molde . . ."

"On the coast? So you have fog in your veins as well!"

He laughed. "I do, but my father and I share a small flat here now. He lives with me when the Storting's in session."

"Rikka said your father's a labor leader."

"Yes. He started in the shipyards but soon rose in the labor movement. But he's not a member of the gentry, despite being in the Storting." Magnus gave her a sad smile. "He's got calluses on his hands."

"My father had calluses, too, Magnus. He did all the planting and tending of his greenhouse."

"But still, Solvi, you know what I mean—my people are not like your people."

She fell silent, not sure how to bridge the divide. Or if she should even try. "Magnus, I'm so sorry."

He held up his hand. "No, Solvi. There's no need." Then he stood up, suddenly awkward with her. "I'll guess I'll see you in class."

"Magnus," Solvi said. "Thank you. You've been so kind to me."

He smiled, but the touch of sadness deepened. "My pleasure," he said, bowing slightly. Then he turned on his heel, leaving her alone in the sun and the wind.

A FEW DAYS LATER, Solvi knocked on the door of Mr. Blehr's office. "Do you have a moment? I have some pictures," Solvi asked.

"Of course, Miss Lange." He shoved his papers aside, and Solvi carefully laid out her photographs of the Vika children. She was proud of them; she hoped he would like them.

He examined them one by one, then looked up at her. "What took you to Vika, Miss Lange?"

"I went with a friend who works with the women's health auxiliary."

Mr. Blehr pushed the pictures around, selecting one, then another.

"These children seem so hopeless, yet they are still children," Solvi said, nervously. "I was trying to show that."

"Children are, by nature, usually hopeful. But this—." He tapped the photo of the children fighting over the crust of bread as they turned to the camera. "This moment of high jinks and the hunger beneath it captures both their hope and their grim reality." He looked at Solvi with a fresh appreciation. "Not everyone can capture that disparity."

"Thank you, sir."

"Nice work, Miss Lange. May I keep these for now? There's a story here, but I need to talk to my writers." He looked through the photographs again. "How do you do it, Miss Lange? How do you get them to let you into their life this way?"

"I'm not sure," Solvi said. "I suppose children are easy. Most people ignore them, especially poor children. If I talk with them, then show them the camera and how it works, they're usually happy to let me take their picture." She stopped for a moment. "They're not ashamed of their poverty, because they know nothing better. Their mothers, though, they are ashamed. It's harder with them."

"Could you get me more, Miss Lange? And try for some of those mothers, as well as the scene down there—the houses, the streetscape. Even the rats, if you can catch them. But mostly more children. Drop the photos off, and we'll talk again."

DOMINIK SMILED and handed Solvi a narrow glass with something fizzing. "Don't drink it too fast—there's brandy in there."

Solvi took a sip, more than she meant to. It was delicious, so she sipped some more. The room, hazy with cigarette smoke, swayed around her. The dining hall of Dominik's residence had been arranged as a nightclub, with the rug rolled out of the way and the tables pushed to the far end. Several musicians played popular tunes while a woman with painted eyes and a fringed dress fluttered a fan and sang.

Dominik led Solvi to a table. "Your gown is very pretty on you," he said. "But why did you put your hair up?"

Solvi patted the French twist at the back of her head. She spent an hour getting it right, hoping to look more sophisticated. "Don't you like it?"

Dominik reached out and, before she could stop him, pulled out the pins holding the twist in place. Her Isolde curls tumbled down around her shoulders. "There, that's better," he said.

"Dominik!" She laughed nervously. "Don't you think you should have asked first?"

"You would have said yes," he said.

"I might not have. I liked it up."

"With your hair down you look wild and free."

"I look twelve."

"Are you older than that?" Dominik pulled back in surprise. "*Quelle horreur!*"

Solvi had never wanted to swat anyone in her life, but she had to sit on her hands to keep from swatting this boy. "Honestly, Dominik . . ."

Two other couples sat down, the girls with their hair piled high on their heads. Solvi combed her curls with her fingers and tried to pull them to one side. She noticed with relief that neither girl was wearing pearls.

Dominik leaned over and whispered in her ear. "You're the prettiest!"

Solvi couldn't help smiling. Why couldn't she stay angry with him?

"Introduce us, Dominik," said a young man with a thin mustache. His date, a plump girl with huge eyes lined in kohl, hung on his arm.

"This is Solvi Lange, boys," Dominik said. "From the provinces, I'm afraid."

"I'm from Bergen, Dominik," Solvi said. She gave him a sidelong scowl but then couldn't help laughing.

The other boys bowed. "Don't mind Dominik, Miss Lange," said one of them. "An Arctic explorer adopted him in Greenland, then sent him to live with the family he claims are his parents here in Kristiania. Don't be fooled! He's really quite a heathen—perhaps even an Eskimo."

Everyone laughed. "And what are you doing here in Kristiania, Miss Lange?" one of the other boys asked. The girls said nothing—just watched Solvi over their cocktails.

"I'm studying at the university," Solvi said proudly.

Two of the boys pulled back in mock amazement. "A university girl," said the one with the mustache. "Dominik, I thought you avoided the smart ones. Didn't you say they talk back too much?"

"Well, I'm trying to modernize myself," Dominik said. "Besides, Solvi hardly looks like your average university girl." He turned to her. "Let's dance, Solvi. Get away from these apes."

He guided her onto the floor and took her in his arms. "Thank you for letting down your hair," he said, tugging it gently from behind.

"You let it down, Dominik."

"That was rather forward of me, wasn't it?"

"Yes. I'm still angry."

"Then I apologize," he said, with a little bow. "I'm famous for doing things without considering the consequences. It's my only flaw."

He stepped on her toe, then had trouble finding the beat again.

"Your only flaw?" Despite herself, Solvi started giggling.

"Now you're laughing at me." He spun her around, then pulled her close. "My plan is to keep you guessing so you don't run off with someone else." He stumbled again.

"Dominik, are you drunk, or is this how Eskimos dance?"

He pulled back and gazed into her eyes. "I wouldn't say drunk. I'm happy, Solvi, happy that you're here with me." He twirled her away.

A FEW HOURS LATER, Solvi glanced at her watch. If she didn't start home soon, she would miss the eleven o'clock curfew. Matron recently extended it just for Saturdays, at the request of the girls, but wasn't happy about it. She'd be quite angry if Solvi was late.

Dominik sat with his back to Solvi, deep into an argument with a friend about the factions in Russia, something Solvi knew little about.

On Solvi's other side, the girl with the kohl eyes chattered about a trip to Copenhagen with her parents. "I don't know why anyone would shop in Kristiania anymore," she said. "Everything here looks like it was made by someone's grandmother."

Solvi tapped Dominik's arm. "I need to go. I've got curfew."

Dominik looked at her quizzically. "Oh, right. Too bad, Solvi. The party's just getting going." He pulled out his cigarette case. "Have another, my sweet, and then I'll take you back, promise."

Solvi already had a headache from several cigarettes and too many cocktails. "Dominik, if I'm not there by eleven I'll get kicked out, and then I'd have nowhere to live. I'd have to go back to the provinces."

"You could live with us here, in the club," said Dominik, lighting a cigarette and taking a gulp of his drink. He had had several more than Solvi and appeared to have lost his jacket and tie. "You could sleep with the servant girls in the attic," he said. "You like servant girls, I think."

He turned to his friends. "Solvi says we have enslaved our housemaids. She's hoping to liberate them. She takes photographs of them doing horrific jobs, like laundry."

Several boys laughed; Solvi flushed, then stood up. "Are you going to be a gentleman and walk me home?"

"I'm sorry, Solvi. Did that make you mad?" Dominik glanced around. "Better find my jacket. Always that north-wind nip in the air." He smiled at her. "Run away with me to the Amazon, Solvi. At least we'd be warm."

"I'm getting my coat. I'll wait at the door."

By the time he appeared, Solvi was walking away by herself. He ran after her, grabbing her hand and then pulling her at a run through the streets.

"We'll make it," he yelled. "Trust me!"

But when they got to the study house, the lights were off and the door locked.

SOLVI STOOD BEFORE THE BUILDING, breathless and angry. "Oh, Dominik, I can't believe you made me miss curfew . . ."

Dominik looked up at the bedroom windows. "Me? I ran as fast as I could, Solvi. You were the slow one, in those heels."

She felt sick to her stomach and shook her head in despair.

"Just kidding, Solvi. Come on, don't be like that. There must be some other way in. Which one is Rikka's room?"

"It's in the back, on the third floor. But perhaps . . ." She crept through the bushes and around the corner of the building, trying to remember if she left her window unlatched.

Dominik crashed after her, tripping on branches. "Maybe we can climb in."

"Shhh," she said, then stopped below her own window. "I need to climb this tree."

"Is that your window?" he said, in a stage whisper. "Is it open?"

"It might be," Solvi said.

"I'll go first," he said, swinging up into the branches. He braced his feet, then reached down to help her. She stepped up onto a branch; her skirt snagged on something, then gave way as it tore. Her heart sank. How did she get here, climbing up to her room after curfew and ruining her first perfect dress?

But Dominik just grinned. "See? Isn't this fun? Bet I can climb higher than you." He swung up to the branch that reached toward the window and carefully shimmied out until he got his toes on the ledge.

The window opened. Solvi, looking up from below, gasped.

"God damn you, Dominik, why did you keep her out so late?" It was Rikka. "Get out of the way so I can help her in."

"Can't I come in too?"

"No, and if you don't move, I'll knock you off that branch."

He slid down to another limb, then helped Solvi to the window.

Rikka looked into her face. "Are you okay?"

"Yes, just . . ." Rikka grabbed her elbows and pulled her in over the sill.

Solvi found her feet, pulled her dress down, and looked out at Dominik. "Thank you for the evening," she said.

He leaned toward her. "Give me a kiss, Solvi, for all my trouble."

"No," said Rikka, elbowing Solvi out of the way. "You don't deserve a kiss. Just be quiet getting out of here." Then she yanked the window closed.

"YOU DIDN'T HAVE TO BE SO RUDE to Dominik, Rikka," Solvi said, checking to make sure Dominik got to the ground, then turning to examine her skirt. It was streaked with dirt and torn around the satin ribbon of the hem.

"Excuse me?" Rikka said, cocking her head. "Did you want to kiss him? I'm sorry. I just assumed—as he brought you home drunk and after curfew, which meant you had to climb a tree to get back into your room—that you probably weren't in a kissing mood."

"How do you know what mood I'm in, Rikka? You're worse than my mother!"

"Well, if you're going to behave like that, then you need a mother! You could have gotten killed climbing that tree in the state you're in."

Solvi tried to shake the ache out of her head. "That's rich coming from you, Rikka. You climb that tree all the time!"

"Yes, but I know what I'm doing."

"Well, Dominik helped me up, and here I am, just fine."

"Except you've ripped your dress," Rikka said, sinking onto the bed with a huff. "When I realized you'd missed curfew, I came up here and waited for you, Solvi Lange, as your friend. What would you have done if I hadn't? The window was latched tight."

Solvi sat and dropped her head in her hands. "I don't know. I'm sorry, Rikka. Thank you for helping, for waiting for me. I just don't want you to be angry with Dominik."

Rikka leaned forward. "Solvi, I don't know why you're defending him.

Dominik is, oh, I don't know—he's irresponsible, he takes advantage of people, he's selfish. He's not good enough for you. Can't you see that?"

"What I see is a handsome, spoiled boy, but a good one underneath. He says and does things before he thinks, that's all. He needs someone like me, someone steady. And he's brilliant, Rikka; you said so yourself."

"I don't see what he has that Magnus doesn't have."

"This isn't about Magnus."

"That's part of the problem. It should be about Magnus."

"Why do you want me to fall in love with Magnus?" Solvi gave her a dark look. "You don't know what's in my heart. I barely do, so I don't see how you could. Besides, I left my mother behind for a reason, so I'm not about to explain myself to you."

Rikka stood up. "Fine, Solvi. Just know that the next time you need that window to be open, I'm not going to be up here looking out for you."

She went out, slamming the door loud enough to wake all the girls on the hall and Matron downstairs.

CHAPTER THIRTEEN

NORA

Spring 1919 ■ *Spokane, Washington*

The newspaper advertisement was getting frayed hidden in the pocket of my apron, but I was loath to put it away. Sometimes I looked at it several times a day, delighting in the images of my children; other days I ignored it, though I could not forget it was there. It had opened a well of worry inside me, but also hope. A hope that was growing.

Perhaps I was reticent about answering because it might not be from any of my children. Perhaps it was from someone else.

If so, then who could it be? The only person I could think of was Tobias.

I stood at the kitchen door considering that possibility, then noticed the sun had set behind the hill. Time to gather the sheep. We brought them in at night to protect them from the mountain lions that roamed after dark. Our faithful donkey stood watch during the day, guarding the flock from coyotes, but he was no match for the big cats.

How different my life was now, compared to those evenings in Vika discussing politics around the fire with Tobias and the other students. I had always wondered if Tobias might seek me out here in America someday. He was the one who kindled my America dream, talking of his own plan to settle in Chicago and teach school or write for a newspaper. I still checked the *Skandinaven* occasionally, to see if he had followed that path, but so far there was no evidence of him. I wrote him a letter when we settled here in Spokane, but I only knew his parents' address. They were elderly and had probably died, so it was unlikely he got my note. I knew he would have written if he had.

I climbed up the hill, listening for the donkey's bell. On second thought, it couldn't be Tobias, because how would he have gotten the photograph to use in the newspaper advertisement? He would have had to find one of the children. Perhaps he went looking for me and found Ivar. Perhaps he convinced Ivar it was time to forgive.

I found the flock and waded through the sheep to the gentle donkey. The children called him Pokey, as he walked at his own pace. I tied the rope to his halter and showed him the apple I had for him. He followed happily, the flock in his wake.

Forgiveness. What a balm that would be.

NORA
June 1881 ▪ *Lac qui Parle, Minnesota*

The birds woke us at dawn the next morning, chattering enough to raise the dead. Except it did not work, not that day. Gustaf, Kari, and Hans still lay in their graves, and we stumbled from the hay ticks miserable and weak. In the bright daylight it was almost too much to bear. We ate our corn mush in silence, and then Mr. Eriksen sent the children to weed one of the fallow fields so we could plant the potatoes. We needed to get one crop in if we were to live through the next winter.

We. Was I part of this *we*, these Eriksens whose prairie experience had brought hardship and death?

Mr. Eriksen sat down next to me as I tended to Tomas. "This tragedy has complicated your situation, Nora," he said. "I'm sorry for that."

We glanced at each other awkwardly, both from such different worlds. "Perhaps there is some other family nearby I could live with," I said.

"There may be, but I dare not ask. If anyone knew we were not married, the town sheriff would put us back on the train. I see no alternative. You must continue to pose as my wife, at least for now."

I turned away. It wasn't that I had to live with this man—what felt like propriety in Norway had evaporated over weeks of shared sea cabins and train cars. It was the playacting and dressing in another woman's clothes. I didn't want to pretend to be Birgitte's mother.

"I know it's difficult, Nora, but I need your help," Mr. Eriksen said. "I realized that in Chicago; I cannot do this without you. Give me one year, help us get on our feet, and then I'll help you get back to Illinois."

"But I don't know if I can do it. Live in the sod house. I'm so—." I choked. "Inadequate. I don't have the strength."

"We have the strength; Birgitte will help you. And we'll fix up the house, clear it of ghosts. If you want me to live in the barn, I will. I don't mean to compromise your virtue."

"Birgitte resents me; she doesn't want me here."

"Birgitte is grieving. She'll learn soon enough to value your help."

"But how will we explain ourselves? You and I are like ox and horse—unsuited to be yoked together."

He flinched.

I started to apologize, but he waved it away.

"I doubt anyone will pry as long as we behave as husband and wife," he said. "If they do, we'll say you are my second wife, Tomas's mother. Not mother to the older ones."

"What will they call me?"

"Nora, as if you were their stepmother. And you must call me Anders. We'll say I met you—a widow—in Kristiania, after Inge died. That's true and explains why you are different."

"What will you say when I leave?"

"Ah. Perhaps that you died. We'll erect a marker next to the other graves and grieve the loss of you." I glanced up to see if he was as bitter as he sounded, but instead his face shone with something honest. "I have little doubt, Nora, that we *will* grieve the loss of you."

He was wooing me. He was afraid I would walk into town and get on the next train.

I fussed with Tomas, thinking. I could leave; I could leave that day. But that wouldn't be fair or honest, and I needed to be fair and honest. Besides, Tomas might not live through the first winter without me.

I sighed. "I will stay, Mr. Eriksen."

"Anders."

"I cannot call you that yet. Please, give me time."

"Of course. But if someone stops by . . ."

"I understand."

He helped me up. "Let's see how the children get on."

I TIED TOMAS TO MY BACK and took Jens's place in the field, so he could help his father gather wood down near the lake. Birgitte moved along the row ahead of me, tearing at the weeds with a hand claw, and I followed, digging out the stubborn ones. It was hot work, and I soon ached from bending. I stood for a moment, gazing out at the lake, and suddenly noticed a man at the edge of a thicket. A strange-looking man, with long black hair hanging down around his shoulders. Otherwise, he looked like a farmer, in a work shirt and homespun pants. He raised an arm and started toward us.

Birgitte looked up, then backed toward me. "Mrs. Solberg—."

"It's all right, Birgitte."

I shouted a greeting to him in English, though his dark skin and hair made me wonder if he was some other race. He didn't answer right away, so I greeted him in French. His face lit up, and he stepped closer. His skin was rough, scarred by a life outside, and he had charcoal eyes. "Are you French or English?" he asked in strangely accented French.

"Norwegian."

"You are Mr. Eriksen's kin," he said, bowing. "He said you were coming. I'm James Renville. A friend to Gustaf and Kari. I am very sorry for your loss."

"Thank you," I murmured. "My husband is Anders Eriksen. And this is Birgitte, and the baby is Tomas." I patted the sling. "We also have another son, Jens. He and his father are down by the lake."

"Is he an Indian?" Birgitte whispered.

"I don't know. He was a friend of your uncle's."

"I saw them fishing," said Mr. Renville. "Are you to take over Mr. Eriksen's claim?"

This last bit I could not decipher. "I don't understand. Do you speak English?"

"Yes, but not good," he said, switching over. "My sister and I learned at the mission school here. But the missionaries left after the Indian War. I picked up more doing business with settlers."

"How did you learn French?"

"It's my native tongue, along with Dakota. My grandfather was the son of a French fur trader and a Dakota wife. He was a border chief and built Fort Renville." He pointed to the distant bank, but I could see only trees.

We heard the wagon rattling up the slope. Mr. Eriksen brought the team to a halt, jumped down, and strode over, Jens on his heels. "Nora, is everything all right?"

"Yes. This is Mr. Renville, your brother's friend."

Mr. Eriksen shook the Indian's hand. "Then you must join us for dinner. Jens, clean the fish. Birgitte, heat the frying pan."

As we shared our meager meal, I translated, switching between languages. The winter was grim, worse than any of the Indians remembered.

Many farmers couldn't get their wheat threshed before the first storm, leaving them little to eat.

Mr. Renville spoke bitterly of the railroads. "You must make the land work for you; it's dangerous to be dependent on the trains."

He asked if Mr. Eriksen would take over Gustaf's claim and what he would plant. When Mr. Eriksen mentioned the potatoes, Mr. Renville nodded in agreement, then told us we would need a garden and some Indian corn, and offered to bring seeds. I was touched by his concern; we didn't seem quite so alone.

Mr. Eriksen sent the children back to finish the weeding, then turned to Mr. Renville. "Please, tell me how you found my brother."

"It was late March, after another big blizzard, still very cold. As soon as I could, I came with supplies, as I knew their food was low, but I was too late. I'm very sorry."

"Thank you for burying them," Mr. Eriksen said, his voice cracking.

"We were surprised to see they had burned nearly everything," I said.

"Yes, but not everything," Mr. Renville said. "I have their valuables, his tools and his gun. I'll bring them to you."

"Thank you," said Mr. Eriksen. "Did he have livestock?"

"They froze in the October snowstorm."

Mr. Eriksen shook his head. "I just don't understand how they became so desperate . . ."

Mr. Renville leaned forward. "Your brother was an able man, Mr. Eriksen, a good farmer. This past winter defeated many, but it's unlikely to happen again. Cut plenty of hay, gather wood, and build your larder. That is what you must do."

Mr. Eriksen nodded, thinking. "We'll need a cow, milk for the baby."

"We're all waiting to restore our stock, but there should be shipments soon." With that he stood. "You're very like your brother. I'll bring Mr. Eriksen's things over the next time I'm on this side of the lake."

"You don't live here?" I asked.

"Many dislike those of us with Indian blood, so I live at the end of the lake, near the old mission. It's abandoned now but familiar land to me." He bowed, then disappeared into the trees.

We spent the rest of the day planting the seed potatoes and hauling water to give them a start. Birgitte did the lion's share, her mouth tight as she registered what my weakness would cost her.

After more corn mush for supper, we prepared for bed.

"Tomorrow we'll clean the sod house," Mr. Eriksen said. "We can't live under the wagon forever."

WHEN I ROSE THE NEXT MORNING, Mr. Eriksen was already gone. Tomas gazed at me from the hay tick, his eyes full of love. He squirmed now with excitement whenever I picked him up and watched me as he drank his milk. It was hard to remember he wasn't mine.

I smelled smoke and looked around. A gray plume rose from beyond the sod barn—someone had set a fire. A moment later, Mr. Eriksen appeared, wiping his eyes. He had pulled the old hay ticks and ragged clothes from the soddie and set them ablaze, he told me. "No need for the children to see those things."

After breakfast we emptied the sod house of what little was left, then swept it out and moved our things inside. We took the *Skandinaven* newspaper I had gotten in Chicago and tacked the pages up around the exposed walls, extending Kari's effort, then hung fresh linens to split the back into two tiny sleeping spaces—one for Mr. Eriksen and Jens, one for me, Birgitte, and the baby. I hung another sheet against the exposed earthen wall, as I could not bear the thought of sleeping against it. We had no bed frames, so the hay ticks had to lie on the dirt floor. I tried not to think of spiders.

Jens found an outdoor fire pit Kari must have used for laundry, so Birgitte and I boiled a huge tub of water and washed our filthy clothes, pounding them with stones as we had no washboard. We spread the clothes on the grass to dry, then took turns bathing. I ran my hands over the stubble on my head and tied the kerchief back in place. By the end of the day my arms were chapped to the shoulder and my back stiff with pain, but we were blessedly clean.

ONCE WE HAD SETTLED in the sod house, however, a dark mood came over me. Our life was so rudimentary, it felt as if we had traveled back in time. Grit sifted down from the roof into our food and hair, and the smoke from the woodstove crept into everything. It made me wonder about Kari, whose shade seemed to inhabit the place. Did she give birth to Hans alone in this filth? Did she miss her family, long to return to Norway? How I wished she were here, teaching me the ways of the house, mothering Birgitte, easing everything.

But when I thought of the Eriksens' loss, I tried to put aside my disappointment. I might not know what Inge or Kari knew about running a farm, but I could still be useful. I took over the cooking chores, along with tending Tomas, and in the evenings I told stories, to fill the silence of this empty land. Jens loved tales of the *nisse*, the mischievous little Norwegian folk people, so I told him their Gudbrandsdalen *nisse* had immigrated with us, hiding in the rosemaled chest. They were to blame for the spilled flour and missing buttons, and they liked to tweak Tomas's ear to make him cry. Jens laughed, then made up his own *nisse* stories.

Birgitte pretended not to listen to our prattle, but one evening she launched into a tale about a *huldra*—an enchantress who lived in the mountains but liked to come down and mingle with people.

"She's uncommonly beautiful, this *huldra*," Birgitte said. "She has rich blond hair and a lovely figure, but if you look closely you can see her long cow tail peeking out from under her skirt. That's how you know she's an enchantress. And we must take care, Jens, for she likes to snatch babies."

I felt my breath leave my body.

Mr. Eriksen gave Birgitte a stern look. "Tomas has been baptized, Birgitte, so a *huldra* would have little power over him. No need to alarm everyone."

When we climbed into our shared bed, I turned toward the hateful dirt wall. Anything to avoid Birgitte's gaze.

THE NEXT DAY Mr. Eriksen went to town to settle his brother's estate but returned undecided and worried. The government would let him inherit the claim only if he paid Gustaf's debts.

"I don't know what to do," he told me. "The banker recommended I mortgage the land to pay the bills, but I hate to start in debt."

"In my experience, debt is a consumption—taking one thing after another," I said. I thought of Krogstad angrily shaking the loan papers in my face when I didn't have enough money to satisfy him. "What can we sell?"

"My brother's wagon and his chest, to start," he said.

"I have some silver forks and a book of Chopin music."

"I didn't know you played the piano, Nora," he said, gazing at me. He used my Christian name now, yet I still stumbled on his.

I went to look through my valise and brought him a stack of things, which he put in a crate. Then he opened the rosemaled chest and rummaged around, finally pulling out the silver spoons and some carved woodenware, including the elegant candlesticks. All, into the crate.

Then he took out a small hand organ.

"Oh, an organ! How wonderful," I said, taking it from him. "Why have you been hiding this?" I started to unsnap the leather clasps, but he stopped my hand.

"I don't have the heart to play anymore, Nora. I did so mostly for my wife's enjoyment."

"But we'll need it, to keep our spirits up."

"It speaks to us of Inge; none of us could bear it." He pulled it gently from my grasp.

"Forever is a long time to grieve, Mr. Eriksen."

He gave me a small smile, but put the organ in the crate.

With that, I handed him my little purse, fat with Torvald's money.

"Nora, that's too generous. You'll have nothing to get started."

I blushed, knowing my pearls lay safely in the seam of my chemise. "Please take it. You can pay me back later. I'll starve with the rest of you this winter if we don't do something."

"Thank you," he said, giving me a searching look. "You keep surprising me, Nora. You carry silver pickle forks, and you play Chopin. What else don't I know?"

Something between us crackled. It was so intimate, our life in this hovel. I stepped back. "Those are all my secrets, Anders," I said, shyly using his Christian name.

He nodded, picked up the crate, and disappeared out the door. When he returned that evening, the homestead was his.

MR. RENVILLE CAME BY A FEW DAYS LATER with the promised seeds. It was a warm afternoon, and Birgitte was helping me make *flotbrod*. From a dense dough we rolled rounds thin as paper, then browned them on the stove top. But I didn't have the knack of sliding the long flat sticks under the rounds to lift them, and Birgitte grumpily patched the holes I left behind. I couldn't tell how long Mr. Renville watched us from the open door. Having him hear Birgitte's admonitions embarrassed me, so I sent her to fetch her father from the field.

Mr. Renville put the bundle of seeds on the chest. "She is not your daughter."

I hesitated, but he could see the truth in my eyes. "No, she's not. Nor Jens. I met their father later. Their mother died in Norway."

"Ah," he said, thoughtfully. "That explains some things but not why you are different."

"I'm from the city, Kristiania—not from a farm."

"Is Kristiania a big city, like Chicago?"

"No, smaller but older, a harbor town."

He thought about that. He was so quiet and sure in this world, I envied him. He unrolled the cloth that held the seeds and identified them—turnips, beets, pumpkin. Then he looked at me. "You are not made for this life," he said. "I think it's too hard for you."

"They're teaching me. I'll learn, and then I can be more help."

Mr. Renville nodded. "Forgive me. Perhaps I am rude."

"No, no." I handed him a *flotbrod*, warm and crispy from the oven.

"Very good," he said, tasting it, then wrapping it in a handkerchief. "I'll take it home to my sister. She thanks you."

"Will we meet her?"

"No. She's sick and does not leave the house."

"Then take another."

He opened the handkerchief, and I added more rounds. He nodded, then stepped out the door.

THE NEXT DAY Anders surprised us with bedsteads built from willow saplings, to get us off the floor. That night I told Jens the *nisse* were angry because they could not climb up the slippery bedsteads to sleep under the quilts with us. He laughed and made up a story about them stealing a coal from the stove to keep themselves warm. Then Anders started singing a song about the fairy people. We all stared at him, astonished. It was so lovely to hear music again that I sang a hymn. Then Birgitte, not to be outdone, recited a poem about a maiden left behind by her lover. We went around our small circle, singing and reciting as best we could remember. For one magical hour I forgot we lived in a sod hut.

Later, curled between Tomas and the earthen wall, a small flame of happiness flickered inside me. Some things about this life I could scarcely endure, but there were also blessings—the beauty of the prairie, Jens and his many questions, Anders's growing confidence in me. And little Tomas. I pulled him close and kissed his warm head.

THE SUMMER UNFOLDED, a string of unending tasks, simple meals, and subtle feelings. Birgitte and I managed the house and garden, while Jens and his father hunted or worked the fields. On our tableland above the lake, the prairie shimmered in the heat, and luminous sunsets lit up the sky. Except for Mr. Renville, we felt utterly alone on the land. Anders went to town occasionally for supplies, but we knew no one there.

In the afternoon I held school outside in the shade of the soddie. I gave the children reading and history challenges and pushed them on their mathematics, which were weak. Next we would open my old English grammar and stumble through conversations. Birgitte, quick and avid to learn, was grudgingly appreciative that I had something to teach her.

One day Mr. Renville brought a tiny harness of leather that he hung from a ceiling pole. He strapped Tomas into it, as Indian mothers do with their children, and soon the baby was bouncing off his toes, crowing with glee.

I was deeply grateful, as the sod house had many hazards for a child starting to crawl. I tended to fuss over Tomas, worrying that he was not gaining weight or running to snatch him up whenever he cried. Birgitte disliked this, often taking him into her own lap and berating me for spoiling him. Still, I was the one he looked for in the morning, and that was enough for me.

AS THE DAYS SLIPPED BY, I grew attached to Jens, this fearless boy with torn pants and unruly hair. He had taken to prairie life as if born to it, which seemed to ease his grief for his mother. He loved to explore and show me what he found—animal skeletons, strange bugs, stone arrowheads. In the evening, he sketched pictures of his collection in a little notebook. He desperately wanted to see a buffalo or a wolf and told me of great panthers Mr. Renville recalled from his childhood.

Jens often worked at his father's elbow, absorbing the prodigious knowledge Anders carried in his head. Without plans or pictures, they built all we needed—furniture, wooden pails, even a little house to smoke fish. I laughed to imagine how Torvald would have treated someone like Anders, lifting his nose in superiority. But Torvald wouldn't have survived a week out here.

Despite summer's beauty, the chores and heat took their toll. Our skin coarsened; our muscles ached. It was difficult to imagine the land covered with snow, yet we were haunted by the legacy of the last winter and did everything we could to prepare. The tasks were legion: cut and cure wood, find a cow, harvest hay, build furniture, hunt and smoke meat, grow our vegetables and potatoes. And make some money, somehow.

ONE AFTERNOON, after too much laundry and wood smoke, I handed the baby to Birgitte and headed toward the lake. I found a flat rock and sank down, grateful for the quiet. Dragon flies buzzed about me, and wild berries beckoned in the dappled sun of the woodland.

I pulled off my kerchief to feel the breeze in my wisps of hair and sat for a long time watching the birds, free in a way I'd never felt before. There were many worries out here on the prairie, but I was not alone with those demons, as I had been for so many years in Norway. Anders and the children and I worked and worried together, everyone doing what they could to make it better. It was so different from my marriage to Torvald, which had been a constant tug-of-war of power and fear, secrets and lies. It made me wonder if I could ever marry again back into that privileged life. As much as I grumbled about laundry day or cooking over the uncooperative woodstove, when I sank into bed each night I felt needed and appreciated, particularly by Anders.

It made me wonder how I would feel when it ended.

I picked a handful of violets and walked slowly home in the dusk.

The others had already supped, but they left a plate for me. I put the violets in a small glass. Mr. Eriksen gave me a sympathetic look. "Was it lovely out there, Nora?"

"Beautiful, Anders. Thank you."

He smiled to hear his Christian name.

A FEW DAYS LATER Anders told me something that took my breath away. He would be leaving in October to work in the lumber mills in Minneapolis. He would be gone until Christmas.

I looked at him in dismay. "Must you?"

"Many of the local men go, once the harvest is in," he said. "We'll run through our money this summer, so I have to do something."

"But I can't possibly cope out here without you."

"You aren't alone, Nora. Mr. Renville has said he'll stop by to check on you every few days. I daresay Birgitte could manage Jens if it were just the two of them. Together you'll be fine."

I bowed my head in acquiescence but still cast about frantically for some alternative. "Maybe I could get a job in town, sewing perhaps."

"You must keep teaching, but maybe some other Norwegian children could join you. I'll ask around."

Teach other children? They might be unmanageable, stupid. I felt like my fragile hold on this challenging life was slipping away. "Of course," I said, with a tight smile.

A WEEK LATER the children and I were studying outside when a team of skinny mules rounded the bend, pulling a wagon driven by a tall, bearded man with two children on the seat beside him. As soon as the wagon stopped, two other children jumped down from the hay pile in the back. They greeted us in Norwegian.

The father looked every inch a prophet, with a full beard and intense eyes. He shook my hand. "Welcome to Lac qui Parle, Mrs. Eriksen. I'm Leif Madsen, and these are my children." The eldest was a girl, the others boys—all thin as their mules and dressed in faded black like their father.

"Thank you. This is Birgitte and Jens."

Mr. Madsen bowed. "Mr. Eriksen said you're teaching school."

"Yes, mostly reading, arithmetic, and English grammar. Birgitte and Jens hope to attend the village school next year but must learn English first. Do your children attend?"

"No, because they don't allow the children to speak Norwegian or read from the Bible. Do you teach the Bible, ma'am?"

"Yes," I said. It was somewhat true, as we used the Bible to practice reading.

"If you'll take my lot here, I'll give you a milk cow as payment."

A cow! We had been unable to find one we could afford, so I didn't even hesitate. "That would be wonderful!"

"They will bring her tomorrow, along with their slates and Bible." He turned to speak to his children, pointing to the sun and the horizon to direct them home. Then he climbed into the wagon and clopped away. They watched him disappear around the bend in the track. How poor and alone they seemed, these four dusty prairie children.

I clapped to start our school day, sat them down, and asked Birgitte and Jens to introduce themselves in English. With shy smiles, the Madsens told us their names. Siri was Birgitte's age and Claus a year behind her. Tosten seemed closer to Jens's age, and Nils was just five.

They soon relaxed, sharing the English they knew. They had little facility in grammar but had picked up many words, and so we patched together a lesson.

The next morning, the Madsen children appeared again, stepping out of the tall grass like fairies. They brought with them the cow—a brown and white spotted beast that became Jens's responsibility. Never having lived around animals, I was nervous, but Jens showed me how to scratch the cow on her neck and speak softly when leading her. I soon came to enjoy her solemn company.

IT RAINED OCCASIONALLY in July and then not again for most of August. The potato plants grew bushy and green, but only because Birgitte and Jens hauled well water up to them every day. The heat intensified, often making the horizon shimmer as if made of molten glass. We Norwegians had never known such heat, and I struggled in the afternoons to keep the children from falling asleep with their slates in their laps.

My students made steady progress, despite the informal nature of our school. The Madsen children had many strange ideas when it came to religion, but instead of discussing them we simply turned to new Bible verses. Gradually, Siri and Claus began to read on their own—helped by Birgitte and Jens and their own competitive spirit—and soon they were reading passages from all the books of the Bible.

We lost track of the days, though we knew it was Sunday when the Madsens did not come. Anders seemed to have little need for the solace of church, and I was secretly relieved. "There will be time for church in the fall," he said, when Birgitte asked about it. "We have too much work right now."

After supper we often sat outdoors in the lingering light. I tatted lace collars to sell in town, while Birgitte knitted socks and mittens. Anders and Jens carved many wooden spoons and bowls, hoping they would sell as well. I prayed we could earn enough that Anders wouldn't go to the mills, but I knew he would go no matter what. Until we could raise some wheat, we would be achingly poor.

As I tended to little Tomas and helped Birgitte with cooking and housework, I seesawed between feeling like a member of the household and daydreaming of a future in Chicago. My favorite escape from the drudgery of chores was to imagine having a room of my own, with a real bed, a wooden floor, and indoor plumbing. In time I might wear a corset and a bustle again.

But when I finished with my daydreams, there would be Tomas, chortling up at me with a broad grin, either hungry or happy. As he grew, he seemed to become my child in a way I could not talk about. The more care I poured into this motherless infant, the more I loved him, but I had to be careful, because Birgitte sensed my feelings and resented them. I only hugged and kissed him when she was not there to disapprove.

OVER THE COURSE OF THE SUMMER, I did my best to weave myself into the family. It was easy with Jens, who taught me many things about working on the farm and caring for the animals, including the rudiments of milking.

With Birgitte, though, everything was harder. When we were busy with the household chores, she lorded over me with her superior knowledge and strength. She knew all the family recipes, including how to make cheeses and butter. She could coax lye from the stove's ashes to make soap, and she knew how to treat a blister or a cold.

But when the baby fussed, I had the final word, and when I was teaching, she knew to be obedient and respectful. I could tell, though, that she didn't like it.

As for Anders, I didn't know quite what to make of him. Sometimes I caught him looking at me with pain in his face, as if I had disappointed him; other times he treated me with gratitude, even tenderness.

To endure this primitive life, I had to forget Norway and make myself into a different woman—one who scrubbed clothes, made cheese, and chased mice from the soddie. The old Nora would have detested these tasks, but the more help I could be, the better I felt about everything, even the dreary little house.

It felt as if we were all suspended in a time that existed outside of time, when we did not need to decide how we felt about each other. We could just go on whittling spoons and feeding the baby and watching the crops grow.

And sometimes I looked up from my work and found myself filled with the beauty of the place—the grass moving in the warm wind, the birds lifting and chittering, the clouds drifting across a deep blue sky. In those moments, I felt as if my soul could expand forever.

THE PRAIRIE TURNED GOLDEN under the August sun, and Anders began cutting hay. We stopped school, promising the Madsens we would start again after the haying, and the children took up rakes to help. It was hot, grueling work. I tried to handle the other chores, and the baby and I brought out sandwiches at noon. They cut hay for days.

Once the hay was stacked behind the barn, Anders packed his rucksack.

He promised to return before the first snowfall. To save money, he would walk the entire way to Minneapolis.

The morning he left, the children and I stood at the head of the path waving until he disappeared. It felt as if the sunlight had been sucked from the world.

That night I let the children pour molasses on their corn mush as consolation, then poured some on my own. For once, Birgitte did not frown at me.

THE FALL DAYS were deceptively warm, yet the nights edged with cold. The brush along the lake soon blazed red and yellow. Great wedges of geese stopped to rest in our lake, flotillas of clamoring birds. I understood then why the French called it Lac qui Parle, the Lake That Speaks.

But even the flocks could not relieve the unyielding silence of the land. Their calls were swallowed up by the vastness of the prairie, leaving us each with our own private loneliness.

In early October it rained heavily for several days, and muddy water dripped through the ceiling onto our heads. Jens did what he could to patch the sod roof, but still we had to cover the food with rags. The gray skies made us feel Anders's absence acutely, and Birgitte turned her unhappiness on me. One day I tried to make *primost*, the traditional caramelized cheese, but in my ignorance I neglected the pot and scorched the precious milk. Birgitte, brittle with disappointment, said I was no better than a troll—carrying my head under my arm rather than on my shoulders where it would be of some use.

I opened my mouth to scold her, but then I saw why she found me so frustrating. "Birgitte, I'm sorry. Your mother could have taught you what you need to know, but I cannot—I don't know how to run a farm. That's what angers you."

Her eyes filled with tears, and she turned away, but when I served the scorched *primost* that evening, she choked it down by way of apology.

THE WEEKS WORE ON. The children and I harvested the potatoes and garden, filling the root cellar and exhausting ourselves. A trickle of resentment began to run under everything I did, as if Anders has broken his promise. This was not our bargain—we were a team, even if ox and horse. I was willing to work hard and live in a dirt house, but not alone.

For months I had managed to keep thoughts of Norway at bay, but now my soul filled with memories, like the tide flooding footprints in the sand. I ached for my old parlor and coal heat—I was so tired of breathing wood smoke and feeding the ravenous fire. And I needed a friend, someone to talk to, like Dr. Rank or Tobias.

When I daydreamed now, it was of walking east with little Tomas on my back, toward a civilized life out from under this great bowl of sky.

THE FROST CAME, and the willow leaves dropped away. We took the wagon and collected windfall down by the lake. The gray days followed one after another. A light snow greeted us one morning but disappeared by noon. The Madsen children still came for school, and Mr. Renville stopped by as he had promised, often bringing a treat of beets or Indian rice from the marsh.

One day I invited him to stay for tea. His otherness always thrilled me a little—his different smell and coal-black hair, the way he sat straight-backed and ready.

"Will it be a bad winter, Mr. Renville?"

"The geese are lingering, so, no. There are never two hard winters in a row."

"Will the lake freeze over?"

"Most years it does, and thick—you can drive a wagon across it."

"I guess it doesn't speak when it's frozen," I said, with a smile.

"No, but it whispers. You'll hear it."

"Whispers?"

"My people, the People of the Leaf, call it the Lake That Whispers, because it's so beguiling. The French trappers did not understand."

"What does it whisper?"

"One's destiny."

"Do you believe that?"

He shrugged. "I only know I can live nowhere but by its side. Sometimes I think of it as wife to me."

I nodded, blushing. There was so little I knew of this man, yet here we sat, sharing tea and speaking of wives. Perhaps he could not take a real wife because he was of mixed blood. Perhaps no one would have him.

"Will there be blizzards?"

"Oh, yes, but they won't come early or stay late. January and February will be the worst. Still, you must watch the northwestern sky. The blizzard cloud comes very fast, and the winds are fierce; the snow becomes ice, like bits of glass. Sometimes you can barely breathe."

"I didn't know the storms were that bad. What do you do if one catches you?"

"Keep walking to stay warm or climb into a haystack if you find one. The most important thing is not to get caught. Don't let the children walk out on the prairie, even if it's clear. The weather can change quickly."

We lingered at the door, each lonely, each shy, not knowing quite how to say good-bye. Finally, he bowed and walked away.

WE WOKE UP ONE DAY near the end of November to howling winds, and when we opened the door a great gust of snow billowed into the house. The children were bitterly disappointed their father hadn't beaten the storm, so we poured out more molasses that night. Anything to keep their spirits up.

The storm blew for two miserable days. It dawned clear and very cold the third day, and we shoveled our way out of the sod house to look out over the frozen prairie. It felt like living at the top of the world—only snow as far as we could see.

The Madsen children stopped coming. Jens and Birgitte didn't mention their father again, but they kept track of the days. In the evening I let Birgitte read to us from one of my novels, a romance about some city girls; it kept us from listening for the door.

Another storm blew through in early December, and the lake iced over. Then, late one afternoon, when we had nearly given up, Anders stumbled into the house. The children threw themselves against him before he could get his coat off, and I smiled at him through the mayhem. He dropped a sack, goods carried all the way from Minneapolis. Perhaps there would be something for Christmas after all.

He plucked Tomas from his harness and sat with him in front of the stove, playing with his tiny hands. I served supper while Anders told us of his long walk across Minnesota and pulling huge logs out of the Mississippi River. He lived in a bunkhouse village with other farmers—Swedes, Germans, Americans, and many Norwegians. Most had families waiting in a sod house somewhere on the prairie.

"Can I go with you next year?" said Jens.

"No," Anders said.

Jens's face fell, making his father laugh. He patted the boy's knee. "If you could see it, you would thank me. It's very dangerous out there on the river with the logs. Best to stay here on the farm."

Anders complimented me on my bean soup.

I was giddily happy that he was back.

THE NEXT MORNING Anders took me aside. "I've brought a few Christmas presents for the children. Can you make a *julekake*?" He handed me two small packets: cinnamon and raisins.

"Yes, how wonderful." We shared a conspiratorial smile; warmth flooded through me.

ON CHRISTMAS EVE, I pulled out Inge Eriksen's traditional *bunad*, with its embroidered apron and vest, and handed it to Birgitte. She buried her face in it. The costume ballooned on her slender frame, and we had to cinch the skirt. But with her apple cheeks and dark hair, she looked like the perfect Norwegian maid. Jens, not to be outdone, put on his father's red felt vest, studded with silver buttons linked with fine chain. We gathered at the table and took turns reading the Christmas story from the Bible. I served goose with turnips and boiled potatoes, and then we finished with tea and *julekake*. Birgitte and Jens ate with quiet reverence.

When we were done, Jens asked if I had made the porridge for the *Julenisse*.

I knew this folk tradition, but I didn't think anyone believed it anymore. I shook my head with a sigh.

"Mama always remembered," Birgitte said. "Else the *Julenisse* won't leave presents."

"Never mind," said Anders. Then he ducked into the bedroom and came out with a stack of packages. "The *Julenisse* crept up behind me in the barn the other day and bit my ankle to get my attention." Birgitte gave him a doubtful look, but Jens's mouth dropped open. "He asked me to give you these."

For Birgitte, there was a book of poems; for Jens, a new notebook and pencil; and for Tomas, a rattle made from a gourd. Then Anders handed me my gift, a carved wooden hand mirror.

I looked up at him in surprise—such an intimate present. "From the *Julenisse*?"

"No. From me."

Birgitte looked at her father, then at me, then back at him.

"Thank you," I said, blushing.

"I hope you'll take it with my gratitude, Nora. I trusted you with the children, and you've done well."

Birgitte got up and started to clear the dishes.

Anders reached for her hand. "We can do that later. I have one more surprise."

"Papa, please."

"What's wrong, Birgitte?"

Tears slipped down her face. "Is it so easy for you to forget?"

"Do you mean your mother?"

Birgitte nodded, then sat, twisting her hands.

Anders reached out and cupped her face with his palms. "Oh, Birgitte, I'll never forget your mother. Every day I think of her, as you do. I know it's hard—the first Christmas without her. Which is why we must have music, in her honor."

With that he pulled from his pocket a small wooden block, raised it to his lips, and started blowing a soft Christmas melody. Birgitte caught her breath. It looked like some sort of mouth harp. "It's called a harmonica," he said, when he was done. "The *Julenisse* gave it to me for my present."

We all examined the little instrument. There was a German name etched on the metal cover and thin reeds inside that hummed when one blew across them. Anders played another Christmas hymn and then all the beautiful old songs we knew. I suspected he had practiced for this night, as he played fluidly with few mistakes.

Tomas stirred in my lap, opening his wide blue eyes. I smiled at him tenderly, not caring what Birgitte would think. I had come so far since that last Christmas with Torvald two years earlier, I could scarcely make sense of it. I thought of our holiday tree blazing with candles, the money I so desperately needed to pay Krogstad wrapped in gilt and hung from the branches. Then I thought of Tobias and the sprig of holly he gave me last year, tied with yarn from his sock.

Somehow, I had washed up on this desolate prairie, living with a family I had known for only seven months. But I was beginning to feel I could belong.

AFTER THAT CHRISTMAS NIGHT, my life brightened. I wasn't sure what had changed, but I felt more confident and apologized less. I started taking more care with myself, pulling my short blond curls back with a ribbon, knitting myself a pretty new shawl. Having a mirror restored something I'd lost—the sense that I was a woman. Some days I even felt like a girl.

Anders also seemed happier. I knew he would always miss his wife, but it felt as if he left the burden of his grief in Minneapolis instead of hauling it back to Lac qui Parle. He told us of the other men he met at the camp, particularly a Norwegian from Lofoten, Lars Hansen, who also came to America after losing his wife. Each night they sat by the bunkhouse stove, whittling and talking, providing the solace Anders had needed.

One day I heard him whistling in the barn. A few days later he offered to haul my share of the water—the chore I detested most—and later that week he returned from town with a beautiful flowered fabric for me to make myself a new dress. Soon, he was lingering with me while I milked the cow or tended to Tomas, often talking of his plans for a large wheat crop and a frame house. I watched him, puzzled. He had grown optimistic and expansive, and he treated with me a fresh appreciation. I was not the only one who saw this. It irritated Birgitte, so I began to think it might be real.

AND THEN, on one of those bright winter days when everything sparkled, he stopped me as I headed to the smokehouse.

"Nora, let us walk down to the lake," he said. "It's so beautiful out."

"But I told Birgitte I would get the fish for supper."

"We'll bring it in when we return," he said. "Please. I need to speak to you."

We headed into the wood, then picked our way through a thin crust of snow down to the edge of the lake. The ice was thick and covered with swirled drifts, like frosting on a cake. I found my favorite granite bench; we brushed it off and sat.

At first he didn't say anything. I waited, mystified. "Anders, please, what is it?"

"Nora, I've been thinking," he said, twisting his hands. "I know you plan to go back to Chicago when your time is done, but if you wanted to stay, we would be happy to have you."

"Stay? Living as we've been? Pretending we're man and wife?"

He shook his head, cleared his throat. "Actually, Nora, I thought we might marry."

My mouth dropped open; my stomach fluttered.

He leaned toward me. "Please don't be offended, Nora."

"No," I said, too amazed to know what I thought, but I didn't want to hurt his feelings. A strange heat rose in my chest. "I am not offended, Anders."

"I know I'm not of your class . . ."

"No," I said again, shaking my head. "That doesn't matter." Now I looked up, into his worried eyes. "I'm so sorry I ever suggested we were like ox and horse. That was unkind."

"But I think it mattered to you," he said quietly.

"I've, well, I've changed," I said. "I didn't know someone could make a life from nothing. It has filled me with admiration for you."

"Thank you," he said. "And I think you love Tomas."

"I adore Tomas, and Jens. And I'm working on Birgitte."

He laughed for a moment but then grew serious again. He sat down next to me. "The question, Nora, is do you think you could love me?"

I just looked at him. Love this man? Then, in that moment, my world pivoted, as if God had spun it like a wheel. Instead of looking east toward Chicago, my mind's eye turned back to this farm. And for the first time I could see a trim white house with a real barn behind it. Horses waiting for their oats, chickens swarming at my feet. Fields of ripening wheat moving in the wind. We could sell my pearls to pay for the lumber.

My heart quickened, and then I began to shiver. No, Lord, no. How could I even think of marrying Anders? I was probably still married to Torvald.

"But, Anders, don't you love Inge?"

He sighed. "I will always love Inge, but she's gone and I've made my peace with it." Now he smiled shyly and took my hands. "When we first came to Lac qui Parle, my heart was like an empty house, but you crept into it." He was quoting a Norwegian poet.

I smiled back, but I didn't know what to say. He watched me, so intent, waiting, hoping. I looked down at our hands, holding each other. "When did you know how you felt?"

"When I came back from Minneapolis," he said. "I was overjoyed to see you. That's when I understood how much you meant to me." He waited for a moment, then asked again. "So, Nora, I realize you may not love me now, but do you think you could learn to love me?"

I looked into his eyes. I felt as if I were being swept downstream in a spring freshet. Then I heard myself whisper one word: "Perhaps."

"Then that is all we need, Nora."

I knew I should smile, but instead my eyes brimmed with tears.

He reached up and wiped them from my cheek. "What is it, Nora?"

"Oh, Anders, it's so complicated," I said. "I'm so complicated! I know I seem like a simple woman, living here with you and the children, but that's only because I've pushed aside everything that came before." I ached to tell him the secret that cowered inside me, but I didn't dare. He would turn away from me forever.

"Is it your dream of returning to city life? Because if it is, Nora, we could consider that. After we build the farm and make it profitable, perhaps we could move to Minneapolis. There's a whole Norwegian community there. I've seen it—clubs, schools, everything you could want!"

I took a deep breath, sucking in the cold air like aquavit. "May I think about it, Anders? Perhaps till spring?"

"Of course, Nora. There's no hurry."

More tears slipped down my cheeks. I wanted so much to be loved.

"Come now, Nora! I didn't mean to make you sad!"

I brushed the tears away, trying to laugh. "No, Anders, you've made me happy today." I gazed deeply into his eyes. What a dangerous fire kindled in my breast. "Very happy. Thank you."

He blushed. "I'm happy, too. But we must be careful around the children. Until we're sure, we mustn't give them any clue. We want to tell them, not have them figure it out."

"Birgitte may be hard to trick, Anders. She's sees everything." Birgitte and God, I thought.

"Then I'll have to be circumspect around you." He squeezed my hands again. "Just know that, no matter how I behave, I still love you."

I nodded, astonished and beguiled by the idea that he loved me. But how could I allow it? "She'll be waiting for the fish," I said. "She probably already suspects."

He helped me stand. "Then let's go back and behave as usual. She'll soon forget it."

ANDERS AND I RETURNED TO OUR LIFE, but everything felt different; each gesture, each word, echoed with meaning and feeling. We tried
to treat each other as we did before, particularly around Birgitte, but if
Anders came into the house and no one else was there, he would sit and
chatter about some new idea, such as buying a team of horses or building
a sleigh so we could go to town in the winter. Love made him talk; I was
surprised to hear what turned in his mind.

As for me, I didn't know what to do. When I thought of marrying him,
joy bubbled inside me, but I was afraid to take the lid off it. Could I marry
him here in Minnesota without anyone suspecting I had a husband in Norway? I had no idea.

But when I told myself, no, I should be honest and tell Anders the awful
truth, then my soul seemed to harden into ice. We felt alone on this prairie,
but there was a Lutheran church in town. Someone might find out.

Perhaps I had to learn to want again.

CHAPTER FOURTEEN

SOLVI

March 1919 ▪ *Kristiania, Norway*

When Solvi went down for breakfast the morning after the dance, her eyes blurry and her head aching, Matron gave her a stern look and handed her another letter.

Dear Solveig: I was quite taken aback by your news and have been debating whether I need to come to Kristiania to save you from your-self. I've decided instead to rely on your better judgment. Your father always said you were a sensible child, and I trust he was right.

I was very disturbed to hear you are clerking in a shop. Indeed, I can only cringe at the thought of you waiting on common people. I cannot imagine what you are thinking. If you need money, ask me. I'm happy to help, but in exchange I ask that you give up this work. These expe-riences, if continued, will coarsen you, Solveig. Independence is one thing, but I fear you've forgotten your breeding—you are a lady, above all else.

Mother

P.S. Our family name was never anything but Fallesen. I can't imagine what you think you know.

For a moment, Solvi could scarcely breathe. If her mother thought clerking in a shop was coarsening, what would she think of climbing in the window after curfew, drunk from too much champagne? Solvi felt as if she'd left her mother in the last century and would never be able to talk to her about anything again. She put the letter aside, but it shadowed the rest of her day.

RIKKA AVOIDED HER FOR THE NEXT WEEK, managing to disappear into the city in a way that both irritated and saddened Solvi. She wasn't sure how to apologize or even whether she wanted to. She wandered through her life alone, feeling estranged from everyone who mattered to her.

Then, one evening, someone started drumming softly on Solvi's door, quite late. It could only be Rikka, Solvi thought, her pulse racing. No one else was that impatient.

It was Rikka, but she seemed oddly disheveled and timid, as if drained of her confidence. She sank down on Solvi's bed, then turned to her with red-rimmed eyes.

"Rikka, what's wrong?"

"Oh, Solvi, everything's awful! We need to be friends again, or I'm going to lose my will to live."

"Rikka, heavens, of course," Solvi said, wrapping her in a hug. "I'm so sorry. I was being stupid that night."

"No, I was wrong," Rikka said, clinging to her in a way that surprised Solvi. "How did we let boys get between us like that?" She tried to laugh but quickly dissolved in tears.

"Rikka, what's happened?"

"I saw something terrible in Vika today," Rikka sobbed. "And I didn't stop it!"

"Slow down, Rikka. Take a deep breath. Tell me what happened."

Rikka blew her nose, then settled for a long moment, as if collecting herself. "I had gone to talk with a woman who desperately needs to prevent more pregnancies. I probably shouldn't have done it, but she already has seven children and nearly died with the last one. So I gave her some condoms. Then, as I was leaving, her husband came in and got very angry." Rikka gulped air. "Before I knew what was happening, he starting beating her, with a ladle!"

"Did he threaten you?"

"No, because I slipped away. I was such a coward! I just left. I knew I should've gone back, but I was afraid he would turn on me." Rikka began to cry again. "Sometimes when I see how these women live, when I see them pregnant with the tenth child, or with bruises on their faces or arms, or how thin they are, I just burn with fury. But there's so little I can do!"

Solvi got her a fresh handkerchief and sat down in front of her. "Rikka, I know you feel you must take on all these problems, but if you let each one into your heart this way, it will tear you apart."

Rikka buried her face in her knees.

"Please don't go back," Solvi said. "You don't want someone coming after you."

"I have to go back. I can't let him drive me away."

"Then don't go alone, Rikka. Tell the auxiliary you need an escort. You can't take on the world by yourself."

Rikka wiped her eyes. "That is rather arrogant of me, isn't it? To think that I can change their poverty."

"Yes," Solvi said. "It is. But then again, you are a heroine of the Great War."

Rikka rolled her eyes. "Oh, Lord, hardly. I mostly cowered when the shells rained down."

"No doubt, but still—the war was your crucible. To be honest, Rikka, it's made you reckless."

"Careful people don't change the world, Solvi."

"But neither do dead people. The war must have taught you that."

Rikka just looked away.

AS PENANCE for letting boys lead her astray, Solvi returned to her studies with renewed fervor and began pulling together her research about the Forgotten One. Before long, Solvi was thinking of her all the time, trying to imagine her life, trying to understand her reasons, trying to get at her shadowy character. Did the Forgotten One live in a dark little room, like Petra, or was it even worse—some broken-down hut in Vika with the sea breezes blowing through the walls? Did she struggle to find food? Did she sit stitching shirts in the back of some store with her stomach growling? And what was so unbearable about her former comfortable life? What drove her out the door?

Then Solvi opened a novel assigned for her literature class, *Constance Ring*, and it felt like pulling back a curtain. Set in 1885, it helped Solvi understand the deadening humiliation of being married to an imperious boor, the constraints of a gossipy and meddling society, the despair of being trapped in a world defined and managed by men. Just before bed, Solvi flipped to the end, curious to see if Constance ultimately set out to find her own life.

But, no. At the end of the book she killed herself.

AT BREAKFAST THE NEXT MORNING Solvi couldn't stop talking about the book.

"It's a novel of such cruel despair," she told Rikka. "But it's all eerily familiar. I felt like I was in my mother's parlor when I was reading it, and one of the characters could have been my grandfather back then."

"Perhaps the Forgotten One killed herself," Rikka said. "It might explain her disappearance."

Solvi frowned. "Goodness, I hope not, although Professor Wolff said leaving her husband would have been nearly suicidal. Is it suicide if one starves to death?"

"Perhaps she ended up like the women in Vika—sick and emaciated with tuberculosis and so poor no one realized she was a lady or cared when she died," Rikka said.

"I just hope my essay leads somewhere more inspiring than to an early grave," Solvi said. But she knew Rikka might be right.

"HAVE YOU MADE ANY PROGRESS finding your grandmother?"

Solvi and Magnus were seated at the pastry shop as usual, but now, for the first time, their conversation felt strained.

"No. I'm too busy researching the Forgotten One, though sometimes I get glimpses of my grandmother's life through what I've discovered."

Magnus just nodded. Solvi had never seen him so quiet.

"Do you think the Forgotten One might have killed herself?" Solvi asked. "I'm reading *Constance Ring* for context and *Madame Bovary* next. They both try to escape their adulterous husbands by committing suicide, and I'm wondering if that's what happened to the Forgotten One."

Magnus gave her a puzzled look. "If I remember correctly, Emma Bovary is the adulterer, not her poor husband. She has several affairs, tries to prostitute herself to pay off her debts, and then ends up taking arsenic because she cannot bear to confess and return to her marriage," Magnus said. "If you reference it in your essay, make sure you have your facts straight."

"I, well, I'm sure you're right," Solvi said, stung by his tone. It wasn't her fault that the matron of her ladies' academy in Bergen had banned them from reading *Madame Bovary*.

Magnus sipped his coffee, then looked at her.

"Magnus, are you angry with me?"

He put down his cup. "I'm sorry, Solvi. Not angry, just, well, disappointed."

He took a breath. "I heard you went with Dominik to a dance at his residence club."

Solvi noticed the flicker of hurt in his eyes. She could see that she had done exactly what she wanted to avoid. "Oh, Magnus, it meant nothing. I'm not even sure I had a good time. Dominik got me home late, and I had to climb in my window to avoid getting in trouble with Matron. It made me rather angry, though it's hard to be angry with Dominik. He couldn't help it; he was drunk—he felt bad that I was late."

"Well, that's your own affair, Solvi," Magnus said, turning a bit red in the face and looking down at the plate of biscuits between them. He took one and fiddled with it. "It's none of my business."

For some reason, that made her heart hurt. "I'm sorry, Magnus," she said.

He gave her a tight smile. "You needn't say anything, Solvi. I understand. The whole world has opened up to you, and I'm sure there will be many young men interested in your attentions."

"But we're friends, aren't we? That's important to me."

He broke the biscuit in half and popped a piece in his mouth. "Of course we are, Solvi. Friends." Then he gathered his books and walked away.

SEVERAL DAYS LATER, Solvi and Rikka slipped out of the study house so early only the milk wagons clattered down the streets. Solvi clutched her camera bag, running to keep up with Rikka, who hurried along in her nurse's uniform.

They were headed to the house of a wealthy family in the Homans Byen section. Petra had arranged it with the servants, but the family knew nothing about it. Solvi would take pictures of the maids, and Rikka would advise them about their sexual lives. Petra had told Rikka so many stories of young maids being raped, then fired when they got pregnant, that Rikka was determined to help.

They were late, because Solvi had second thoughts that morning. It was one thing to do this in Bergen, where she knew the families, but here in Kristiania it felt like trespassing. In fact, it was trespassing.

Rikka listened, then sighed and waved that away. "We're not stealing anything, or hurting anyone," she said. "You've got to be willing to take a little risk, Solvi, if you want to make a difference in the world. This is nothing. If you're careful in your pictures to obscure the identity of the maids and the place, no one will ever know we were there."

They found Petra on the corner stamping her feet against the cold. "I thought you lost your nerve," Petra said, pulling her shawl tight around her shoulders.

"Oh, goodness, no," said Rikka, glancing at Solvi. "Plenty of nerve, right, Solvi?"

"Sure," said Solvi, though she felt nervous and queasy.

They caught a tram and jumped off in a neighborhood of stone row houses and stately mansions. With Petra in the lead, they trudged up a hill, then ducked down an alley and through a gate left open for them. When they knocked on the basement door of one elegant mansion, a young scullery maid let them in, her finger on her lips. She led them through a busy kitchen to a storage room stacked with china.

An older maid who seemed to be in charge came in with two chairs. "Rikka, you can talk to the girls over here," she said. Rikka took off her coat and pulled out her stethoscope, a stack of pamphlets, and a box of condoms.

"And Solvi, take whatever photographs you want," the older maid said. "But don't forget, you must be gone in a half hour. The family rises early."

Solvi took her camera into the work area, her hands shaking. She quickly shot a photo of the cook hacking at the carcass of a lamb, the table slick with blood. Then she shot a scullery girl polishing a large copper kettle scorched with use. After that, Solvi moved into the laundry and photographed a housemaid ironing sheets and another struggling to operate a huge wringer. Solvi carefully obscured the girls' faces and, in several photographs, purposefully cut off their heads, catching only the labor of their thin bodies, arms tensed, backs bent and straining.

Petra wandered about, watchful, listening for footsteps on the stair.

After a bit, Rikka poked her head into the laundry, pulling on her coat. "Come on, Solvi, we'd better go."

"Just a moment," Solvi said. There was one last photograph she wanted. She talked to the maid, who nodded and then, using huge tongs, pulled a wad of steaming sheets from a deep pot.

Suddenly, Solvi heard a male voice in the other room. "Who the hell are you?"

Petra started to speak, but Rikka interrupted. "We're nurses with the Health Auxiliary, checking the girls for tuberculosis," she said. "Lucky for you, they all look fine."

The laundry maid turned to Solvi. "In here!" she hissed, opening a large closet filled with brooms. Solvi grabbed her camera and slipped inside. She heard Rikka say the authorities had every right to test domestics for tuberculosis, and the young man countered that any respectable health organization would ask permission first. Rikka pretended that they had; perhaps his mother didn't tell him, she said. This offended the young man, who took their names—Rikka and Petra gave false ones—and sent them out the door. Solvi held her breath.

After a few minutes, she cracked the door of the broom closet. The laundry maid stood stock still, looking toward the kitchen.

"Do you know who they are?" the man said, coming into the laundry. Solvi shrank back into the closet.

"No," said the maid. "I was just doing the washing; I didn't know they were here. I didn't talk to them, I swear." Solvi couldn't see the young man, but she could see the maid looking up at him anxiously. "Please, Edvard, I knew nothing of it."

Then Solvi saw his hand snake around the girl's throat. "I want to believe you, Greta, but something tells me you're lying."

The maid began to cry. "Please, Edvard, I wouldn't lie to you."

After a long moment, he let go of her neck but pinched her cheek, hard. Her hand flew to her face, but she took the punishment silently.

"Ask the others who they are and report back to me," he said. Then he stomped away.

Solvi heard him go upstairs and slam the door. She stepped out of the closet. The maid held her cheek and just looked at Solvi, tears running down her face.

Solvi lifted her camera. "Move your hand, Greta. I'll make a record of it. Evidence, in case you want to make a complaint."

Greta looked at Solvi, her eyes huge. Her hand dropped; the pinch stood out as an angry welt. Solvi clicked the shutter.

A minute later, she was out the back door, running to meet Rikka and Petra, who were waiting in the alley. They hurried to the street, then made their way to a main thoroughfare. A tram pulled up; they climbed aboard, breathing hard.

Rikka started to giggle.

"It isn't funny, Rikka," Petra said between her teeth. "This isn't a schoolgirl's prank."

"But he has no idea who we are," Rikka said. "There's no need to worry."

"Hush," Petra said, glancing about the crowded car.

"He threatened the laundry maid," Solvi whispered. "He pinched her face, badly."

Petra shook her head. "Doesn't surprise me. I just hope you got some good photographs."

Rikka elbowed Solvi. "This is our stop. Petra, we'll see you later."

"Hopefully, we can get inside another home next week," Petra said. "I'll let you know."

Solvi sighed. That was the last thing she wanted to do.

A FEW DAYS LATER, Magnus sat next to Petra, helping her edit her newspaper story, while Solvi laid out her photographs of the maids. Petra had refused to meet them at the students' café but grudgingly agreed to the pastry shop. Solvi felt a little stab of jealousy watching Magnus and Petra with their heads together, talking quietly.

"Magnus, which of these do you like?" Solvi asked.

He looked up, scanned the pictures, and picked up one of the laundry maid struggling to turn the crank of the giant wringer. Solvi had photographed only her shoulders and arms straining with the effort, water running everywhere. "This one is very evocative, Solvi," he said, giving her a small smile. He seemed to have forgiven her.

"They're good, but we need more," said Petra. "Mr. Blehr wants at least twenty so he can choose the best. I've gotten permission from a young woman to have you photograph her family's maids next week, while her parents are in Italy. We won't have to sneak around."

"Sneak around?" said Magnus, glancing at Solvi. "Did you sneak around to get these photos?"

Solvi glanced at Petra. "Well, it was arranged with the maids, but the family didn't know. We went early one morning. Unfortunately, a young man of the house came down and caught Rikka and Petra. The laundry maid hid me in a closet, and I got out later." She felt breathless as she said this and watched Magnus for a reaction. Perhaps her mother was right about coarsening.

Then Magnus laughed. "I would never have imagined you cowering in a closet, Solvi. But you two should be more careful. I don't want to have to bail you out of jail."

"Sometimes Rikka scares me," Solvi said. "She's afraid of nothing."

"Well, Rikka has little to lose and no one to advise her otherwise," Magnus said.

"I think she's courageous," said Petra. "Few can match her. But don't worry, Solvi. It's impossible to tell who these maids are or where they work."

Solvi took another photograph from her satchel and laid it on the table: Greta's tear-stained face with the welt.

"What is this?" Magnus said, peering at it.

"The young man at the house in Homans Byen got angry at the laundry maid and put his hand around her throat, then pinched her hard. I took a picture, in case she wanted to make a complaint."

"Are you going to publish this photograph?" he asked.

Petra took it from him. "We should, Solvi. People need to see what happens."

Solvi shook her head. "No, it's Greta's to do with as she will. I just need to find a way to get it to her."

"I'll take it to her," Petra said, reaching for it.

Solvi hesitated, not sure she could trust her but not brave enough to ask. "Thanks, Petra."

A FEW DAYS LATER Solvi was hanging up photographs to dry at the photography shop when Mr. Stenberg knocked on the darkroom door.

"Miss Lange, I've found something astonishing. Come out as soon as you can."

She finished and emerged into the light.

"Look at this," he said, leaning over a large photo album. It was a collection of formal portraits from the past, the pages faded and cracked along the edges. Mr. Stenberg pointed at one particular photograph. "There."

It was a picture of a beautiful woman with honey-blond hair in a dress very like the one Solvi's grandmother wore in the photograph of Solvi's family. Solvi peered at it. It *was* her grandmother, an individual portrait likely taken at the same sitting. Underneath the photograph was a title: *The Notorious Nora Helmer, 1879*.

Solvi glanced around the rest of the page. The other portraits were from the same period, and many of the names sounded vaguely familiar.

Mr. Stenberg flipped to the front of the album, where someone had written a title page in flowing script: *Famous Personages: Kristiania, 1872–1890. Compiled by Mr. Otto Stenberg.*

"What is this?" Solvi asked.

"I believe my father put this album together from photography sessions he did of famous Norwegians."

"But what is my grandmother doing in there? And why is her name Nora Helmer? Her name was Solveig Fallesen." Solvi's knees went weak; she grabbed for a chair. "And what did he mean by notorious?"

Mr. Stenberg shook his head. "I don't know, Miss Lange. But the different name and the word *notorious* both point to some kind of, well, family embarrassment. And here she's Helmer. That must mean Helmer was your family name at the time the portraits were taken. It became Fallesen only later."

Solvi looked at him in dismay. "But I'm from a genteel family, an old Bergen family." She covered her face with her hands. "None of this makes any sense."

"I've found life to be far more complicated than most people pretend," he said gently.

Solvi looked up at him, and something clicked into place. She jumped to her feet.

"I'm sorry, Mr. Stenberg, but I can't stay today. I, I need to do something. I'll come in this weekend to finish the developing. May I take the photograph?"

"Yes, of course. Just bring it back to me when you're done with it."

Done with it. Solvi might never be done with it.

She grabbed her coat and flew out the door.

SOLVI RAN ACROSS TOWN TO THE CAFÉ, desperately hoping Magnus would be there. Inside, she looked madly about, finally spotting him in the back with some friends. "Magnus!"

He looked up from his toasted cheese. "Solvi, what's wrong?"

"I need your help. Remember how you said we should look through the parish records?"

"Yes ..."

"If you have time—." She stopped. "I know I don't have the right to ask, but I'd be very grateful if we could go today. Right now." She took the picture of her grandmother out of her purse. "Because now I know my grandmother's real name."

He stared at her, then pushed the rest of his sandwich in his mouth and stood up. "Good-bye, comrades. The lady awaits."

They headed for the cathedral, Solvi telling him about Otto Stenberg's album of famous Norwegians.

Magnus whistled. "Boy, I'd love to see that! But why was your grandmother in there? Was she famous?"

"More infamous, I'm afraid. Now that I know her actual name, I need to find out if she really died. I don't know why my mother lied to me about her name, but she must have."

"So what are we looking for in the records?"

"Whatever we can find for both Helmer and Fallesen: marriage records, birth and death records. We should be able to find my uncles' and my mother's birth records from the 1870s. My grandparents probably married just before 1870—maybe there's a record of that."

"Their marriage would be recorded in the place where they married," Magnus said. "Did they marry here?"

"I don't know! I just learned my grandmother's real name a half hour ago."

"Right. Okay." He stopped for a minute and tugged on her hand. "It will be okay, Solvi, really."

But she didn't believe that. She felt like the floor of her life was falling away, right out from under her.

INSIDE THE CATHEDRAL they were directed to a library below the nave. A white-haired cleric listened to their request, then disappeared into shelves of ledgers. After a few minutes he reappeared with several large tomes. They took them to a table by the window.

Solvi opened the first, a record of births in Kristiania from 1870 through 1880, and her pulse quickened. The old-styled handwriting, the dates and names of the babies, all of it felt like unlocking time itself. Magnus opened a record of deaths in Kristiania for the same decade. They started scanning for the two names, turning the pages slowly, the dust of the old books making them sneeze.

All of a sudden a familiar name materialized before her eyes. *Helmer, Ivar, a boy, born September 9, 1872. To Torvald and Nora Helmer.*

Solvi gasped. "Look, Magnus. A boy, born to Torvald and Nora Helmer! My uncle!"

He leaned over. "Ivar. He'd be, ah, forty-six today. Old enough for you to have cousins."

"If he's still alive," Solvi said, writing down the information. She kept scanning and soon found another boy born to Torvald and Nora Helmer, Robert, in 1874.

"Two down, just your mother to find next," Magnus said.

Then, several years further into the ledger, Solvi gasped. A girl, Emma, also born to Torvald and Nora Helmer, on April 16, 1877. Her mother's name and birth date.

"Magnus, I found my mother!" She looked at him; tears rose in her eyes.

"Solvi, are you all right?"

"Yes," she said, wiping her face with her sleeve. "But it's so strange, that different name. Why did my mother lie about my grandmother? It's as if she didn't want me to find out anything about her."

"And you've seen no births under Fallesen."

"Nothing under Fallesen," she said. "How about you?"

"Let me search more carefully in the death register, now that we know everyone's name. How old are the boys in that picture?"

Solvi thought for a moment. "Ivar's about seven or eight, and Robert five or six. If they had gone off to school a few years later and died, they would have been about ten and eight, maybe a little older." Solvi did a quick calculation in her head. "So check for their deaths in 1881, 1882. My mother made it sound as if they died at the same time—from cholera or diphtheria, something sudden."

Magnus skimmed carefully through the ledger, but there was nothing. "Maybe the boys didn't die here in Kristiania." He asked the clerk a question and sat back down. "He said that if the boys' family lived here, their deaths would have been recorded here, in this parish." Magnus went back to scanning but then abruptly stopped.

"This is odd," he said, pushing the book in front of Solvi. "Look at this entry."

Solvi squinted—the handwriting had faded a bit. *Nora Helmer, born 1850, declared dead by court order, November 18, 1885.*

She looked up. "What in God's name does that mean? Oh, Magnus, she's dead!"

He shook his head. "Not necessarily. They do that when someone vanishes without a trace."

"Like she drowned or something? Like there was no body?"

"Yes," he said, "or she left Norway, and no one knew." Then he grabbed the ledger of marriages. "I just thought of something." He opened to the year 1886, and there it was. "Torvald Helmer married Johanna Moller the next summer, July 1886. That's why he had your grandmother declared dead. She must have been missing for a while, and he only went to the trouble when he wanted to remarry."

Solvi looked at him, and the room began to sway around her. Then everything went black. She started to topple off her chair.

"Solvi!" Magnus caught her and settled her back on the seat. "Here, put your head between your knees and breathe, big breaths."

Solvi dropped her head and closed her eyes. She could barely think of her grandmother—the elegant woman in the photograph, who radiated such intelligence and warmth—dead at the bottom of a fjord or possibly murdered and left to rot. It was too much. Her grandmother was supposed to be alive, alive and waiting for Solvi to find her. Not dead. Solvi lifted her head, looked at Magnus, and wept.

"Oh, Solvi, let's go." Magnus returned the books, gathered their things, and helped Solvi outside. The sun was setting, lighting up the clouds, but the beauty of the sky meant nothing to her. Her grandmother had died—not quite as her mother said, but she must have died nonetheless.

Magnus walked Solvi back to the study house and promised to check on her the next day. She slipped upstairs and into bed, weepy and broken. How she had longed to find her grandmother alive, someone who might understand her, who could explain her thorny family.

She felt like an orphan.

LATER, Rikka tapped on her door. Solvi let her in, showed her the photo Mr. Stenberg found, and explained how she and Magnus discovered the court declaration of her grandmother's death in the parish records.

Rikka listened to it all, then gave her a consoling hug. "I'm so sorry, Solvi. This must be quite a shock."

"I was so excited, then, just hours later, we found that she died. It was awful."

"But maybe she didn't die," Rikka said. "It's just a court order, not a death certificate."

"But that's what they do when the body can't be found," Solvi said. "She was probably murdered and dumped somewhere, or she committed suicide. She's probably moldering under a pile of leaves right now."

"Listen, don't torture yourself," Rikka said. "Now we can work on finding your uncles."

"But Magnus says there's no sign of them here in Kristiania, not working as professional men. If they're alive, they're somewhere else. I don't think I can search the whole world."

"Perhaps they've left a trail you could follow. Maybe they are the ones waiting for you somewhere."

Solvi nodded, but it was little solace, as she had nothing to go on. Rikka said goodnight, and Solvi fell back into bed, sad in a way that surprised her.

There were losses that could happen before a person was born, losses that cast grief over a family for generations. How much had she wanted to change that.

CHAPTER FIFTEEN

NORA

Spring 1919 ■ *Spokane, Washington*

Maybe Emma was searching for me. Perhaps she found some evidence that I was alive and had grown curious. Perhaps her own children made her think of me in a different way.

When I had my first baby, I began to wonder more about my lost mother. There was something about holding my infant child in my arms that made me ache for what I had been denied growing up without a mother. Perhaps Emma had that same revelation—the sudden understanding that losing me shaped her more than she had thought.

I examined her baby face in the photograph, but there were few clues. The last time I saw Emma she was twelve years old, a surly little beauty. She wouldn't have anything to do with me. I always hoped that would change one day. Every year when her birthday came, I imagined her more grown-up, more mature. By now, no doubt, she was living the privileged life of an elegant lady. I could just see her ruling her household with a confident hand, knowing what she preferred and how it should be done. I often wondered whether she found a good husband, someone worthy of her, someone who would respect her concerns and treat her like an adult. But perhaps Torvald got in the way.

The truth is, I had no idea what kind of woman she had grown up to be. I sometimes imagined her playing my piano, using my books of Mozart and Chopin, yet I had no evidence that she enjoyed music, as I did. Did she have close friends beyond her family? Did she take baskets to the poor? Did she have a favorite child, or was she fair-minded and careful not to prefer one above another?

I wondered what it would be like to meet her on the street. Would I be intimidated by her or drawn to her? She had been a bossy baby, willful and demanding. As a young teen she appeared mannered but suspicious—uninterested in anything or anyone that was not part of her world. What kind of woman had grown from such roots?

I wrote to Emma when she was eighteen, telling her where I was, but I never heard back. Most likely Torvald burned the letter before she even saw it.

Maybe she had placed this ad. Maybe she was the one who wanted to find me.

NORA
February 1882 ■ *Lac qui Parle, Minnesota*

The days were lengthening, but the winter cold deepened, leaving the sky clear and cloudless. One day Anders said he and Jens would take the wagon down to the lake to gather wood while the weather held. "Only for a few days," he said, smiling. "Mr. Renville said we could stay in the abandoned mission."

I packed them blankets and food. Birgitte and I watched the wagon disappear into the woods.

Later that night she sat down next to me by the stove. "Nora . . . may I ask, what happened to your husband and children?"

"My family?" I stopped to knot a thread, biting off the ends to give myself time to think. "It was an accident, Birgitte. Terrible. I try not to think of it." I fell silent, wondering if that was a lie. There was an accident—the accident of my being blackmailed and discovering that my husband wasn't the man I needed him to be.

"How long ago?"

"Several years," I said tersely. "I'd rather not discuss it."

"I am asking, Nora, because I wonder how long a person should grieve."

I softened. "Oh, of course. Some losses you never get over; others fade more quickly."

"Will you miss Tomas when you go?"

"When I go? Why, yes, Birgitte, but I'm prepared for that." I stuffed my sewing in my bag and stood up. "I'm looking forward to starting my life in Chicago."

"You just seem so settled here, with us," she said, an edge to her voice. "Jens thinks you will stay forever."

"Perhaps I should talk with him, so he understands."

"And talk with Papa," she said, more boldly. "He must understand as well."

"Your father understands, Birgitte. Now, we best get to bed, as we have all the chores to do ourselves in the morning."

THE CONVERSATION left me unsettled. The next day I helped Birgitte in the barn, tossing out the soiled hay and bringing in fresh, but we didn't talk. Instead of a lesson, I gave her some Bible passages to translate while I mixed and kneaded the bread, as I was reluctant to engage her.

Then a knock sounded on the door. We both jumped.

When I opened it, Siri Madsen stood there, wrapped against the wind in two shawls.

"My goodness, Siri, come in!"

Her teeth chattered, and she moved quickly to the stove. "Please, Mrs. Eriksen, you must come. The boys are sick, very sick, and Mama doesn't know what to do. She said to come for you, as you are educated and will know how to help them."

I might be educated, but I knew nothing of medicine. "Isn't there a doctor in Lac qui Parle village?"

"No. Papa went to Montevideo to fetch one, but he's been gone two days."

Birgitte looked at me. I didn't know if I could help, but Dr. Rank often talked to me of his cases; perhaps I would remember something. I darted outside to check for blizzard clouds, but there was only bright sunshine. I didn't see how I could refuse.

I went back inside and nodded to Siri. "I'll come. Let me get a few things."

"No!" Birgitte cried out. "Papa would never want you to leave us!"

"Birgitte, your father said that you could easily handle things here if I needed to go into town for some reason. So I'm going to the Madsens'. It's not that far, and I'll be back tomorrow." I moved around the house packing a small bundle—extra socks, iodine, baking soda, the brandy. But the truth was, I had no idea what I needed.

Birgitte stared at me. "Father said that?"

"Yes. He has every confidence in you, as do I. Now, you know what to do for Tomas? He's safer here with you."

"Yes, but, but . . . What do I do if a blizzard comes?"

"Bring in the rest of the woodpile, leave the stock plenty of hay, and melt snow for water. You'll be fine." I threw on my coat and Inge's shawl. "Goodbye and be careful!"

SIRI AND I TRUDGED ACROSS the frozen prairie as quickly as we could, our heads deep in our shawls. It was a relief to get away from Birgitte's prying comments, and I was pleased the Madsens had turned to me, even if I knew little about nursing.

The family lived west of our farm in a low sod house that stood out in the middle of the flatland with little protection from the weather. Siri glanced at me as we pushed through the door, as if in warning.

I should have braced myself, as the air inside the soddie reeked of illness and soiled linen. A wave of nausea swept over me. In the dim light, I could see Mrs. Madsen in a rocker, crooning to a child that lay limp in her lap. Racking coughs echoed from the beds in the back.

Siri sank to her knees in front of her mother. "Oh, *Mor* . . ."

Mrs. Madsen looked up at me, weeping. "He's gone! I couldn't do anything for him, and now he's gone!"

It was Nils, my youngest student; my heart clenched. "Here," I said gently, "let me take him." I gathered him up and laid him on their wedding chest. Siri, leaking tears, fetched an old muslin sheet, and we wrapped his small body.

I sat down beside his mother. "I'm so sorry, Mrs. Madsen. What do you think this illness is?"

"I don't know, Mrs. Eriksen! I've never seen this before. They have fever and a very sore throat. Nils could barely breathe. He gasped so!" She began to weep again, and Siri glanced at me, ashamed. She hadn't wanted to say how bad it was for fear I wouldn't come.

Behind a curtain I found Claus, Tosten, and two-year-old Per together in one bed, clutching each other in fear and misery. I held a candle close and looked down their throats. They all had something that looked like a patch of white leather across their windpipes, and Per was hot to the touch.

I mixed baking soda and water to quell their stomachs, but they barely swallowed any of it. I boiled tea; again they took little. A memory flickered in my mind of Dr. Rank talking about the Trondheim throat sickness, a disease that struck children, often killing several in a household. Or it could be scarlet fever, though none had a rash. I prayed it was not scarlet fever.

When I had dosed the boys as best I could, I helped Mrs. Madsen wash and change into fresh clothes—she probably hadn't rested in days—and then I made her lie down. Within minutes she was asleep.

Siri and I cleaned up, sweeping, washing dishes, and boiling the dirty sheets, which she stoically took outside to pin on the clothesline. After that she sank, exhausted, into bed as well. I dozed in the rocking chair. Some-time before dawn Mrs. Madsen awakened and went to sit beside Nils's little body, muttering prayers in Old Norske.

In the morning the older boys seemed a bit better and could take some gruel, but little Per was worse and gagged as if being strangled. I wrapped him in a blanket and rocked him by the stove. By early afternoon I grew worried. Birgitte expected me back, but I hated to leave before Mr. Madsen returned. I stepped outside to check for storms and spotted a wagon com-ing over the southern horizon. I prayed the doctor was with him.

But when Mr. Madsen came through the door, he was alone. His wife rose, sobbing, and collapsed in his arms, telling him about Nils. He held her for a long moment, then went to his dead child and knelt beside him.

I gathered my things to go. "I need to get back to my own children," I said.

"It may be diphtheria, or scarlet fever," he told me. "Something is sweep-ing through western Minnesota. The doctor couldn't come because so many in town are sick."

"I'm very sorry for your loss."

He just nodded, resigned. I left them to their grief.

I HURRIED HOME, glancing over my shoulder, but the sky remained blessedly clear. The sun slipped below the horizon, and I made it back just as the world went dark. When I came through the door, Birgitte jumped up with a cry of relief and helped me unwrap.

"Thank you, Birgitte. How's Tomas?"

"Fine. He's napping. I made *primost*. There was milk for it, without every-one here. How are the Madsens?"

I sat down, stiff from my labors, and warmed my hands by the stove. "It's sad news, Birgitte. Little Nils died last night. I don't know if it is scarlet fever or diphtheria, but all the boys are ill. I fear their baby will not live another day."

Her hands flew to her face. "No! How awful! Did they get medicine? Did a doctor come? And what about Siri?"

"Mr. Madsen returned with some medicine, but the doctor was too busy tending sick children in Montevideo. Siri, so far, seems fine; I hope she can resist it."

We ate our beans with *primost* on bread, and I spent the evening with Tomas in my lap, so glad to be back in our neat little house with these healthy children. I could feel the despair of the Madsen household like soot on my clothes. After putting Tomas down for the night, I washed and slipped into bed for a deep, comforting sleep.

TWO DAYS LATER, Anders and Jens appeared just before dusk, the wagon loaded with firewood. They were cold and tired, so we ate right away. Then I told them about the Madsens.

Jens fell silent when I mentioned Nils.

Anders turned to me. "What was this illness?"

"I'm not sure, but it may have been scarlet fever or diphtheria, what they called the Trondheim throat sickness back home. The boys could scarcely breathe, with white lumps in their throats."

"Yes, I remember hearing about that." He looked concerned. "I hope you didn't bring the illness home."

I glanced at Tomas, sitting in my lap and kicking at my hands. "Oh, I don't think so."

"Did you bathe before touching him?"

Birgitte and I looked at each other. "No," I said. "I held him in my lap until bedtime, then washed up. Would that matter?"

A shadow crossed Anders's face. "Let's hope not."

My stomach seemed to fall away. I thought of Nils's cold body lying atop the rosemaled chest. Please, God. Please.

Anders stood and patted my shoulder. "I'm sure he'll be fine, Nora. Let's just keep him warm and well fed. We mustn't worry about it."

LATER THAT WEEK, however, Tomas woke up hot to the touch. Birgitte brought him to me, saying he was fussy and sweaty. When Anders heard that, he snatched the child, took him over to the lamp, and peered down his throat. The baby coughed and fussed. "It looks a little red," he said. "And he's feverish. How many days since you were with the Madsens?"

"Five? Six?"

"Let's see if he'll drink his milk," Anders said.

While I got the flask, Anders checked both Jens and Birgitte, looking down their throats and feeling their foreheads. They seemed fine, but Tomas was clearly sick with something. He turned from the flask, as if drinking was painful.

Anders and Jens tended to the chores in the barn, taking longer than usual. When they returned, Anders started pulling the blankets off the beds.

"If this is diphtheria, Jens and Birgitte and I must live in the barn until it passes."

"What?" I looked at him, aghast.

"Diphtheria is very contagious among children, Nora, so we must quarantine you and Tomas here in the house." He dragged one of the hay ticks to the door.

"You'll leave me to nurse him alone?"

"I've no choice, Nora. I've got to go to Montevideo for medicine."

Panic rose like bile in my throat. "Please, Anders, please don't leave me alone with the baby. What if he weakens? What if he dies? Please!" Yet I clutched Tomas to my chest, as if the fairies were after him.

Anders turned to Birgitte. "Birgitte, take the hay tick to the barn, and these blankets."

"But, Papa ..."

"Now. Do as you're told."

She shouldered the tick and went out the door.

Anders came over to me. "Nora, you must understand that I have no choice. It breaks my heart to leave you here alone with the baby, but I could lose them all if I don't quarantine you. I couldn't survive that." He took a deep breath. "We won't be able to come back into the house until it's over, one way or the other, and you've cleaned the house of the contagion. I'll talk to you through the door."

My hands shook. "What if it's not diphtheria but something that might sicken me? Would you leave me to die with him?"

He looked at me—I could see the turmoil in his eyes. "I wouldn't do that if I thought you could get what he has. Adults are usually unaffected by diphtheria, and that must be what it is, as there are no other illnesses around."

"But how was he exposed?"

"He could had gotten it from your clothes or your hair, even your breath."

Something inside me crumbled. "Am I to blame?"

"No. Nora, you did what you could, what any kind person would do. You didn't know how contagious it would be, or you wouldn't have gone." He couldn't quite look at me as he said this last bit.

Now he glanced around the kitchen area, anxious to get what he needed and retreat.

"Take some dried fish, and the skillet and cornmeal," I said, piling things into a crate—spoons, bowls, crocks.

He carried out the crate and bedding. A few minutes later I heard him shouting at Birgitte to stay away from the house.

"I want to see him!" she screamed.

"No! Birgitte! Come away!" I heard a scuffle, then Birgitte's fading sobs as her father dragged her down the path to the barn. A few minutes later he returned to say good-bye to Tomas. He dared not touch the child but leaned over him. "Sweet Tomas," he whispered, lingering for a long moment.

Then he turned to me. "Try to make him drink—water and milk with a little brandy. Whatever you can get down his throat. I'm leaving now for Montevideo and should be back late tomorrow with the medicine. I'll have Birgitte or Jens come by every hour to see what you need. But don't let them in, no matter how they plead."

He banged out the door.

I WARMED MILK MIXED WITH BRANDY, but Tomas—listless and flushed—drank little. I rocked him until my arms ached, only putting him back in bed when Birgitte left me a bowl of corn mush.

After I ate, I lay down, curling myself around his fevered body, as if I could shield him from death. As the night wore on, his breathing grew more labored, and in the morning there was the telltale white membrane in his throat. By noon I noticed swollen lumps on both sides of his neck, and his temperature seemed even higher. I bathed him in cool water and vinegar to bring the fever down, but he cried through the ordeal and kicked in misery. I wrapped him back up, and he slipped into an exhausted sleep.

As I watched him worsen, dread built inside me. I tried to think of him healthy, playing peek-a-boo with my apron or watching me from his harness. He had been mine for less than a year, yet was as dear to me as my own. It seemed strange, now, that I was never allowed the closeness of caring for my own children, protected as I was by Torvald and Anne-Marie. Could I have left them if I had? I doubted it.

And now I was losing this one.

BIRGITTE KNOCKED ON THE DOOR every few hours, asking about her brother. I didn't want to tell her the worst, so I just said he was sick but resting. With each small lie, my isolation grew. I was the only one who knew what was happening.

As his breathing grew more tortured, I wracked my brain for anything that might help but could think of nothing. Later that evening, as Tomas gasped for breath and burned with fever, Anders knocked on the door. "Nora, I'm back. I brought medicine. How is he?"

"Oh, Anders, he's fighting for every breath!"

"Quickly, then. The doctor said to mix a spoonful with a little water. Here, I'm leaving it by the door. I'll check back in an hour."

I waited a few moments then snatched the packet off the ground. My hands shook as I opened the precious envelope and mixed the powder with water. I took a sip—it was exceedingly bitter, so I stirred in some molasses. I poured the medicine down Tomas's throat, but he gagged and spit most of it back up. I tried again, finally holding his nose so he would have to swallow to breathe. He struggled and cried but finally took most of it. I laid him back in bed, then poured myself a dram of brandy to calm my nerves. When Anders came by later, I told him Tomas had taken the medicine. I feared, however, that it was too late.

My sweet boy had one last night, a torment of racking breaths I hoped never to witness again. I could feel him drowning but was powerless to save him. By morning his pulse was so low I could barely find it, and his breath came in shuddering gasps. When Anders knocked on the door, I just said he wasn't much better. I knew he would die, but I could not say it.

All that day I rocked and sang to him. Tomas seemed a bit calmer when I did so, and it eased the knot in my chest. Late in the afternoon, as the light faded away, he took his last gasping breath. A long moment of silence followed, and then his little body slumped in death, his head rolling toward my breast.

I held him for a long time. I had taken on his care as a sacred trust, and now it had come to this. A fine mother I turned out to be.

I FINALLY ROSE, the cold urging me back to life. I wrapped him in a blanket and laid him on his father's bed.

Then, a knock. "How is he, Nora?" It was Anders.

I could not answer. I stood frozen in the middle of the room.

"Nora! What's happening?" His voice rose in panic.

"Oh, Anders, Tomas has, he has . . ." I could not say it. I could not make myself say it.

"Nora, has he died?"

I finally croaked out a yes, then shouted it, not knowing if he had heard. "He's gone! Oh, Anders, I'm so sorry!" All I could do was weep.

I didn't know what hell Anders experienced outside the sod house. It was very still. I listened at the door. "Anders, are you there?"

"Yes, Nora." His voice was cold and flat, like death itself.

"I tried everything, but the medicine came too late!" I was weeping again and could speak no more.

"Nora, Nora. Calm yourself. God does not blame you, nor do I. Please."

I tried to pull myself together. "I've wrapped him in his blanket."

"I'll build a box for him. And, Nora, put the medicine packet outside the door. I'll give the rest to Birgitte and Jens, just in case."

"Yes."

"You must clean the house, Nora, from top to bottom. The doctor gave me alum powder. You mix it with water and scrub everything. Burn Tomas's clothing and blankets, then you must boil the other clothing and bedding in the house. But first, get some rest. In the morning Birgitte will get the water and wood you need and leave it out here. You'll need to strip and burn the newspaper from the walls, then wipe the walls with the solution."

"Yes, of course," I said. I couldn't imagine how I would find the strength, but I couldn't let the others die.

"I'm going to tell the children. Don't forget the medicine."

I grabbed the packet and set it outside the door. A few minutes later I heard muffled shouts and cries from the barn, then later the hammer blows as Anders began building the tiny coffin. They echoed through the night.

I SLEPT IN FITS AND STARTS, chased by snatches of dreams, some of Tomas, some of my own children. Many were gentle, but a vivid image of crows picking at a child's body woke me just before dawn. I got up and stoked the fire, then forced myself to heat water for tea and porridge. I had little appetite, but if I didn't eat, I wouldn't have the strength I needed.

Anders knocked and said that Tomas's coffin was ready.

"Must we bury him so soon?" I couldn't bear the thought of putting him in the ground.

"Yes, Nora. His body carries the contagion. Mr. Renville helped me dig a small grave."

"Will we have a service?"

"In a few days, when we can."

I waited a few minutes, then opened the door to find a beautiful little wooden coffin, with Tomas's initials and a Gudbrandsdal flower carved on top. I brought it in and lined it with one of his mother's old skirts, making a comfortable nest. He was stiff now, and cool; I laid him in the box, then blew him a gentle kiss and put the lid back on. It was all I could do to set the coffin outside and shut the door, as if leaving him for the wolves. I was relieved to hear his father return and take him away.

BEFORE LONG BIRGITTE KNOCKED HARD, yelling that the water and wood for the laundry was outside. She was angry—blamed me, no doubt. In a fog of sorrow, I pulled the buckets and wood inside, then built up the fire and stuffed Tomas's clothes into the stove. I was tempted to keep his little red knit hat, but I could not risk it. All, into the flames.

I scrubbed and boiled all that long day, finally bathing in the last of the rinse water. I napped and then ate a little supper and started peeling the newspaper off the walls so I could wipe them down.

And that was when I found the letter, pushed into a crack between the sod bricks.

Norwegian, in a feminine hand. I caught my breath. It was addressed to Anders.

Dear Anders, Gustaf died three days ago—lung fever. Hans and I are now very weak, from hunger and illness, and it is still snowing. Hans lies beside his father's body and cries. We've nothing left to eat save the pages of the Bible. I don't know if you'll find this note, but please know I did my best. I cannot watch my son suffer any longer, and so I will take him outside to meet his Maker. The blizzard will rage through the night; by morning it should be over. How dearly I wish we'd never left our beautiful valley in Norway. Good-bye, dear family. Kari

Dread filled my chest. Did she take her son out into the storm to freeze? There was something evil in this land, something that lived now in this house. I slipped her letter into the stove. Anders needn't know that she watched his brother die and took her son's death into her own hands. I thought of her and Hans huddled in the blizzard and wept for her. And as I mourned, something of her took root in me. Everything felt useless, hopeless, sad beyond bearing. It was all I could do to wipe down the furniture and walls with the alum, then sprinkle the floor and sweep it dry. Finally, I opened the door and let the cold wind in, weeping as winter swirled through our little home.

After a while, Anders brought the children and their bedding and food back inside. We shut the door and lit the stove again. Anders asked Birgitte to get our supper and went back out to the barn to do the evening chores.

I threw on my shawl and followed. I knew how it looked, but I couldn't help it.

Anders put down his hay fork. "Nora, why have you come out into the cold?"

I moved toward him, leaking tears, my arms open. "Please, Anders, hold me. It was awful—you have no idea."

But he backed up, his eyes intense with pain. "Nora, I cannot. You may still carry the contagion, and I don't want to take it back to Birgitte or Jens. I don't mean to hurt you."

"Don't you love me anymore?"

"Please, not tonight. I cannot bear anything tonight."

My heart stopped. He saw this in my face.

"Nora, dear Nora, bless you for caring for him. You saved the other two, I swear to God." He turned away; he didn't want me to see his grief, or his anger. "Just give me time."

I wanted to sink through the floor. Instead, I went back to the soddie and climbed into bed. I could not face any of them.

AFTER TOMAS DIED, the snows returned. Winter gripped the land, and the cold and darkness settled in my breast. Nothing moved in that frigid world except what the wind gave life to. Once a day, if weather permitted, I bundled up and staggered through the drifts to the little graveyard. Only the tops of the wooden crosses poked through the snow, and often Tomas's small cross could not be seen at all.

Sometimes it almost felt as if I had imagined him, that he was never a real child who babbled and laughed. But when I closed my eyes I could see him—peeking out over my shoulder on the dock in Kristiania, staring into my eyes when I fed him, falling asleep in the crook of my arm. It felt as if my own child had died. No, it was worse—it felt as if my only surviving child had died. Stripped of my three, I had turned to Tomas for comfort, and somehow he knew his part. I was able to come to America and learn to live on this godforsaken prairie because I had him on my hip. Now that he was gone, I couldn't bear anything.

Sometimes I would look away from the graveyard out across the frozen lake and listen for my destiny. I could feel the lake beckoning me, just as the fjord had beckoned the night I left Torvald. It was all I could do not to turn from Tomas's grave and follow the path to its frozen edge.

But I could not allow myself such indulgence. I pulled my shawl tight and trudged back to the hateful sod house and my responsibilities inside.

ANDERS DIDN'T LIKE ME GOING TO THE GRAVE SITE but said nothing. None of us said anything about Tomas; indeed, we rarely spoke at all. I didn't talk because I feared anything from me would make it worse.

At first I could not understand this winter of the soul. Then I started to think that Anders and Birgitte thought I had no right to feel what they felt, as I was not Tomas's mother. And because they did not cry, I could not cry. We all grieved silently behind our stoic faces.

I knew they blamed me. I risked the family's health for others, and the worst happened. Birgitte's resentment soon took root and flared in a thousand subtle ways. She blocked me from talking with Jens; she ignored me during lessons; she elbowed me out of the easy chores. And I let her, because she was right—I was a fraud. I knew little about caring for children and should never have pretended otherwise.

She soon grew bold and started speaking rudely to me in front of her father. I expected him to come to my defense, but he just muttered admonitions and turned away. None of us was any help to each other.

And poor Jens drifted through his sorrow alone, like a child clinging to a spar in a vast sea. I saw him suffering but dared not comfort him. Never again would I mother a child; he was better off seeking comfort from his father and sister. It was too dangerous to be close to me.

AT NIGHT IN THE BED I shared with the simmering Birgitte, I turned to the dirt wall and considered what was left of my life. I had lost my country, my class, my family and friends, and now my purpose. Without Tomas, Anders didn't seem to love me anymore. He sank into his grief, avoiding my eye and my company. The cord that bound me to the Eriksens loosened with a jerk the day Tomas died, and now it dropped away.

MY DEPENDENCE BEGAN TO CHAFE. I imagined that they resented having to feed me, so I ate only small bits. I moved my chair back from the stove, out of the family circle. Our lessons died away. I did my chores—most of the cooking and sewing—but little else. Anders spent as much time out of the house as he could, working in the cold barn on his carving. Jens followed him like a puppy, now that he was discouraged from spending time with me, and Birgitte went as well, since she disliked being left with me. Alone, I wept silently as I went about my work.

My mind took on a life of its own. One day, I picked up the butcher knife and pushed the tip against my skin, pricking enough to draw blood. I imagined that cutting my arm would release the tremendous pressure trapped inside. I pressed again until it hurt, then stopped, but the idea did not frighten me.

And then there was Kari Eriksen. First she showed up in my dreams, a gaunt figure leaning over our stove, making a dreadful-smelling stew. She seemed to haunt the sod house; I imagined her slipping behind a curtain at the edge of my vision, or bringing in a load of wood when I heard Birgitte open the door with a grunt. Kari didn't frighten me any more than the knife did. By imagining her here with us, I felt I could give her something in death that no one gave her in life—understanding and sympathy. I was particularly consumed by her last days, watching her husband die and making her fateful decision. I began to feel I was becoming Kari—isolated, miserable, alone.

Mr. Renville stopped by one day with more of the Indian rice, to boost our health, he said. Birgitte elbowed her brother, and they slipped out to the barn. I was glad to get a chance to talk with him privately, so I made tea while he warmed himself, then asked if he could tell me about finding the Eriksens' bodies.

Mr. Renville looked up from his cup. "Why do you want to know?"

"I found a letter Kari wrote but left behind, hidden in the wall."

"What did it say?"

"She said Gustaf died of lung fever first and that they had no food left, and she couldn't bear to watch Hans die of hunger, so she . . ." I choked and could not go on.

"So that's why she took him outside that night."

"You found them there?"

"Yes, their bodies were just beyond the barn, where it's less protected.

That puzzled me at first, but when I saw that Gustaf had died earlier, I understood." He looked into my sad eyes. "I'm sorry you had to find that letter."

"I burned it, as I didn't want Anders to know. It's been so difficult for him, losing his wife, his brother, and now Tomas. Please, don't say anything to him."

"Yes, Mrs. Eriksen, if you think that best."

"Anders carries his grief inside, but it's a heavy burden, and I fear it might defeat him if he knows the worst."

He nodded, pensive. "Thank you for the tea, Mrs. Eriksen."

THE EMPTY PRAIRIE turned people in on themselves, and if that was not a safe haven, then woe to them. One day I was thinking of Kari and her terrible decision, and the next day I envied her. If the Church fathers were right, she and little Hans were together now with Gustaf. I didn't know if there was a heaven, but I hoped her soul had joined those of her son and husband, which might be all the heaven she needed. When I knelt in the snow beside Tomas's grave, I prayed he was with his mother; otherwise the afterlife would be a lonely place for a child.

I slipped Emma's embroidered cap inside my chemise and kept it there against my thinning breast, in my grief likening Tomas to my own baby. I also put Ivar's stone—still strangely comforting—in my apron pocket, where I could hold it when I needed to. I walked to the graveyard, thinking of Tomas, then looked out across the frozen lake and thought of Kari. She escaped this life, this awful dirt house, this evil land. Maybe I could escape, as she had—free myself from the pain and sorrow.

And so I drifted away from everyday life into the bleak world of my weakened mind.

ONE DAY IN LATE MARCH I noticed the ground softening beneath my feet, mud mixing with the snow, and from the hill I could see water puddling on the lake ice. Spring was coming; slowly, but it would come. I squeezed Ivar's stone in my pocket.

A few days later Anders and I argued over the best way to treat an infected cut Jens had on his hand. Anders wanted to rub cow liniment into it; I thought we should bathe it in hot water with salts. I pushed too hard—Birgitte came to her father's side and shouted me to silence. I turned to

Anders, but he just looked away. His refusal to reprimand her left me burning with shame; I had come to nothing in his eyes. I slid behind the curtain and crawled into bed.

The next morning Anders said he and the children would take the wagon north to gather wood. Birgitte packed bread and dried fish, saying they wouldn't return until dark. My pulse began to race. I said no more than a simple good-bye as they closed the door behind them.

I left my pearls as payment, with a note, tucked in the pocket of my apron. Perhaps now they could afford the lumber for a house. I patted Emma's cap to make sure it was there inside my bodice and then put my baptism certificate, the photograph of my family, and the letter from my children into my drawstring bag, which I tied around my waist. Finally, I put Ivar's stone in the pocket of my coat.

Outside, I headed first to the cemetery, where I whispered over Tomas's grave until I wept. I then turned down the path toward the southeastern end of the lake. I moved as if in a trance, clutching at branches to keep from slipping in the soft snow.

A desperate longing to withdraw built inside me. It was not that I wanted to run away—I wanted to vanish, leave no trace, melt into water with the spring snow. Because only then would I find peace. If I lived, I would just hurt more people with my lies and pretending. I lied to my father to get away from his prying; I lied to Torvald to evade his authority; I had lied to the priests and police and all my friends. And I lied to Anders so I could cling to what he had—a ticket, a baby, a family. But no more.

It took me a long time to find the right spot, my body growing numb in the chill. I didn't think—just pushed down through the undergrowth to the lake edge, thorns snagging my clothes, skidding through the mud. When I reached the bank, I stopped to breathe, but just for a moment. There was open water farther out but, close in, the ice still hugged the shoreline. The woods were quiet and still. The lake whispered its promise.

I stepped out. The ice, spongy and dense, creaked beneath my weight. I brought Ivar's stone to my lips. I meant to kiss it good-bye but instead slipped it into my mouth, as if to stop the lies. I shuffled out a few more feet; nothing. Then a few more and a few more.

The ice gave way; I plunged into the water.

For the first moment it felt like a comfort, but then the cold hit—an intense pain that shot through me and shattered my trance. I tried to let myself sink, but every muscle in my body wanted to fight. I could feel grass around my legs, then my feet hit bottom. I looked up. Sunlight filtered down through the hole, beautiful and serene, but under the ice there was a murky blackness unlike anything I had ever seen—the color of death. Terrifying emptiness. I felt Ivar's stone, heavy on my tongue, and suddenly remembered stopping by Torvald's apartment and my wolf-like hunger to see my children.

For the first time in weeks, I thought of them.

I spit out the stone and gulped in lake water. Spots danced before my eyes. I wavered between two worlds. Then, blazing across my mind like a comet, came Torvald's terrible lie: that he would tell the children I died. And here I was, despite the distance, doing what he wanted, playing the role he wrote for me.

But it was not what my children wanted, those sad creatures I locked away and tried not to think about. The children who still lived and breathed, who deserved to have a mother.

I struggled out of my coat, then kicked off the bottom with all my strength. I grabbed the ice edge and managed to get my head above water and take a breath. But the softened ice quickly gave way, and I went under again. I pulled out a second time, took another breath, got my arms up onto the ice, and crashed through again. I breathed in water, coughed, and sputtered, but it was shallower now. Desperate, I threw myself toward the trees, which reached for me like silent helpers. Somehow I pulled myself out and collapsed onto the wet snow of the bank. I looked around. There was no one. I called out to the quiet wood. Nothing but the drip of melting snow.

I laid my head on my cold arms, so tired I could scarcely breathe. Gently, tenderly, the world went black.

CHAPTER SIXTEEN

SOLVI

April 1919 ■ *Kristiania, Norway*

When Magnus slipped into his seat next to Solvi in history class, he squeezed her hand. "Are you all right?"

She smiled sadly. "It doesn't make sense, feeling bereft over a grandmother I never knew, but I do."

"But Solvi," he said, "you don't know for certain that she died."

"If she was alive, don't you think my mother would have heard from her?" She shook her head. "She must have died years ago. I need to let her go."

"If your grandmother is gone, let's try to find your uncles," Magnus said. "There's no evidence that they died."

"That's what Rikka thinks, but how on earth would we do that?"

"With an advertisement."

Solvi looked at him, puzzled. "What do you mean? What kind of advertisement?"

"We prepare an advertisement to be posted in a newspaper, one that includes the photograph you have of your family. Mr. Blehr could probably help us."

"But you said my uncles aren't working here in Kristiania, so what would be the point?"

"The point would be to run the advertisement in an American newspaper, one the Norwegians read."

She stared at him. "Do you think my uncles are in America?"

"Yes, I do," he said. "Otherwise, I'm sure they would have contacted your mother."

"Even if they didn't know her name?"

"If they are alive, I suspect their last name has also been Fallesen for some time."

At that moment, Professor Wolff banged into the room, and there was no more time to talk. Solvi hoped Magnus would have time to go to the pastry shop after class, but instead he picked up his books, gave her a small smile, and walked away.

A FEW DAYS LATER, Matron handed Solvi a card. "Delivered by a constable, Miss Lange," she said. "I hope you aren't in any trouble."

Solvi turned away to read the note.

I've found information about the Helmers. At your service, Officer Farstad

SOLVI TOOK RIKKA WITH HER, someone to hang on to if she got bad news.

But when they arrived, Officer Farstad greeted them with an eager smile and bustled them over to a counter beside a bookcase of ledgers.

"I've got to say, Miss Lange, it looks like your relatives—your grandparents, I'm guessing—got into a marital tiff," he said, opening a musty old police docket. "Here's the first item, from June 1881: *Torvald Helmer, a bank manager, requested police assistance in finding his estranged wife, Nora. Blond, medium figure, attractive. His private investigator followed Mrs. Helmer to a rooming house at Filosofgangen and Vinkelgaden, in Vika. Mr. Helmer suspects she has fallen into a state of hysteria and should be under the care of doctors at the asylum. She appears to be living with a group of young anarchists; he fears she may be engaged in prostitution.*"

Solvi stared at the entry, struggling to believe this Mr. Helmer could have been her grandfather. It was so tawdry, so humiliating. How could such a thing have happened to her grandparents?

"And here's the second," Officer Farstad said, flipping the pages to later in the month. *Nora Helmer picked up in raid on rooming house at Filosofgangen and Vinkelgaden last night. She refused to inform on the residents at the rooming house. She had lice; head was shaved. No charges brought. She was released into the protection of her husband, Torvald Helmer. She could possibly be persuaded to testify against the residents if necessary.*"

Rikka and Solvi looked at each other. "Prostitution, hysteria?" Solvi whispered. "And they shaved her head?"

"Routine in those days," Officer Farstad said. "Especially if a woman wasn't behaving herself." He coughed. "There're two more, some years later." He opened another ledger.

The first entry was June 5, 1885. *Torvald Helmer requests an investigation into the disappearance of his wife, Nora Helmer. Officer Sandvik assigned.* Then he flipped to the last one, a few months later: *Investigation into the whereabouts of Nora Helmer closed. As there is no evidence of her living anywhere in Norway, nor record of her leaving the country, it is presumed she has died. Registered with the court for a declaration of death, November 18, 1885.*

"That's it, all I could find," Officer Farstad said.

Solvi handed him a crown. "Thank you, Officer."

She and Rikka stepped outside. "That explains it, doesn't it?" Solvi said, giving Rikka a grim look. "I just never imagined it would involve prostitution and hysteria. Maybe it's better that my grandmother is dead."

"No, Solvi," said Rikka. "If you're after the truth, it wasn't in that police docket. Nothing proved she was either a prostitute or insane. I'll bet she didn't even have lice! They probably shaved her head to punish her for protecting her friends."

Solvi gave her a dubious look. "Do you really think so?"

"Yes," said Rikka. "We have no idea what the true story is. Maybe she was a hero, Solvi. I'll bet she was a hero to those young men."

"My mother would never think of her as a hero," Solvi said.

"Perhaps not, but you can think of her that way."

A FEW DAYS LATER, Solvi stood before an elegant mansion, dread filling her chest. Ever since Dominik invited her to Sunday dinner at his family's house in Homans Byen and she saw the address, Solvi had wondered. Could the house where she hid in the laundry closet be Dominik's house? She knew it was on the same street, but she didn't know whether this was the house. Maybe all mansions looked alike.

Dominik answered the door. "We've been waiting for you."

He led her to the parlor, where his parents were sipping drinks. Dominik's mother, her hair in a French twist, swept forward to shake Solvi's hand. She was older than Solvi's mother, not as beautiful, though her gown was expensive and trimmed with exquisite lace. She looked Solvi over, then smiled, as if Solvi had passed some sort of test. She was right to wear the silk her mother had picked out.

"Welcome, Solveig," she said. "Come sit and tell me of your family."

Dominik's father handed her a glass of sherry and gave her a nod before stepping over to a desk on the other side of the room and moving some papers around.

Dominik poured himself a drink and sat down next to Solvi, smug as a cat as she answered his mother's questions. They were gently probing, the questions Solvi had heard a hundred times in the parlors of Bergen. Who were her father and his Danish family? Who was her mother, and where was her family from? And, finally, who was her grandfather, and which bank had he managed? All asked with a charming smile.

But for the first time these questions made Solvi stutter. She wasn't sure, anymore, where her mother was from, or even if she should answer honestly. She smiled back at Dominik's mother, to cover up what she didn't want to say.

The door to the parlor opened, and a young man entered. He was older, smartly dressed, with dark eyes and his nose held high, as if he were sniffing the air. He reminded Solvi of Stefan Vinter.

"Ah, Edvard, come meet Solveig Lange, Dominik's new girl," said Dominik's father.

He shook her hand. "Nice to meet you. Dominik's been telling us about you. Apparently you're a photographer."

Solvi went still. It was the same voice, the voice of the man who put his hand around Greta's neck. This *was* the house.

Dominik elbowed her. "Tell them how you took pictures of plants for your father."

She looked at their faces. There was no sign that anyone recognized her or knew anything about the photographs she took in their kitchen. Poor Greta seemed to have covered for her.

"Well, my father studied rare plants, and as he didn't like to dig them up, he taught me to take photographs in the field. When he died, he left me his camera. I mostly take landscapes and pictures of my friends." She couldn't look at Dominik, as she was terrified he would mention her pictures of the housemaids.

"She took a picture of me the other day, up near Akershus Fortress," Dominik said proudly. "I suspect you've got it pinned up near your mirror, eh, Solvi?"

She didn't know what to say, so just sipped her sherry. How much she seemed to need it at the moment.

"Let's go in," Dominik's mother said, standing. They passed into a beautiful dining room, the walls papered in a damask rose, the mahogany table and china gleaming. Dinner was just as Solvi had expected—a beef roast from England, champagne, a French torte for dessert. Solvi and the serving maids glanced at each other in recognition, and from that point on Solvi tried to look only at the food and her hosts. She laughed; she answered more questions; she listened. She behaved as her mother had taught her and thought of nothing else.

LATER, Solvi stopped by Rikka's room, flinging herself on Rikka's bed in despair.

"It was the same house?" Rikka said, her eyes wide. "Are you sure?"

"Dominik's brother, Edvard, was the one who pinched Greta. His mother called him by name, and it was his voice," Solvi said. "Besides—the serving maids and I recognized each other."

"Good God, I hope you didn't stare."

"No. I spent a lot of time cutting my dinner into tiny pieces." Solvi sighed. "Oh, Rikka, now I'm afraid we shouldn't use those photographs in the article. This is why people shouldn't trespass!"

"No, this is why we need to do this story: to protect housemaids from people like Edvard," Rikka said. "I assume you told Dominik you can't see him anymore."

Solvi sat up. "What do you mean?"

"Well, obviously he's from a bad family."

"Rikka, that's not fair. His brother's the bad one. Dominik's harmless."

Rikka went quiet, then shook her head. "I just don't see why you like him."

"He's fun, and he challenges me to think in new ways. When it's just him and me, it's nice; I think he really likes me. He gave me a book, *Albertine*. It's the story of a young woman who gets tricked into being a prostitute."

Rikka gave her a sidelong look.

"No, it's not what you think. It's background for my essay about the Forgotten One. He's trying to help me, and I want to help him back. I think he needs someone like me."

"Saint Solvi, needing to save someone," Rikka said.

"That's the pot calling the kettle black, don't you think?"

"Maybe, but it's a bad reason to fall in love, Solvi."

"Why?" It annoyed Solvi how patronizing Rikka could be, treating her like the kid sister who didn't know anything about the world.

"Because love shouldn't be confused with heroism," Rikka said. "Trust me; I know."

THE NEXT TIME Solvi and Rikka went to Vika, they wrapped themselves in heavy shawls to obscure their youth. They stopped at a ramshackle cottage on a narrow lane, one of the poorest houses Solvi had ever seen. Inside, a barefoot young girl stirred a kettle over an open fire, a toddler on her hip. The mother, thin and weak, tried to rise from her bed but could not.

Rikka went to help her while Solvi turned to the girl. "Here, I'll take the baby for you," she said, pulling the toddler into her arms. "Watch your feet there, around the coals."

But the girl just looked at her with a haggard face and went back to stirring. Solvi could see bits of burned potato floating in the soup. The little boy gazed up at Solvi with big, serious eyes. She bounced him; a small smile played on his face.

Rikka sat beside the mother, talking to her quietly. The woman was hopelessly frail and wracked with rattling coughs. Rikka urged her to go to the sanatorium to recover, but she just shook her head.

"There is no one to care for my family," she said, looking around the small, dark room.

"Do you have a husband?"

"No," she said, without explanation. She looked away from Rikka.

The little boy squirmed in Solvi's arms. "Ma'am, may I take a picture of your children?" Solvi asked. "I'll give you a print."

The woman shrugged, too sick to care. Solvi handed the toddler back to his sister, then positioned them beside the open door, in a wash of gray light. The girl canted her hip to the side to hold her brother, just as any mother would, making her look strangely adult. The little boy twisted away, whining; the girl looked into Solvi's camera, wistful and resigned. Old before her years, Solvi thought. She pressed the shutter.

Rikka gathered her equipment, then gave the mother a pamphlet about the sanatorium. "Maybe we could find someone to care for your children," she said. "I'll be back in a few days to see what you've decided."

The woman nodded. "Thank you, miss. And you'll bring the photograph?"

"Of course," Solvi said.

As they walked to the next house, Rikka shook her head. "She's a prostitute, I'm sure."

"She is?"

"You can tell when they don't explain how they lost their husband."

SOLVI SAT DOWN that evening with the book Dominik had given her, curious now in a way she hadn't been before. Albertine's story started with poverty and exhaustion. She worked at home as a seamstress, laboring for hours over her hand-operated sewing machine, sometimes sleeping in her chair. Her sick brother was dying, her aging mother mired in despair. Albertine—beautiful and principled but pessimistic about her future— thought obsessively about her sister, Oline, who had brought shame to the family by becoming a prostitute.

In time, Albertine tumbled as well, tricked by a policeman who drugged her and then raped her. Fate, it seemed, had no escape for poor Albertine. She ended up in Vika, a swaggering, laughing, unashamed whore, even worse than her sister.

Solvi read the novel in one night.

At the end of the book she was surprised to find reproductions of a series of paintings. The author, Christian Krohg, was also an artist and painted scenes from the book. Solvi paged slowly through the plates, some of which she recognized, though she'd never understood before where they came from. There was Albertine sleeping in her chair before her sewing machine and Albertine's dying brother propped in a wheeled chair. Then Albertine being chastised by her mother. Later there was Albertine, demure in her skirt and shawl, being ushered into a clinic for women with sexual diseases, surrounded by prostitutes in cheap gowns. And after her fall, Albertine in a thin shift sitting on the edge of a rumpled bed, her head in her hands.

Solvi took the book to Rikka and told her all about Albertine. Together, they examined the plates.

"I hate it when the heroine becomes a prostitute at the end of a novel because, believe me, that's not the end of that woman's story," Rikka said.

"I have an idea," Solvi said. "This might sound strange, but I think it would get people's attention. We try to find several prostitutes to help us re-create some of Krohg's *Albertine* scenes, which I photograph. Then we show them to Mr. Blehr."

Rikka looked at her with surprise. "Is this your mother's daughter talking?"

"Albertine still lives in Vika. People need to know that."

Rikka jumped up and gave her a hug. "Let me work on it."

A FEW DAYS LATER, they set out. Solvi brought money, and Rikka carried a basket of food—cheese, biscuits, and fruit. The two women were waiting for them in the rough rooming house where they lived. One had a child, a small girl who sat on a low stool and stared.

Rikka handed her an apple. The girl took it silently and held it in her lap.

"You can eat it, love," said her mother, a delicate woman with a frail, sickly body. She wore a torn Chinese robe over a shift and slippers, her stringy blond hair piled haphazardly on her head. Rikka pulled out her stethoscope and listened to her lungs.

The other prostitute, younger and stronger, with dark tresses around her shoulders, wore a narrow skirt and a frayed blouse open at the neck. She treated the older woman as someone under her special care, offering her the best bits from the basket.

Solvi talked with them first, trying to understand how they had come to live this way. The stories were bleak—hunger, little schooling, fathers who beat them and worse. One came from a long line of prostitutes that started with a great-grandmother abandoned on the wharf. The other woman, the mother of the child, fell into prostitution when she lost her mother as a young girl. Solvi scribbled notes and assured them she would obscure their identity in anything she might write for the newspaper.

Then she took pictures that would echo the *Albertine* paintings. First, Solvi shot the delicate one in just her shift sitting on the edge of her bed, her head in her hands. Then Solvi had the women face each other, with the younger casting her eyes down in shame, the other berating her. Next, she seated them at a table before a heap of knitting, leaning back as if they slept in their chairs. For the last shot, she put a blanket over the lap of the little girl, whose blond hair glowed white in the light of the window, and photographed her straight on, just as Krohg had painted Albertine's dying brother.

When she was done, she promised to bring them copies of the pictures when they were developed. Rikka handed them a box of condoms.

Solvi and Rikka walked home quietly, subdued by being with these women and their resignation and shame, their hunger, the child. Baskets were never going to be enough.

LATER IN THE WEEK, Solvi and Magnus visited Mr. Blehr for help placing an ad in an American newspaper. He recommended the *Skandinaven*, published in Norwegian from Chicago. Read by Norwegian immigrants from East to West, he assured Solvi. He even knew the name of the editor.

By the end of the afternoon, the advertisement was readied and sent off to Chicago. That evening, Solvi told Rikka about it. "I have no idea if it will work," Solvi said, "but I feel better doing something. At the least, maybe some Norwegian in America will recognize them and send me some information. Even that would be something."

Rikka tipped her head to the side. "Will you tell your mother about it?"

"Lord, no," Solvi said. "I may never be able to tell her any of it. Even if I find them."

Rikka nodded thoughtfully. "It was very kind of Magnus to help you with that."

Solvi chewed a hangnail. "Yes, it was. In fact, it was his idea. We will see if anything comes of it."

A WEEK LATER, against her better judgment, Solvi went with Petra and Rikka to a second wealthy home. Fortunately, this one was easy since the family was away on holiday and only the staff was in the home. With no need to rush, Solvi got better pictures. Her favorite showed the maids in a line, all holding kitchen pans in front of their faces, like masks. Their uniforms and aprons—wrinkled, stained, streaked with dirt and flour—told the story of their labor.

When she was done, Solvi chatted with them as she waited for Rikka to finish distributing condoms and advice. One of the girls asked if Solvi would someday write a newspaper article, as Petra was doing. Solvi heard herself say yes and told them about the Forgotten One. They listened, rapt.

When she was done, Solvi looked around the table. "And here's the strangest part of it: the Forgotten One was never heard from again. She disappeared, and no one has any idea what happened to her."

"Maybe she became a famous actress," one girl said dreamily.

"Maybe she went west," said another. "Maybe she got kidnapped by Indians and learned to shoot buffalo."

The others giggled, except one older maid polishing silver at the end of the table. "No," she said. "It's a sad story, losing her children like that."

The elderly cook shook a pan at the stove. "I've always thought it a sad story, myself."

Solvi turned to her. "Do you know this story?"

"Aye, I've known it a long time," the cook said. "I have a friend whose mother was nurse to the children of this woman when she left her husband."

Solvi nearly choked on her coffee. "You knew her nurse?"

"Well, I know the nurse's daughter, and she told me this story years ago."

"Is the nurse still alive?"

"No, she's been gone for years. But her daughter, my friend Louiza Olsen, is right here in Kristiania."

"Would she talk to me?" Solvi asked.

The cook turned to look at Solvi, sizing her up. Finally, she shrugged. "I'll ask her. If you come back next week, I'll let you know."

"Thank you. I've been searching for someone who knew her."

The cook gave Solvi a solemn look. "It's not a pretty story, Miss Lange. She left those children bereft. My friend, if she's willing, can tell you what it looked like from the nursery."

Rikka emerged from the dayroom, pulling on her coat. "We'd better get going."

One of the housemaids wrapped two warm pastries for them in a bit of newspaper. Rikka and Solvi thanked the women and headed out the door.

"You'll never believe what I just heard . . . ," Solvi said.

IT WAS A SOFT SPRING DAY when Solvi knocked on the door of a small apartment in an old tenement building far from the center of town. She carried a small bouquet of narcissus flowers, clutching them nervously, unsure what sort of reception she would get.

A thin woman with hollow cheeks and a loose twist of gray hair behind opened the door and looked her over. "I suppose you're Miss Lange."

"Yes, good day, Miss Olsen. Thank you for meeting with me." She handed the woman the flowers.

The woman nodded in a formal way, then stepped aside and let Solvi enter.

Solvi stood awkwardly in the middle of a small room, waiting for an invitation. After a few minutes, she edged toward a chair. "May I sit?"

"No one is stopping you," Miss Olsen said, then shook herself a bit. "I suppose I could get some tea. I've got the kettle warm, so it's no trouble."

"Yes, please. If it's no trouble."

"That's what I said, miss," Miss Olsen muttered, shuffling off to her tiny kitchen.

Solvi swallowed hard. She had high hopes for this interview, but already it felt like something had gone awry. Maybe Solvi shouldn't have worn her short skirt and nice jacket.

She took out her notebook and looked about as Miss Olsen rattled things in the kitchen. Everything indicated a life lived with barely enough, but it was still a respectable life. Nothing like the squalid conditions of the poor prostitutes in Vika.

For a moment Solvi wondered if this woman could be the Forgotten One herself, but no. Solvi could see that Miss Olsen was not born upper class, as the Forgotten One was. Still, their fate might have turned out much the same.

Miss Olsen returned carrying a tray with an elegant tea set, oddly out of place in her spare room.

"What lovely china," Solvi said. She picked up one of the little cups and turned it about, admiring the delicate pattern of red blossoms. "So fine, and beautifully kept."

"I rarely use it," Miss Olsen said. "It was given to my mother by a friend."

"Thank you for seeing me, Miss Olsen. I'd begun to think this woman, this Forgotten One, was just a myth."

"Oh, she was real, miss. I know because my mother devoted her life to her."

Solvi took some notes. "So, please start at the beginning. How did your mother come to work for the family?"

"My mother nursed the woman when she was a baby, in Hamar. Her mother died in childbirth, so they needed someone."

"Did you grow up with her in the same house?"

Miss Olsen stared for a moment, then shook her head roughly. "Oh, no. My mother had to give me over to be raised by strangers in Kristiania so she could take the job of caring for the princess. That's how it was done in those days."

"The princess?"

"Well, she wasn't a real princess, but that's what I called her. Her father was wealthy, bought her whatever she wanted, my mother said, just like a princess."

"You kept in touch with your mother?"

She nodded. "And after the princess married and moved here to Kristiania, she brought my mother with her, to nurse her own children. My mother stayed with me on her days off."

"What was your mother's name?"

"Anne-Marie Olsen."

"Do you know why the woman left her family?"

Miss Olsen sighed. "There were troubles between her and her husband. He was an upstanding man, but he treated his wife like a child, my mother told me. He loved her dearly but was also fond of humiliating her."

"Did he try to get her to return home?"

"He hired men to find her and fired my mother after he discovered she'd corresponded with her. But then he rehired her. Those children were lost without their nurse, and he knew that."

"Yes, I can understand. How did they react when their mother left?"

"To my recollection it was hardest on the boys, as they were older and had more memories of her. Their mother tried several times to talk with them in the park or on the street, and that was very upsetting for them. Frankly, it would have been easier for everyone if she had died. Her husband finally told the children she *had* died so they could grieve and get over her."

"But was that true?"

Miss Olsen poured more tea, then stood. "I'll fetch some biscuits." When she came back a few minutes later, Solvi felt her withdrawing.

"I hope these questions aren't too intrusive," Solvi said. "She's an important figure to the feminists, one of their first heroines, but no one seems to know her fate. Do you remember her name?"

Miss Olsen hesitated, then pursed her lips. "It was Solberg, Mrs. Solberg."

"Solberg!" Solvi wrote it down. "Thank you! That should help."

Miss Olsen gave Solvi a searching look. "I'll be frank with you, Miss Lange; I don't know why anyone would consider her heroic. My mother loved her like a daughter, but it broke my mother's heart when she abandoned those children. My mother tried hard to hold them together, but it was difficult." She stopped for a moment, fingering her teacup. "Maybe I was jealous; the princess had a rich father and my mother for her nurse. Later she married a rich husband and had those beautiful children. That should have been enough for her. Put that in your notebook."

Solvi scribbled away, then finally looked up again. "Is there anything else you remember? Do you know where she might have gone, I mean, if she didn't really die?"

Miss Olsen shook her head. "That's the most I want to remember. I don't like to talk of it. I just thought I could be of some help."

"Of course, you have been," Solvi said, rising. And then she had an idea. "Miss Olsen, could I take a photograph of you and your beautiful tea set?"

Miss Olsen blushed, then patted her hair. "I'm not sure why you would want to, but all right." She picked up the tray and stood beside her small ceramic stove. Solvi shot her looking into the lens, her face stern but proud.

"Thank you, Miss Olsen. I'll drop off a print in a few days." Solvi packed up her camera and notebook, then put on her jacket. "Just one last thing, Miss Olsen—Mrs. Solberg didn't die, did she."

"No. Not as far as I know. But then, I wouldn't, would I? I was just the nurse's child."

CHAPTER SEVENTEEN

NORA

Spring 1919 ▪ Spokane, Washington

A few days later I was sitting with Jens and Katrin's youngest child, their only girl, making up silly rhymes with her. She's a quick-witted one, fond of bouncing between Norwegian, German, and English to see if the rest of us can keep up. She's only five but rules my heart.

She was working on her next couplet when she tilted her head and pursed her lips; and in that moment she reminded me so much of my son Bobby that I almost let out a sob. He loved rhymes and songs as well and often asked for a special one just for him.

In the photograph in the advertisement, it is Bobby who leans lovingly against me. When I left home those many years ago, it was Bobby who knew just enough to feel wrenched from my arms and not enough to understand any of it.

Perhaps Bobby was looking for me. If his father had died, maybe Bob now had enough money to journey to America, to go on an adventure that might solve the mystery of his lost mother. When Ivar discovered I was still alive, he made sure Bobby knew. And when I saw Bobby shortly after that, when he was still not quite of age, he had none of Emma's disdain. He only knew that his mother had, finally, wonderfully, returned.

And then it all fell apart. Most likely Ivar told him the terrible truth, and that extinguished his love for me.

But maybe not. Maybe that was what this advertisement was about. Bob had packed his rucksack at last and now needed to know where to find me.

The child in my lap tweaked my ear. "Listen, *Bestemor*. Are you listening?" Then she clasped her hands together and recited her little poem.

NORA

March 1882 ▪ Lac qui Parle, Minnesota

Someone rolled me over. My eyes fluttered. Sky above me, flat and white, traced by bare branches. I gasped and coughed. A dark face hovered; someone pounded my chest. I closed my eyes. Please, just leave me.

And then he slapped my face, shouting in French. "Breathe!" It was Mr. Renville, trying to lift me up. "Cough! You must cough up the water!"

I tried, but I shook with cold. He dropped me back into the snow, disappeared, returned with a blanket, and rolled me into it. Then, with a great heave, he lifted me over his shoulder and scrambled up the bank to where his Indian pony waited. He dropped me onto the little horse and told me to lie against its neck. It was all I could do to grasp the shaggy mane.

I SCARCELY REMEMBER our trip around the lake. He told me later he was checking traps when he saw someone walk out onto the ice and fall through. He came as quickly as he could. When we arrived at Mr. Renville's log cabin, he carried me inside and sat me in a rocking chair. It was blessedly warm, with a fire in an open hearth. After a moment, a woman stepped silently from the back room. She was coffee skinned, like Mr. Renville—the sister I'd never met. He gestured to her with his hands, then walked out.

She smiled, kindness shining from her eyes, but said nothing. Probably she didn't speak English. I tried to greet her in French, but my teeth chattered too much. I had no more strength than a baby. She untied the drawstring bag from my waist and peeled off my soaking layers, stopping to examine Emma's cap. Then she rubbed me hard with a rag. She fetched a heavy flannel nightdress and dropped it over my head, then wrapped me in a dry blanket and put a hot brick beneath my feet.

This generous care made me weep, my thoughts slopping from relief to shame to dread. I could still taste the horror that coursed through me under the ice. I feared Mr. Renville would be angry, that he would fetch Mr. Eriksen.

She held a bitter tea to my lips, and I drank as best I could. Then she opened my drawstring bag, taking out my treasures and doing what she could to save them. My baptism certificate might dry, but the photograph and the children's letter were ruined, so with a tearful nod from me she tossed them into the fire. Then she combed the lake grass and leaves from my hair. She didn't ask about my short locks, barely long enough now to tuck behind my ears. She didn't seem surprised by me at all.

Mr. Renville returned and sat down beside me, his face grim. "Oh, Mrs. Eriksen. First Gustaf's wife, now you. This land is not meant for white women."

I didn't know what to say. I felt as if my soul had floated a long way beyond our crabbed life here on the prairie, and I couldn't bear to bring it back.

"Why would you do such a thing? Your family—what am I to tell your husband?"

I gazed at him in confusion, then remembered. "He's not my husband." Having spit out Ivar's stone, I was ready to tell the truth.

"What?"

I blushed; I knew it was shameful. "We're not married. He hired me to care for the baby after his wife died, in exchange for my passage."

Mr. Renville pulled back with a soft grunt, watching me intently. "I didn't understand you and Mr. Eriksen. Now I do."

"I had to pose as his wife on the voyage, as I traveled on her ticket and papers," I said, stopping to cough. There seemed to be water in my lungs. "I was to live with Gustaf and Kari when we got here, but they were gone, so we went on as if we were married. There was nowhere else for me to live and take care of Tomas."

He nodded. "You loved that child so, I never imagined he wasn't yours."

"I lost my own children back in Norway. Tomas meant everything to me."

"Did you hope to marry Mr. Eriksen?"

I blinked, then felt tears in my eyes. "I didn't . . . He doesn't want to marry me. He and Birgitte could never forgive me for losing Tomas."

"So you walked out onto the ice." He stood. "I must tell him where you are."

"No, I beg you! I left him my jewelry to pay off the rest of my debt to him. I cannot go back there."

"But I must tell him you're alive."

"I left a note saying I was going to Chicago. He won't think I am dead. He won't come looking for me."

His eyes burned into mine. "I don't like to carry lies, Mrs., Mrs. . . . I don't even know who you are."

"I am Nora Solberg."

"So you'll go to Chicago?"

"I'd like to, but I don't know how I will get there. Perhaps I can walk to Minneapolis."

"Will you go back out onto the ice?"

"No. It was terrifying." I began coughing again, the water coming up in spurts. I coughed until I bent over. Mr. Renville's sister pushed him away.

"Ann says you must rest," he said. "I am going upriver for a few days to check my traps. When I get back I'll try to find you help. I'll only tell Mr. Eriksen once you're gone."

"Thank you."

"One thing you should know—my sister cannot hear or speak. She was very ill as a child, and her hearing was taken from her. But she understands many gestures."

ANN RENVILLE PUT ME TO BED, and I fell into a deep sleep. A burning fever brought me out of my coma the next day, but I could barely lift my head from the pillow. I coughed incessantly. Ann helped me sip more bitter tea, but I soon slid back into sleep. Later, I remembered waking to find Ann rubbing a foul-smelling paste on my chest and pounding my back. The next few days were a blur of burning fever and shaking chills, with a deepening pain in my chest. I was haunted by hallucinatory dreams—the faces of my children floating in dark water, a blanket of grasshoppers crawling over my bed, Anders turning his back and disappearing into a forest.

But each time I surfaced, there was Ann, bending over me.

It took me several weeks to recover, and during all of it Ann tended me with silent dedication. I lay under the quilts and watched her. She looked more Indian than her brother, with two thick braids tied together at the ends. She wore homespun skirts but deerskin moccasins on her feet. She was not limited by her lack of hearing or speech. Her gestures were clear, and she shared a hand language with her brother. I envied their quiet understanding.

My body began to recover, but my soul refused. Brought back from the edge of death, I had to shoulder again all that dragged me down, and with it came a fathomless sadness. I worried that Anders would find me, then the next day that he wouldn't. My sorrow at being alive but separated from him surprised me. Did I love him? Was it his coldness after Tomas died that drove me out onto the ice? I turned my face to the wall and tried to forget.

Ann saw that I was troubled and handed me yarn and knitting needles. When I was better, she took me outside to pull weeds from her garden. It helped to be useful and feel the sunlight around me.

But as I healed, new worries surfaced. How would I repay the Renvilles, and how would I get to a city and find shelter and work? I had nothing but the clothes I wore into the lake, now filthy and torn—even my coat was gone. The only thing I had of value was Torvald's wedding band. Perhaps the Renvilles would take it as payment for all they had done.

ONE EVENING Mr. Renville sat down to talk with me.

"I found help for you. A German that lives near Milan has a Norwegian wife, and they've helped many people around here. He's wealthy, and kind. I told him about you."

I gasped. Above all I needed to stay hidden.

"No," he said. "It's all right; he won't give you away. He lives on the other side of the lake from Mr. Eriksen, in the next county, and doesn't know him. He has a plan for you."

Mr. Renville took several bills out of his pocket. "This is money for a train ticket to St. Paul and directions to a mission for immigrant women. They can give you shelter and help you find a job." Then he tossed a coat of warm wool on the bed beside me. "This is from his wife."

I pulled it to my chest, astonished by this largesse. "How will I ever repay him? What is his name?"

"Herr Gippe. He doesn't expect you to repay him. He and his wife were quite moved by your story."

"Did you tell them I lived with the Eriksens outside of marriage?"

He nodded solemnly. "It was the only way to explain your situation, Mrs. Solberg. But don't worry; they don't judge you and will keep your secret. Write to them from St. Paul. All they want is word that you've found your way."

I nodded. Ann came up behind her brother with a broad smile. I slid Torvald's ring off my finger. "Please, take this in payment for your kindness."

But they just laughed. "No," Mr. Renville said. "You will need it."

That night Ann mended and ironed my skirt and blouse, then helped me wash my hair. The next morning she gave me a beautiful woven shawl to cover my head, and I hugged her good-bye. Mr. Renville, solemn as always, drove me to the train in Montevideo in a cart hitched to his pony. The first spring wildflowers ran lacy fingers through the grass, and my grateful soul expanded under the prairie sky.

When we got to the station he shook my hand. "You are a strong woman, Mrs. Solberg. I'm sure you will find a place of service and belonging." With that, he helped me aboard, then walked away without a backward look.

Something in me died at that moment, as I doubted I would ever return to the lake that whispered, or to the Renvilles or the Eriksens. My heart, like a ravenous vine, had wound itself around these people and their beautiful land, and I didn't see how I could live without them.

Before I was ready, I was flying east, back to civilization.

THE TRAIN pulled into St. Paul late, and I hurried across town to the West Side mission before it grew dark. The mission was little more than a rambling old house with faded shingles behind a broken picket fence and a garden of weeds. I rang the bell; a young woman in a dirty apron opened the door.

She looked me over, puzzled. "Have you come to hire a maid, ma'am?"

"No. I need a room for the night. Herr Gippe in Milan said you could help me."

"Best come speak to Matron."

I followed her to a parlor, where a prim older woman in a starched black dress looked up from her papers and reached for my hand. "Welcome to the St. Paul Women's Mission. What can we do for you?"

"I need a room. I've a bit of money and can pay what it costs."

"Well, ma'am, we're a place for the truly destitute, those who otherwise might be preyed on in the streets. Tell me how you've come to us."

"I've nothing but a few dollars. I've been working with a farm family in Lac qui Parle. I immigrated with them, as the mother had recently died and left an infant child."

"You immigrated with a farmer? But your English is good."

"Yes, I am educated, from Kristiania. But I lost all that. I met the family on the docks and agreed to care for the infant for a year."

"And so your year is up."

"Yes," I lied, then stopped. "Actually, it's more that my debt is paid. Now I need work."

"Do you have any skills?"

"I speak French and German and could be a governess or seamstress. I've also worked for a shipping agent, managing his office and books."

"We place most of our girls as domestics. Are you willing to go into service?"

Service—my father would turn in his grave. "Yes," I said.

She nodded and made some notes. "And you care for children, I assume?"

"I'd rather not."

She tilted her head to the side. "May I ask why?"

"The infant I was caring for died of diphtheria. I was unable to save him . . ." My voice faltered.

"I am so sorry," she said. "It's a dreadful disease. Even the doctors cannot save them, in my experience." She stopped and looked me over again. "Are you a widow?"

Why did the world make it so difficult to stop lying? But there it was: I could not tell her the truth and expect to get a position. "Yes," I said.

She nodded her condolence, then smiled. "You may stay, though you'll have to work in the kitchen for your board until we find you a placement."

"Thank you, Matron."

"Yes, well, see that you do your part." She looked at me again. "What happened to your hair? Lice on the ship?"

I hesitated, then nodded. My truths were just too damning.

I went straight into the kitchen to help dry the supper dishes, while the cook bustled about preparing the next day's breakfast. When she realized I'd missed dinner, she gave me a bowl of cold porridge. I ate it quickly, then went upstairs to my bunk and sank into an exhausted sleep.

I WORKED AT THE MISSION for several weeks, sometimes on my knees scrubbing the floors, sometimes helping Matron with her correspondence. I did whatever was asked and was grateful for a bed and meals. Most of the others were young girls who immigrated with no one to rely on and found America harder than they imagined. I felt infinitely old as I listened to their easy chatter, but I enjoyed their laughter. One of them was quite pregnant. I was relieved there was a place for her, and for me.

One morning I was called to the parlor, where a well-dressed gentleman sat talking with Matron. He looked a bit like Torvald, successful and overly tidy in his dress. But when he turned, his face was deeply creased with distress.

"Mrs. Solberg," Matron said, "this is Mr. Burnley. He's looking for a companion for his wife, who's nearing her next confinement but not doing well." The gentleman shook my hand, his eyes quickly scanning my face.

"Is your wife ill, sir?"

"Yes, but not in body," he said. "She's ill in spirit, quite despondent. She's convinced she will die in childbirth."

Such a fear was hardly unreasonable; most women worried as their confinement neared.

"Have you brought in a doctor?" I asked.

"Yes, several, but they give contradictory advice. My sense is she needs someone to sit with her, read to her, distract her."

"That's why I thought of you, Mrs. Solberg," Matron said. "You would make an excellent companion."

I hesitated, wondering if I was strong enough to help someone else in despair. But it was a job, with a private room and good wages, he said, and would earn me a reference if I did well.

I smiled. "When shall I start?"

Mr. Burnley shook my hand again, relief flooding his face. "Thank you, Mrs. Solberg. Can you come with me now?"

I fetched my coat. Mr. Burnley met me in the front hall. "No bag?"

"No," I said. I was stripped of everything but what I carried in my head.

He helped me into his buggy.

WE PASSED MANY FINE HOMES as we crossed St. Paul, but when we stopped in front of the Burnleys' house, I had to pinch myself. The three-story limestone mansion towered over its neighbors and a small park of flowering trees across the street. We were met by a maid, who led me up two flights to an attic room with a gabled window looking down into the Burnleys' garden. The room had little more than a bed and a washbowl but was blessedly private. "I'll leave you to get settled," she said.

I took off my boots and lay down on the bed, gazing out at the trees just beginning to green. Such gentle surroundings—lace curtains, ironed sheets, real soap. I ran my hand across the soft quilt. Perhaps this place could heal me.

The maid knocked. "Mrs. Burnley is ready for you, Mrs. Solberg."

"I'll be right down." I put my boots back on and washed my face, but I still looked like a street urchin, with my boyish hair and worn clothes. I hoped I would do.

The maid led me to a door, knocked gently, then opened. The room was quite large, with tall windows facing the street, but the drapes were shut tight against the afternoon sun. In the dim light I could see a huge bed with someone under a mound of blankets. A low fire burned in the fireplace, though the room felt stiflingly hot.

"Ma'am, this is Mrs. Solberg," the maid said.

From the bed, nothing, though I could see that Mrs. Burnley was awake. The maid retreated.

I looked about. There was a breakfast tray, untouched, and a pile of clothing on an armchair. I walked to the window and pushed the curtains aside. Sunlight spilled across the floor.

"Spring is just over the horizon, ma'am," I said. "It's quite warm today, for April."

Mrs. Burnley just turned to the wall.

How many mornings in the sod house had I longed to stay in bed. But I had to carry my weight—make breakfast, wash the laundry. Still, I understood wanting to lie silently all day. I pulled a chair up to her bedside.

"Mrs. Burnley, I am Nora Solberg. Please call me Nora."

She kept her head turned away. I picked up a volume of poetry off her nightstand, chose a poem, and started reading aloud. When I was done with one poem, I read another, then another. After a while I stopped and sat in the stillness of that sad room.

Finally, she spoke. "You're Swedish, or Norwegian. I can hear it."

"Norwegian, from Kristiania. My husband was a bank manager, but I lost my family, so I came to America to start a new life."

"Where did Mr. Burnley find you?"

"At a mission for immigrant women."

"How long have you been a domestic?"

"Most of my life I've had servants of my own. My father was a businessman and gave me an academy education. But since coming to America, I've had to make my own way."

"You'll have a hard time of it," she said.

"Making a life in America? Yes, but I think the worst is over."

"I mean helping me. My husband says I don't want to be helped."

"What do you say?"

Now she turned to me. She was quite beautiful, with curly black hair, pale skin, and dark-blue eyes with black lashes. But she also had crescents of deep shadow beneath her eyes and gaunt cheeks, despite her pregnancy.

"I don't say anything because I cannot explain it. If he knew what plagued me, he wouldn't say such things."

"Yes. That I understand."

She gazed at me, I at her. "What happened to your hair?"

"Lice—on the ship," I said, standing up. I needed to take charge. "First, I'll tidy your room a bit, then get some fresh air in here. Perhaps you should sit up. Have you eaten today?"

She turned away again but spoke clearly. "No. Food frightens me."

"Frightens you?" I moved about the room picking up clothes and putting them into closets and drawers.

"I am afraid of the baby, and the food seems to be for him. So I don't eat."

I stopped. "You don't want this child?"

She looked at me over her shoulder, then turned away again. "This is why I don't speak."

I came back to her bedside. "Because no one can bear to hear what's in your heart?"

Tears slipped down her cheeks. I handed her a handkerchief. "They would lock me up if they knew the truth about me," she whispered.

"Yes, well, men would like to lock many of us up, if given half a chance."

She turned her damp eyes toward me in disbelief. Good, I had piqued her interest.

"Birthing children is a hardship, I grant you," I continued. "How many do you have?"

"Four living, and I've lost two already—one stillborn, the other when he was barely two. Each time I near my confinement this fear comes over me, but it is worse this time. My sister died in childbirth a few months ago." I took her hand and held it tight. "I fear these are my last months," she stammered.

All I could think to do was to smooth the tangled hair from her brow. Then I noticed a pull chord, so I rang. The maid appeared.

"Please bring us some beef broth, a bit of cheese and bread, and something sweet."

"Yes, ma'am. There's custard from the children's supper last night."

After she left, Mrs. Burnley looked at me, despondent. "I cannot eat."

"Then I'll have to eat it. I haven't had anything since breakfast."

The lines around her eyes softened. I brought a damp cloth and wiped her face, then brushed her hair and pinned it back. The food came; I set the tray on the edge of the bed and nibbled at the cheese and bread. She watched me.

"I'll tell you a story," I said, taking a spoonful of the rich broth. "Once upon a time there was a beautiful maiden raised in comfort by a doting father. She lost her mother at her birth but had a kind nurse and many friends. With them and her father, she was never lonely."

"This is your story."

"It's someone's story, that's true. So the maiden grew into a lovely young woman, and a fine man came along and took her for his bride. She was a good wife and gave him three perfect children and did everything she could to make him happy and safe. But then a great misfortune fell upon the household, illness and debt. She did her best, but still, she lost everything—her children, her husband, her home."

Mrs. Burnley watched me intently.

"She wandered for a time, trying to find her way," I continued. "She lived in poverty, then took a journey across the sea to a new land. There she found another home and another family. It wasn't her family, but she grew to love the children, especially the littlest one. Then one terrible day the baby died, and the woman sank into despair. After many dark weeks, she walked out onto a frozen lake and fell through the ice."

Mrs. Burnley's eyes were fixed on my face. "Did she die?"

"No, not that day. A surprising thing happened to her. Once she was sinking to the bottom of the lake she realized she didn't want to die after all. So she swam and pulled herself out."

"But how could she?"

"She used all her strength, and a kind friend saw her struggling and saved her. Another kind friend, a woman, nursed her until she was better. And do you know what was most interesting about this nurse?"

"What?"

"She could not hear or speak."

"Not a word?"

"Not a word. It didn't matter, though. They understood each other well enough. Sometimes women just do."

She gazed at me. "So you've lost your family."

"Yes, twice over."

"Yet you talk and laugh like a normal woman."

"Today I do. You will too, someday. I promise."

Mrs. Burnley suddenly spooned a bit of custard into her dainty mouth. But no more. I acted like it didn't matter and called for the maid to remove the tray. Her husband came in at supper time, but she refused to go downstairs. Still, we'd had some success. Perhaps tomorrow, I thought, I could get her out of bed.

OVER THE NEXT FEW WEEKS I worked to lure Mrs. Burnley out from under her paralyzing fear. She was certain she would die when the child was born and was angry no one took this seriously. She refused everything that gave life—sunlight, food, water.

I sought first to win her trust, then gradually brought life back into her somber bedroom. I ate all my meals at her bedside, savoring delicacies and nudging her to try things. We debated the opening of curtains, the reading of poetry, the need for a walk, and I always pushed for more. Each day I fixed her hair, helped her wash, made her put on a clean nightgown.

I wasn't sure what guided me in this work. I felt like I had crawled out of the lake a different woman, able for the first time to forget myself and think only of the other person. It was an astonishing relief.

On my first day off, I pawned Torvald's wedding ring and bought several new blouses and a fashionable skirt, discarding the worn homespun that had defined my days with the Eriksens. I also bought new shoes, soft leather heels with a strap. The first glimmer of a smile I got from Mrs. Burnley was when she saw me in my new clothes.

As we became friends, she asked about my life in Norway. I didn't talk about what happened with Torvald, but I did tell her about our dinner parties and Norwegian holidays, my singing and dancing. One day she asked me to play the piano for her. We went down to the empty parlor where I found a book of Chopin and sat down at the keyboard. I stumbled at first—it had been so long, my hands trembled with the effort—but soon the tender melodies returned to me, unspooling into luminous sound. Mrs. Burnley sat still as a cat, tears sliding down her face. After that I played for her every afternoon.

She went into labor one evening in early May. She grew quite terrified, but the midwife stationed me at her side, talking and breathing with her. Within a few hours a tiny, wizened baby girl slipped from her womb. Mrs. Burnley, overcome to find herself alive, took the child tentatively into her arms. When the wet nurse arrived, she let go of the wee thing with reluctance.

After the birth, Mrs. Burnley began to eat again, though not without a struggle, as her body was not used to food. When I asked her about this, she said, "I eat only so they won't worry."

As Mrs. Burnley improved, so did I. By the time summer arrived, I could finally think about the Eriksens without weeping. How I wished our time together had ended differently.

WITH HIS WIFE PAST HER CRISIS, Mr. Burnley began looking for another post for me. I considered going on to Chicago and even sent a letter to Tobias at his parents' home in Norway, hoping they would send it on to him if he was in America. But I never heard back. I worried I didn't have enough money saved and grew reluctant to leave Minnesota, as the only friends I had in America were there. When Mr. Burnley told me of another St. Paul lady suffering from despondency, I took the position.

The next woman was older, mired in grief after losing two daughters to tuberculosis, one right after the other. I did the same things: told her stories, walked with her beneath the elms, read to her when it rained. After a few weeks she no longer muttered under her breath, and I soon moved to another home.

ALL THAT LONG SUMMER I tended to sad women by day, then lay awake at night in some hot attic room, lonely and empty. I may have found a purpose caring for these women, but belonging eluded me. No one else had welcomed me as the Burnleys did; the others considered me a nurse— there to serve and clean up. Every few weeks my position changed, and I worried, always, about the next job.

Sometimes I imagined myself back on the prairie under that endless sky, and my heart ached. What might have happened if Tomas hadn't sickened and died? I thought of my summer with the Eriksens the year before, sewing and carving outside in the evenings. And I thought of the short, sweet time that Anders loved me.

Before I could stop myself, I was spinning dreams of a life back at his side. Sometimes we kept a tidy frame house up on the tableland, with lace curtains in the windows and a coal stove. Other times we lived in Minneapolis, and Anders worked as a carpenter while I opened a school for girls.

But then I would come to my senses, and my stomach would knot. How could I marry Anders when I might still be married to Torvald? I tried to release Torvald the night I left him, saying we were no longer bound to each other, but I never knew if he agreed to that. If he wanted to remarry, perhaps he had gotten permission for a divorce, but I didn't know. Still, these hopes flickered in my mind.

If he hadn't released me, however, I was then bound to him forever, with little chance of anything more than a lonely spinsterhood. And that made me angry. Without a divorce, the Church and the law said I was Torvald's wife, but if I didn't live with him or make any claim on him, how could I be wife to him?

When I thought of growing old alone, I could feel despair creeping up on me again. I wanted to be loved by someone good, someone true. I wanted to be part of a family again. I wanted that web of commitment and consideration I had with the Eriksens—Jens asking me his questions, Mr. Eriksen smiling when I served supper. I could even live with Birgitte if she forgave me for Tomas. Perhaps all of us could pretend again.

I put myself to sleep each night thinking of Anders and woke up in the morning to my forlorn existence.

ONE DARK DAY I was practicing the piano at a new home, waiting for the woman I was tending to rise from a nap, when her husband came up behind me and slid his hands around me in an embrace. I jumped up, startled, and he backed away.

But later that night he rattled the locked door of my room. "You'll let me in, Mrs. Solberg, if you want to keep working in St. Paul."

I braced a chair against the doorknob, then resigned the next morning. The Burnleys took me back in and tried to find me another placement, but for the first time no one needed me. I returned to the mission. Matron offered me room and board in exchange for managing her correspondence and helping in the kitchen. I was back where I started, unsure what to do next.

Every morning I combed through job placements in the newspaper, and one day I noticed a surprising announcement. My old heroine, Aasta Hansteen, was visiting Minneapolis and would be speaking at Nordens Hall in two weeks' time.

I remembered her talk in Kristiania—the mob, the yelling, our escape out the side door. Would it be like that?

I asked Matron what she thought, and she laughed. "You should go, Nora. I am sure Miss Hansteen would be pleased to talk with a Norwegian lady like yourself."

The night of the talk I put on my only dress, a blue worsted gown with lace trim down the bodice, and walked to the hall. There were mostly Norwegians in the crowd, and some Swedes. When Miss Hansteen stepped onstage she appeared older and less confident than she did in Kristiania, but once she started to speak her strength shone through.

She came to America, she said, to better understand the legal protections for American women so that such laws could be proposed in Norway. She had concluded that the American marriage laws, which allowed women to get divorced and keep inheritances, offered better protection to women than the paternalistic Norwegian marriage laws. She also spoke with admiration of American suffragettes and their remarkable freedom of thought and said she hoped to bring their message back to Norway to serve as inspiration for a new generation of Norwegian women.

When Miss Hansteen finished, there was only polite applause. No angry men, no shouting. Afterward, she greeted people she knew, and I waited patiently for a moment with her. Finally, I shook her hand and asked if we could talk privately.

She gave me a questioning look and told her hosts she would meet them later. They nodded and left us alone.

"I've long wanted to meet you, Miss Hansteen, but I always thought it would be in Norway."

"And who are you, if I may?"

I hesitated, then leaped. "I am Nora Helmer."

Her brow wrinkled. "The Nora Helmer who left her husband in Kristiania?"

"Yes."

She shook her head in surprise. "Why, Mrs. Helmer, imagine finding you here in Minnesota! No one would believe it! You're quite the heroine among freethinking women in Norway. Does anyone know you're here?"

"No, Miss Hansteen. And, please, they cannot know. You must keep my secret."

She hesitated, then finally smiled. "Of course. But how did you get here?"

"I immigrated with false papers—as the wife of a poor farmer whose own wife had just died, leaving him with two children and an infant. I agreed to care for the infant for a year in exchange for passage. I posed as his wife on board ship."

She sucked in her breath. "My goodness, Mrs. Helmer. What an adventure! You're lucky you weren't stopped."

"Yes, but I had to leave Norway. Mr. Helmer was threatening to have me committed to an asylum."

"Because you left his protection?"

"Yes, and because I wanted to see my children. He could not abide the thought, and so he had me arrested."

"Were you jailed?"

"Only overnight. They shaved my head, then released me in the morning. I left Norway that very day."

She considered me now with fresh appreciation. "It is a great honor to meet you, Mrs. Helmer."

"Mrs. Solberg. I go by my maiden name and tell people I am a widow."

"How sad that you must hide that way, even here."

"Perhaps, but here at least I have a life. I work in St. Paul with women who are despondent."

"How do you help them?"

"I care for them and talk with them. Sometimes all they need is someone to listen."

"I commend you. I wish more women would reach out to each other rather than setting themselves up as rival queens in their overdecorated parlors. That's part of what drove me out of Kristiania."

I nodded, then leaned forward. "Miss Hansteen, may I ask your opinion about something?"

"Of course."

"I enjoy my work here, but I am a servant in these homes. So I am thinking of remarrying."

"But you are still married to Mr. Helmer, are you not?"

"I don't know. I asked him to petition the king for a divorce, but I don't know if that has happened. Do you think I dare marry here?"

She gazed at me. "God would know, Mrs. Solberg, and the Norwegian Church might find out."

"But I've heard you say that God understands when women do something for love."

"Yes, but still . . ." She considered me for a moment. "I've always said that if the laws do not meet the needs of women, then women must write their own laws."

"Oh, yes! I've always believed that myself!"

She sat back. "Mrs. Solberg, have you ever thought of speaking out about these things? Your case is inspiring; you could be an important voice for Norwegian women here in America."

Inspiring? I worked in a mission because I had nothing. I thought of my life in Minnesota, the narrow ledge of civility to which I clung. How dare I stand before other women and encourage them to follow my lead? For a moment I felt a pang of anger. Who could I have been if I'd had a little wealth or been given the chance to earn my way to a bigger life? Perhaps I could have been someone.

At the same time, though, my obscurity had protected me, and it was better to stay hidden. "Miss Hansteen, I am doing my best just to survive. I don't know what I would say to other women."

She sighed. "Well, Mrs. Solberg, I think you should follow your own instincts. You know what's best for you. And I suspect that, out here in the West, no one cares as much as they do back in Kristiania."

"You don't know what that means to me. Thank you."

She shook my hand. "Good luck to you, Mrs. Solberg. I'll keep your secret, but someday Norwegian women must know what became of you. I look forward to that day."

I walked out into the warm evening, and my heart soared.

I CONTINUED TO WORK at the mission as the leaves of the maples flamed with color, then dropped to the ground. I waited until I was sure the harvest was done. Then, one morning, I headed across the city to St. Anthony Falls.

The famous falls—and the lumber mills powered there by the river— were easy to find, as trams filled with men flowed in that direction just like the Mississippi itself. The men glanced at me with curiosity when I got off with them at the main gate, as I was one of only a few women in the crowd.

At first I just stood aside, overwhelmed by the vast site. The mill buildings sat on platforms out over the Mississippi River, so that the churning water could turn the huge saws. Upstream, great pine logs blanketed the river in a tremendous jam. Men scrambled over them with long pikes, jumping and pulling, trying to corral the logs into booms to prevent them from going over the falls uncut. Saws whined; mist and wood dust hung in the murky air.

I scanned the crowd, coughing, my pulse hammering, but it was hopeless. There were hundreds of millworkers.

A man stopped and tipped his cap. "Are you looking for the kitchen, ma'am?" He pointed to a building behind me. Workers streamed in and out of a long, low shack.

"Yes, of course, thank you," I said, turning toward it. Everyone must eat, after all.

Inside, the tables were packed with men hunched over metal plates. Others waited to be served by women doling out food.

I slipped behind the serving table. A woman in a calico apron staggered from the kitchen lugging a huge pot of porridge. "Are you here to volunteer, ma'am?" the woman asked. "If so, could you take the empty in to wash?"

I picked up the pot, heavy even with nothing in it, and pushed through the door. I could not imagine lifting it full. In the kitchen, women stood at a line of cookstoves, stirring huge cast-iron kettles, while others peeled potatoes and apples or worked at a long sink stacked high with dirty plates.

One of them grabbed the empty pot and tossed me a dish towel. "We could use help with the drying, if you don't mind."

I nodded, then took off my coat. Perhaps this would be best. I could help out here in the kitchen for a few days, then ask to work at the serving table. If he was here at the mills, he was bound to come through.

That day I dried hundreds of plates, peeled heaps of apples, and rolled out enough pie dough for an army.

"Don't be too generous with the sugar," one woman said, watching me mix the apples. "They're so hungry they'll eat anything."

I had never seen so much food produced so quickly and marveled at the women who could haul great buckets of water and stew. Some seemed to be working for wages, but I was not the only volunteer. Several better-dressed girls nodded to me politely.

At the end of the day, I could barely stand, but when I got back to the mission I spoke with Matron, and she agreed to let me work the morning shift at the mill kitchen as long as I did my office work for her later.

AT THE MILL, I had to peel potatoes and wash dishes for nearly a month before I was allowed to serve. When I could get a short break, I lingered in the yard outside the kitchen watching the crowds. And once I was portioning out the corn mush, I looked at every face that appeared before me.

But still I didn't see him.

Then one morning, as I was scraping the pot to gather the last bits, someone reached across the table and grabbed my wrist. I knew it was him even before I looked up.

We locked eyes. I fought back tears, then began to smile.

"Nora, is it really you?" he whispered.

I nodded, unable to speak.

"I, I am glad to see you," he said. "But why are you here?"

The next man thrust his empty plate at me, and I served him a spoonful. "Because I hoped you would be here," I finally said.

"Let's keep the line moving," someone shouted.

Anders stepped aside. "Where will you be tonight?"

"I live at the St. Paul Women's Mission, on Grace Street."

"May I stop by?"

"Yes, of course." I gave him a spoonful of mush, then a little extra.

His serious eyes searched mine for clues. "Tonight then, after supper."

I nodded, going weak in the knees. What had I started? "Yes, Anders, tonight." I gave him a small smile, then he was gone, back into the sea of men. I spooned out mush the rest of the morning, barely breathing.

AFTER SUPPER THAT EVENING, I washed and put on a fresh blouse, watching myself in the mirror. Now that I had found Anders, I wasn't sure what to say to him. I longed to tell him the entire truth—about Torvald, my children, my leaving them—but how could I? If I told him everything, he would vanish from my life as irretrievably as if he had died along with Tomas.

And I knew by then I couldn't bear that. Just because I left Torvald, should that mean I would never be allowed to love anyone else, never be permitted to share a bed again, never sit at a family table? Did I come all the way to America only to wear the shackles of Norway?

I did not.

I brushed my hair until it shone and pulled it into a small knot, as it was finally long enough to gather and pin. Neither God nor man would deny me this chance.

WHEN ANDERS APPEARED at the door of the mission, he didn't say anything. He just looked at me and turned his felt cap in his hands.

"Please, come in," I said. I thought he would be happier to see me. I led him into the small parlor. He perched awkwardly on the horsehair sofa.

"How, ah, how are the children?" I asked.

"Fine, I hope. I didn't want to leave them, but they made me go. Birgitte's very capable, and we need the money."

I nodded. "I thought you would be working at the mills. But I was so overwhelmed when I first went down there. There seemed to be thousands of men. Then I found the kitchen."

"I couldn't quite believe it when I recognized you at the serving table," he said. "To be honest, I spotted you a few days ago."

My heart sank. "Why didn't you come forward then?"

"I, well, I don't know, Nora. I had to consider it."

I looked down at my hands. "Perhaps you never wanted to see me again."

"No, Nora, don't think that," he said. "I always hoped to see you again. I just, well, I thought you were in Chicago. I never expected to see you serving mush at the mill kitchen in Minneapolis."

I could only nod. There was so much to say but nowhere to start.

"Are you happy here?" he finally asked. "I am sure the city is more your kind of life."

Now I looked up, into his eyes. "I've been working as a nurse, for despondent women, as a servant. But even that work has disappeared. Now I am stuck here, at this mission."

He winced. "I would never have thought of you as a servant."

"I didn't feel like a servant with you. We all worked together, as a family. This is different. Here I belong to no one."

"But I am glad to see you alive and well, Nora. After Mr. Renville told me what happened, I, well, I feared for you." Now he took my hands. "I am so sorry, Nora. I had no idea you'd taken Tomas's death to heart that way."

My eyes filled. "It wasn't just losing Tomas, Anders. He was the last in a long line of children taken from me. I couldn't bear it."

"Yes," he said. "I am sorry I didn't understand that. Talking of these things has never been my way, but I see that I must change."

I nodded, falling silent again.

He tugged on my hands a bit. "What I couldn't understand was why you walked out onto the ice."

I sighed. There was a raw place inside me that would never fully heal, and I didn't like to think of it. But I could see he wanted to understand. "After Tomas died, I fell into a terrible hole that I couldn't crawl out of. I didn't just lose him; I lost my purpose. There was no one I mattered to. It broke me."

He squeezed my hands hard. "Then that was my great failure, Nora, because you mattered to me, deeply, despite everything." He shook his head. "The weeks after Tomas died were the worst I've ever lived through, because I thought God was punishing me. That he took Tomas to punish me. I couldn't see anything beyond my own sin."

"But why would God punish you, Anders?"

"For falling in love with you so soon after Inge's death."

"But, Anders, does God work in that way?"

He shook his head. "I don't know anymore. When I saw you at the serving table, it made me wonder what God meant by sending you." He was quiet for a moment. "I hadn't even dared wish for that."

"Oh, Anders, what if all this has nothing to do with God?" Suddenly, I knew what to say. "Inge died after childbirth like many women, and Tomas died because of a terrible illness known for killing children. I don't believe either was God's will. And I came looking for you of my own accord, not because God sent me. This is about you and me, Anders, not God or Inge or even Tomas."

His eyes burned into mine. "But why did you come, Nora?"

"Because I missed you! I missed you all, the children, the chores, even the cow! I missed what we had."

He looked at me for a long moment, then finally smiled softly. "May I come see you on Sunday? I have the afternoon off."

"So do I. We could walk."

"I'd like that," he said, rising. "Until next week, Nora."

WHEN MR. ERIKSEN ARRIVED Sunday afternoon, he greeted me warmly, but I could tell he was nervous, so we went out for a long ramble. It was snowing gently, a fall dusting. We walked past the elegant houses of Summit Avenue, lamps glittering in every window.

"Some Americans are so wealthy," Anders said. "There must be great opportunity out west here, though I doubt it's in farming."

"Did you plant wheat this year?"

"Yes. We had a good crop, despite the crows. Next year I'll plant more."

"What will you do with the money?" I asked.

"I've already spent it."

"Really! On livestock? A team of horses?" I stepped out to cross a street.

"No, Nora. On a house."

I stopped dead in the roadway. He pulled me to the other side, laughing at the look on my face.

"I built a frame house, Nora, with help from Mr. Renville," he said. "It's white with green trim."

"Are the children there now?"

"Yes. It still needs more furniture, but I can build some this winter."

"Where is it?"

"Up on the flat but not far from the well. With another crop, I hope to build a real barn."

"Oh, Anders, what an accomplishment!" I wondered for a moment if he sold my pearls to help pay for the lumber, but dared not ask. That was his business, not mine.

AFTER THAT HE CAME BY EVERY SUNDAY. When the sun shone, we walked outside; other days we sat in the parlor. A week before Christmas he visited one last time before returning to Lac qui Parle.

We sat side by side, not talking much at first. The wood snapped in the fireplace.

Finally, he gave me a shy smile, then took a tiny box out of his pocket. "Here, Nora, for you." I unwrapped the present with unsteady hands. Inside was a silver locket engraved with an elegant N. When I opened it, there was a tiny dried violet under glass.

"It's beautiful, Anders. Thank you." My throat tightened. I could not endure the thought of his walking away.

"Nora, I asked you once if you would marry me, and now I ask you again. Do you think you could? Perhaps in the spring? I know it's a difficult question; you needn't answer today."

"But what about the children," I said, scarcely breathing. "Do you think they could accept me?"

"I wrote to them, explaining that I had found you and hoped to bring you back as my wife." He smiled gently. "Birgitte can't quite admit it, but they have both missed you. I think that, in time, all will be fine."

I laughed, and then I was crying. "Then it's an easy question, Anders, and I don't need to wait until spring. Yes, I'll marry you. I've been so afraid you would never ask me again!"

He stared at me with surprise, and then his face softened and he leaned forward to kiss me.

"Shall we do it this week? Are you ready to go back home?"

"Yes, please."

A FEW DAYS LATER Anders and I stood before a simple altar in a Lutheran church in North Minneapolis and pledged our troth. I used my maiden name and told only one lie—that I was free to marry. Everything else, promising to love and honor and obey, I swore with a clear heart. By then, I was more sure of love than truth. For who was to say where the truth lay? Was I still Torvald's wife? I didn't even know. But I knew I loved Anders, and my desperate hope was that our marriage would become true over time.

And if this was selfish, I didn't care. I felt beholden to no one.

THAT NIGHT, in a musty hotel room, we took each other into our arms for the first time, timid and shy. He found it harder than I did, whispering at first that he felt unfaithful to his wife, but after a while his hesitancy faded. It felt so strange to lie with a different man, yet better. I had no idea it could be such a comfort, so gentle. As the barriers between us melted away, I was more confident I had done the right thing.

The next morning Anders surprised me by pulling out my string of pearls.

"These are yours, I believe. Would you like them back?"

I gazed at the beautiful necklace, so out of place in this drab hotel. I thought of the night Torvald gave them to me, but then shook the thought away. "No, I meant them for you, to help improve the farm. There are jewelry stores here that would take them, and then we could use the money for whatever we need next. Perhaps more cows."

"Jens wants to raise pigs."

"Pigs, then," I laughed. "From pearls to pigs!"

We sold the strand for a nice sum and bought Christmas gifts and new shoes for the children, as well as a green gingham traveling dress for me with a straw hat to match. Then we sat for a wedding picture and sent it to the children, telling them when to expect us in Lac qui Parle.

A few days later we boarded the train. Shifting emotions flickered through my mind as we rumbled west across the brown prairie. I felt shy with Anders but also buoyed by his quiet strength. I looked forward to seeing the children but was nervous about Birgitte. And I knew I would have to take on the heavy chores again, learn the things I still didn't know.

Yet now I was a wife. I would never be alone again.

WE REACHED MONTEVIDEO just before supper and got a room at the hotel. The next morning Anders went off to negotiate for several sows he would retrieve later in the week. I went to the general store to buy more gifts for the children and silk thread for lace collars. I looked forward to taking up my needles again.

We set out walking, as there was little snow, and didn't approach our homestead until quite late. The full moon helped, and Anders knew the track well. When we reached our wheat fields, my stomach clenched, but instead of heading toward the sod house, we turned west, and then I could see something looming in the dark. A real frame house, with carved trim and a green door. A lamp burned in the window.

We came in quietly, but within an instant Jens tumbled down the attic stairs, his sister following. Jens gave me a ferocious hug, while Birgitte dutifully kissed my cheek and offered her congratulations. After a few minutes, their father sent them back up to bed. They slept in the attic, Anders said, and we would sleep . . . here. He opened a door. Inside was a beautiful little bedroom with a dresser and bed built into the wall. The bedstead was carved with flowers in the Norwegian fashion. I sat down and ran my hand over a rich new quilt.

"Mrs. Madsen made it for you," he said. "She was sorry to find you had gone but insisted we keep it in case you returned."

I recognized the traditional Norwegian pattern, embroidered roses with green and maroon borders on a white lawn. "Did the rest of her children survive?"

"Yes, miraculously. She credits you, Nora. It was a kind thing you did."

I looked away. I couldn't think about that time. It was hard enough being here again.

But he understood and gave me a hug. "Tomorrow, I'll show you everything. It will be better now, Nora. I promise."

CHAPTER EIGHTEEN

SOLVI

May 1919 ▪ *Kristiania, Norway*

Spring came slowly. The flowers seemed hesitant to emerge after the hard winter and the trees reluctant to unfurl their leaves. To Solvi, everything felt unresolved—from the mysteries she was chasing to the relationships around her. She wasn't sure how she felt about anything or anyone— neither Dominik, nor Magnus, nor the Forgotten One, nor the puzzle of her family.

For the first time since leaving Bergen, she ached for her father and the gentle advice he often gave her as they hiked the upland meadows. She pined for him, and she missed the wide outdoors.

So when Dominik invited her a few days later to picnic with him in Frogner Park, she jumped at the chance, despite her uneasy feelings about him. "What a nice idea," she said. "I love a long walk."

He gave her a cryptic wink. "Just you wait."

ON SATURDAY MORNING, she waited for Dominik outside the study house. She couldn't quite believe her eyes when he appeared on a yellow bicycle, one with two seats and two handlebars.

"This thing's a bit hard to manage without a partner," he yelled, careening into the curb. "Hop on, Solvi."

"But I've never ridden a bicycle," Solvi said. "My mother thought it improper."

"If you're with your boyfriend, it's perfectly acceptable," he said, patting the second seat. "Don't worry. I'll steer—you just pedal."

Solvi climbed gingerly aboard, tucking her skirt beneath her. Then Dominik pushed off. They veered across the street but then picked up speed and began to even out. It took Solvi a few blocks to trust it, but soon they were flying along, her pulse thumping with excitement. It felt like rid-ing a horse, only smoother.

"It must be fun to ride by oneself," Solvi yelled. "Is it hard to learn?"

"Most people pick it up quickly," he said. "But I'd rather do it together."

He headed up the hill to the park. Solvi pedaled hard, enjoying the exer-cise, watching his strong shoulders and legs. Her long hair streamed out behind her, tangling hopelessly.

When they got to the top, they stashed the bicycle behind a blackberry bush and walked up into a meadow of tall grass and wildflowers. As if over-night, everything had started to bloom. There were other people about, some picnicking on the lawn, others walking through the trees beyond. Solvi breathed in the smell of the grass and closed her eyes to listen to the bees.

"I'll show you my favorite spot," Dominik said. In the distance, the meadow sloped down to a lake with a stand of weeping willows at one end. The willows were so old, their branches swept the ground in the light breeze. He took her hand and headed toward them.

Solvi expected him to spread out the picnic blanket beside the lake, but instead he ducked between the willow branches, pulling her with him.

Solvi looked around. Behind the branches, they were completely hidden.

"Isn't this great?" Dominik said, taking the blanket out of his rucksack and spreading it out. He patted a spot next to him. "Come, sit, Solvi. We've got our own private little room. Just us and the birds."

But Solvi just stood, watching him. Something felt wrong. She wasn't sure if she should sit with him under the tree like this. He ignored her and set out the lunch—sandwiches, strawberries, wine, and chocolate. He had obviously gone to some trouble. How could she disappoint him? She finally sat on the blanket, as demurely as possible.

He poured the wine, then handed her a glass and raised his in a toast. "To my girlfriend, Solvi Lange!"

"To my friend, Dominik," she said back, then took a long sip.

He looked at her, surprised. "Not your boyfriend?"

"Well, I don't remember agreeing that we were girlfriend and boyfriend, Dominik. It isn't so just because you say it."

"But I took you to meet my mother! Didn't that mean anything?"

"Yes, but something that important should be discussed, between you and me," Solvi said, taking a strawberry. "What would it mean to be boy-friend and girlfriend?"

He leaned down on one arm. "It would mean that you're my girl. That you cannot go out with other boys."

"I often go to a pastry shop with Magnus after class, to get coffee. Could I still do that?"

"You go for coffee with Magnus, every week?"

She nodded, even though it was no longer true. They hadn't been to the pastry shop since their fight after Solvi went to the dance with Dominik, but she didn't want Dominik to know that. "Magnus is just a friend, Dominik. He's helping me with my essay."

"I've been helping you with your essay. How much help do you need?" He sat up and scowled at her. "I'm not sure I like that."

He reminded Solvi of her mother forbidding her to walk about Bergen. She reached for a sandwich. "Come on, Dominik, let's not argue. It's such a pretty day."

"Well, I don't like it, Solvi," he said, but after eating half a sandwich and drinking more wine, he brightened up again. They talked and laughed. Soon they had finished the bottle of wine and opened the chocolate.

Dominik took a piece and held it up to Solvi's lips. "Let me feed you," he said, smiling.

She flushed; she didn't really like this but opened her mouth and took the chocolate with her teeth. Then, before she knew what was happening, Dominik leaned over and kissed her.

"Now are you my girl?" he asked, with an impish grin.

"Dominik, I really think . . ."

"Oh, Solvi, don't you know when to stop talking?" With that, he took hold of her hair, wrapped it around his wrist, then pulled her backward, down onto the blanket.

"Dominik!" she cried out, struggling to get up, but with his hand in her curls she couldn't twist away. He leaned over and kissed her again.

Now she pushed him with both hands, and he finally let go. She sat up, twisting her hair into a rope and stuffing it down the back of her blouse. "Dominik, that wasn't fair."

"But now I think you have to be my girl, because you don't want it getting around that you'll kiss every boy."

She put her hand to her lips. Her first kiss. She wished she had wanted it more. "I think we should go," she said.

"You're being rather cold about this," Dominik said. "I thought you'd like it." He started to pack up the lunch.

"Perhaps I'm just not ready," Solvi said, feeling bad in every possible way. "Why didn't you ask my permission?"

"Permission spoils the mood. It's a bit rough on us lads if you lead us on but don't mean anything by it," he said. "You sure know how to ruin a nice day."

They walked back to the bicycle, pulled it out of the bush, and headed down the hill. For Solvi, sitting behind him and unable to steer or set the pace, the joy had gone out of it. She wished she were riding on her own.

When they got to the study house, Solvi tried to be polite. "I'm sorry, Dominik. It was lovely up there. Thank you."

But both of them knew she didn't mean it.

AFTER DOMINIK PEDALED AWAY, Solvi turned toward town, heading straight to a barbershop. The barber refused at first, but when she offered to pay him double, he did as she asked. He left just enough of her hair to cover her ears.

When he was done, she tried to pull her hair back, but it was too short to hold. Good, just what she wanted.

WHEN SOLVI APPEARED at dinner with her new haircut, Rikka could only stare. The other girls fussed over her, saying they wished they had the courage, but not Rikka.

It was only after they were seated that Rikka whispered in her ear. "What happened?"

Solvi grabbed a roll. "I'll tell you later. I'm starving. I rode a bicycle today, with Dominik. A bicycle built for two."

Rikka looked at her. "Was it fun? You don't look like you had much fun." "No."

UPSTAIRS LATER, Solvi told Rikka what happened under the willows. "You were right, as much as I hate to admit it," Solvi said, running her fingers through what was left of her curls. "It was a mistake to trust Dominik."

"I'm sorry for you, Solvi. I know you liked him. But some boys seem to need to make others do their bidding. Maybe it comes with their privilege, that sense that other people should bend to their whims."

Solvi sighed. "Perhaps. I just wish he and I could have talked about it. I wish he had asked permission."

"If you find a guy like that, marry him," Rikka said. "In the meantime, your bob looks smashing."

LATER THAT WEEK Solvi took her new photographs of the maids to the newspaper office, swallowing her misgivings. Rikka was right, she thought. There was no progress without risk.

Mr. Blehr looked through them, then shook Solvi's hand. "Excellent work, Miss Lange." He handed her several crowns. "The story will be out in a few days, as soon as we can make engravings from the photographs."

She looked at the money. "Mr. Blehr, I have more photos. Do you have a moment?"

"Of course."

Solvi pulled out her copy of *Albertine*. "Do you know this book?"

He took it. "Ah, yes. Most of these were burned within days of publication," he said, then looked through the plates in the back. "I've seen some of these paintings. For some reason, the authorities didn't burn them. I suppose they thought paintings were not as dangerous as books."

"Well, I'm not sure they were right," Solvi said, surprised at her own boldness. "My friend who works for the health auxiliary in Vika introduced me to several prostitutes who helped me re-create Krohg's paintings."

He looked at her, dumbfounded. "Re-create?"

She laid out the photographs. "See? Albertine still lives, in Vika."

"My word," he said softly, picking up each one and comparing it with Krohg's version. "How clever, Miss Lange. Very interesting."

"I also talked with the women about how they ended up working as prostitutes. They're quite hopelessly poor, and most are sick."

He scooped up the photographs and the book. "May I keep these? Let me talk to the other editors. Excellent work, Miss Lange."

Solvi smiled; then, just as quickly, her smile vanished. She had just thought of something, something that worried her.

"When the housemaid story comes out, Mr. Blehr, will my name be in the newspaper?"

"Absolutely; I want everyone to know who my talented photographer is."

"Even if one's mother might be horrified?"

He looked at her over his glasses. "You still have a mother, Miss Lange? I would never have guessed."

"Well," she said, "this may be the last week."

AS IF ON CUE, a letter arrived from Solvi's mother that same afternoon.

Dear Solvi: I have been thinking of your circumstances in Kristiania and have decided you need the guidance of a mature female presence. To that end, I have contacted an old school friend of mine, Mrs. Klausen, who lives in Briskeby, just a tram ride away from the university. She is widowed now, with room to spare. She has generously offered to have you live with her until a better solution can be found, as it is clear the matron of your study house exerts little control over you girls. Mrs. Klausen said some company would do her good.

I trust this arrangement will meet with your approval. With the money you save living with Mrs. Klausen, you can give up that frightful job at the photography studio. I am happy to help with your expenses.

I hope you understand how difficult this is for me, alone here in Bergen and fearing for your safety. I trust you will take pity on your grieving mother and offer me some relief. Please tell me when you will be ready to move to Mrs. Klausen's so I can let her know.

Mother

Solvi went straight to Rikka's door.

"Hey," Rikka said, kicking aside a pile of clothes. "What's wrong?"

"Read this."

"Oh, I just love other people's mail," Rikka said, grabbing it and reading it through. Then she looked at Solvi and put her hands on her hips in mock disdain. "Really, Solveig, what were you thinking, working in a photo shop? You should be ashamed of yourself."

Solvi sighed. "Now she's cooked up this Mrs. Klausen, as if it's my responsibility to keep some old widow company."

Rikka tossed her head. "Just refuse, Solvi. You're making enough money to keep living here. This is your life, your decision."

"But what if my mother never speaks to me again? She's my only living relative, as far as I can tell."

"You won't lose her," Rikka said. "Call her bluff."

"This is what I get for being honest with her, trying to close the gap between us by telling her what I'm doing."

"Did you tell her about me?"

"No, you're much too alarming."

Rikka laughed. "So there it is. You're your own person now, Solvi. Congratulations."

SOLVI SAT DOWN to respond that afternoon, before she lost courage.

> Dear Mama: Thank you for your concern, but I will not go live with
> Mrs. Klausen. The study house is as safe as a private home, and I do
> not need guidance from a mature female presence. Please tell her
> thank you but that I am fine where I am.
>
> You must understand this is my life, Mama. I am different from
> you. I am not sure why, but I have always felt it and I need to be free
> to choose as I will.
>
> I hope you can find a way to trust me. You are my only family,
> Mama. We need to be happy with each other, but that can only
> happen if you let me live my own life.
>
> Your daughter, Solvi

Solvi didn't tell her mother what she had learned about her grandmother. She wasn't sure why, except that she felt somehow her mother
didn't deserve to know. Her mother hadn't tried to find her own missing
mother and didn't seem to care what had happened to her. Solvi could feel
herself clutching her grandmother's story—thorny, confusing, haunting—
as if it were her own secret treasure. It didn't belong to anyone else.

WHEN IT CAME TIME to write her history essay, Solvi holed up in her
room, coming out only for meals. She worked hard to bring the Forgotten
One to life, describing the legal and social restrictions for women at the
time and what they would have meant for someone in her circumstances:
her thin purse, the ache of missing her children, the shame that would have
left her unemployable and friendless; how she must have had to live in the
shadows, how hard it would have been to resist falling into prostitution.

As she wrote, the sorrow Solvi felt for her lost grandmother seeped into
the essay, giving it a tender, tragic edge.

When she was done, Solvi carefully wrote out a copy. She wanted to
show it to Magnus, but she wasn't sure she had the right. The truth was,
she didn't know what to think or feel about Magnus.

A FEW DAYS LATER, the newspaper published the housemaid story.
Solvi ran out early and bought several copies, glancing nervously inside to
see which photos Mr. Blehr had used. There was the picture from Bergen
of the scullery girl with the long braid down her back washing stacks of
dishes, then several from Kristiania—the maids with the pans, the cook

hacking the lamb carcass, the young girl brushing ashes from an enormous fireplace. In each photograph the maid's face was obscured in some way, but below them all stood Solvi's name, in bold type.

And there, at the bottom of the page, was the photograph of Greta and the ugly welt.

Solvi swore softly. Petra must have given it to Mr. Blehr instead of to Greta. How could Petra have defied her? She looked closely at the picture. Fortunately, Solvi had shot Greta's cheek up close, so it was impossible to see who she was, and Petra hadn't named Greta or Dominik's family. Her article talked of how maids worked long, exhausting hours and often suffered physical and sexual violence. The picture of Greta's welt proved her point. At the end, Petra called for the Storting to pass wage and workday standards for housemaids, as well as legal protections.

Solvi sat back with a sigh. She understood why Petra had done it; she just wished she had asked permission.

She brought the newspapers to breakfast, and Rikka jumped up to show the other girls before Solvi could stop her. They congratulated her, but several glanced at her with an edge of discomfort. Most probably grew up with housemaids.

"I think you've intimidated them," Rikka said later. "Few would have the courage to do something like this. You've stepped out of the privilege of your class, Solvi. I'm very proud of you."

"It's exciting, Rikka, I'll admit, but I'm angry with Petra. I told her not to give the photo of Greta to Mr. Blehr."

"But you can see why it was necessary."

"Yes; I just hope we don't get into trouble over it," Solvi said.

"How would we get into trouble? No one can possibly know we were there."

"I don't know, Rikka. I just have a bad feeling about it."

"That's silly; enjoy your celebrity, Solvi. You earned it. Maybe I need to find another bottle of champagne." Rikka gave Solvi a sly smile. "If we had some rope, we could haul it in from outside."

Solvi couldn't help but laugh. "Rikka, you're not going to quit until we're both booted out of this place, are you?"

"Probably not."

WHEN SOLVI WALKED INTO the photo shop later that day, she found Mr. Stenberg leaning over the newspaper.

"Congratulations, Miss Lange! These are excellent. I'm quite impressed."

"Thank you," she said. "I couldn't have done it without your encouragement. You were the first to appreciate what I was trying to do."

She retreated to the darkroom, a relief after the hubbub of the morning, and sank into the quiet process of moving the photographs from one pan to the next.

After several hours, Mr. Stenberg knocked. "There's someone to see you, Miss Lange. A young man."

Her stomach flipped. Dominik. She washed up, her hands shaking, then took a deep breath and emerged into the light.

But it wasn't Dominik; it was Magnus.

"I didn't mean to disturb you, Solvi. I just wanted to congratulate you, and I knew you'd be here." He held the newspaper in his hands. "The photographs are very moving and powerful. I'm so proud of you and Petra."

"Thank you, Magnus. But do you think it's a problem, the photo of Greta?"

"I saw Petra this morning and asked her, because I was surprised to see it. She said Greta gave her permission. Petra found her a better job in another house."

"Ah," Solvi said, and then she turned to Mr. Stenberg. "Would you mind if I finished the developing tomorrow?"

"Of course not," he said with a smile. "Enjoy your moment of glory."

Outside on the sidewalk, Solvi looked up at Magnus. "Could we go to the pastry shop again, like we used to?"

His face brightened. "I thought you'd never ask."

SOLVI BOUGHT their usual packet of sweets as Magnus claimed the table in the window. Now that the spring equinox had passed, the afternoon light lingered. The buildings glowed pink in the sinking sun, and the trees, finally leafed out, bent gently in the breeze.

"Thank you for stopping by, Magnus. I was hoping to see you."

"I've missed our talks, Solvi."

"Me, too," she said, looking into his eyes. "I need to tell you something, though I'm not sure it will matter to you. I don't want to presume."

"What is it?"

"I'm not seeing Dominik anymore. He, well, he . . ." Her voice caught.

Magnus put his hand on hers. "You don't need to explain; I understand. Dominik is a strong fellow."

Her eyes brimmed. "It's a mess, Magnus! I haven't told you yet, but Greta was one of the housemaids for Dominik's family!"

"What? Was the house you sneaked into Dominik's home?"

"Yes, though I didn't know it at the time." Then Solvi told him about Edvard threatening Greta and about being invited later for Sunday supper with Dominik's family. She explained how she identified Edvard and blushed when she recognized the serving maids who brought in the food. Magnus listened thoughtfully.

Solvi sighed. "Now I'm worried Dominik and Edvard will put two and two together and go to the police."

Magnus cocked his head. "I suspect Edvard will be too embarrassed to say anything. If Greta doesn't make a formal complaint, he'll probably stay silent." Magnus opened the newspaper and looked at the photographs again. "There's hardly anything here that could tip off Dominik's parents, unless they get suspicious and look at the photos carefully and compare them with their kitchens and their maids' aprons and shoes. They would never recognize them unless they were looking for it."

Solvi sighed.

"Really, Solvi, don't lose sleep over this," Magnus said.

She took a deep breath. "Between Edvard, Dominik, and my mother, it's hard not to worry. I wish I could enjoy it more."

Magnus laughed. "And I'll bet Edvard and Dominik are the least of it!"

Solvi rolled her eyes. "I expect my mother to show up any day now, unless seeing my name in the paper gave her a heart attack right away."

"But she should be proud of you, Solvi. I certainly am." He smiled. "You're a surprising girl, Solvi Lange. I'm glad we're friends again."

"Me too," she said, her soul filling with light. She had no idea how much she had missed him.

THAT NIGHT, Rikka and Solvi met at the café for supper. Solvi noticed Dominik across the room, but he didn't look her way or come over. She hadn't spoken to him since their picnic and was relieved to find he was keeping to his own circle.

When they were done with their soup, Rikka stayed behind talking with her many friends, but Solvi, exhausted, headed home alone. She glanced at

Dominik one more time as she slipped out the door. He didn't seem to have noticed her.

The streets were dusky in the remaining light, and Solvi trailed along dreamily, thinking of Magnus and all he had said. She was happier than she had been in some time.

She turned the corner into a darker street, then suddenly heard someone running up behind her. She started to look around, but before she knew what was happening, someone grabbed her and pushed her hard against a building.

Edvard.

"Solvi Lange, the great photographer," he grunted, pushing his face into hers. "You were there that day, weren't you? You and your friends trespassed in my family's home, and you a great friend of Dominik's!" He squeezed her arms hard behind her. "I can't believe my family hosted you for supper, you ungrateful bitch!"

"Edvard, I didn't know, I didn't mean . . ." Solvi twisted away from his eyes and breath.

His hand closed around her throat. "You'd better keep quiet about what you think you know, Solvi Lange. If Greta files a complaint, I'll need you to come to court and deny it. I hope you're ready to explain to the police why you were trespassing."

"Photographs don't lie," she croaked, her voice little more than a whisper.

He spit in her face. Then, in a moment of inspiration, he pulled her satchel off her shoulder.

"Is your camera in here?"

"No!" she screamed, though it wasn't true. She lunged to grab the satchel, but he kicked it away.

Then someone else came running and shouting. Dominik.

"Edvard, stop! You said you wouldn't hurt her!" he cried, scuffling with his brother and pulling him off Solvi. She stumbled from the wall, scrabbling across the pavement for her satchel. But Dominik snatched it first.

She straightened slowly, wiping the spittle from her cheek. "Dominik, please, you know what that camera means to me." She looked into his eyes and held out her hand.

He hugged her satchel tighter. "Then explain it to me, Solvi. Explain why you did it." His eyes burned into hers. "Why would you hurt my family when we were so kind to you?"

"I'm sorry; I didn't mean for Greta's photograph to be in the newspaper. Greta gave it to the editor, not me."

"But why did you trespass?"

"I didn't know it was your home. It was before you asked me to come for supper. But you are right. We shouldn't have gone in without permission."

Edvard tugged at the satchel. "Come on, Dominik. Let's throw it in the fjord. That'll teach her to snoop."

"Permission, Solvi," Dominik said. "You wanted me to ask permission, but you couldn't be bothered. It cuts both ways, doesn't it?"

Tears ran down her face. "You're right, Dominik. I apologize. And I'm sorry, sorry about everything."

He frowned and looked down at her satchel for a long moment, then abruptly pushed it back into her arms.

"God damn you, Dominik!" Edvard said, giving his brother a sharp push. "You're going to regret this!"

"Shut up," Dominik said. "I'm not going to bully her, Edvard, and neither are you, so just shut up."

Solvi slipped the strap of the satchel over her head.

Dominik hesitated, looking at Solvi now with pain and sadness.

"I'm so sorry, Dominik," she said.

"Just go, Solvi. Please go. But keep quiet about this, or you'll be even sorrier."

Solvi backed away, crossed the street quickly, and then hurried around the next corner. Her heart didn't slow down until she was safe inside the study house.

SOLVI RAN UPSTAIRS and rapped on Rikka's door, then elbowed her way in and sank onto her bed, fighting back tears.

"Solvi, my goodness, what happened?" Rikka asked.

"Edvard attacked me as I was walking home. He was so angry—he wanted to throw my camera in the fjord! He grabbed my satchel, but Dominik gave it back to me."

Rikka pulled her to a stand. "Let me look you over and make sure you're not hurt."

Solvi rubbed her neck. "He grabbed me by the throat, but it's not bad, thanks to Dominik. If he hadn't come along, I'm not sure what Edvard would have done."

"I hope Dominik isn't your hero now."

"No. But he was right; we never should have trespassed at their home."

Rikka ignored that. "Will you see him again?"

"No. I think he hates me now," Solvi said. "But I'm worried that Edvard might still go to the police."

"You should tell Mr. Blehr. He'll know what to do; it's his newspaper, after all."

Solvi sighed. "I wish I were braver. You probably would have gouged his eyes out."

"I'm not brave, Solvi. I'm angry," Rikka said. "It makes me so angry that men have that power over us. Anger is my sword."

Solvi looked at her for a long moment. "I need a sword."

"Yes, you do. If you're going to be a journalist, you might need a cannon."

CHAPTER NINETEEN

NORA

Spring 1919 ■ *Spokane, Washington*

Ivar. Maybe it was Ivar who was looking for me. I gazed at the advertisement again, at the image of my eldest standing there like the stalwart boy
that he was, and my stomach knotted. Of my three children, he was the
one I most needed to see. I had grown old, past seventy. It would be painful
to go to my death without his forgiveness.

Ivar was my first-born, and our relationship was a revelation to me. He
was the first person I loved in an uncomplicated way, without having to
perform for him as I did for his father, without worrying whether he loved
me back. Because that was without question—he was my child, and I was
his mother. Our bond was simple, true.

I had little time to indulge my delight in him, however, as Torvald
became ill with tuberculosis shortly after his birth and my father soon
developed his bad heart. I felt torn between the three of them: a demanding father, a weakening husband, and my baby boy. Each one needed more
of me than I could give, and so I managed to disappoint them all.

Ivar survived, as babies do, even though we dragged him to Italy while
his father convalesced. He learned to walk on the filthy streets of Rome
among the flowerpots and heaps of dung. It was all I could do to keep him
safe and healthy that year. Between Torvald and Ivar, there was little time
for anything other than tending and worrying. Would Torvald survive?
Would Ivar catch malaria or totter in front of a cart? I hovered over them
both, guardian angel and mother and wife. I barely slept the entire year.

When Ivar grew up anxious, I was not surprised. He learned it at my
knee.

THE TRUTH WAS, I didn't know whether it was Ivar, or Bobby or Emma. But it must be one of them. And I could see that this was my chance, my one chance to patch my life back together again.

I sat down at the kitchen table that afternoon with a fresh sheet of paper. I was too old to be afraid anymore.

> *Dear Child of Mine,*
>
> *I am not sure which one of you posted the advertisement in the "Skandinaven," but please know I am so grateful. For years I have longed to find my way back to all of you, and it appears now that might be possible.*
>
> *Please write to me at post office box 216 in Spokane, Washington. I await your response with happy anticipation.*
>
> *All my love, your mother*

I folded the letter and slipped it into an envelope, to mail the next day when we went to town.

Then I walked down through the orchard to where my patient husband was working, to show him the advertisement and tell him what I had done.

NORA
January 1883 ▪ Lac qui Parle, Minnesota

Now that I was married to Anders, I could begin my life on the prairie anew. The frame house proved a revelation—carefully crafted and filled with comforts, including rocking chairs and glass windows. Birgitte surprised me by helping sew curtains, and one day brought out the rag box so we could braid a rug. Around me she was quiet and solemn, but no longer angry. I tried to be as kind as I could.

As we sorted through the rags, I noticed strips of the calico curtains from the sod house.

"I'm sorry, Nora," said Birgitte, pulling them out. "I thought we burned these." She turned toward the stove.

"No," I said, stopping her. "We need to remember, don't you think? We mustn't forget him."

We held each other's gaze for a long moment, and then she tossed the strips on top of our pile and returned to our task. I could feel her opening to me.

A FEW DAYS LATER, I walked with Jens over to Tomas's grave, where the sparse snow glittered around his small cross. I would always miss that baby boy, but life had surged onward, in its relentless way. I was surprised by what a blessing that was.

Mr. Renville soon stopped in to welcome me back, and the next day I walked around the lake to visit his sister. She greeted me as if I had never left, showing me her weaving and brewing me a cup of her herb tea. Once the ice left the lake, Mr. Renville took me across in his canoe to visit Herr Gippe, the gentleman who gave me the money to get to St. Paul. His Norwegian wife and I sat together over coffee, and when I told her about caring for women with melancholy, she said there might be local women who needed my help. She promised to send her husband for me if she heard of anyone.

With spring, our pigs arrived, three sows with swollen bellies who soon gave birth to a passel of noisy piglets. Jens took charge, cleaning their pens, watching for escapees, and making sure the runts got milk. When he thought one was being cheated, he brought it to me, and I would sit in the hay with the old suckling flask, cooing to the piglet as I cooed to Tomas. It helped heal the hole in my heart.

In the warming evenings we took our chairs outside and watched the sun sink toward the horizon. Sometimes Birgitte or I read aloud, or Jens and his father played checkers, a game Anders had learned in town. He knew more people, as the county filled up, and on Sundays now we went to the Lutheran church. I did my best to attract little attention.

In many respects I settled in well, but still—it felt strange to be married again. Memories of Torvald nagged at me, like ghost limbs that ached with imagined pain. I sometimes found myself telling small fibs or hiding something I should tell Anders, as I did with Torvald. Then I would make myself confess so I could live with a clearer conscience. I worried that I could never be the helpmate Anders needed, but he was patient with me and appreciated my efforts. Anders's love was different from Torvald's— quieter, less demanding—and by the time Indian summer arrived, memories of Torvald had faded away.

That fall we had a good harvest—pulling in a healthy wheat crop and selling pigs to new settlers. Anders celebrated by going to town and returning with a team of horses. He was curing wood to build a small sleigh, so that we might attend church in the winter. Birgitte, who was nearing fifteen, needed to be confirmed.

Once the harvest was finished, Birgitte and Jens returned to the village school, walking off down the track with their lunch sacks and books. The days were lonelier for me but not without their pleasures. Anders taught me to paint the traditional rosemaling so that I could decorate the bowls and spoons he sold in the general store, and I learned to drive the horses.

One day, Birgitte came home talking of the licensing exam for teachers. I agreed to help her study, and her dream soon became our common mission.

IN THIS SHELTERED WORLD, six years passed. Anders and the children and I toiled to make the farm prosper, but it was never easy. Some seasons were contented ones; others were shadowed by hardship and worry. Late the second summer, after the August winds had dried the grass to parchment, a great fire surged across Lac qui Parle County. We awoke that morning with smoke in our lungs and leaped from our beds. Anders plowed a line around the house first, then the fields, but by the time the flames rose in front of us, it looked hopeless. Jens climbed out on the roof and hauled up buckets of water to wet it down, risking his life but saving the house. In the midst of the mayhem, Birgitte's skirts caught fire. Without thinking, I grabbed a wet blanket and flung myself against her, rolling us both on the ground. Birgitte's legs were quite badly burned, and she spent weeks in bed healing, tended by me and Ann Renville. By the time she walked again, she was a different girl—older, wiser—and we were finally friends.

When Birgitte turned sixteen, she passed her examinations and went to live and teach in the town of Madison, ten miles away. Her visits home were happy times, and we encouraged her to save her earnings so she could attend the new college for Norwegian immigrants in Northfield, south of Minneapolis. Jens, who was not a student like his sister, developed into a carver almost as good as his father. He, too, sold his woodenware in town and gladly added his earnings to Birgitte's college fund.

IN THE WINTER AFTER THE FIRE, many families struggled. One cold day a sleigh pulled up with Herr Gippe at the reins. A young mother needed my help, he said. I packed a small bag, and soon he dropped me at a very poor farm. Entering the humble soddie I was overcome by the familiar dank smell but mustered myself to do what I could. The woman sat silent as a post in a corner, a letter in her hand. I stayed three days, cleaning, cooking, and helping with her children, while she wept for her parents back in Norway, who had recently died. When I returned a few weeks later to check on her, she was better, and grateful.

Others soon learned of my skill, and when an anxious child or husband appeared at our door, I knew it was time to gather my bag and go. Prairie women fell to grief in every season, on dark winter days when the wind was howling and soft summer mornings when the meadowlarks sang from the fence posts. By the time someone sought my help, the women were often far gone, gaunt with sadness and weak from sickness and hunger.

I did what I could to ease their burden, usually starting with the women themselves, much as Ann Renville had done with me—bathing and changing them in their beds, feeding them by hand if they wouldn't eat, brushing their hair. Anything to make them feel better.

Eventually, they would fall asleep, relaxing at last because someone was there to cook for their families. And so I did, getting the children to help me tackle the dishes, sweep the house, cook, and bake.

Many women sank into despair after losing a child or suffering an injury, tragedy piling on top of their unremitting poverty. Herr Gippe fetched me one day to help a couple whose three children had recently died of scarlet fever. I stayed with them for a week, until they recovered their equilibrium and sent me home. I heard later that the mother burned the house down shortly after I left, on a beautiful April afternoon.

There was something about the prairie—the heavy silence, the blank horizon, our fragility in the face of nature's will—that intensified everything. One woman told me she often imagined she had traveled back to Narvik to visit her dead sister, and feared her soul might refuse one day to return. Another woman believed a storm would someday blow away all they had—their shanty, their wheat, their children. When the weather threatened, she felt compelled to drink brandy until it passed. Another told me she walked out on the prairie at night but knew not why. Her husband had gone after her several times. "I know there's nothing," she said, "but still I must go."

The women asked if I thought they were mad, but what they feared was often real, so I told them no. Most got better when they overcame their Nordic reticence and shared what haunted them.

Occasionally, I found wives with bruises or black eyes. They blamed homestead accidents, though the tension in the house often suggested a different story. When I asked if their husbands hit them, they said, "Only when he drinks." The men denied drinking, though Anders said few could resist the saloons when they had money in their pockets.

At first I cared for the women with my mouth shut, but in time I started urging women to stand up to husbands who hurt them. To take the children and go to a neighbor's house or hide in the barn. For those burdened by many mouths, I even hinted at ways to protect themselves from more pregnancies, though few could hear this advice. Most believed it was their sacred duty—to accept another child or death, whichever was the will of God.

Husbands sometimes caught echoes of what I said. Anders reported grumbles around the stove in the back of the general store, often tied to my friendship with *the Indian* Ann Renville. He defended the Renvilles when their names came up, but fear of Indians persisted in this region. Few befriended them as we had.

As for the women I helped, they were usually too ashamed by what they told me in their darkest hours to welcome me for coffee after they recovered. I felt like my work had purpose, but it did not open the community to me. I remained an oddity—strangely well educated and refined, too ladylike to be feeding chickens on a prairie farm. Because I was not like the Norwegian farmers who settled our county, I was never fully trusted.

I was happiest in Ann's silent company.

I NEVER AGAIN suffered the deep despair I felt after Tomas's death, but sometimes sorrow crept up on me. If Anders and I had had a child, it might have filled the void, but we agreed to manage our love in such a way that I would not get pregnant. Neither of us could risk losing a child again.

When I was sad, I thought obsessively of my own children back in Norway. I finally sent a letter to my old nurse, Anne-Marie, praying that she was still alive. I begged her to write with news of the children and whether she knew if Torvald had remarried. I also enclosed a letter for the children, asking her to mail it to them when Ivar turned fifteen. But I never heard back.

And, to be honest, the lie I told Anders—that I was free to marry—festered like a wound that would not heal. Because of it, I felt unworthy of his love and was afraid that if I opened my heart to him completely, my secrets would tumble forth and ruin everything. In time I came to understand the terrible bargain I had made: if I was to see my children again,

I would have to tell Anders of my falsehood, but if I did that, my marriage would be destroyed.

I learned to start each day thankful for my bowl of porridge and the quiet husband across from me, as that might be all I would ever have.

THEN, ONE DAY, a miracle happened. A miracle with a thousand ripples.

It was a warm spring evening in late May of 1889. I sat outside shelling peas, the breeze playing around my skirt, the scent of manure and rebirth thick with the new season. Anders and Jens were washing up by the well, tired after a day in the fields. I rose and went inside to put the peas to boil.

By then, Birgitte was teaching school in Lac qui Parle, living behind the schoolroom and enjoying the bustle of town. She was our most American child—an impressive young woman with excellent English and a scholarly bent. She usually came home only on Sundays, but this Wednesday evening she appeared in the doorway, breathing hard.

"Birgitte, what is it?"

"Nora! I came right away! There's—."

Anders and Jens came in behind her. "Why, Birgitte, you're just in time for dinner," Anders said. Then he saw her face. "What's wrong?"

She glanced at her father, then back at me. "There's a young man in town, from Norway, and he's asking for Nora Solberg!"

I looked at her, puzzled; then my knees turned to water. I grabbed a chair. A fierce longing flooded my heart.

"What does he look like?" I said, starting to tremble.

"Well, that's the strangest part—he looks like you. There's something about his eyes and coloring."

Anders turned to me. "Nora, who is this?"

My pulse began to race. "How old is he, Birgitte?"

"About my age," she said. "Good-looking. A city boy."

"Did you speak to him?"

"No. I stopped by the store, and he was there talking with the men. I thought I should tell you immediately."

Anders tugged hard on my hand. "Nora, who is this young man?"

I could not speak. I wanted it to be Ivar more than I had ever wanted anything else, but if it was, my worlds would collide. Or perhaps it was Tobias, but, no—he looked nothing like me. It was Ivar; I knew it.

"Anders, I must go to town." I untied my apron. "Right now. I'll walk back with Birgitte."

"Nora, we will eat first, and you will explain," Anders said. "Then I'll hitch up the horses."

I sat on the edge of my chair. Birgitte got our supper, the peas and potatoes, the *flotbrod* and butter. Anders watched me over his plate, waiting for an explanation, but I didn't know what to say or where to start. I forced myself to eat a few bites.

"I don't know who it is, Anders," I finally said. "It might be a cousin, or the boy who befriended me at the boardinghouse in Vika. He meant to immigrate to America."

"How would he know where to find you?"

"I wrote to him several years back, telling him where I was." I tried to sound nonchalant, but my hands shook. Anders kept a troubled eye on me until we finished.

He brought the wagon. Birgitte needed to get back to town, and Jens insisted on coming, so we all climbed in. Bouncing over the rough track, I shivered with anticipation. Saying it might be a cousin was untrue, as I had no family in Norway other than my children. And if it was Ivar, perhaps he brought terrible news—that Bob or Emma had died.

And how, in God's name, could I explain this to my husband?

Anders kept glancing at me in the fading light and finally put his arm around my shoulders. "Nora, it will be all right. Whoever it is."

I nodded, but tears slipped down my cheeks. How little he knew.

WE STOPPED FIRST at the general store. The stranger wasn't there, but he had left a note. I took it from the storekeeper and stepped away from everyone, ostensibly so I could see better by the oil lamp in the window.

Mother, I dearly hope it is you, as I've come so far. I'm staying at the Lac qui Parle Hotel, across the street. Come immediately, day or night. Your son, Ivar Helmer

Heat rushed up my body, as if I had caught fire. I stuffed the note up my sleeve and tried to compose my face.

I turned to Anders. "It's my cousin's son!" Then, before he could say anything, I darted ahead, running across the street and bursting through the door of the hotel.

And there was Ivar, sitting in the lobby calmly reading a newspaper. He looked up.

I would have known him anywhere—the broad cheekbones and

blue-gray, wide-set eyes, the tousled dark-blond hair. Me, him—mother, son. I could see Torvald's success in the quality of his sturdy tweed jacket and leather breeches, in the fine Norwegian boots on his feet. But I also could see how much he was still my child, despite everything.

He stepped toward me and pulled me into a desperate grip. I could feel him trembling with emotion.

I whispered in his ear. "Ivar, oh, Ivar, I am so happy to see you! But please, darling, let me do the talking, I beg you. Say nothing of your father until we're alone. Then I'll explain everything."

At that he pulled away; then he saw Anders, Birgitte, and Jens standing behind me.

Anders stepped forward to shake his hand. "Anders Eriksen, Nora's husband."

Ivar glanced at me, then nodded solemnly and took Anders's hand.

I jumped in, before Ivar could speak. "This is Ivar Helmer, my cousin's son," I said. "From Kristiania, now, I believe." I smiled at Ivar.

"Yes," he said, but that was all. He looked lost and suddenly very young.

I pulled the others forward. "And this is Birgitte and Jens, Mr. Eriksen's children."

They said hello, then stepped back again, shy before this well-dressed stranger. Birgitte kept looking at me.

I turned back to Ivar. "And how are your brother and sister, Bob and Emma? As you know, I haven't seen them in years."

"They're fine," he said cautiously, searching my face for clues. "Bob is in his last year of school, and Emma is twelve."

"And your mother?"

At that, his face clouded over in confusion, and pain. "She is, ah, well enough," he said slowly. "And Father. Thank you for asking after them."

"Good. Please tell them both that I miss them," I said, smoothly, though my heart still raced. "It was kind of them to send you all the way out here to visit me." I sat down on the nearest sofa so that I wouldn't collapse. I had no idea where this pretense was going.

Everyone sat down as well, all of us awkward with each other. My mind galloped in circles, trying to figure out what to do.

Anders, polite and unsuspecting, asked Ivar about his journey. Ivar said he had been traveling for only a few weeks, as the steamships were faster now, the railroads more direct than a decade ago, when the Eriksens and I made the passage.

I watched my boy, dazed to see him grown, dazed by the surge of long-ing and happiness and confusion to see him again after all this time.

Jens asked if he could milk a cow, which made us all laugh. Then Birgitte asked if he was immigrating or if he was just touring and planned to go back to Norway.

"I don't know," Ivar said. "I thought more about coming than what I would do when I got here. Everyone in Norway either wants to visit Amer-ica or wants to immigrate."

I stood up, before the conversation could get me in trouble. "You must be very tired after your journey, Ivar," I said, picking up my bag to signal it was time to leave. "It's lovely to see you. I'm glad you have a room here, as it is far more comfortable than our farm. Why don't you get a good night's rest, and I'll come to town tomorrow morning so we can visit."

He looked at me, dumbfounded. I leaned forward and gave him a chaste kiss on his cheek. "I'm sorry, darling," I whispered.

Anders clapped his hands and stood. "Well, young man, I guess we are off. Perhaps you could come out and see our farm tomorrow."

"I would like that," Ivar said cautiously, glancing at me again. "Good night, um, Aunt."

I turned to Anders and the children. "Go on ahead and get the wagon ready. I'll be out in a moment." They nodded, surprised that our visit was so short, but headed out at my urging.

I turned back to Ivar, who stood stone-faced in the middle of the lobby.

"What have you done?" he said, his voice strangled. He was no longer the boy he had been; he was a young man and capable of upsetting my world.

"Darling, in the morning, please, I'll explain everything."

His eyes burned into mine. "It's just not—it's not what I expected."

"I know, and I am sorry. Tomorrow, when it is just you and me. I promise."

"You are much altered. If I didn't know it was you . . ."

"I'm sure it must be a shock. The prairie ages us. It can't be helped."

"It's not that, Mother; it's him."

I could barely stomach the look on his face. "Please, don't judge me yet, not until I can explain." Tears rose in my eyes. "Please."

He stepped back. "Tomorrow morning, then. Aunt."

I turned out the door, heartbroken to leave him there alone but fighting to regain my composure. I didn't want Anders to see me like this.

I could see by the look on her face that Birgitte had a million questions, but I just gave her a quick hug and said good night.

Anders helped me into the wagon. "Are you all right, Nora?"

"Oh, yes; it just is so sad to think of my cousin and her family, whom I haven't seen for so long."

"He seems a nice fellow," Jens said. "Maybe he could stay with us for a while. I could teach him to milk."

Anders said nothing until we were clear of town and rattling slowly back to the farm, but I could sense that his mind was turning. Finally, he spoke: "Did this boy's mother, your cousin, live in Kristiania when we left?"

"Oh, no," I said, crafting a tale. "They were in Alesund. We both lived in Hamar when we were little, but she moved away when she married. She and her children are my only kin; there's no one else that I could call family." I looked away into the darkness of the prairie, searching for something familiar that would restore my equilibrium, but there was only the endless grass. "I wrote to her some time ago, letting her know where I was. It's such a surprise that Ivar should come to visit."

Anders cleared his throat. "I had no idea you were sending letters back to Norway. Why didn't you invite him out to our farm, Nora? That's what one should do for family."

"I, well, I haven't seen him since he was a small child, Anders. I honestly have no idea what kind of person he is. I thought it best for me to talk with him more, and then we'll see."

"He appears to be a fine young man, Nora, if a bit citified. But still, Jens and I could use help. If he wants to stay in America and is looking for a place to start out."

"That's very kind of you, Anders. I'll think about it."

THE NEXT MORNING I put on one of my better dresses and walked back to town. It felt like dreaming when my son came down the stairs from his room, but then I saw his troubled face. We hugged, but he said little. I sat with him in the dining room, where they served him porridge and eggs and coffee. The sun poured in; the muslin curtains stirred in the breeze.

"Mother," he said, finally putting down his spoon and looking up with an unhappy scowl, "I just don't know what to make of it. I'll be honest, it makes me angry."

"I'm so sorry, darling."

"I mean, how can you be living here in this godforsaken place, out in the middle of nowhere like this? And with them? It's so primitive!"

He didn't just mean the dusty town and the sod houses that still marked the landscape. He meant the farmers who took me in. It was almost as if Torvald had spoken.

I took a deep breath. "Ivar, don't judge Anders Eriksen. You may judge me but not him. He's an excellent, honest man; he and his children saved my life."

"If he's so honest, why did he marry someone who already had a husband?"

I hesitated for a long moment.

"Because he didn't know, Ivar."

He squinted, as if seeing me for the first time. "You didn't tell him?"

"I thought your father would have gotten permission to divorce me by then. I knew he wanted to! And, out here? It didn't seem to matter what was true in Kristiania."

Ivar took a few gulps of his coffee before he responded. Then he cocked his head to the side. "How do you swear at an altar if you don't know whether you're free to marry? Don't they have laws against that sort of thing, even here?" He looked down at his food; he pushed the plate away, then looked up at me again. "Doesn't marriage mean anything to you?"

I glanced nervously around the hotel dining room, wondering if there were people in the parlor who could hear this. "Please, Ivar, don't raise your voice."

He leaned forward, his face contorted with pain. "Please, Mother. Don't marry other people," he whispered hoarsely. "Honor your vows, for God's sake!"

I pulled back, stung. But it was the least I deserved.

He took two photographs from his coat pocket and slapped them down on the table. The first was Bob, quite grown up. He looked like both Torvald and my father—darker than Ivar or me, an intensity in his eyes and brow. And then the second was Emma. I gasped—she looked almost exactly like me as a girl. She was very prettily dressed, with a large white bow in her blond curls and an expression of self-satisfaction on her hauntingly familiar face. Me and yet not me.

Now Ivar looked into my eyes, and I could see his anger hardening. "I just don't understand, Mother. How could you have left us for them?"

"Ivar, it wasn't like that. I didn't know the Eriksens until later, much later."

His mouth worked. "So you left us for nothing? Just to be alone?" He looked away, blinking hard. "How could you not have loved us?" he finally croaked.

"Oh, Ivar," I said, my eyes filling with tears. "I always loved you and Bob and Emma, and I have missed you terribly. It's the tragedy of my life that I couldn't stay and be your mother!"

"But why couldn't you? Yes, I realize Father is difficult, but was he that bad? What could possibly have been so awful about your life with us?"

"It was complicated, Ivar."

"I've come all this way to understand it, because it is my tragedy, too. So, please, explain it to me."

"It will take time."

"Nothing else matters."

I nodded and stood up. "Then come with me. We'll head to the farm."

WE WALKED A LONG WAY before I could begin, each of us in our own wheel rut, the grass rustling in the breeze around us. When the track forked toward our house, I hesitated, then led him away, down the trail toward the lake. I knew by then that I couldn't take him home.

But I did want to explain. I started by telling him why I left his father, beginning with Torvald's illness and the cursed loan, including my forgery and Krogstad's subsequent blackmail. He kept silent, though I could tell he was offended by some of what he heard—he had inherited a portion of his father's moral rigidity. I told him how hard it was to make a living in Kristiania, my poverty, and how I ended up living in Vika with the students and working for the shipping agent. Then, because it was the fulcrum of the story, I told him about his father's threat to send me to the asylum and the night I was arrested.

At that, he stopped walking and reached out to take my hands. By now we were down near the edge of the lake. "I had no idea, Mother."

"There's more," I said, leading him to a fallen tree where we could sit.

He coughed. "This is difficult to hear, Mother. It's so far outside the life you could have had, with us, with Father."

"I know, Ivar, but it's my truth."

And so I continued, telling him of the Eriksens and my journey out of Norway. Finally, I told him about the prairie and the terrible winter Tomas died. Ivar grew quieter and quieter. I didn't burden him with the story of falling through the ice, though I did tell him of my flight to St. Paul and my work with despondent women.

I had never told my story this way and was surprised to find the fragments knitting into a coherent if painful whole. At the end, I tried to explain why I married Anders—my desperate loneliness, my hope that Torvald had divorced me, my abiding belief that love was truer than the law.

We sat in silence for a long while. I could sense him struggling with this tale, finding it hard from his limited experience to understand how difficult it was to be female and unprotected in a harsh world. But he had a tender heart, and I could also feel his sympathy. Along with it ran a strong current of sadness. Both of us had lost so much.

"When Father told us you died, I didn't believe it," Ivar said. "I was sure you were alive, and I looked for you around every corner. I decided Father just didn't know where you were because I heard him speaking with men in his study about trying to find you. And then I found the letter you sent Nurse."

"Anne-Marie! So she gave you my letter?"

"Well, her daughter did. Nurse died a few years ago, but her daughter got the letter and tried to pass it to me. But Father intercepted it, because I didn't see it until one day last fall when I was looking through his desk and found it. When I confronted him, he was furious, but I didn't care anymore. By then, I was angrier than he was."

Ivar told me next about growing up with his overbearing father—how Torvald refused to let Ivar take the matriculation exams for the university and refused to help him find a job in the bank or any other business.

"Instead, he made me work as his personal secretary so he could keep an eye on me," Ivar said bitterly. "He didn't want me leaving home because he knew I'd try to find you."

"Perhaps you can understand then how I felt," I said. "I thought I would die if I stayed with him."

Ivar nodded. "It must have been impossible, or you would have stayed with us, yes?"

"Yes, darling."

He coughed again, looking out over the lake. "There's something I should tell you, Mother. Father also married again."

I grabbed his arm. "When? Ivar, when did he marry?"

"A year after he said you died. I was thirteen, so in 1885, I think. The wedding was in July; then they went to Europe. Anne-Marie left when they returned."

That would have been two years after I married Anders. So Torvald must have gotten a divorce—but when? Could my marriage to Anders be legal after all?

"Did he get a divorce from the King?"

"No." Now Ivar looked down at his hands, which were twisted together. "I'm sorry, Mother, but he had you declared dead!"

"Dead?"

"No one could find you in Norway, and there was no record of your leaving the country. They assumed you had died or been killed somewhere."

My head swam. I was supposed to be dead?

"But I knew you weren't, and I knew that Father always knew you weren't. And then I found the letter you sent Anne-Marie."

"Who did he marry?"

"Johanna Moller. She's half his age, and she's spoiling Emma."

I recalled a young girl we met once at a party. "Are they happy together?"

Ivar winced. "I suppose, but Father has become quite stupid around her. I can barely stand it; it's part of why I left."

Then he kicked at the dirt with his toe. "There's something else, something important. After I found the letter, Father and I had quite a row. I insisted that, since you were alive, you deserved to know about your legacy."

"Legacy?"

"Your legacy from Dr. Rank. He left you his fortune, Mother, all those years ago. And it's quite a sum, according to the solicitor."

"What? How could that be? I was still in Norway when Dr. Rank died; why wasn't I told of it?"

"The solicitor must have notified Father; apparently, that's why the police went looking for you. But when Father had you declared dead, the legacy passed to me and Bob and Emma."

My head buzzed. "The money didn't go to your father?"

"No. Dr. Rank prohibited that in his will. It made Father quite angry. Even now the solicitor Mr. Paulsrud administers the money, which drives Father crazy."

I closed my eyes. Dr. Rank tried to take care of me. The very thought made me ache. How I wished Dr. Rank had told me himself, so I could have thanked him. And there were so many times we could have used that money—the winter after the fire, the year we needed the new plow. And there it was, all that time, waiting for me in Kristiania.

Then I remembered those last few days in Norway, my arrest, Torvald fetching me from the police station. Was he about to tell me of the legacy that night in the cab as we drove toward our flat? I will never know. Instead, I offered him my deal: I would disappear into America, and he could make of that what he wanted. I had no idea a legacy was at stake.

"Did Mr. Paulsrud give you the money for your passage?"

"Yes. He's hoping I find you, so the rest can go to you. He's with Nordlands Bank."

"But he doesn't know you've found me."

"No, Mother," he said with a wry smile. "I only found you yesterday."

"Does your father know you're here?"

"He knows I booked passage for America. In fact, he kicked me out after I told him I was coming to find you."

"Oh, Ivar. I'm sure he would take you back if that is what you wanted."

"He's a stubborn man, Mother. Surely you know that."

I nodded. "Did he read the letter I sent Anne-Marie?"

"Yes; he knows where you live, if that is what you're wondering." At that, Ivar pulled out an envelope. "The solicitor sent money for you to return to Norway. I changed it in New York." He handed it to me.

I looked inside—it was more than I had seen in a long time. The blood pounded in my ears. "I, I must talk with Anders," I stammered. "There's so much to explain."

"There's one other thing—Bobby needs to see you."

"Did you tell him I was alive?"

"Yes. He needed to know in case something happened to me. It shocked him to hear it, and infuriated Father, but now Bob's desperate to see you."

"Where does your father live now?"

Ivar named a street of elegant row houses in a wealthy part of Kristiania. I could see it all, as if I had moved there myself.

"I was half afraid Bobby would try to follow me," he continued. "Bob often acts before he thinks. If you came back to Norway and saw him, that might keep him from doing something rash. Besides, you must collect the rest of your money."

Norway? I looked around the dappled wood where we sat, the birds chattering, the lake glistening. I could not imagine going back to Norway. It was so far, and who could say what might happen? If I claimed the money, would I be declared alive again? Would I still be married to Torvald?

And, worst of all, could I be arrested for marrying Anders?

I looked at Ivar and began to weep, for I saw what I must do.

"Mother, what is it? I know all of this is distressing." He patted my shoulder hesitantly, not knowing how to comfort me.

My weeping overtook me. I buried my face in my hands. At long last, I tried to stop, gulping air and wiping my tears away. "Ivar, oh, Ivar. Don't you see? I have no choice."

"What do you mean? No choice about what?"

"About you."

He went pale.

"I wish I could take you back with me to the farm, but I see now that I cannot take you into my life here, darling. I cannot claim you as my son!"

"What are you talking about? I am your son!"

"But Anders doesn't know I have a son, or other children, or a husband who's alive. And he cannot know!"

"Why the hell not?" Ivar shouted, jumping to his feet. "We came first! We're your children!"

"Yes, darling, yes, but he is my life!" As soon as I said it, I understood how completely I had knitted myself around my quiet husband, my ally and my anchor. And I could see how much the news Ivar brought with him threatened that world.

I looked at my perfect boy. "I need my husband. If you came back to the farm, Anders would figure it out, and if he found out about your father, it would destroy my marriage."

"But with the money from the legacy, you wouldn't need a husband," Ivar said, looking at me in disbelief. "We could go live somewhere, maybe Chicago, maybe London or Ròme. After you claim the legacy, we could go anywhere. We could bring Bobby and Emma with us."

"I will not leave my husband, Ivar. He is everything to me."

"Even for us? You will choose a bigamist farmer over your own flesh and blood?"

"But you are an adult now, Ivar! You don't need me anymore. You will marry and have your own life, as will Bob and Emma. And then I would be alone again!"

And hated, I thought to myself. No one would love me by then, I was sure of it.

"Don't tell me what I need, Mother," he said bitterly. "You don't have that right."

"I apologize. But surely you must see how dangerous this is for me. If anyone found out I had a living husband in Norway, I would be driven from town, possibly tried and sent to prison. I would be cast out; I would have nothing!"

"But how would they find out?"

I looked at him—how naive they are, even when they think they are grown. "Your father will not let you go that easily, Ivar. If he thinks you have stayed here with me, he might alert the authorities. Indeed, I am sure he would."

"But he has also remarried."

"But he had the law on his side, Ivar. I did not."

Ivar's face grew pinched. "Can you live without me?"

I felt as if I was falling into a well of grief from which I would never emerge. I just looked at him, unable to speak.

After a long moment, he took that as my answer and stepped backward, repelled by me. "Is that it then? I came all this way for you to deny me?"

My heart cracked; I could only weep. My terrible choice was carrying him away from me so swiftly, it took my breath away.

He watched me, his face hardening. "Well, then," he said, brushing the dust from his pants. "I can choose as well, Mother. I don't want to have anything to do with a bigamist mother, so go back to your farm and your farmer."

"Please don't call me that, Ivar!"

"But it's true, isn't it? You knew you were probably still married to Father, but you went ahead and married this man anyway." By now, he was weeping as well. "As if morality and laws and the Church didn't matter!"

"Ivar, please!"

"Good-bye, Mother," he said, his voice strangled. Then he turned on his heel and headed back up the path toward town.

I sank to the ground, sobbing, as he walked out of my life. He disappeared into the woods without even a backward glance.

I DON'T KNOW how I managed to stumble home after Ivar left me. When I came through the door, the house was blessedly empty. Anders had left a note: he and Jens were hunting up on the tableland for prairie chicken and wouldn't be home until supper.

I heated water for tea, then washed my dusty, tear-streaked face. I put the packet of money Ivar had given me on the kitchen table, then took my mug and sat outside in the soft afternoon light. I thought of those early days when Birgitte and Jens and I held our little school in the shade of the sod house, baby Tomas on my lap. Did I have any idea back then how happy I was? What an astonishing choice I made to give up my own children and come to America with the Eriksens, yet it had saved my life. I was sure of it.

But at what cost?

And it wasn't just about Ivar. It was also about Bob and Emma, those children in the pictures. The children who had every right to know me.

I stood and went to the window. Outside, the chickens bickered; a yellow-headed blackbird perched on the well crank. My beautiful prairie world. How much I would miss it.

Because I had to return to Norway. I wanted both: my life with Anders and a life with my children. Before now I had never thought it possible, but maybe it could be. The key to all of it was Torvald.

"WHERE IS YOUR COUSIN?" Anders said when he came in hours later. "I thought for sure you would bring him home with you today. Did you see him in town?"

Then he spied the envelope of cash on the table and picked it up. "Good Lord," he said, feeling the weight of it. "What is this, Nora?"

"It's part of a legacy that was left for me a long time ago."

"And Ivar brought it to you?"

"Yes; that was the purpose for his visit. We had lunch and talked. I tried to get him to come out here for a longer stay, but he wanted to get back to Chicago. I think perhaps our life here was a bit too rough for him."

Anders listened to this with his head cocked to one side. "I'm sorry to hear that. He seemed like a nice young man." Then he narrowed his eyes. "Did you say part of a legacy?"

"Yes, Anders. Please sit down."

He took a seat, then picked up the envelope again and counted the bills. "That's a lot of money, Nora. Why did Ivar give it to you?"

"It's complicated. Apparently, there was a legacy left for me shortly after we immigrated to America. But as no one could find me in Norway, or any record of my leaving, they had me declared dead, and the legacy passed to my cousin."

"And Ivar's come all this way to share it with you?"

"His mother sent him. Once she knew where I was, she felt it only right."

Anders fetched a glass of water for himself, then sat back down. He suddenly had a wariness about him. "You said part of a legacy. Is there more?"

"Yes, quite a bit more, at Nordlands Bank, in Kristiania. But I would have to go back to claim it."

His eyes grew wide. "You're going back to Norway? Is that what this money is for?"

Then, before I could answer, he leaned forward with another question. "Did you know about this money? Did you ask your cousin to send her son?"

"No, Anders. I had no idea there was a legacy, or that Ivar would bring it to me."

"Was this part of your husband's estate?"

"What?" I struggled for a moment to remember how little Anders understood of what was true. "No. He left me nothing."

"Then who left you this money?"

I swallowed hard. "A gentleman in Kristiania."

He pulled back, his eyes narrowing. Then he got up and walked across the room and stood at the window, as if he couldn't bear to look at me.

"A gentleman, you say."

"A doctor."

Anders turned. "What was this man to you, Nora?"

"He was a friend, Anders. An elderly friend."

"Why do I feel, Nora, as if I have no idea who you are all of a sudden? Where are all these secrets coming from?"

"It's not what you think, I swear to you. His name was Dr. Rank. He was my husband's physician and our friend. He was much older than me. I was kind to him; that was all. By the time my husband was gone, Dr. Rank was very ill with tuberculosis. I worked as his companion toward the end, and he died a few months later."

"Did he love you?"

"Oh, Anders, it was so long ago! Does it matter?"

"Did he love you, Nora? I need to understand."

I sighed. "Yes, he probably did, but only from afar. I never allowed it to be more."

"Did he tell you he was leaving you money?"

"No, but he had no family."

He stood considering me for a long moment. "So you are going back."

I held his gaze. Then I saw something that hadn't been clear to me before: I had to be as honest with Anders as I could. If I was to keep Torvald a secret, everything else had to be true.

"Yes. This legacy could make a great difference in our life, Anders."

He stepped away again, and it felt like he was slipping from my grasp, just as Ivar had. It felt as if a flood was sweeping through my life, taking everyone who mattered to me.

"I need to know, Nora—are there others you want to see, back in Kristiania?"

"Yes, Anders, but please don't ask me about them." Tears rose in my eyes. "Please! It will not help us!"

He looked at me from across the room, across the abyss. His face grew sad. "If you return to Norway, you may never come back, Nora. I don't know who you still have in Norway, nor do I have any idea why you were so desperate when I met you down near the docks. But I know now that there is more you aren't telling me."

"There is," I said, trying to keep from weeping. "Which is why I need to go back. I need to settle these things and collect my money. And then I will return, and we can have our life again. Our happy life, Anders."

He shook his head. "You could collect your money and make your life there. I know you miss your cultivated world, and you probably have old friends to return to."

"Anders, my life is with you. I swear to you I will come back."

He ran his hands through his hair. "I wish I could believe you, Nora, but you leave me in the dark, so what am I to think?"

"Then come with me! There's money enough for us both!" I said this before thinking of the consequences, but I couldn't bear the way he was looking at me. As if he no longer trusted me.

"Back to Norway?" He shook his head. "I cannot return."

"Why not?"

"I wouldn't dare, because I'd be engulfed by regret, Nora! For the mountains, the fields, the hills. I would need to visit Inge's grave and go see my brother in Gudbrandsdalen. I might not be able to leave again."

"Do you feel that pull here, on our farm?"

"No, because I don't indulge it. But in my heart I'm still Norwegian. I'm split in half, Nora, and I'll never be one again. It's the immigrant's curse, I think."

"I didn't know you felt that way."

He looked at me. "You're adaptable, Nora, like water—you change to fit any vessel. I am built of rock. It's much harder to reshape me."

"Then if you won't go with me, you must trust me to return."

"It will depend on what's in your heart."

"You're in my heart, Anders. You, the children, this farm."

He considered me for a long moment. "I think you are unhappy here, Nora. Your cousin's son has kindled a longing in you; I can see it in your eyes."

"I am not unhappy here, Anders."

"But someone pulls you back," he said, watching my face. "Someone you love."

"I need to settle something, Anders."

"You can't settle it from here?"

"No." I put my head in my hands. "You have no idea what I've given up."

"Ah," he said. Then he relented and sat down next to me. "I'm sorry, Nora. This is just so bewildering. But you are free to do what you must. I will not stand in your way."

At that moment Jens came in from the barn, hungry and unsuspecting. I rose and gathered dinner together, then put it on the table. But I could barely eat.

After supper, I could not bear to sit with Anders and Jens as I usually did. Instead, I slipped into bed. But sleep would not come. When Anders later climbed in next to me, I curled up against his warm back. "I'm sorry, Anders. I'm sorry I cannot tell you everything yet."

But he didn't turn to me as he usually did. "I don't like having secrets between us, Nora."

"Anders, please. I will explain it all when I return. There are things I don't understand, which is why I need to go back."

"No doubt," he said. "But if you return, you must be ready to tell me everything, the complete truth. No more lies, Nora." Then he pulled away.

I turned toward the window, where the stars shone down like bits of ice. The complete truth. He knew not what he asked.

A FEW WEEKS LATER, I left for Norway.

Anders took me to the train on a clear summer morning, helping me aboard with a kiss, then waiting until the train chuffed out of the station.

And so I journeyed back across America in the dust and soot of the railcars to St. Paul, Chicago, Cleveland, and finally New York. I spent a night there and bought some better clothes, including a hat with a short veil. For my passage, I presented Inge Eriksen's papers, stamped when I immigrated as her back in 1881. On the ship I traveled second class and kept to myself. I didn't want to have to explain who I was. Sitting on deck looking out over the Atlantic, I remembered watching for icebergs with Jens, Tomas sleeping in my lap. How innocent that time seemed to me now.

The ship sailed first to Bremerhaven and then on to Norway. After several weeks of travel, I stood at the rail once again as we steamed up the Oslofjord in glittering sunlight.

I THOUGHT I KNEW KRISTIANIA, but when I stepped off the ship that afternoon I found the city quite altered. The streets and neighborhoods had been tidied up, and there were new stone buildings where rows of humble houses used to stand. Aside from the cityscape, there was also something different about the people, a new confidence and boldness— the influence from America, it seemed. More money and the fresh winds of progress. The exodus had become an exchange.

I pulled down my demi veil. It felt unnecessary, as no one who knew me would believe this prairie woman could be the former Nora Helmer. Still, I was supposed to be dead, so best to stay hidden.

I checked into a small hotel and settled into a room filled with gleaming furniture, velvet curtains, and brocade upholstery. I walked about the room examining these luxuries. I had nearly forgotten the feel of silk and down. But when I passed the window, bright with sunlight, the room instantly felt claustrophobic. I went back outside, heading down Karl Johans Gate and hoping I might spot Bobby and Emma. The young were everywhere; I searched their faces as I passed but with no luck.

The midsummer light lingered, and the coffeehouses stayed open. I found the bakery that sold those wonderful macaroons, but as I gazed at the display case nostalgia washed over me, and in my confusion I could only point. I sat at a table by the window and tried to let my feelings settle as I watched the people outside. So much was familiar—the language, the broad streets, the polite parade—yet it felt strange and uncomfortable as well. I thought of our spare world in Minnesota, where the beauty and drama lived in the sky and the sweeping land, and ached with homesickness. I finished my coffee and returned to the hotel, lonelier than I had been in years.

THE NEXT MORNING I met with Mr. Paulsrud, Dr. Rank's solicitor, a man I had met years ago at several dinner parties but never knew well. It was a risky step but necessary to learn the truth.

When I was ushered into his office, he gasped first, then reached out to shake my hand. "My God," he whispered. "It is you. I can see it, despite . . ." He stopped to regain his composure. "Forgive me, Mrs. Helmer. I hoped Ivar would find you, but, well, it's a big world."

"Yes," I said, sitting down. "I never thought one of my children would show up in Minnesota, but I couldn't be happier. Thank you for helping him get to America. He's traveling around for a bit before deciding what to do next."

"Of course. No doubt he told you about the legacy. I knew you'd come if Ivar found you, as it's quite a nice sum." He smiled. "I'd given up looking for you, especially as your husband was so little help. They had you declared dead."

"Yes, Ivar told me."

"No one knew you'd gone to America, including the authorities." He raised his eyebrows. "It was quite puzzling. And then Ivar showed up and solved the mystery."

"I had to flee Kristiania, as Mr. Helmer was threatening me. I went to America on another woman's ticket, on her papers. In fact, I'm traveling on her papers now."

"Now?"

"Because, Mr. Paulsrud, no one must know I am here."

"And why is that, Mrs. Helmer?"

"Because I am no longer Mrs. Helmer. I'm Mrs. Eriksen. I married in America. The papers I carry are those of Inge Eriksen, who died as her family started their emigration journey. They were from Gudbrandsdalen. She had just borne a son, and her husband hired me to care for the child and let me travel on her ticket. And then, some years later, I married him."

His mouth opened with surprise; I had rendered him speechless.

"And I need to know when Mr. Helmer had our marriage dissolved," I continued, "because when I married Mr. Eriksen, I didn't know the precise date."

He shook his head quickly for a moment, as if repulsed by something. "This is all quite astonishing, Mrs., ah, Eriksen. But let me see; I think I have a copy of the death decree in the file, but . . ." He pushed some papers around on his desk in agitation, then gave me a look of rebuke. "Why in

God's name did you marry someone else when you were married to Mr. Helmer?"

"I didn't think I was married to Mr. Helmer," I said evenly, though my stomach tightened into a knot. "He said he would get a divorce, and there was little Mr. Helmer put his mind to that he didn't achieve."

"But he never asked for a divorce, Mrs. Eriksen. As you are still alive, you're still married to Mr. Helmer!" Mr. Paulsrud jumped up and started pacing behind his desk. "Oh, this is complicated, very complicated." He opened a file drawer, peered at the labels, then pulled out an envelope. "Here, this is your death decree, null and void, as you sit here before me in perfect health."

My hands shook as I took it, scanning quickly. It was dated November 1885. Two years after I married Anders.

"Well, perhaps we can just let it lie, Mr. Paulsrud," I said, smiling as if none of this worried me. "I will just take my legacy and return to America. No one needs to be the wiser."

He coughed into his handkerchief. "Mrs. Eriksen, I don't think you understand. The truth is, to claim Dr. Rank's legacy, you must appear before a judge and provide evidence that you are who you profess to be. And then everyone will be the wiser." He gave me a pointed look. "Not just me."

"Is this an issue of the law or the Church?"

"The state would charge you with bigamy, Mrs. Eriksen." His face grew stern. "If the authorities here in Kristiania knew you were alive, they would no doubt arrest you."

Awful words again—*arrest* and *criminal*, now *bigamy*. Somehow, I was always outside the law.

"Well, I didn't come all the way from Minnesota to be arrested in Kristiania, Mr. Paulsrud. If my claim to this legacy jeopardizes my freedom, then I will let it pass to my children."

He sat staring at me for a long moment. "You would return to America, back to your bigamous marriage."

I lifted my chin, in a way I hadn't done for years. "Mr. Paulsrud, what I do in America is no business of yours. I will disappear and never set foot in this country again."

He blinked a few times, then pawed through his papers again. "Well, then, of course, but . . . there might be a fee for, well . . ." He gave me a sharp look. "For securing my confidence."

"Excuse me?"

"So that no one would ever know you appeared in my office in June of 1889."

My heart sank. Blackmailed once again. "Of course," I said. "How much would that be?"

"Well, Mrs. Eriksen, confidences are not cheap."

I sighed. "No, I'm sure they are not."

"Come back later in the week, and I'll have it worked out. And keep your head down. No one must recognize you." He smiled now. No doubt, this was the most interesting thing that had happened to him in months.

Then he pulled a small envelope from the file. "From your friend Rank," he said with a salacious glance, as if he understood all about me and Dr. Rank.

I slipped the letter into my bag, ghosts rising all around me.

ONCE OUTSIDE I lowered my veil and sought the comfort of the little coffeehouse. I ordered macaroons, then retreated to a table in the back and opened the letter.

> Dearest Nora: Although you would never let me say it again, you know
> I always loved you. Now that you're in such difficult circumstances, I
> hope this legacy will allow you to put sweets in your pocket and share
> your life with your children without having to beg from Torvald.
>
> In deepest gratitude, Dr. Rank

I closed my eyes, overcome. How different my life might have been if I had known he was leaving me this legacy! My children, my station, everything lost when I left for America. And it would have helped just to know he tried to take care of me. How much had I needed to know, back then, that I was loved.

I sat for a long time thinking of him and how I still missed his puckish humor and warm attention. No one had ever listened to me quite like Dr. Rank.

I walked to the cemetery and consulted the ledger in the guardhouse. When I found his grave, I knelt down, whispered my thanks, and tucked the last macaroon under the leaves against his stone.

AFTER MEETING with Mr. Paulsrud, I considered my alternatives. It would be safest to board the next ship back to America, but I couldn't bear to be this close to Bobby and Emma and not try to see them. I decided I would appear at Torvald's door on Sunday after church. He would be shocked and angry, no doubt, but I would make him understand that we must work together. His marriage was just as illegal as mine.

Sunday dawned cloudy and cool. I woke up jumpy as a squirrel, so I walked to the harbor to clear my head. I could see Vika in the distance, looking smaller, as if the authorities had winnowed it down. I wondered if Tobias was still in Kristiania but had no idea how to find him. Those days in the rooming house, so full of talk and company, now seemed like little more than a figment of my imagination.

I was drawn to the water, so I walked out a long pier and gazed down the fjord. Anders felt closer, as if he was just over the horizon. I stood there a long time, the wind whipping up the spray.

By the time I headed to Torvald's, the sun was peeking out. I found the house, and when a servant opened the door, I told him my name was Nora Solberg. His brow furrowed as he tried to place me and finally went to check.

I trembled, with both fear and excitement. The door opened again, and there was Torvald, so much the same it was as if his world had stood still while the rest of us had gone tumbling forward.

He uttered a cynical laugh. "Why, Nora, it is you. Not a new washerwoman after all. I suppose I shouldn't be surprised. Ivar found you, didn't he?"

"Yes, he showed up in our village in Minnesota."

Torvald stepped outside and closed the door behind him. Apparently, I was too dangerous to invite inside.

"Did Ivar come back with you?" he asked.

"No. He's traveling around America. He had no interest in staying at our farm with us."

"You live on a farm? That's quite, well . . ." His hands flailed as he tried to find words. "Remarkable, I must say; I can't believe you would be much help on a farm."

"Torvald, being married to you was the only time in my life I had little purpose. Since then I've lived through things you could scarcely imagine. And they have made me strong."

He smiled bitterly. "You boast, Nora."

"Hardly. You've no idea."

His smile faded, a hint of steel rising in his eye as he registered my seriousness. "What do you want, Nora?"

"To see Bob and Emma."

"That's impossible. They think you're dead."

"Bob doesn't. Ivar said he told him the truth before he left."

Torvald glared at me. "I don't want to quibble with you, Nora. You have no right to see them, and I won't allow it. It would upset them terribly. Bob may believe you are alive, but he certainly isn't expecting you to pop up at the dinner table."

I realized something: Torvald was afraid of me, afraid that I would disrupt his perfect world. I had power over him again, at long last.

"I thought you might try to block me, Torvald, so consider this. If you won't let me see the children, I'll authorize Mr. Paulsrud to tell the court I'm alive. Once I'm safely out of Norway, that is. You could be arrested for bigamy, as you've known all along I was in America."

His face hardened, but his hands started to twitch, as if he had a palsy. "You would destroy my life? Haven't you done enough damage already?"

"I don't mean to destroy your life, Torvald, but I must see the children. They're older; let them decide."

"My wife is pregnant, Nora. It would be a great shock to her; it could endanger the child."

"Then let me tell you this, as a peace offering, so you'll know I'm not trying to ruin your life. I've remarried as well and have two stepchildren."

His brow crinkled. "When?"

"After you had me declared dead," I said, twisting the truth a bit. "I went to see Mr. Paulsrud."

"So you claimed your adulterous legacy?"

"Torvald, don't dishonor Dr. Rank that way, or me. There was never anything between us, and you know that."

"Well, Nora, all I can tell you is that his will—when it was read in court—was deeply humiliating to me. You have no idea what Kristiania thinks of you."

"Kristiania must continue to think I'm dead, Torvald. I trust you can keep your wife and the children quiet, as the truth jeopardizes all of us. Mr. Paulsrud has agreed to keep my visit confidential, for a fee, and I will give up the legacy. It will pass straight to the children."

His eyes narrowed. "It could be quite difficult for you if the townspeople in Minnesota—or the Lutheran Church—discovered you were married to two people."

"We share that shame, Torvald, you and I. Don't forget that."

He glared at me for a long moment, and then something inside him seemed to give.

"Let me see them, Torvald, just for a few minutes. That's all I ask. I beg you."

He looked away, his jaw working. "I don't like it, Nora. But I suppose Emma should know that you are alive. It might do her good to meet you, to see what you are." He scowled. "But I need time to talk with the children, and my wife. Tomorrow would be better."

I suddenly had a vision of the police waiting for me if I let him delay. "No, Torvald. Today. Now."

He grumbled but yielded, escorting me into the parlor, then disappearing out the door. I looked around. The house was much larger than the apartment we had shared all that time ago, and the room was handsomely furnished—Torvald had done well. There was my old piano against the far wall, with the paintings of Italy above it. The drapes were a dusky blue silk, the armchairs luxurious, tasseled. A woman's touch.

The door creaked. I turned, and there was Bobby, my sweet boy.

He stopped. "Is it really you?" he said, his voice thick with feeling. He had grown up dark like his father, all curly hair and hungry eyes.

"Yes, darling."

He stared at me. "Tell me something only you and I know."

"Ivar threw a stone at me once."

He went pale. "Yes," he whispered. "That was the last time I saw you."

I held out my arms. He hesitated, then finally stepped into my embrace, leaning against me like a falling tree. "Mother!" he said, and it sounded like a sob.

"I'm so very glad to see you again, Bobby. So glad."

We stood that way for a long minute, forgetting all else.

When I looked up, Emma was standing in the doorway, her chin tucked as she eyed me suspiciously.

I didn't approach her, but I smiled. "Hello, Emma. How you've grown! But you still look as I remember you."

She said nothing and walked stiffly to the sofa, where she perched on the edge. Torvald sat down beside her like a protective hawk. She was dressed in layers of white cotton trimmed with lace, her blond curls tied back with lilac ribbons. An image of Birgitte at this age flashed in my mind—competent, knowing, clad in her homespun skirt, the baby on her hip. I wasn't sure what to make of this girl-child before me, so alien and yet once so dear.

"Emma, don't be rude," Bob said. "Say hello to your mother." He brought me a chair and plunked down on the floor by my knee. I couldn't help but smile at him. My boy, restored to me. It was overwhelming.

"Hello," Emma finally said, though there was little welcome in her face. She clasped her hands in her lap, her knuckles white.

"My wife will not be coming down, Nora; I'm sure you understand," Torvald said. He meant that I was too sullied to be introduced to her, but I didn't care because I was with my precious children, even if one of them was scowling at me.

To break the ice, I pulled out a package wrapped in tissue. "This is for you, Emma. I was embroidering it when I had to leave home. I always hoped to give it to you someday."

"A present for me?" She relaxed a bit and reached for it.

"Yes, in a way."

She unwrapped the package—it was the small flowered cap I had carried with me for years. She examined it, then gave me a quizzical look. "It's so small. Is it for a doll?"

"It was for you, originally. I thought you might want it. To keep for when you have a child of your own. I've kept it close to me all these years to remember you."

She turned it over in her hand. "How old was I when you left?"

"Just two. A toddler, but you were already talking a torrent."

She looked at the cap again and shivered slightly, like an animal that smells the hunter. Then she flung it to the floor. "I don't want it!"

"Now, Emma," said Torvald. He picked up the cap and turned to me with a triumphant gleam in his eye.

"I don't mean to be rude, Papa. But I don't understand!" She glared at me. "How could you leave a baby? How could a mother do such a thing?"

I looked at her with sympathy, but I wasn't sure what to say. "It was complicated, Emma, but it never meant I didn't love you."

"It might've been one thing if you had died—that made sense to me. But this, this coming back from the dead! As if you have any right to be alive!" She jumped up and turned to Torvald. "May I be excused? Please, Papa."

Torvald squeezed her hand. "Of course, my pet." She bowed briefly in my direction, the slightest nod of the head, just enough to register her manners. Then she ran from the room.

"Well, Nora, I told you it wouldn't be easy," Torvald said.

"Don't be offended, Mother," said Bob. "She doesn't like surprises."

"I'm not offended. I knew this first meeting would be hard."

"This will be the only meeting, Nora," said Torvald, standing up. "It's been quite a shock for her, learning you're alive. I think you've tortured her enough."

"I should have waited until she was old enough to understand."

"It would've made little difference, Nora. She's never known you and apparently has no inclination to correct that. I'm surprised you expected more." He stepped to the door. "I should see to Emma. Bob, we have an appointment at half past."

"Yes, Father," Bob said.

The door closed. I looked at him, my darling boy, so tall and strong.

"Did Ivar find you, Mother? Is he living with you now?"

"Yes, he did find me. In the town where I live, out on the prairie. It's a beautiful farm, with horses and pigs and cows and chickens."

"A farm? We visited one once, one summer. Up in the mountains. It was very, well, very poor. Do you milk the cows?"

"I do milk the cows sometimes. I live there with a nice farmer and his two children who are a little older than you."

His brow furrowed. "Are you a servant to them?"

I laughed. "No. We all share the work. We are servants to each other."

He shook his head, as if he couldn't understand such a world, but then he smiled. "I'd like to see it, Mother. I'd like to come visit and see Ivar."

"Well, Ivar must not have liked it much because he didn't stay. I think he's gone to Chicago, which is a big city on a lake so large it looks like the ocean."

"Still, I'd like to come to America and see you again."

I didn't know quite what to tell him. "I'm not sure your father would allow it."

"He didn't allow Ivar, but Ivar found a way to go."

"Maybe you should go to university here in Norway first, Bob, then come to America later, when you are on your own."

He nodded, then looked at me wistfully. "But will I ever see you again, Mother? It's a bit rough on a boy to see his mother for a few minutes, then never again." He looked down and scuffed at the rug with the toe of his boot. "Since Ivar told me you were alive, I've been hoping you would come back to Norway and live here, where you belong. This is your home, Mother, isn't it?"

I sat back. "Oh, Bobby, I wish I could stay here in Norway, but I cannot. It makes me very sad because I'd like to be near you and Emma, but this isn't my home anymore. I have responsibilities back in Minnesota."

"Can't they hire someone to milk the cows?"

"Darling, it's much more complicated than that. But this doesn't mean we won't see each other again," I reassured him. "Either you will come to America, or I will come back to Norway again, when you are older. I promise."

"How will I find you in America?"

"Ivar will know where I am. He will tell you."

He nodded again, then frowned. "I'm sorry about Emma, Mother. She has no memories to help her. Besides, she's very fond of Papa."

"Maybe it's better she has no interest in me. It's my fault, not hers."

"I was angry with you, too, because you didn't look sick when we saw you in the park, so I didn't understand why you couldn't come home. But then Papa said you died, and I cried for a week because I hadn't believed you." His face darkened. "How could you leave us, Mama? I just don't understand!"

"I can't explain it right now because it's a long and grown-up story. But when I see you again, I'll explain everything, and I hope someday you can forgive me. It never meant I didn't love you or want to be with you. Please know that!"

Tears rose in his eyes. "I forgive you, Mama. Even if I don't understand."

I kissed his cheeks and rumpled his hair. He wrapped his arms around me, and I pressed my head against his.

The door creaked again. "It's time for you to go, Nora," said Torvald. "Your visit has upset Emma considerably."

I gave Bob one last hug, then took Emma's cap and put it back in my bag. It had meaning only for me.

Torvald handed me my wrap and guided me out the door. On the step, I turned. "I told Bobby I would return to Norway, which I will do when they are a little older. I hope Emma will consent to see me again someday."

"I cannot stop the boys from chasing after you, but I can stop Emma. She's an obedient girl. She has a sweetness she didn't get from you."

"Well, there must be some shred of rebel in her, Torvald, as she is my child."

Now he gazed at me for a long moment. "I would never have recognized you, Nora; you're so brown and weathered."

I laughed. "Everyone on the prairie is brown and weathered, and it doesn't matter. My husband loves me deeply, and we work well together. We have a true marriage of equals."

"You mean a marriage of inferiors. You married a farmer from the hills of Norway, and there you've found your level. Your father must be turning in his grave."

I looked at him. How stunted he was, how tight and small-minded. I would have to wait to bring my children back into my life, but now I had hope, a tiny flame I could nurture and grow. They had seen me; they knew I lived.

I RETURNED to the solicitor's office to ensure that the legacy went to the children uncontested as soon as each reached their majority, shaving off a considerable chunk to secure Mr. Paulsrud's confidence. I also left my address in his folder, so that the children could find me in the future if they cared to do so. Then I bought myself a return ticket for America.

The next day I took a hansom cab to the wharf. As we bumped across Kristiania, I wondered how this familiar terrain could now feel so foreign to me—the broad esplanade, the Akershus Fortress, the green hills, and beautiful fjord. But it didn't sadden me. The American West was big enough to accept an outcast like me, and I was grateful.

I didn't need Norway anymore.

CHAPTER TWENTY

SOLVI

May 1919 ■ *Kristiania, Norway*

The morning after the scuffle with Dominik's brother, Solvi woke up to a sharp knock on her bedroom door.

"Miss Lange!" It was Matron.

Solvi climbed wearily out of bed, her body aching and her head heavy. She cracked the door.

Matron thrust a telegram at her. "This came early. I hope no one has died," she said, as if that might be Solvi's fault.

"Thank you, Matron." Solvi said, her heart beginning to race. She shut the door and ripped the telegram open.

Saw newspaper yesterday; very alarmed. You must be desperate for money. Am giving you a legacy. Go to Nordlands Bank and see solicitor Munk. Please quit photo shop, newspaper, and friends who led you astray. Mother

Solvi sank back into bed, clutching the telegram. A legacy? Who could have left a legacy, and why would her mother have hidden such a thing from her? For a moment Solvi wondered if it was even true, then shook the thought out of her head. If not, why would her mother send her to Nordlands Bank?

She rose and began to dress. She would go to the bank but only because she was tired of mysteries, tired of not understanding her maddening family. And if there were no answers there, then perhaps she would give up trying to find out what happened. She would put a black border around the photo of her grandfather's family and tuck it away for good.

AT THE BANK, Solvi asked for Mr. Munk. A few minutes later, a rotund little man bustled toward her across the lobby.

"Miss Lange, it's a pleasure," said Mr. Munk, ushering her into his office. "I was quite surprised to get the telegram from your mother about the trust this morning. I had hoped to meet her, but she has signed everything over to you, so I suppose she won't be coming in."

"She lives in Bergen," Solvi said, taking a seat, more mystified than ever.

"Yes, well, that's not a problem; I have the documents I need," Mr. Munk said. "So, Miss Lange, do you know anything about this trust?"

"No, Mr. Munk. This is all a surprise. I didn't even know there was a trust."

"Well, it's an old trust, which I took over from the original trustee, Mr. Paulsrud, several years after your uncles were given their shares when they came of age in 1889 and 1891. I've waited thirty years for your mother to claim her portion."

Solvi leaned forward. "My uncles were given shares in 1889 and 1891? They were alive then?"

"Yes, apparently, but that was many years ago, Miss Lange, before you were born." He coughed. "Perhaps I should start at the beginning."

"Please. Who is the legacy from?"

"A Dr. Theodor Rank, a friend of your grandparents, left this legacy for your grandmother Nora Helmer when he died in November of 1880. The legacy was written so that, if not claimed by your grandmother, it would pass equally to Ivar and Robert, your uncles, and Emma, your mother."

Solvi watched him intently. All of this confirmed what she had discovered.

"This was unusual," he said, glancing at her. "At that time, bequests to women normally became part of the husband's estate and bequests to children were managed by their father. This legacy purposefully blocked that."

"Why would Dr. Rank have written the legacy that way?"

"Miss Lange, I do not speculate about such things. Clearly, Dr. Rank meant to keep the legacy out of the hands of your grandfather Torvald Helmer." Solvi's chest tightened. She thought of the police report; something bad must have happened.

Mr. Munk picked up another document. "Apparently, your grandmother Mrs. Helmer refused the legacy when she visited the bank in 1889. That is why it passed down to her children and, because your mother has refused her share, on to you."

Solvi nearly came out of her chair. "My grandmother was here in 1889, here at this bank?"

"According to this record, yes." Now Mr. Munk picked up another document. "But this is the complicated part. Look at this, Miss Lange." He pushed a death certificate before her. *Nora Helmer, born in Hamar, Norway, 1850, declared dead by court order, November 1885.*

"Yes, I found that in the parish records," Solvi said. "But if your records show she was here in 1889, that would mean the death decree had it wrong. That she was still alive!"

Mr. Munk shuffled the papers about and extracted a handwritten note. "Yes, and this is what explains it," he said. "It's a memo from Mr. Paulsrud, dated June 23, 1889."

He started reading out loud. "To Whom It May Concern: Nora Helmer appeared in my office, alive and well on this day. She has been living in Lac qui Parle, Minnesota, since leaving Norway in 1881 and is married to a Norwegian farmer named Anders Eriksen. She says she married Mr. Eriksen in America after she was declared dead by the courts in Kristiania in 1885."

Mr. Munk couldn't help looking up at Solvi for an instant, his face clouded with rebuke; then he continued reading.

"Mrs. Helmer/Eriksen reported to me that when she left Norway in 1881, she traveled on the papers and ticket issued to Mr. Eriksen's first wife, Inge Eriksen, from Gudbrandsdalen, who had recently died. Mrs. Helmer/Eriksen said she had traveled back to Norway in this year, 1889, still using Inge Eriksen's documents.

"These facts presented a problem, in that Mrs. Helmer was never divorced from Mr. Helmer. If the state knew she was alive, she would still be considered married to him. We discussed the implications of this, and she agreed to let the legacy pass directly to her children rather than claim it in court, which would have alerted the authorities. For my assistance and confidence, she agreed to a consultation fee of 300 crowns. My understanding is she returned to America as soon as possible on Inge Eriksen's papers."

Solvi stared at him. "Does this mean she was married to two people at the same time?"

Mr. Munk took off his spectacles and rubbed his eyes. "Apparently, Miss Lange."

Solvi sat back, suddenly unable to breathe. A grandmother with two husbands? Hysteria, prostitution, that whiff of revolution, and now—bigamy? Her head swam. Yet a hope kindled inside her; perhaps this strange, confounding grandmother was alive, alive and living in Minnesota!

Mr. Munk pulled out other documents. "And here's a notice that your grandfather Torvald Helmer changed his family name to Fallesen, by court order in 1891, and moved to Bergen." He shook his head. "Little wonder." Then he glanced at Solvi with an odd smirk on his lips. "Quite the story, isn't it, miss?"

"Excuse me?" Solvi said, heat rising in her face.

He coughed again. "Beg your pardon." He pushed things around on his desk. "Now if you'll just sign these papers, Miss Lange, we can transfer the remainder of the legacy into an account for you here at the bank."

Solvi signed where he indicated, then noticed the amount. "This can't be right," she said. "This is much too much."

But Mr. Munk just muttered something about investments in sawmills and the need for lumber during the war. "You are a wealthy young lady, Miss Lange," he said. "I would be happy to discuss investment opportunities with you if you would like."

Solvi blinked at him. "Could I come back later to talk about investments? I need to think about all this."

"Of course. Understandable." With that, he slapped the folder shut. "That completes the disbursement of Dr. Rank's legacy. Thank you for coming in."

Solvi stood up but instantly felt faint and had to grab the chair back. What a relief it was that her mother had not been present for this, the reading of legal documents detailing her grandmother's scandalous behavior.

Then Solvi understood. Her mother already knew, knew all of it, and had probably known for a long time. That was why she hadn't come. It would have shattered her to hear it discussed by the likes of Mr. Munk.

For the first time in months, Solvi felt a surge of sympathy for her.

"Are you all right, Miss Lange?" Mr. Munk asked.

She pulled herself together and lifted her chin. "Of course. I am fine."

SOLVI FOUND RIKKA in the library.

"Where have you been?" Rikka whispered. "Matron said you got a telegram before breakfast."

"I've been at Nordlands Bank," Solvi said, dragging Rikka upstairs so they could talk in private. As soon as they closed the door of her room,

Solvi pulled out the telegram and handed it to Rikka. "It was about a legacy originally left for my grandmother, but now it's mine."

Rikka scanned the telegram. "This was Nora's legacy? The woman they thought was hysterical, that consorted with radicals, that got her head shaved?"

Solvi started to smile. "Yes, and she may be alive."

Rikka shook her head. "But if she's alive, why do you get the legacy? Isn't it hers?"

"It's complicated. And, honestly, Rikka, it's a sordid tale."

"Well, let's look at the facts. Where is she living? Do you know that?"

"Well, she immigrated to America, to a place called Lac qui Parle in Minnesota."

Rikka stared at her. "Minnesota?"

"Yes. And she married a Norwegian farmer after she got over there. In fact, it appears she made the passage with this farmer."

"But she was a lady."

Solvi nodded. "Yes, but that's the least of it."

Rikka sat down. "The least of it?"

"Yes. So my grandmother Nora must have left her family, the ones in the photograph, when my mother was very young, probably soon after the picture was taken. And it sounds like Nora may have gone to live with another man, a gentleman. The money in the legacy is from him, a Dr. Rank. He left his money for Nora when he died. He would have been quite a bit older than her."

Rikka's eyebrows rose, but she said nothing.

"Later, Nora immigrated to Minnesota and eventually married the farmer. The only problem was that when she married him, she was still married to my grandfather back here."

Rikka's mouth dropped open. "You mean she's a, a bigamist? Oh, Solvi!"

"Yes, it's all quite scandalous," Solvi sighed. "But it makes so much sense now, the way my grandfather condemned people for moral lapses, the way my mother didn't seem to care whether her mother was still alive. It explains the big void and the name change, everything." Solvi suddenly wished she had known and understood all this while her grandfather was alive, while they were all still together. She would have tried to be a better granddaughter.

"How much is the legacy, Solvi?"

"Enough; no, more than enough. Plenty," Solvi said. "It's all such a shock."

She sank onto her bed, holding her head in her hands. "So much has happened in the last few weeks, everything's jumbled in my brain. Writing about the Forgotten One, taking the pictures of the prostitutes, now my grandmother's scandal . . ." Suddenly Solvi went still, very still. Something was rattling around in her head, something trying to come together.

She looked at Rikka. "Oh, my. Could it be?"

"What?"

"Rikka, could my grandmother be the Forgotten One? She left her husband and children in about 1880; then she vanished!"

Rikka's eyes grew wide. "Is that possible? Look at your notes. What do you know about the Forgotten One?"

Solvi pawed through her bag and pulled out her notebook. "Let's see . . . At the talk we heard that she was the wife of a gentleman, had seven children . . . But my grandmother had only three."

"Well, three gets exaggerated in the public imagination into seven. Makes her seem more of a witch, leaving behind seven inconsolable children," Rikka said. "Ignore that. What else do you know?"

"That she left her family in about 1880 and tried to find work. Then from the newspaper articles, I know that the feminist Aasta Hansteen took up her cause at a public lecture, which turned into a riot. Then from Professor Wolff I learned that she would have lost her place in society, become classless, would have had a grim time trying to find work, that she probably left Kristiania to escape her scandal. Then, from the daughter of her nurse, I learned that she was born in Hamar, that her nurse was named Anne-Marie . . ." And then Solvi stopped.

Anne-Marie. Her mother had said, *I was raised by my nurse, Anne-Marie . . .*

Solvi jumped up. "I know how to solve it. I'll be back!"

PROFESSOR WOLFF was just locking his office door when Solvi ran up, out of breath. "Oh, I'm so glad I caught you," she said. "Do you have a minute?"

"Miss Lange! What is it?"

"I have to talk to you—show you something." She opened her purse, pulled out the photograph of her grandmother's family, and handed it to him.

He glanced at it, then looked at Solvi with a tender smile.

"Yes," he said.

"Yes?"

"Yes, that's her, your Forgotten One."

"But that's my grandmother!"

"I know," said Professor Wolff.

"How could you possibly know?"

"I knew the first day you came by my office. That's why I told you her story."

Solvi's head swam. "I'm sorry. It's been a difficult day. Which story?"

He unlocked his office door. "Here. Come in," he said, pulling off his coat and offering Solvi a chair.

She sat down. "Do you mean the story of your friend who taught you to sew?"

"Yes. Remember I told you how much you reminded me of her, the well-educated and mannered lady? I knew then that you were probably her granddaughter, as you looked so much like her. The part about being from Bergen threw me at first, but the longer you talked, the more I could see it: the tilt of your head, your eyes, your gestures. And then, just as you left, you said your family had been from Kristiania before you were born."

Solvi listened, then shook her head again. "But when did you realize she was the Forgotten One?"

"Oh, well, I've always known that. She and I went together to the talk by Aasta Hansteen that turned into a riot. I helped her escape."

Solvi stared at him. "I'm confused. Miss Olsen, the daughter of the woman who was nurse to her children, she said the Forgotten One was a Mrs. Solberg. My grandmother was Nora Helmer."

"Solberg was her maiden name; she used it after she left your grandfather."

Solvi shook her head. "But you made it sound like she wasn't real. Why on earth didn't you tell me? Why haven't you told other people?"

He put his fingertips together. "I wanted you to find out on your own, because that's how you'll become a better historian, Miss Lange. As for why I haven't told anyone else? That's because she swore me to secrecy."

"When?"

"The day before the police raided our rooming house, back in 1881." He looked at Solvi for a long moment. "I'm only telling you now, Miss Lange, because I know how much she would want you to find her."

Something welled up in Solvi, a great surge of longing, something that could sweep her away. "But my grandmother has had such a, well, such a compromised life, it's hard to . . ."

"Yes, I'm sure it's been challenging for her. She was trying desperately to get out of Norway when I last saw her because her husband threatened to commit her to an insane asylum."

Solvi sucked in a breath. "My grandfather was not a bad man, Professor Wolff. Stubborn, yes, and very old-fashioned, but he must have loved her. Why would he threaten to commit her?"

"Because she refused to return home to her marriage, and she kept trying to see her children. She would wait for them in the park and on the street. One of them threw a stone at her once. It was an untenable situation."

In a flash Solvi could see her grandfather, bearish, desperate, trying to hold on to his wife, trying to protect his children. "Do you think she was insane?"

He shook his head. "Heavens, no. She was one of the sanest people I knew. I suspect your grandfather thought the threat of the asylum would force her home."

"I found in the police records that she was picked up in a raid on the rooming house. Were you there that night? Were you one of the anarchists?"

He cocked his head. "You went through the police records from back then?"

"Well, I paid a policeman to do it."

"Impressive, Miss Lange. I was there, though I wouldn't say I was an anarchist. The police clubbed me on the head, so I don't remember much. That was the last time I saw her."

"The police report said she refused to inform on the students from the rooming house. They shaved her head, then released her to my grandfather."

"They shaved her head?" he said, his voice hoarse. "Those thugs!" He turned away, lost for a moment. "She had the most beautiful golden hair."

"Maybe you can help me understand something. I don't know what happened to her that night," Solvi said. "The police record said she was released into the protection of her husband, but instead of going home with him she seems to have disappeared."

"I doubt she went home with him, as she might never have gotten free again. No, I suspect she made a deal with your grandfather. She planned to leave on a boat the next morning for America."

"With the farmer," Solvi said.

"Yes. How do you know that?"

She told him briefly of the legacy, the memo from Mr. Paulsrud, the death decree, and the complications of her grandmother's remarriage. Solvi didn't use the word *bigamy*, but she didn't have to.

He listened with astonishment, then chuckled. "I tried to dissuade her from going with this farmer, as they were headed to a primitive homestead out on the prairie. I thought it extremely risky, but apparently it worked out fine." He shook his head.

"Except for her children; I would think it impossible to leave one's children," Solvi said, her voice cracking. "Do you know if she loved them?"

He gave her another tender look. "Oh, yes, Miss Lange. It was her greatest sorrow, that she had to leave them to save herself. In the beginning she hoped her husband would let her keep the children in the summers or see them on Sundays, but he forbade all of that. He thought it better for them to think she had died. And he had the law on his side, after all. She finally realized she had to bow out of their lives and allow them to grow up in peace, and the best way to do that was to go to America."

He shook his head again. "When the rest of us were released the week after the raid, your grandmother was gone. The landlady said she had returned, retrieved her bag, and walked off in a homespun skirt with a shawl over her head. I've always thought of her that way, walking into the unknown dressed as a farmwife. It was so different from her usual elegance, a measure of how much she had given up."

He gazed at the photograph again. "She was such a beauty, and those children. Look how they settle into her, as if they lived in her lap. How hard it must have been for all of them."

Solvi closed her eyes. Grief filled her chest, pushing the air from her lungs. She looked at the professor. "Is it possible to miss someone you never knew?"

"Ah," he said, with a wise smile. "Grief gets handed down, Miss Lange. I suspect a world of it got handed to you, as much as they may have tried to protect you."

Solvi looked away for a moment. A resolution was forming in her mind. "I need to go to America to find her."

"How would you do that, Miss Lange?"

"Magnus Clemmensen helped me put an advertisement in a Norwegian newspaper published in Chicago, the *Skandinaven*. We used this photograph and asked for information about the people pictured. Apparently, the paper is read by Norwegians all over America. I'm desperately hoping she sees it and responds."

"Also impressive, Miss Lange."

"And if that doesn't work, I'll just go to the town in Minnesota where she settled with the farmer. They are probably still there."

"You should try to find her, and soon," he said. "She's old now, in her seventies. She won't live forever."

Solvi nodded, thinking. "Have you read my essay, Professor Wolff?"

"Yes. Nicely done. I gave it a strong mark."

"I might submit it to *Dagbladet*. I could solve the mystery of the Forgotten One."

He looked at her for a long moment. "Or perhaps your grandmother should write her own story, Miss Lange—all of it. Why she left, where she went, how she survived."

Solvi's eyes went wide. "Yes, but . . ." She hesitated. "She's so, well, compromised, isn't she? There's so much about her history . . ."

Professor Wolff leaned forward. "Don't you see, Miss Lange? She was a true rebel! It didn't matter to her what the law or the Church said. She told me once she did everything for love, for reasons women would understand. I suspect that's how she ended up on the prairie married to a farmer when she was still married to your grandfather."

"So she wasn't a prostitute or an anarchist or some kind of lunatic?"

"No. Those were things other people said about her because they didn't understand." He looked away, wistful. "I'm glad she found someone worthy of her love. I always thought I might go to America and try to find her, but I couldn't leave my obligations here."

Solvi stood. "Thank you, Professor. I can't tell you what this means to me."

He handed her his card. "Please, if you see her, ask her to write to me. I've missed her these many years."

WHEN SOLVI RETURNED to the study house, Rikka and Magnus were huddled in the front hall.

Magnus took Solvi's hand. "Are you all right? Rikka's been telling me a crazy story about a legacy, your mother, your grandmother . . ."

Solvi just looked from one to the other. "There's so much to tell you."

"Where did you go?" asked Rikka.

"To see Professor Wolff. You will never believe it, Magnus, but my grandmother is the Forgotten One! Professor Wolff suspected it all since the first day he met me!"

"What?" said Magnus. "Slow down—start at the beginning."

"Professor Wolff knew Nora Helmer, my grandmother, and he knew she was the Forgotten One. They were friends back in Vika many years ago. He suspected I was her granddaughter because apparently I look very much like her. Remember the riot that broke out when Aasta Hansteen talked about the Forgotten One? Professor Wolff was with Nora at that talk. He helped her escape!"

Magnus let out a low whistle.

Matron, working behind the desk, looked up. "Dinner is being served, girls. Best say good-bye and go in."

Magnus grabbed his coat. "Come on, you two. I know an omelet house not far away. I'll have you back by curfew, I promise."

A FEW MINUTES LATER they were seated at a wooden table before an old hearth, low beams overhead, oil lamps glimmering from the walls. Magnus ordered cider and mushroom omelets.

Solvi started with her mother's telegram and the legacy, then told them how her grandmother immigrated to America and married a farmer, including its shameful interpretation. Then, finally, Professor Wolff's account of the Forgotten One. Solvi hesitated only when she got to the part about her grandmother's bigamous marriage, watching Magnus to see if he would be repelled. But he listened to all of it with a gentle smile.

When she was done, Magnus nudged her plate. "Eat up, Solvi. You've hardly touched your omelet."

She took a large bite. Had she had lunch? She was ravenous.

Rikka, who had been unusually quiet, spoke up. "Magnus, I think you're hiding something. You look like the cat who ate the canary."

"I was just going to let Solvi eat before I tell her."

"Tell me what?" Solvi asked, her mouth full of egg.

He reached into his jacket pocket and pulled out a letter. "We got a reply to the advertisement."

Solvi dropped her napkin and snatched the letter. It was from a Nora Eriksen in Spokane, Washington. She looked up at Rikka and Magnus, her lower lip quivering.

Silently, reverently, she opened it up and began reading out loud.

Dear Child of Mine,

I am not sure which one of you posted the advertisement in the "Skandinaven," but please know I am so grateful. For years I have longed to find my way back to all of you, and it appears now that might be possible.

Please write to me at post office box 216 in Spokane, Washington. I await your response with happy anticipation.

All my love, your mother

Solvi reread it, then clutched it to her chest. It was everything she wanted, the long-lost grandmother reaching for her with open arms. And even though her grandmother didn't know yet that she existed, Solvi felt remade. All her life she had been like a rowboat dragging anchor, but now, finally, the anchor had caught and held.

She turned to the others. "Ivar and Bob and Emma aren't the only ones; I am also a child of hers."

Magnus smiled. "I'm so glad it worked! I had no idea anyone would even notice the advertisement. So, Solvi, now we know where she is. Do you think you might want to go to America to see her?"

Solvi looked at Rikka, then back at Magnus. "Yes. It's far away, but I have to meet her, to get to know her. No matter what she has done. At this point, it doesn't seem to matter anymore. I just need to know her."

Magnus nodded. "I understand, Solvi. It will be a great adventure."

"And now I can afford it, with the legacy," Solvi said. "Professor Wolff urged me to go this summer, as she's getting old."

"Well, if you're going, I'm going with you," said Rikka.

Solvi turned to her. "Rikka! Really? Would you?"

"Well, I'll go as far as New York. There's a woman there I'd like to work with this summer, an advocate for birth prevention. I'll stay in New York while you go visit your family out west. Then we can travel back together."

"Oh, Rikka! That's a wonderful plan! When did you think of it?"

"Just now. It seems like a good time to leave Norway." Rikka glanced at Magnus.

"What do you mean, Rikka?" he asked.

Rikka and Solvi looked at each other. "I suppose we should tell you what happened last night," Solvi said.

"What?" he asked, his brow furrowing.

"As I was walking home, Dominik's brother, Edvard, came running up and pushed me against a wall," Solvi said, watching his face. She didn't mention the hand on her throat or her arms pinned back. "He wanted to throw my camera in the fjord. He was angry about the pictures in the newspaper and told me to keep quiet about Greta or he would report us to the police for trespassing."

"Did he hurt you?"

"Only a little; mostly he scared me. Fortunately, Dominik came along— he must have followed him. He pulled Edvard off me and returned my camera."

"I'm so sorry, Solvi," Magnus said. "We'll have to tell Mr. Blehr."

"I meant to speak to him today, but then all this happened," Solvi said.

Magnus squeezed her hand. "We'll talk to him tomorrow. Mr. Blehr can speak to the family and make sure Edvard doesn't bother you again. Until then, I think you two should stick together. Don't go out alone at night and be sure to stay on main streets."

They finished and headed back to the study house, but when they got there, Magnus took hold of Solvi's hand.

Rikka noticed, gave them a big yawn, and stretched her arms over her head. "I'm exhausted! See you two tomorrow."

She went inside, leaving Magnus and Solvi alone.

THEY SAT DOWN TOGETHER on the steps of the study house. The sun hovered low on the horizon, giving the world a soft, dusky light.

"That is quite the story about your grandmother," he said. "I wonder if meeting her might be a bit disappointing. She could be very different from the woman in that picture."

Solvi shrugged. "You're right; it's a strange story, but in a way it makes sense to me. She must have been desperate at every turn. I think she was trying to survive and, in the end, needed someone to love." Solvi looked at him. "You come from a big family, don't you?"

"Yes, and my grandparents live with us. There's hardly a quiet spot in the house back in Molde."

"You've no idea how lovely that sounds." Her eyes brimmed. "See, I needed more family, especially after my father died. And ever since I found that photograph, I've wanted to find the missing pieces. It doesn't matter to me if they aren't perfect. I know my grandmother has lived a life of difficult compromises, but I still need to find her."

Magnus took Solvi's hand. "I see a future for you filled with people, Solvi, loving people. I don't think you'll be lonely much again."

She nodded, unable for a moment to speak. "Do you think you'll go back to Molde when you're done with university?"

"No," he said. "I want to see the world—Alaska, South America. I also want adventures."

Her eyes filled again. She suddenly saw that she, too, would never go home again, except to visit.

"Solvi, what's wrong? What did I say?"

She wiped the tears away. "No, it's nothing you said, Magnus, other than you unearthed my truth before I knew it myself."

"Which truth?" he asked in a soft voice.

"I just realized I'll never go home again, either, certainly not to live there. It's both exciting and sad."

He gazed at her. "That's exactly how I feel, Solvi. It's the curse of the educated; we don't fit into that familiar world anymore."

She laughed. "My mother told me a university education would make me unmarriageable. Maybe this is what she meant."

"No, Solvi. You may not be able to go home again, but it definitely has not made you unmarriageable. Not at all." He looked at her. "I have a question."

She went very still. "A question?"

"Do you think you'll ever want to introduce me to your mother?"

"Why do you say that, Magnus?"

He held his hands out to her, palms up. "Calluses, Solvi. I chopped wood for money during the coal shortages. I have the telltale calluses of the working class."

She took his hands in hers. "Well, Rikka says I'm my own person now, so it's my decision who matters to me, not my mother's. And I admire your calluses."

He smiled. "Then I have another question."

She held still as a mouse.

"May I kiss you, Solvi Lange?"

Warmth flooded her body. "I thought you'd never ask."

THE NEXT MORNING Solvi wrote her mother a letter.

Dear Mama: Thank you for the legacy. I now know what happened to your family. I am sorry you have had to carry this secret for so long. I understand that it has been difficult.

You will be surprised to hear that I have found your mother, my grandmother, Nora Helmer. She lives in Spokane, Washington, with her husband, Anders Eriksen. She sent me a short letter. I need to meet her, so I am going to spend some of the legacy to travel to America this summer. I know you may be unhappy about this plan, but it is what I need to do. I promise I will return to Kristiania by the end of the summer to finish my studies.

I must tell you that I will also continue working at the photography studio and selling my photographs to the newspaper. Because this is what I do, Mother: I take pictures of things that are important, either problems that need to be corrected or mysteries and beauties that would otherwise go unappreciated. I am good at it, and I trust that, occasionally, my work will make a difference in the world.

I hope you can forgive me and, along the way, perhaps you can forgive your mother. If you want to come with me this summer to visit her, I would be thrilled, but that is up to you.

Love, Solvi

Over the next few weeks, Solvi and Rikka finished their classes and prepared for their trip to America. After hearing nothing in return from her mother, Solvi packed a small bag and boarded the train to Bergen. It was late May, and the snow was melting from the high plateau, swelling the streams into torrents and sending a thousand waterfalls over the cliffs into the fjords. Solvi watched her beloved landscape pass by and marveled at how much she had changed since her journey to Kristiania the November before.

When she stepped into her childhood home, her mother dropped her book with a small cry and wrapped her daughter in a hug.

"I knew you would come, darling," Emma said. "There was too much to say. I couldn't write because I knew I would never be able to stop."

Solvi understood and let her mother pick the time. A few days later, they sat down together after supper in the parlor.

"Mama, please tell me what happened, everything you know. It's a terrible humiliation, Grandmother's story, but it will be better if you share it with me. We will weather it together."

Emma took a deep breath and arranged her silk gown around her. "I suppose you're right. I've tried all my life to protect you from the shame of your grandmother, just as Grandfather tried to protect me, but it's been a terrible burden."

"I am sorry for you, Mama. But please tell me. I want to know."

"My mother, Nora, left us when I was two. Remember the photograph you found? That must have been taken a few months before."

"Do you know why she left?"

"No. I suppose she and Grandfather had a terrible fight about something. I don't remember any of it, just Ivar and Bob whispering about it years later. When Dr. Rank died and the incriminating legacy came out, it was assumed Nora left us to be with him, though he was at death's door. Dr. Rank had been a trusted friend of your grandfather's, indeed his only real friend, so Grandfather took the announcement of the legacy very badly. All this I was told only years later."

"Did you ever see her again?"

"Once, when I was twelve. Ivar had left us that spring to go to America, which was upsetting enough. Then Nora appeared. I thought she was dead, so it was quite a shock to have her show up at our house."

"It must have been strange," Solvi said.

"It was awful. Grandfather invited her in, though I'm not sure why because he was angry that she had returned to Kristiania. She was so ugly—all brown and wrinkled and badly dressed. I had no memories of her and didn't want to think such a woman could be my mother. Bobby remembered her, though, and was very happy to see her, which was also unsettling."

Emma stopped, lost in that time. "She gave me the most disturbing present, a little embroidered cap. She said she'd been working on it when she left and had kept it to give to me someday. But it had yellowed and was so small, as if made for a doll. It troubled me; she left when I was still just a baby. I threw the cap on the floor."

"What happened to Ivar and Bobby?"

"Before Ivar left for America, he had found a letter from Nora. He fought with Father about it, then booked his passage to New York. Apparently, he went to see her on the farm in Minnesota where she was living and told her about the legacy. That was why she came back. But there must have been a complication, because she signed the legacy over to us. Bobby took his share a year later and followed Ivar to America."

"Are they still there?"

"As far as I know."

"Have you never tried to find them?"

Her mother shook her head. "Why should I go looking for them? They chose her over us, your grandfather and me. They abandoned us, just as she did." She stopped to breathe. "Your grandfather never got over it. He refused to let me answer their letters or take any of the legacy. He was desperate to keep me out of her clutches, especially after it was clear she had committed bigamy."

Solvi watched her mother carefully. "Yes, I was shocked to hear that."

"The shame of it," Emma said, shaking her head. "It was bad enough that she left us, but then to commit such an abomination, and at an altar before God. Grandfather spoke quite bitterly of her."

"But didn't Grandfather remarry as well? Someone named Johanna?"

"Yes, but his marriage was legal because Nora had been declared dead years earlier when she couldn't be found. No one knew she was in America until her letter came."

Solvi thought of the grave site at Our Saviour. "What happened to Johanna?"

"Johanna was pregnant, and we were all excited a new baby was coming. But the day after Nora appeared, poor Johanna started hemorrhaging. She lost the child and bled to death a few days later. It crushed your grandfather. He blamed it on your grandmother's visit, as Johanna grew quite upset when she found out Nora had come to the house." She stopped for a moment and closed her eyes. "She was very kind to me, Johanna."

Solvi thought of her grandfather—his heavy-handed manner, his secretiveness, his bond with her mother. Puzzle pieces shifted into place.

"Was that when he changed the family name and moved you to Bergen?"

"He did that after Bobby left. That was the final straw. Grandfather said he couldn't hold his head up in Kristiania after that."

Solvi took a deep breath. "Why do you think Grandmother left?"

"Because she didn't love us," Emma said, without hesitation. "If she had loved us, she couldn't have done it. I knew that for certain once I had you."

"But what if there was some reason she couldn't live with Grandfather? What if her leaving was a terrible, painful choice? I mean, it could've been a brave thing that she did."

"Brave?" Emma said now, sitting up in her chair. "Brave, Solvi? How is any of it brave? I thought her a coward to slink back into Norway dressed in her cheap American clothes, offering to love us when we had finally gotten over her. I was deeply troubled and confused by her return. Then she stole Bobby's heart and upset Johanna so badly she miscarried and died." Emma shook her head. "Everything your grandmother did hurt us. Everything, except leaving for America. That was the only thing I was grateful for."

Solvi rose and paced about. She could feel this bitter story wrap around her, like ropes at her ankles. How could the elegant woman in the photograph, the grandmother who looked so knowing and strong, how could she be the person her mother described? How much Solvi had wanted this grandmother to prove herself fine and uplifting, worthy of Solvi's effort to find her, worthy of redemption.

She felt it like an ache in her stomach, unrelenting. "Mama, maybe that's just one side of the story. If you came with me to America, we could find out together. Perhaps she is an awful person, but perhaps not! Maybe she had to leave for reasons you never thought of. Maybe it broke her heart to leave you!"

Solvi's mother just looked at her, grim-faced.

"And you could forgive her," Solvi said. "It might do you good to forgive her. I'm sure she misses you."

"She has my brothers, Solvi. That should be enough for her."

"But that's not true, Mama; she doesn't have them. She doesn't even know where they are." Solvi took out the letter from Nora. "See? I don't know why, but they are not with her."

Her mother read it, then gave Solvi a look. "Because of the bigamy, no doubt."

"But she's not a bigamist anymore. Not since Grandfather died."

"That hardly absolves her," her mother said, rising and taking the letter to the stove. "Perhaps we should burn this, Solvi, just forget she ever sent it. We could go on with our lives."

"No, Mama, don't!" Solvi jumped up and snatched the letter from her hand. "I can't, Mama. I'm going to America, to Spokane. I've already written to her."

"But why, Solveig?"

"Because I think she deserves to be forgiven! Or at least she deserves to be understood. I don't know what happened between her and Grandfather, but it must have been awful if she had to leave. And think of all she lost, how harrowing her life must have been! I think she's worthy of our sympathy, and I need to know her story. I need to."

Her mother looked at her now with a sad smile. "See, this was always my concern. I've tried, more than anything, to protect you from her."

"Protect me from my own grandmother?"

"You were always rebellious, Solvi, even as a small child, questioning things, resisting my rules, wanting to make your own way. Sometimes your grandfather would take me aside, concerned you were turning out to be like her. We tried to make sure you never knew anything about your grandmother, but I can see now that effort was useless."

"People can't help who they are meant to be, Mama."

"I suppose you're right," Emma said. Then she leaned over and tugged gently on Solvi's short hair. "See what I mean? Rebellious. But I'm learning to live with that. You need to make your own way, Solveig, I know that now, and in a way I admire you. Going to Kristiania, starting your studies, taking those photographs, though I will never understand what you have against employing housemaids. But I see now that it is your life, to do with as you will. Your father was right; you are a mostly sensible young woman."

"So will you consider coming with me to America?"

"No, darling. That is your adventure, not mine."

"Do you want me to take her a letter from you?"

Her mother bowed her head. "I wouldn't know what to say."

Solvi sighed. "You could forgive her, Mama. It would mean everything to her."

Her mother turned and went to stand at a window, looking out into the midsummer dusk. After a few minutes, she finally spoke. "This is how I'm forgiving her, darling."

"What do you mean?"

"I am giving you to her."

A MONTH LATER, Solvi and Rikka checked their luggage at the steamship office in Kristiania and walked with Magnus to the foot of the gangplank. He had been so good to Solvi, convincing Mr. Blehr to talk with Dominik's family, then helping her write a story to accompany her photographs of the prostitutes in Vika. Solvi was proud of her work but also a little bit relieved she would be out of the country when the story ran. Magnus had promised to buy a hundred copies.

Now that everything was settled, Solvi was beginning to regret leaving him behind.

He gazed at her with sad eyes.

"Good gracious, Magnus, you look like an abandoned puppy," Rikka said.

"I feel like an abandoned puppy," he said, still looking at Solvi.

She smiled up at him. "I'll write to you, Magnus. I promise."

"No, there's something else," he said.

"What, Magnus?" Solvi said. "What's the matter?"

"I'll just check our luggage," Rikka said, sliding away.

Magnus took Solvi's hands in his. "I'm worried you won't come back. Perhaps you have an America dream, like so many others. Maybe you'll move in with your grandmother and learn to ride a cow pony, or stay in Chicago to sell photos to the *Skandinaven*. I'm terrified I'll never see you again!"

Solvi burst out laughing, rose up on her toes, and gave him a kiss. "Don't worry, Magnus. I'll come back. At least long enough to get you."

CHAPTER TWENTY-ONE

NORA

June 1889 ■ *Lac qui Parle, Minnesota*

The trip back across the Atlantic proved sunny and calm, but as I watched the water roll by, I began to worry about what to tell Anders. I was returning empty-handed, having left the legacy behind, and I had no idea how to explain it. I was deeply grateful to have seen my children and glad that Bob had forgiven me. But I knew I must pack them up tight in my heart again until Torvald died. There was no alternative—I could not talk about them or tell Anders anything until my first marriage ended. I crafted a simple explanation about the legacy and hoped that would suffice.

The journey, however, gave me too much time to think, and before long my conscience began to take me to task. What kind of woman had I become? How often had I believed myself bigger or more important than I was? I had donned costumes, pretended to know more than I did, imagined myself heroic when I often just blundered. I even considered myself a good wife to Anders, yet I had not been honest about the most important thing.

Over the years, I told myself I had my own moral code built on love, but there had been a cost to it all—marrying Torvald, forging the loan, lying to Anders so he would marry me. I saw now that I had also lied to myself— lied about the pain I had inflicted, lied about who I was and what I had done, lied before God and the minister and the man I loved.

I was not bigger than life; I was small and misguided. Out here on the empty ocean, I also felt inconsequential, which was the only thing that brought any relief. I began to think it unfair to burden Anders with my bigamous shame, that it would be kinder to never return.

Perhaps I should get off the train in Chicago, I thought, and try to find Ivar. With his portion of the legacy we could set up housekeeping. He could attend university, and I could tend to women again, but as my own person with my own home to return to each night.

It was cold comfort, but the possibility flickered in my mind.

WE DOCKED IN NEW YORK, and within hours I was on a train, rattling west. Watching out the window I spotted farm after farm—women with chickens around their feet, boys driving cows, farmers harnessing their horses. Each scene made me homesick.

I grew nervous as we approached Chicago, unsure, my heart aching. But as soon as I stepped off the train, I knew I could not stay. I made my way to the western station and bought a ticket to Minnesota. I needed to see Anders again, feel his arms around me, return to our quiet life together.

I made a choice the day I sent Ivar away, a terrible choice but a necessary one.

Now I must learn to live with it.

WHEN I ARRIVED at the end of the line in Milan, I hired a buggy to take me home. The driver let the mare do the work, pulling his hat down and leaving me alone with my knot of worries. The hot prairie wind washed across the grass. I watched the western horizon for storm clouds, as it was that kind of day, but there was only the shimmering heat.

I came through the door just as Birgitte was putting dinner on the table. I knew she had come to stay with Anders and Jens while I was away, and I was grateful to see her. She gave me a hug and a kiss.

Then I noticed that she had set just two places at the table, for her and her brother.

"Birgitte, is your father away?"

"Yes; he's hunting up the river. He said he wouldn't be back till tomorrow."

I could scarcely breathe. I never thought Anders would not be here to greet me.

Jens came in a few minutes later, giving me a hug and telling me all the news from the barn. Birgitte pulled the cornbread from the oven. I was suddenly famished for it all—the simple meal, my familiar home, the company of these two who meant so much to me.

We talked of Norway and my trip; I smiled and answered as best I could, but I was anxious now. Perhaps Anders had decided not to take me back; maybe that was why he was away.

Before she headed to bed, Birgitte gave me another hug, as she could see I was troubled. "You must be very tired, Nora. I'm sure everything will look better in the morning."

"Thank you, Birgitte." I closed my bedroom door, washed off the grit, and slid into my own bed, a place of so much tenderness. Would it ever be that way again?

THE NEXT MORNING I rose early and made biscuits to give my nervous hands something to do. As I placed the pan in the stove, my husband appeared in the doorway with the milk bucket.

We looked at each other across the room, across the abyss. This was the moment—my life could tip either way. He set down the bucket; I wiped the flour from my hands. And then we both stepped forward at the same instant and sank into each other's arms.

"I've missed you, Nora," he said, gruffness in his voice. "I am very glad to have you home again."

I wanted to stay buried in his chest, to say nothing, to just hold him. Because the moment we started talking, I feared everything would teeter and crash.

But he pulled back, holding me by the shoulders and looking deep into my eyes. "Are you ready to tell me the truth, Nora?"

I nodded, but my throat was a vice.

He led me to a chair, then sat beside me. "Tell me of your journey. How was Norway?"

I smoothed my skirts because it was hard to look at him. "Norway was beautiful, Anders, very green. But it was also confining. I felt closed in all the time. You can see the influence from America. People dress differently, and there's new wealth. I can't quite describe it."

He listened but said nothing. He was waiting.

"I don't have the legacy, Anders. I couldn't get it."

He frowned slightly. "No? What happened?"

"It was complicated. Because the court had me declared dead some time ago, I could not claim the legacy without going back to court to prove who I was, and if I did that I risked legal trouble for having left the country on Inge's papers."

He looked at me, puzzled. "You would be in trouble for that, after all these years?"

"Yes, for that and for using her papers to get back into Norway," I said.

"In Kristiania, there is no Nora Solberg. She is dead, and there is only Inge Eriksen. But if the court looks into Inge's papers, they will find she is also dead."

He sighed.

"In the end, I let my cousin keep the money," I said. "They are my kin, after all, and it has helped them substantially."

I could see the disappointment in his face, as the money would have helped us substantially as well. It could have sent Birgitte to college, helped Jens find a livelihood, and helped support us as we grew old.

I took his hand. "I am so sorry, Anders. I know you were counting on it. But I couldn't risk going to court; I was afraid I might never get back to you."

He nodded solemnly.

"The entire time I was over there, all I wanted was to return to you," I said. "I missed you every day. The only place that brought me solace was standing on the dock looking down the fjord, because that was the way home to you."

He gave me a sad smile. "I understand, Nora, and perhaps it's for the best. I didn't like the idea of money that came to us through another man's affection for you. Our lives will continue as they were, as if Ivar never found us."

As if Ivar never found us—that was how I should proceed. But at that moment, in the pale, disappointing present of that prairie morning, I wasn't sure I had the strength to keep my children a secret until Torvald died. Everything inside me seemed to be collapsing.

"And who did you see while you were there?" Anders asked.

I hesitated. I desperately wanted to tell him of my joy in seeing Bob and Emma, the possibility that the future might bring me close to them again. But I couldn't.

"I stayed with my cousin and her younger children for a few days. They were very kind to me."

"Did you see others? Perhaps the young men you knew in Vika?"

"No. I didn't know how to find them, and I had to keep myself hidden."

"Do you think you will want to return to Norway again, Nora?"

Tears filled my eyes. "Oh, Anders, I can't imagine why I would. There's no one there for me anymore."

At that moment the scent of scorched biscuits drifted across the room. I jumped up and took them out—burned, all of them. I began to weep.

This was my life now; I must find a way to make my peace with it.

Anders pulled me silently into his arms. We could hear the children stirring overhead. It would have been a happy sound if only mine were here with us.

I wiped my eyes and set the table.

THE NEXT FEW DAYS I struggled to return to my settled life. I forgot to feed the chickens one morning, then failed to soak the beans the next. Anders seemed to have accepted my explanation about the legacy, but he kept his distance, spending more time in the barn than usual, as if he was working something out. Perhaps he suspected I had not shared the whole truth; perhaps he was more disturbed over the loss of the money than he let on. When he came in, he carried his disappointment on his shoulders.

I also found it impossible to pack my own children away in my memory again, as I had in the past. Having seen them older gave me rich new scope to think about their lives and experiences, and my imagination chased them across Kristiania. Hope could be a terrible master, especially when it refused to be snuffed out.

In the midst of all that went unsaid, Anders and I orbited around each other like lost stars.

SEVERAL DAYS LATER, on a still summer night, we were working quietly in the parlor when we heard footsteps outside, then a loud knock. Anders went to open the door, and I came up behind him to see if it was a family in need of help.

But instead of a poor homesteader, it was Pastor Aasen, the Lutheran minister, with several of the church fathers.

"Pastor, brothers, please, come in," Anders said, stepping aside to let them pass.

But Pastor Aasen shook his head. "We cannot enter a house such as yours, Anders Eriksen, I'm sorry to say." The others nodded in agreement, and two of them glared at me.

My blood went cold.

Pastor Aasen pulled a paper from his breast pocket. "We received this today from the Lutheran Synod in Minneapolis with information from Norway. It says that a woman known in America as Nora Eriksen and wife to Anders Eriksen is married to another man who lives today in Kristiania,

Torvald Helmer. Nora Helmer has committed the sin of bigamy by marrying you, Mr. Eriksen."

Anders stood motionless, staring at Pastor Aasen. I stumbled back. Did Torvald go to the authorities after all?

"Given that you have entered into a bigamous marriage," the pastor continued, "you both are now excluded from Church membership." He waved a certificate of some sort. "Your marriage has been annulled by the Synod, and we have applied *kjerketukt*. You may not attend Lutheran services, and no God-fearing Lutherans will speak to you from this day forward. You will be shunned."

Anders grabbed the certificate.

"But Mr. Helmer said he would divorce me!" I cried out.

Anders turned and looked at me with disbelief. "Divorce you? You said your husband was dead!"

Pastor Aasen shook his head. "Mr. Helmer has sworn before the dean of the parish that he saw you recently in Kristiania. As he never secured a divorce, you are still married to him."

"Nora, is that why you went back to Norway? To see your husband?" Anders said, his face going ashen.

My pulse hammered. I couldn't answer Anders, not in that moment. I turned instead to the pastor. "But Mr. Helmer must have divorced me, because he has married again as well!"

Pastor Aasen squinted at a letter he also held in his hands. "According to the dean, Mr. Helmer believed he was free to remarry because the court had declared you dead. Mr. Helmer's second wife, however, has recently passed away. So, as you see, Mrs. Helmer, you are the one in the bigamous marriage."

I felt the ground give way beneath my feet. There would be no defending myself from this.

Now one of the church fathers spoke up. "You must return to your husband in Norway, Mrs. Helmer. We will not have one such as you in our midst!"

Anders looked at me again, hurt but also defiant. He shook himself and stepped forward. "Just a minute! This is a free land, sir. You have no right to banish my wife from our farm. You are not the law in America."

"No, but we can bring the law, if that is what you prefer, Mr. Eriksen," the pastor said. "I have no doubt the sheriff will be as concerned as we are. Bigamy will not be tolerated by either Church or state."

"It's not fair to expel Mr. Eriksen from his land," I said. "He knew nothing of any of this. He married me in good faith."

"Nora, hush," Anders said. He gripped my hand.

Pastor Aasen turned to me. "If you leave, Mrs. Helmer, we will reinstate Mr. Eriksen to the Church. But if you stay, well, God help you." He looked at Anders. "We trust you'll do what's right."

With that, they turned and disappeared into the night.

WE STUMBLED BACK INSIDE and bolted the door. Birgitte and Jens hovered nearby, but I couldn't look at any of them. I turned toward the bedroom. There was only one thing to do.

"Nora," Anders said, his voice shaking.

"I'm going to pack my bag, Anders."

"No, Nora," he said, setting out a chair. "Sit and explain every last shred of truth. I need to understand what I'm dealing with."

Then he looked at Birgitte and Jens. "Go check on the stock. Make sure they're inside."

"Yes, Father," they said in unison, quickly slipping out.

Anders pulled out a chair for himself and sat in front of me, just as Torvald and I had sat in the darkened dining room the night I left him all those years ago.

"Please just let me leave!" I said, trying to stand. "Let me go, and you won't have to worry about any of this anymore!" I couldn't bear the pain in his face.

"Nora, look at me! I need to understand, or I'll never be able to live with it."

"You won't love me if you know the truth. You will hate me!"

"I could never hate you, Nora, but you have not been honest with me, and that is hard to accept. I know you had a difficult life in Norway. I never understood why a beauty like you was in such desperate circumstances when I met you on the docks. Just tell me what's true. Are you married to this man Helmer in Norway?"

"I don't, I . . ."

"Tell me, Nora! No more lies! Did you have a husband when you married me?"

"Oh, Anders, I thought he had divorced me, but I didn't know, not for sure!"

"How could you have married me when you didn't know!" he thundered.

I pulled back. Anders had never raised his voice with me in all our years together.

"My husband said he would divorce me, Anders, and I was sure he would do it. He was that kind of man. But it turned out that to divorce me, he had to find me." I stopped to gulp air. "As I had already come to America with you, on Inge's papers, they couldn't find me in Norway or in the emigration records. That's when they assumed I had died and had me declared dead instead of giving him a divorce."

"But you said at the altar that you were free to marry me, Nora! How could you lie about such a thing, and before God?" His face filled with pain. "And the priest blessed our union! Why didn't you tell me the truth back then?"

I started to say I did it for love, but something stopped me. I had said that so often in my life, excused so much with it. Instead, I reached for the deepest truth, which came out as a savage cry. "Because I would have lost you," I howled. "Because I couldn't bear to let you go! I was so alone in the world, Anders. I wanted to belong to you again, to have what we have here—our whole life together!"

"Even if we're living in sin?"

"I don't care! I don't care what the Church says, and I don't care what others think. I only care what you think!"

"But now we could be arrested!"

I covered my face with my hands because I couldn't look at him. "That is why you must let me go. They will not arrest you if I am gone."

He pulled my hands away. "Look at me, Nora."

I glanced up for a moment, but it was impossible to hold his fierce gaze.

"These are difficult truths, Nora. To realize how much you've deceived me."

"I am so very sorry, Anders, and I understand now how much this matters. But when you asked me to marry you, I didn't see it. My marriage to Torvald was long dead, as if it happened to someone else rather than the Nora who worked in St. Paul, alone in the world, with no one. Torvald and Norway seemed so far away. I never imagined my former life would find me here."

He sighed. "These must have been painful secrets to hold, all this time. Tell me how this happened. Why you left your husband."

"You will not love me if you know the truth."

He looked at me sideways. "Is this about the older gentleman?"

"No! It has nothing to do with him, and it's not what you think. But still, you will not love me."

"Nora, I will always love you. And if you leave me, I'll never get over you. But I need to know what's true. How could this happen?"

I swallowed hard. "When I met you in Kristiania, I was running from my husband, this Torvald Helmer."

"But you told me you lost your husband and children. You dressed as a widow!"

"Yes, and I apologize. I know I wasn't honest with you, but I was desperate, as you said. I had left my husband because I couldn't be married to him anymore, and then he refused to let me see my children."

He shook his head, as if bothered by a fly. "Your children? Nora, are your children also alive?"

Sudden relief flooded through me. I could tell him. I could tell him all of it. "Yes. Ivar is one of them."

He looked at me, his eyes widening. "Ivar? Your cousin's son?" Then he jumped to his feet and walked to the other side of the room before turning to me again. "Did you send him away, your own son?"

"Yes," I said, bursting into tears. "I had to! I couldn't claim him as my son without risking our marriage! I had to send him away because of my terrible secret, and it broke my heart!" I doubled over, sobbing in earnest.

Anders sat down again and took my hands. "Nora, Nora. Calm yourself. And where are the other children?"

"In Kristiania, with their father. I saw them, Anders. You can't imagine what it's meant to me. My younger son, Bobby, was very glad to see me."

"This is all very bewildering, Nora. You have three children and a husband in Norway. I never would have imagined."

I wept. I had lost my children, and now I would lose Anders and his children. Everyone I loved.

He came and sat down again before me. "Leaving your children behind in Norway doesn't sound like you, Nora. How could such a thing have happened? Tell me so I understand."

My story. He wanted to hear my story.

I took some deep breaths, then told him how I came to marry Torvald, and about Torvald's sickness and my forging of the loan, and how I worked for years paying off the loan surreptitiously, the anxiety and anguish of that burdensome secret. And then the Christmas when it all came crashing down—the blackmail, our fight, my sudden realization that Torvald could never accept or understand me. How painful it was to leave my children but that I knew I would die if I stayed with Torvald.

He sighed. "Like you nearly died here, on the ice?"

"Yes. One night I went down to the wharf in Kristiania, but the fjord was so cold. A constable found me."

"Did Torvald beat you?"

"No. He never hit me, but he treated me like a child—no, worse, like his little doll. Not the way you treat me, as your partner. He could never accept me as his equal; he couldn't even imagine it. He had to be my master in everything—what I said, what I ate, what I thought. After I left him, he threatened to find me and send me to the asylum because I kept trying to see the children. The only way to escape him was to leave Norway. But I couldn't afford the passage."

"Ah," Anders said. "Then you met me, with a baby that needed care and a ticket I couldn't use."

"It felt like an act of God, Anders," I said. "But then Torvald sent the police after me, and I was desperately afraid I wouldn't get free from the prison in time to go with you. When the police handed me over to Torvald, I knew that was my only chance to escape, so I offered him a promise. If he agreed to let me go to America, I would not contact the children until they were grown."

He listened but said nothing.

"I couldn't tell you the truth in Kristiania because you wouldn't have taken me with you," I said. "I know that was wrong, Anders, but I don't regret it! Because of you, I escaped the asylum or having to live for years as my husband's property without my own freedom." I started to cry again. "I am so grateful, Anders; you saved my life."

Finally, he spoke. "Didn't you think about seeing your children again?"

"Yes, but that seemed so far in the future. It wasn't until after you and I married that I saw the trap I'd created. I dreamed of returning to Norway to see them when they were grown, but I realized I couldn't do that without confessing everything to you. And then I would have lost you! It's been a torture, and it's drawn me away from you. So I hoped for a miracle. To be honest, I prayed that Torvald would die."

He looked at me, as if seeing me differently.

"I knew that was a sin, but I didn't care. And then a miracle happened, but it wasn't what I expected. It was Ivar." I looked down; I was twisting my apron mercilessly. "You've no idea, Anders, how it felt to have Ivar find me."

"It must have been like having him return from the dead."

"Yes, it was. But then I had an agonizing choice: you or Ivar. It felt like one of God's cruel jokes."

"It pains me to hear you speak of God that way, Nora."

"Forgive me, Anders." I tried to fold my hands in my lap, to resign to my fate.

"You should ask for God's mercy, Nora."

"Anders, I am not a God-fearing person, you know that. And now that I've lost my way in the world, I doubt God can help me. I must help myself, not depend on others anymore. That's why you must let me leave."

He looked at me, so troubled. This man who could not lie, tied to a woman who struggled, always, with the truth. He pushed the hair out of his eyes. "It would be a great sorrow to lose you, Nora. I wrapped you around me like a bearskin, and it was only then that I could build a life here. What would you have me do?"

"Let me go to Chicago. Put me on the train tomorrow. Then you can think about whether you want to stay on the farm or join me. In a big city I think we could continue to live as man and wife, and no one would know the difference. It would be up to you and me to decide what we are to each other."

"But isn't that best left to the ministers? My life has been built on their guidance and authority."

"If we are shunned by the Church, then we must decide what God would have us do."

"God wants us to abide by his laws, Nora."

"But God's laws are different in different lands. There are great debates about God's laws, many opinions. There's no one law, Anders, not that I can see."

"And so you would make your own morality, Nora?"

I hesitated—this was the question Torvald asked the night I left so long ago. I didn't have an answer, then, but now, baring my soul to the man who meant everything to me, I realized that a moral code built on love was the only one that felt true.

"Yes," I said. "I believe a marriage is what two people build together, and you and I have such a marriage, one that supports two other people and a farm. I cannot see what good would come from breaking us apart. Why would God wish such a sorrow on us and the children, after all our other losses?"

"Perhaps you're right, but, still—it's hard for me to accept, to see the world as you do. It doesn't feel honorable."

I sighed. Must it always be honor on one side and love on the other? My life kept leading me back to this choice, over and over. "Anders, I considered staying in Chicago when I returned from Norway. I thought that would be the honorable thing to do. That if I really loved you, I would release you."

He looked at me, his gaze intense. "And yet you came back."

"Yes. Because in every way that matters, I am your wife! I know what it means when you sigh; I know when you need my help. I know your history and your sorrows and joys. We have a thousand bonds, Anders! This farm and the many responsibilities here, Birgitte and Jens, even our grief for Tomas. I've been safe with you in a way I've never been with anyone else. My marriage to Torvald was a sham—not like this, a partnership where I'm loved and appreciated. Even if I never see you again, you will be my husband until I die. There can be no other."

A sad tenderness stole across his face. "Nora. Dear, complicated Nora." He hesitated for a long moment. "I understand what you're saying, but my honor stands before me like a stone wall. I don't know how our marriage got built on a lie. Perhaps my silence has prevented us from understanding each other. There's so much we should have said to each other, Nora, starting on the dock in Kristiania." He put his head in his hands. "Truly, I don't know what to do."

"I will go. And if you want me, sell this farm and join me in Chicago."

"I don't want to make you leave. This is your home, as much as it is mine."

"I've lost the right to live here, Anders. That is my sorrow to carry. Only join me if you can choose me."

And with that I went into my room to pack.

AN HOUR LATER, we heard a commotion approaching our house—many footsteps this time, shouting, and, just as Anders reached to open the door again, another loud knock. Birgitte gasped. There were men with torches outside the kitchen window.

Anders turned to me quickly. "Go in the bedroom, Nora, and shut the door." He snatched his rifle from the corner. "Jens, come with me."

I retreated but left the door ajar so I could see and hear. Anders stepped out onto the stone stoop, and Jens stood behind him, blocking the doorway.

"Anders Eriksen, you must take your family and leave this county!" shouted a rough voice. "We will not have bigamists here!"

Other voices took up the cry. "Leave, bigamist! Go!" I could see the torches flickering, hear boots and horses stamping. Then a fresh voice among the others, louder. "It's that witch who must go. She's the one who has sinned!"

I pulled out my bag and started throwing clothing into it. My mind tumbled.

Then I heard Anders's voice. "Quiet! Let me speak!" The shouting died down. "If you say my wife is a witch, then you forget what she's done, how many women she's helped!"

"But she heals by black magic!" shouted someone else. "She must have one of those black books, the devil's medicine. That's how she heals when the doctor can do nothing!"

"And she consorts with that *svartz*, the one that doesn't speak," yelled another. "We see them in the woods together!"

"Yes, she's friends with Ann Renville, but that's not against the law!" Anders shouted.

I put on my traveling dress, though I could scarcely button the front, my hands were shaking so. I stuffed my sewing bag in my suitcase and snapped it shut.

"There is confusion about the status of my wife's first marriage in Norway," Anders said. "That is true. And I need to talk with the Church fathers in Minneapolis to sort it out. But we have lived among you peacefully for six years, and there is no reason we should be forced to leave at this point."

"Besides," he said, "Nora has helped many of your wives." He started to pick people out in the crowd. "You, Pieter, didn't Nora help your wife when she lost the last baby? And you, Lars Mark; she stayed with your family for two weeks when your wife could no longer cook or clean. Do you people have such little gratitude? Don't you recognize a woman of God among you?"

"But she preaches disobedience!"

At this my stomach clenched. Anders didn't know how often I told women to stand up to their husbands or leave if they hit them. All my subtle preaching was catching up with me.

But Anders abruptly laughed. "Is that it? That your wives have become disobedient? Perhaps you should tend to them with more affection. Then you might not need her help."

There was a silence, then another voice. "This is about bigamy, Eriksen. We won't go until you promise to leave."

"I swear that if the law of the land—not this crowd—requires we leave, we will leave!" Anders shouted. "But not a moment before. You, my friends, are not the law."

I carried my bag to the door, squeezed past Jens, and stepped into the yard, facing the crowd. Anders reached to pull me back, but I shook him off.

"There's no need for this; I'm leaving," I said in a loud voice.

Anders grabbed for me. "Nora, no!"

"Please, Anders, just get the wagon. We'll wait at the station in Milan, and I'll take the train in the morning."

"We'll take her to Milan, Eriksen!" Some started to laugh.

"Absolutely not!" Anders yelled, pulling me back toward the door. "Don't give in to this ungrateful mob, Nora!"

"But they're right—I should go!"

"Tomorrow, we'll go together tomorrow. But don't let them . . ." Now Anders raised his voice again. "It's late; no one's going anywhere tonight. If you disband, I won't have you charged with trespassing, and I give you my word I'll speak to the justice of the peace tomorrow." He waved his rifle at them.

There was grumbling, muttering, a few more shouts. One man pushed forward and shook his torch at us. "You wouldn't want to lose your barn, now, would you, Eriksen?"

Anders froze. "Are you threatening my animals?" I could see torchlight glinting off several bottles in the crowd.

Someone grabbed the man with the torch and dragged him away. "Just keep your promise, Eriksen, or we can't say what might happen," someone said. The figures backed off into the darkness, the torches moving down the path toward town. We turned inside and closed the door.

I fell against Anders's chest. "Oh, Anders, no one has ever defended me before!"

He wrapped me in his arms. "Nora, Nora." After a long moment, he pushed me away so he could look into my face. "Listen, we must leave tonight, as soon as we can pack. We cannot wait for the law to come to us."

"No, Anders. I don't want you to give up the farm! Tomorrow I'll go. It's for the best."

He looked at me. Then he looked past me and out the back window. "The henhouse!"

We all turned—my chicken coop was aflame.

Anders grabbed the hatchet and shouted orders. "Jens, water! Birgitte, Nora, the sackcloths!" We grabbed what we could and ran outside, but the coop was already engulfed. I tried to get to the door, but the heat came toward me in a sickening wave, filling my lungs with smoke. Anders pulled me away, then managed to hack a hole in the back wall, but only flames came licking out. There was no hope. Anders and Jens went to calm the horses, while Birgitte smacked at the cinders in the grass with wet rags.

I sank to the ground and wept into the folds of my dress.

THE HENHOUSE BURNED to ashes in a few hours. Anders stationed Jens at the smoking ruin with the sackcloths and the gun—to keep an eye on the embers and the road. Then he took me inside, into our bedroom, and gently started to unbutton my traveling dress.

I pushed his hands away. "I need to leave, Anders. Once I'm gone they'll have no reason to hurt you."

He looked at me with great tenderness. "No, Nora. We'll go together. Change into your work clothes, for we must pack. I'll never have peace here, not now. It shocks me that they would threaten us this way. It's a measure of their resolve."

"But you cannot lose the farm! You've worked so hard for it!"

He shook his head and helped me step out of my dress. "No, it's you I cannot lose. I saw that tonight. You're right; we're husband and wife. There's no abandoning each another now."

I looked at him, speechless. I was forgiven.

He dropped my day dress over my head and gave me a kiss. "Come."

We stepped back into the main room, where Birgitte was making sandwiches.

"We must all pack," says Anders. "We're leaving at dawn."

"Where are we going?" asked Birgitte,

"West," said Anders.

"Not back to Minneapolis or Chicago?" I asked.

"No. West, where there's still land and we can escape our history."

"How far west?" said Birgitte.

"To Alaska territory, if that's what it takes," Anders said. "Pack your woolens."

WE FELL TO OUR CHORES—sorting, packing, and tending to the animals. I opened up Inge's rosemaled chest and filled it with our books and better things, carefully stowing Anders's woodworking tools and my beautiful quilt from Mrs. Madsen in the bottom. Most of the cookware and household things, however, we had to leave behind. Along with our chest, each of us would carry just a bag of clothing and a rolled blanket.

We soon heard a horse approaching. Birgitte shot me a nervous glance, but when I looked outside it was James Renville, pounding up on his pony.

I rushed out. "Mr. Renville!"

He jumped down, taking in the half-filled wagon. "Nora, are you all right? There was a nasty crowd in the saloon—it's all over town." He sniffed. "What's burning?

"They torched my henhouse and my poor chickens."

He strode around the side of the house to see the ruins, and I followed, though it was hard for me to look at the smoldering pile.

Mr. Renville shook his head in dismay. "Nora, how could they turn on you, you who've done so much for them?"

"Anders and I are not legally married, not according to the Church. We've been shunned and must leave. They threatened to burn the barn, so I think we got off lightly, at least in their eyes."

Anders appeared with a crate for the wagon. "Well, James, I guess you heard. You're the only friends we have left in Lac qui Parle."

"You'll always have us," Mr. Renville said. "Must you go?"

"Yes, we're heading west," said Anders. "Can we stop with you for a day or so, just until we get things sorted out? We're not safe here."

"Of course. Ann will want to say good-bye."

"You may have our animals," Anders said. "We can bring the cows with us now, but you'll have to come back for the pigs."

"And there will be many things left in the house," I said. "Ann can take what she wants."

Mr. Renville sighed, then turned to help Anders with the stock.

There seemed to be no words for what we were all feeling. It was shocking how quickly our life on this beautiful piece of prairie had unraveled.

WE LEFT OUR FARM in the pale light just before dawn, the wagon heaped with luggage, the heifers plodding behind. Anders didn't look back, but I could not steel myself that way. I twisted on the wagon seat, gazing at our graceful green-trimmed house, the garden and barnyard, the corn and oats ripening in the distance. Everything spoke of toil and care.

Perhaps this was our paradise, I thought in that moment, my stomach knotting with despair. Perhaps it would never be that good again.

We stopped at the graveyard to say good-bye to little Tomas, then headed toward the lake and the Renvilles' cabin. I realized, then, that I would never return to either of my two homes. I could never return to Lac qui Parle, and now that the authorities in Norway knew I was alive, I could never return to Kristiania.

And if I couldn't return, my children would never be able to find me.

TWO DAYS LATER, after hiring a lawyer to sell the farm for us, we said good-bye to Lac qui Parle. Ann just smiled into my eyes, nodding gently. Our farewell was like everything else between us—deeper than words.

Mr. Renville drove us to the station in Milan under a bluebird sky. It was too fine a day to leave, he said wistfully, then he bid us safe travel and clattered away.

"I'll get the tickets," Anders said, turning toward the ticket booth.

"Wait!" said Birgitte, stepping forward. "I'm not going west with you."

"What?" I said, clutching my stomach. I wasn't sure I could survive more losses. "Birgitte, what do you mean by this?" Anders asked.

She squared her shoulders. "I want to go to Minneapolis and work until I have enough to enroll at St. Olaf. I want to be a teacher, not a farmer."

We stared at her, our robust girl, brimming with health and purpose. The breeze rose, filling our skirts and tugging at our jackets. How much she had become a child of this vibrant land, this American place.

Anders reached for her hand. "I'd always hoped for this, Birgitte. We'll miss you, but you're an adult now and must make your own life."

I wasn't so easily mollified. "Are you sure?" I said. "You could work out west until you have enough money to enroll."

"Yes, come west with us!" Jens begged. He looked stricken by her decision.

"It's best if I stay here in Minnesota," she said. "I've already written to the college. I'll miss you all, but I'll come visit. I promise."

I took her into my arms. "Truly, you will make an excellent scholar. I'm so proud of you."

"We will send what money we can," Anders promised her, with a tender kiss on her forehead.

"And you best come visit at Christmas," Jens said, punching her on the arm, then grabbing her in a bear hug. "The *Julenisse* won't come unless you're with us."

She looked around with a sad smile. "I'll write as soon as I am settled."

I told her where to find the mission in St. Paul, in case she needed help, and we agreed to send letters to each other through the Renvilles until we settled.

Anders went to buy our tickets, and we waited, talking softly about the mysteries ahead for all of us. The westbound train arrived first. Birgitte helped us board, then clung to each of us one last time. It broke my heart to say good-bye to her, this girl who at first refused to accept me and then grew to be my closest friend. How strange life is; how big it makes us.

As our train pulled out for the Dakotas, Jens and I leaned out the window, waving back at her. Before I was ready, her dear figure resolved to little more than a silhouette. Then the station was swallowed up by the wide land.

I finally pulled back into the car and sat down, wiping the soot and tears from my eyes. Anders took my hand.

Wherever we were going, I hoped the sky was vast—the very vault of heaven.

July 1919 ✳ *Spokane, Washington*

NORA

Memory is a fickle muse, one day comforting, the next condemning.

My granddaughter wants me to write my story, *the true story of Nora Helmer*, she calls it, but I sit frozen before the empty page, unable to begin.

I can't even say when everything started. Was it the morning I married Torvald, the day I forged my father's signature, or the night I walked away? I gave up making sense of it when Anders and I left Minnesota. To unearth it now, after finally finding a place of peace, seems unwise. Besides, how can I say what is true? I've had trouble with the truth my entire life.

AFTER WHAT HAPPENED IN LAC QUI PARLE, Anders and I never again questioned whether we were husband and wife. When we arrived in Spokane, we went on living as we had, keeping our heads down and trying to avoid suspicion. A great fire burned through the city a year later, which destroyed most of the downtown and gave the townspeople other things to worry about.

We never again dared to go to church, and I knew Anders felt the loss of that. Sometimes I found him reading sermons or the Bible he brought from Norway.

Instead of Bible verses, I planted my morality in an effort to be scrupulous with my word, though it sometimes cost me. Still, Anders seemed comforted by my effort. We wore each other like old cloaks, grateful for the warmth.

Our love never felt like sin to me, even if it meant I couldn't return to church. But then, I never felt God's presence in church anyway, even as a child. I tried looking to the hills for God, but the prairie taught me that nature is indifferent to my troubles and can be merciless in its fierce beauty.

I didn't find God until I returned to working with women. Instead of helping in private homes, I work in a mission for immigrants who have landed in Spokane penniless and alone. The women come from all the corners of Europe, and even from the East, dressed in outlandish costumes and speaking strange languages. But if I look past their haunted eyes and bad teeth, I see the light of God. Because every woman wants what I wanted—her family around her, meaningful work, and the freedom to live honestly in the world. We are all the same, and that is how I've come to know, finally, that God is true.

ANDERS AND I ARE OLD NOW, and the dry western wind has left us wrinkled as gnomes. Our life is spare, but our work and children remind us the world is rich. We keep a happy home, particularly with Jens and Katrin and the grandchildren here. In the evenings, Anders plays a hand organ I bought him, and Katrin teaches the children to dance. After we settled at the orchard, Anders found and repaired an old piano, a great pleasure for me. Sometimes I play Chopin and wonder if Mrs. Burnley still lives or has gone to her grave.

Birgitte went to live in St. Paul and eventually enrolled at St. Olaf College, her longtime dream. When she graduated, she married a fellow student and moved to Wisconsin to teach. They've given us several more grandchildren and keep a home filled with books and learning.

I wrote to Emma when she was grown, telling her where I was, but I never heard back. Most likely, Torvald burned the letter before she even saw it. I've thought of her often over the years, wondering whom she married, but it was difficult to imagine her as an adult. She would always be a baby to me.

As for her brothers, I do not know where they are. I hope they are happy in their lives.

AND THEN ONE SPRING DAY, after the Great War was finally over, I found that astonishing advertisement in the *Skandinaven*. Soon after writing my answer, I received a letter in return. But it wasn't from Ivar or Bobby or Emma. It was from a granddaughter I didn't even know existed, Solveig. It turned out she was the one who put the advertisement in the newspaper, this surprising girl. She told me her grandfather Torvald died of complications from the Spanish flu in October of 1918, but her mother—Emma—was fine and living in Bergen. At the end of the note she said she was coming to America and asked if she could visit us here in Spokane.

I WROTE TO THIS MYSTERIOUS GRANDDAUGHTER, welcoming her to our home. A few weeks later, Anders and I took the train to Seattle to be married before a justice of the peace. Jens stood up as our witness, and at the end of that day I was finally, honestly, Mrs. Nora Eriksen.

WE DROVE INTO TOWN to meet Solveig's train on a bright July day. As we waited I realized I was expecting Emma—that I had confused my granddaughter with my daughter. I could not deny a longing that Emma might be with her, though I knew better. My gloved hands twisted together. I had no idea who this child would be.

When the train arrived, Solveig stepped from the carriage all modern and confident, in a short skirt and cloche hat, a camera bag on her shoulder. We spotted her first, and my heart, nervous all day, leaped in gladness. All I could think was, yes, this was my own, my granddaughter. I would have known her anywhere.

We called to her in Norwegian. She turned, scanning the crowd, then saw me. She stared for a long moment, then her modern facade crumbled and she was a child again, a lost child. Tears slid down her dusty cheeks as she stepped, hesitantly, into my arms.

"Grandmother! I, oh . . ."

I held her until she was ready, and then she pulled back, laughing through her tears. "I'm sorry. I've just, well, I wanted you to be alive so much, and you are, you are! It's almost beyond belief."

She was an only child, raised mostly by Emma and Torvald. I could just imagine her lonely life.

I smiled, my own feelings surging in a way I hadn't felt in years. I wasn't quite sure what I expected from this mysterious granddaughter, but I could already see she was not her mother.

"Welcome, Solveig," Anders said, handling the niceties. "I'll go fetch your luggage."

Solvi and I just smiled and clutched each other.

Anders decided to leave us at a hotel for lunch and headed off to do errands, so we could be alone. Solvi dried her tears and ordered competently in English, looking at me all the while. In my worn clothes I knew

I appeared more authentically American than she could have imagined. Still, she leaned eagerly across the table, chattering in Norwegian.

I tingled with joy just to behold her, this daughter of Emma, but I soon understood that her visit wouldn't be easy. She pulled a photograph from her purse—the one from the advertisement. Torvald tried to burn it just before he died, she told me, showing me the scorched edge, but fate intervened. The picture was the first evidence that her mother had been part of a larger family, and ever since Solvi saw it, she said, she's been searching for me.

In the beginning she thought her uncles and I would be in Kristiania, or at least in Norway, but she could find no trace of us. Then she heard a story, something about a forgotten woman who became an iconic figure in Norway, and she was haunted by it. Now she was convinced I was this forgotten heroine who slammed the door on an unhappy marriage and started a revolution.

I stared at her, astonished.

"I'm an old story, Solvi," I said. "No one remembers me."

"Oh, but they do, Grandmother." Then she opened her purse and pulled out a card. I peered at it. *Dr. Tobias Wolff, Professor of History.* My old friend!

Solvi smiled. "He's my professor. He helped me figure out that my missing grandmother and the Forgotten One were the same person."

I just stared at her, astonished.

"He asked that you write to him. He still misses you, after all these years." Now she leaned forward again. "And there are others, many who are curious about you. They call you the woman who first said no!"

"Who calls me that?"

"The feminists, the women who have changed Norway! It started with you and Aasta Hansteen, but you are just a shadow because no one knows what happened to you. I'm hoping I can convince you to write your story, so everyone will understand."

How strange. I have lived in America nearly forty years. How could I become important to Norwegians in my absence?

I gazed at her across the table, taking her measure. She had more of Torvald in her than she would likely admit, the high forehead, the certainty—but, no. I mustn't blame her for her grandfather. He was my mistake, not hers. Still, she was the most precious gift, with her bobbed blond curls tucked behind her ears—fresh, unbent, a crusader. She had been to university; that was the problem.

I couldn't hold the intensity of her eyes, so I looked down past the tea cakes to the frayed sleeve of my jacket. I reached out, my gnarled hands palms up in supplication. She took them in her own fair hands and rubbed the knobby skin with her thumbs.

"This is why, Grandmother, because your life is much more interesting than the story they're parading about," she said. "Why, no one even knows you're alive! They think you're dead and so say whatever they want. You must write the true story of Nora Helmer, so they'll understand what you endured, how you survived."

The true story of Nora Helmer? I shook my head. When I left Torvald, I wondered who would prove to be right, me or the world. I still didn't know. And even if I were sure, I would probably dress it up, make myself virtuous, imply wisdom and forethought when there was little of either in what I did. I would make myself a myth whether I wanted to or not, because all that had happened seemed to make sense only as myth, something larger than life.

And yet, and yet. My drab clothes reminded me of our orchard home and the humble mission where I worked, listening to women poorer yet more mythic than I could ever be. Some had escaped the czar; others had run from pogroms, or soldiers, or the hunger of the Great War. So who was I? Just Nora.

TO HUMOR HER, I said I would consider it. "But, first, Solveig, you must help me understand the family. I left a long time ago. Tell me what I missed."

"Of course," she said, smiling. She wanted to help.

I rummaged in my bag and pulled out something dear to me: Emma's cap. "I was embroidering this for your mother when I left. Please tell me about her. When I visited thirty years ago she refused to speak with me."

Solvi fingered the little cap. "Mother told me about this. I was not surprised she wouldn't talk to you back then. No one in the family ever spoke of you, because Grandfather wouldn't allow it. She was quite shocked that you reappeared when she'd been told you were dead."

"She had no memory of me to help her," I said. "I was a stranger to her."

Solvi nodded sadly. "I tried to get her to come with me to America, but she doesn't venture far from her parlor in Bergen." She paused, looking into my eyes. "I begged her to forgive you."

"Shush, child; it's enough that you're here."

A long moment passed before she spoke again. "That's what Mama said—that I was her gift to you."

Tears rose in my eyes. I was forgiven; it nearly took my breath away.

"So tell me about your mother. I've really only known her as a small child."

Solvi gave me another sad smile. "She is loving, beautiful, conventional, and stubborn. I think she got that from Grandfather. She seems to hate all things modern." Solvi paused. "I know it's disrespectful of me to criticize my mother," she finally said, "but we must be honest about life, don't you think?"

"Yes, but we must also be understanding."

"Of course," she said, measuring her words. "Mama was very precious to Grandfather; we lived with him in his house. He and Mama almost seemed like an old married couple sometimes, the way they sat and talked while my father retreated to his study. It made me angry for Papa, but he was resigned to it." She stopped to breathe. "Mama also got very sick with the influenza, and when Grandfather died I was terrified she would too, just because she couldn't live without him. At the worst moment, when we both thought she was dying, she asked me to promise I would marry the boy Grandfather had picked for me. But I couldn't do it." Solvi looked at me with anguish. "It was her deathbed request, and I said no."

I squeezed her hand. "Sometimes we face harrowing decisions in life, Solveig. But choosing whom to marry and to love must come from our own hearts."

She nodded fervently. "Oh, I've always believed that! But Mama—well, after that I couldn't stay in Bergen anymore. I actually ran away to university."

How alike we were, this child and I! "Have you reconciled with her, Solveig?"

"Yes. I went to visit her before I came to America. It wasn't easy, but I think we understand each other better now."

For all her confidence, I sensed how difficult this was for her. She was one of mine, after all, one of those I injured. She wanted my story so she could understand her own.

"The strange thing about my mother," Solvi said, "is that I never quite felt like her child. We are so different. Sometimes I imagined myself an orphan she had adopted, someone whose real mother had left her behind."

"As your mother was left behind, as I was. We've been lonely children, Solvi dear. You, me, your mother."

"Oh, Grandmother," she said, pulling out her handkerchief and dabbing at her eyes. "Don't you see? There's so much I need to understand, or I'll never know who I am. Please write your story. Why you left Grandfather, where you went, how you survived. If not for the others, please, write it for me."

SOLVI

The first night at the orchard Solvi found herself swept into the family embrace. Jens and his wife, Katrin, brought supper and their four children for a noisy evening filled with laughter, music, and a staccato mixture of Norwegian and English. Solvi spent the evening answering the children's questions, taking their pictures, and letting the littlest sit in her lap and eat her pie. Whenever Solvi looked up from the mayhem, there was her grandmother, smiling at her.

Over the next few weeks Solvi helped in the kitchen, walked with her grandmother in the orchard, and photographed the children climbing the trees, monkeys all of them. Slowly, she told her grandmother the full story of solving the mystery: following her trail in the newspaper clippings, talking with Anne-Marie's daughter, searching cemeteries and parish records. Nora listened with astonishment, asking the occasional question, but mostly just nodding and sighing. She appeared to remember everything, yet there was an emotional guardedness, it seemed to Solvi, a reluctance to go back to the world she left behind. Solvi sat with her sometimes just holding her hand, retreating to the love that was wordless. They were kindred, but also strangers.

AFTER THE FIRST WEEK, Solvi sat down to write her mother a letter, but when she could not even pen the first sentence, she realized she must tell her in person, when she would be able to see her face and watch for tears. Solvi knew it wouldn't be easy for either of them.

But she could tell Magnus, and so she wrote to him.

Dear Magnus: There aren't enough words to describe how wonderful it's been—the voyage across the Atlantic with Rikka, traveling through the endless expanse of America to reach Spokane, seeing my grandmother for the first time, and settling in with her and my American family at their beautiful orchard outside the city. The other grandchildren are a passel of blond imps, three stair-step boys in knee britches and a fearless, pinafored little girl who follows her brothers around like a wolf pup, sneaking about and playing tricks. Their father, Jens, runs the orchard for my grandmother's husband, Anders. Their mother is Katrin, an able farmwife with a lovely singing voice and laughing manner. When I'm surrounded by them at dinner each night, I think of your vision of me having a life full of people, as it seems to have come true. These are evenings of sublime happiness for me.

Their life is very rustic. I feel as if I've stepped back in time, especially when I ride in the orchard wagon, which is pulled by mules, or light the oil lamps in the evening. There is no electricity and few modern comforts. And yet, the farm is cozy and happy. It can be quite hot during the day, but at night a breeze blows down from the mountains, cooling everything. The land is dry, but there are green pines and spruce on the hills.

My grandmother is quite wrinkled but beautiful and elegant nonetheless, with her gray-blond hair swept up on her head and her lace collars (all handmade). Anders has shown me every kindness. We sit and talk of Norway sometimes; he has a nostalgia for the fjords and mountains that she doesn't share and enjoys hearing of my days tramping the uplands with my father. My grandmother has told me of some of her adventures in Norway and here in America, and they are by turns grim and fascinating. She has worked for many years with grieving, despondent women and now helps immigrant mothers settle into America. She believes this is her special calling. I went with her yesterday to the mission, and it was sobering to see the poverty of these women. My grandmother moves like a swan among the most squalid figures, dispensing advice, medicine, packets of knitted goods, and hope. She reminds me a bit of Rikka, though she's much better behaved.

I'm trying to get my grandmother to write her story, as Professor Wolff suggested—so that Norwegian history can make a place for her and the feminists of Kristiania can finally claim her as their sister. I'm not sure I've convinced her, though. I haven't had the courage to ask why she left my grandfather, or why she married Mr. Eriksen when she was still married to someone else. I'm not sure I have the right. My grandmother is silent about many things, a silence learned, I suspect, from a lifetime of secrets and living on the prairie. There's no way to *describe the distances here, how empty the horizon can feel here in the West. You'll just have to come back with me someday and see it for yourself.*

So, dear Magnus, I am being changed. Finding my grandmother and living for a time in her pioneer life has stretched me in ways I never imagined. I've taken many photographs. The world is so much bigger than our little country, perched there on the Arctic Circle, and humanity is so much more varied. America seems filled with those who are different—Chinese, Indians, Africans. I'm sure you'll find it quite exhilarating when we travel here together someday.

I don't ever want to leave, but I look forward to my return. Will life always be made of these contradictions? Maybe you can help me make sense of that.

Your affectionate, Solvi

NORA

Solvi is gone now, headed back to finish her studies in Norway and to see her mother and her beau, Magnus. I miss her with an ache that will not quiet. When she told me how she searched for me, I was quite moved by her hunger and her deep intuition that I was alive. At first I didn't feel worthy of it, but the longer we were together, the more I understood the deep bond between us—not just of blood, but of spirit and heart. She completes my life; she is the ending of my story. I may never see Emma again or the boys, but, despite that sorrow, I feel whole.

We finally talked of Ivar and Bobby. Neither of us knows where they are, though Solvi said her mother assumed they were in America with me. No doubt they have gone on to have full lives, possibly somewhere in this great country. Solvi promised to try—along with her beau, who works as a journalist—to find them, wherever they are, and attempt to reunite us. I smiled at her naive belief that such a thing would be easy, but it is possible there are more miracles to be revealed.

As for her hope that I will write my story, by the time we said good-bye, we had come to an agreement. I would write it, and she would get it published. I finally realized that Aasta Hansteen was right: it might help other women to understand my experience, to hear my truth. I couldn't speak out before, when she asked me so many years ago back in St. Paul, but I can now.

SO HERE I SIT, pen in hand, a virgin notebook before me. Anders has fashioned me a little desk and placed it by the window in our bedroom so I can work in peace. Yet there is no peace in this project. To find the beginning I must unearth the memories of my life with Torvald, and as soon as I scratch at the surface, it all rushes back—the slanting light of those winter afternoons I sat eavesdropping on Torvald and Dr. Rank at the study door, the children bouncing in their chairs around the kitchen table as Nurse served their supper, Torvald putting a proprietary hand on my back when we went out so everyone would know I was his.

And I can feel, even now, how hard it was to breathe.

So, perhaps that is where I'll start: with that frigid night so long ago, when I took my first real breath.

APPRECIATION

Any serious work of historical fiction is built on considerable research. I would like to thank the many people who helped me understand the work of Henrik Ibsen, the Norwegian diaspora and the conditions in Minnesota during the late nineteenth century. In Norway, I would like to thank Dina Tolfsby and Benedikte Berntzen at the National Library of Norway, Astrid Saether of the Center for Ibsen Studies at the University of Oslo, Knut Dju-pedal at the Norwegian Emigrant Museum in Hamar, as well as the guides at the Ibsen Museum and the Norwegian Folk Museum in Oslo, and the Bergen Art Museum. In Minnesota, I was ably aided by Jeff Sauve of the Norwegian American Historical Association in Northfield, Billy and Ann Thompson of the Arv Hus Museum in Milan, Janet E. Liebl of the Lac qui Parle County Historical Society, the staff of the Minnesota Historical Soci-ety, Katherine Linstrom for her presentation on Helga Estby, the delightful grandmothers of the Sons of Norway in Montevideo, and Mark Odegard for his family's immigration story.

My agent Ann Rittenberg was very helpful in shaping the narrative, and editors Carolyn Carlson and Liz van Hoose provided additional useful insights. My thanks to all of you.

This book was also improved by the close reading and comments of var-ious friends, relatives and colleagues. Some of the best advice came from my "sister brigade," including Anne Swallow Gillis, Laura Swallow, Penny Dwyer, Carrie Shepard and Andra Georges. Among other readers and advi-sors, special thanks go to Betty Miller (who read at least eight versions), Susan Kellam, Sandra Eskin, Amy Eisman, Kathleen Eisman, Beth Brophy, Ann Keniston, Irene Tudor, Carolyn Oxsen, Steve Piacente, Carol Francis, Jane Hall, David DeLong, Almut Hennings, Maggie Heyward, Dara LaPorte, Julie Stewart, Liza Tucker, Edward Robinson, Marcella Gillis, Mary Swal-low, Cadi Simon, Josephine Shepard, Ben Shepard, Fred Williams, Joe

Williams, Christine Bachman, and Joanne Lipman. Kathleen Szawiola was one of my earliest and sharpest readers, and she also designed the book and managed the production. Many, many thanks to her, and my skilled copy editor Annette Wenda, as well as Kimberly Glyder, who created the luminous cover. I am deeply grateful for all the frank discussion, thoughtful assistance, and encouraging words.

Thanks, as well, to my mother Edie Swallow, and all the Swallows and Shepards who bore witness to the long process of writing this book, especially my boys Ben, Joe, Sam and Geoff. But my deepest gratitude goes to my husband Charlie Shepard, who supported me for the ten years it took, always believed in my vision for Nora, listened tirelessly as I worked out the plot and characters, and took copious notes on our trip to Norway.

I could never have persevered without the support and wisdom of everyone here.